I THOUGHT I KNEW

I Thought I Knew

MELISSA TROMBETTA

Flawed & Funny Publishers

Copyright © 2024 by Melissa Trombetta

All rights reserved.

No part of this book may be reproduced in any manner whatsoever without written permission except in the case of brief quotations embodied in critical articles and reviews.

This book is a work of fiction. The characters and events in this book are fictitious. Any similarity to actual persons, living or dead, is purely coincidental and not intended by the author.

Cover design by Jessica Coffin of Jessicacoffindesign

ISBN: 979-8-21833-625-7 (ebook)

ISBN: 979-8-21833-622-6 (paperback)

flawedandfunny.substack.com

First Printing, 2024

To The Elsas ~
May you forever be empowered to be strong and confident
in your convictions and decisions.
I love you more.❤
~ Mommy

CONTENTS

Prologue   1

PART 1

1	Nicole	4
2	Nicole	9
3	Nicole	15
4	Nicole	19
5	Jamie	22
6	Nicole	29
7	Nicole	33
8	Nicole	38
9	Nicole	42

10	Nicole	47
11	Jamie	51
12	Nicole	61
13	Nicole	68

PART 2

14	Nicole	82
15	Nicole	90
16	Nicole	95
17	Nicole	100
18	Jesse	107
19	Nicole	113
20	Nicole	122
21	Nicole	129

22	Jamie	139
23	Nicole	145
24	Nicole	148
25	Nicole	161
26	Jesse	163
27	Nicole	168
28	Jamie	175
29	Nicole	188
30	Nicole	193

PART 3

31	Jesse	206
32	Nicole	219
33	Jesse	236

34	Nicole	249
35	Jamie	261
36	Nicole	273

EPILOGUE

Resources	291
Acknowledgments	293
About the Author	295

"STRENGTH DOESN'T COME FROM WHAT YOU CAN DO.
IT COMES FROM OVERCOMING THE THINGS YOU ONCE
THOUGHT YOU COULDN'T"

—RIKKI ROGERS

Prologue

May 18, 1995

After an infuriating night out at MacArthur's Pub, he went home the long way to burn off the anger still raging inside. He was almost at the edge of Wheeler's campus when he heard a woman's voice cursing in the distance. "Screw you!" she yelled. Faint laughs followed, echoing off the brick exterior of the dorms bordering the driveway that snaked up to his feet. *Nic?*

He turned toward the sounds and saw her pacing in the dim light of the streetlamp at the bottom of the hill, hands on her hips, smile on her face. Alone. He stood firmly out of the glow, staring at her beauty. *I've loved you since the day we met.* He swallowed his affection. *But you've never seen me.*

Gravel shifted underneath his sneakers as he moved a few steps, giving himself away. Like prey being stalked in the night, she tensed.

He could have called out, announcing his presence, easing her fears. But the fury he tried to walk off earlier was blistering his insides. His mind went blank. Before he realized what he was doing, the adrenaline pumped through his veins, propelling him down the driveway at full speed toward her. Her quiet cries caressed his ears a split-second before he tackled her onto the lawn.

The night sky was more than black, and he could barely see her shape lying on the ground. She groaned in pain as he rolled her over. Her breathing labored. He had knocked the wind out of her. She was hurt. And for once, he didn't care.

Working recklessly to push up her skirt, howls from a pack of drunk guys staggering home cut through the air. For a fleeting moment, he considered stopping, but his rage intensified. He didn't have an off switch.

Her wheezing cries regained his attention, sending icy panic through his extremities. Hastily, he slapped his sweat-drenched hand over her mouth to muffle her sobs. He needed to think.

With the guys finally gone, he scrambled to his feet, dragging her by the ankles deeper into the darkness, when a dumpster enclosure at the base of the driveway caught the corner of his eye. *Better coverage.*

He dropped beside her in a heart-racing second, wrapping one arm around her shoulders, hooking the other underneath her knees. Scurrying across the lawn, his chest heaved as he carried her limp body like a bride about to span the threshold of her new home.

Inside the pen, he gently laid her down on the wet pavement in the narrow space between the fence and the dumpster, taking care not to drop her head. The rancid smell of garbage stung his nostrils as he knelt by her feet, bunching her skirt around her waist. Fumbling to unzip his pants, he ignored the faint clanging of something metal bouncing along the pavement near his leg.

She whimpered groggily as he climbed on top of her, his knee wedged between her legs. Terrified that she was coming to and would recognize him, he palmed the side of her face and drove her line of sight toward the dumpster. *Now or never.*

Using his other hand, he tore off her panties and forced his way through the friction to get fully inside of her. She wriggled underneath him, trying to buck him off. *You're stronger than I gave you credit for. I'm almost done, I promise.* He bore down harder, lifting her thigh to his hip, ignoring the biting pain from the pebbles digging into his knees as he moved against her, pumping inside her while she lay there, still, no longer fighting. *There you go.*

At the point of no return, he barely flinched when she vomited. It was a small price to pay to be with her. *Finally.*

"Nic," he quietly groaned at his release. "I've waited so long to be with you."

PART 1

| 1 |

Nicole

Two hours earlier

That night, the night Nicole was attacked, started like most Wednesdays at Wheeler College—at MacArthur's Pub for dollar shots and two-dollar beers.

Three days before college graduation, an electric charge of anticipated freedom ricocheted through the bar as Pearl Jam's "Better Man" crackled through the jukebox over the buzz of the crowd. Nicole slid onto the barstool beside Megan, hoping her old boyfriend Matty wouldn't see her. He had been trying to corner her all night. She knew he was looking for one last hookup and didn't have time for his nonsense. She was too consumed with her paper that was due by Friday. Without it done, she'd fail the class, and that meant she wouldn't graduate on Saturday with everyone else.

"Last call!" the bartender yelled, turning on the barroom lights.

Megan squinted at the room with her shot glass at the ready. "When did all the ugly people get here?" she asked, perched on the barstool beside Nicole. Megan wore her variation of the downtown college uniform—Guess overalls with one side hanging open, a fitted Nirvana tank top, and a black watch plaid flannel tied around her waist.

Nicole clinked her glass. "Don't worry, Megan, you're beautiful in any light," she joked just before they threw back their last shots of

Aftershock. The familiar burn of the cinnamon syrup slid down Nicole's throat, causing her face to contort. Megan's face, though, remained calm as she slammed her shot glass down on the bar with a *thud*.

"You know, as trashy as this place is, I think I'm gonna miss it," Nicole said. *That is IF I get out of here. If I fail my class, I'll be stuck here all summer retaking it. Where would I stay? How would I pay for all that? What if I lose my job offer?*

"See, aren't you glad you came out with me tonight?" Megan asked.

With the lights on, Nicole saw how low she was willing to go to be with her friends at Wheeler—smoke-filled room, sticky floors from God only knows what, unusable clogged toilets, puke in the corner, cigarette butts put out in half-filled cups of swill beer. Nicole would be willing to pay a ransom to get out of a place like that in any other situation. But somehow, there with Megan, it felt like home.

"I still don't know how you convinced me. I should be in my room working on my paper instead of sitting on this stool," Nicole said, chewing on her bottom lip. "If I want to graduate on Saturday, anyway."

"Oh, would you stop with the bullshit, please? Call your sister, Jamie, in the morning. You said she could help you," Megan reminded Nicole as she motioned to the bartender for one more round.

"But Dr. Bernina was *such* a dick to me this afternoon. His face got all red, and he kicked me out of his office when I told him I already had a job and that my new boss probably wouldn't care if I 'incorporated Dr. Bernina's feedback' into my final paper. I literally used air quotes. He may not let me graduate out of spite alone."

"You need to stop. You're killing my buzz with all this schoolwork talk. Deal with it tomorrow," Megan said, handing Nicole a bottle of Bud Light. "Tonight, we celebrate! Cheers to the class of ninety-five, baby!"

Nicole slouched. "Fine. Cheers."

Amusement crossed Megan's face. "Oh, and perfect timing. Look who it is, Nic," she said, tipping her head toward the person standing over Nicole's shoulder.

Nicole turned to find Matty O'Connor, her ex-boyfriend, hovering too close, wearing an intoxicated grin. Her stomach twisted at the sight of him. Great. Exactly what she didn't need.

Megan stood. "I'm going to the bathroom. You kids have fun," she said, giving Nicole a wink before disappearing into the crowd.

Nicole blew out an exasperated sound from the back of her throat.

"Hey, Nic," Matty slurred, breathing heavily on her neck. "You look hot tonight."

"What do you want, Matty?" she asked, standing to move further away from him, accidentally bumping his beer cup on the way. "Oh, shit, sorry."

"No problem, I was ready for a new one anyway. This one was warm . . . and now gone," he realized, eyeing the bottom of his cup.

"Want anything?" he asked, pointing to the bar.

Nicole held up her beer. "All set." She smiled flatly.

He turned toward Nicole, new beer in hand. "So, what are you doing later?" he asked, guzzling a mouthful of his pint. "Wanna get outta here?" he shouted in her ear, struggling to enunciate his words.

Nicole side-eyed him. "Definitely not."

"C'mon, Nic. It's our last week here. One last quickie for old-time sake. It'll be fun," he garbled, holding her arm for balance.

She was swift to respond. "Yeah, no. I don't think so," she said, tugging her arm. "Think you can loosen your grip a little here?"

"Oh, sorry," he said without adjusting his hold.

Desperately scanning the room, Nicole caught the eye of Jesse Young—a fellow Wheeler senior and family friend from home. "SAVE ME," she mouthed, begging with her eyes.

Jesse tilted his head with his face scrunched up.

"Did you just mouth 'Save me' to that guy?" Matty slurred accusingly.

She curled one side of her lip when she glanced at Matty—eyes half closed, rocking to the blaring music, spilling his beer on the floor.

Nicole turned her attention back to Jesse, who had a faint glimmer of delight on his face. She had known Jesse for nearly a decade, meeting him for the first time shortly after her dad died when they weren't quite teenagers. Nicole's mother was forced to sell their house, and Jeanie, her best friend, and Jesse's mom took Nicole's family in for the summer at her home on Lake George. Nicole and Jesse warmed up to each other after a few days, and by the Fourth of July, they were inseparable. He was like the brother she never had—her *summer sibling.*

"Hey, Nic! Over here!" Jesse called out across the bar, waving his hand, pretending to catch her attention.

Nicole gave Jesse a nod and then turned to Matty, still swaying like a buoy in rough waters. "I gotta go," she said, peeling his hand off her arm and plopping him onto a stool.

"So, is that a 'no?'" Matty asked, leaning in for a kiss goodbye.

Nicole pulled her face out of reach. "It's a definite no."

"I should have guessed." His smile disappeared. "You were always such a dick tease."

"Classic," Nicole said, shaking her head, walking away.

She crammed through the pack of people, finally making it to Jesse. "Oh my God, thank you! You're a lifesaver!" Nicole said, gripping his forearm.

"Good friend of yours?" he asked sarcastically.

"Yeah," she scoffed, letting go of him. "Very drunk ex-boyfriend."

"Oof. The worst kind," he said.

She emulated his smile. "Exactly."

As Nicole glanced over Jesse's shoulder to where she had left Matty, Jesse relaxed against the bar and clinked Nicole's bottle with his. "It's good to see you, Nic. What are you up to after graduation? My mom said something about a job in Albany."

Distracted, Nicole half listened to Jesse's words. "Oh good, he's gone. And there's Megan. Perfect timing," she said, spotting Megan through the thinning crowd. Nicole looked up at Jesse and blew out a breath. "Coast is clear. I can go now."

His face dimmed. "Oh. Right," he said flatly, taking a sip of his beer. "Better go then."

Nicole stepped to leave when Sarah Clemson, an acquaintance from several of her business classes, blocked her path by draping herself over Jesse like a tapestry covering a dorm window. "Hey, Jesse," she slurred. "I thought I lost you." She looked Nicole up and down, rubbing her free hand along his torso as if she was gluing a bulletin board on his abs that read, 'he's mine.'

"Who's this?" Sarah asked as if she didn't know already.

Nicole never understood why women defaulted to being threatened by other women. *Wouldn't it be better if we supported each other instead?*

Jesse peeled Sarah's arms off him before Nicole could promise Sarah she had nothing to worry about. "Nicole. She's a family friend. She was just leaving."

Nicole met his glassy stare. "What?" she asked, scrunching her eyebrows together.

"Go," Jesse said. His tone was short. "You don't want to keep your friend waiting."

"Oh, right." She nodded, side-stepping the two of them. "Well, thanks for rescuing me."

"Sure," he said faintly as she walked away to meet Megan.

| 2 |

Nicole

"You ready?" Megan asked Nicole, her eyes flitting from guy to guy. "The bartender wouldn't let me sneak one more in. We're cut off."

"Absolutely. Hey, what happened to your lipstick?" Nicole asked, noticing the ruby-red smears on her face. Nicole's question was a rhetorical one. She already knew what had happened. What she didn't know was with which guy. "Wait, you can't leave looking like that. Let me help you," she said. Megan stood there like a child, letting Nicole rub the lipstick off her cheek with the cuff of her shirt.

Nicole wasn't always so judgmental of Megan. Early on, they had always been on the same page—schoolwork was the priority. But over the last year or so, Megan had been drinking and hooking up so often that Nicole realized that it wasn't just a phase of reckless behavior. It had become a problem.

Out of concern, Nicole quietly became Megan's caretaker after their nights out. It was easier than confronting Megan about her problem. But if Nicole was honest, it was getting old and often in the way of what she needed to do for herself.

"I think I got it all, beautiful. We can go now."

Following the crowd to the exit of MacArthur's, they found themselves in the center of the mob, squeezing through the narrow doorway. The plug of people eventually broke free, spilling out into the streets of downtown Wheeler like an unclogged drain. "Shit, it's freakin' cold out here." Megan shivered.

It was mid-May, and while it had finally started to warm up by Upstate New York standards, snowbanks still lined the streets, and it was less than forty degrees outside. "Jesus, it must be sixty-degree cooler out here. Look at my arms. They're steaming," Nicole said in bewilderment. She untied her shirt from around her waist and pulled it over her tank when Megan did the same.

"Ready? I need to get to bed. Gotta get up early tomorrow," Nicole said.

Megan held up her finger. "You mention that paper again, and I will throw you into that snowbank!"

"But . . ." Nicole started, but Megan cut her off with a zip of her fingers across her mouth.

"We're not leaving without one last slice of Bono's pizza for the walk home."

"Oh, God. That is the last thing we need," Nicole said, holding her stomach. "It's so heavy."

"But so good," Megan cooed. "Hey, if you don't want pizza, it's totally fine if you want to head back to campus. I'll find someone to walk home with." Megan gave Nicole a cunning smile.

Nicole knew she would have no time or patience to take care of Megan the next day. She needed to get Megan safely to her room that night so she could concentrate on her schoolwork in the morning without interruption. "No. I'll go," she said.

A few minutes later, slices in hand, they walked in silence, toggling between stopping to take bites and concentrating on not slipping on the thin glaze of ice that had formed on the sidewalks since sundown.

"All right, it's game time," Nicole declared.

"Hit me," Megan said with her mouth open, steaming from the hot bite resting on her tongue.

"Would you rather go out with a strong eight, with zero personality, or a three with a wicked sense of humor?" Nicole asked.

"Please," Megan said in an exasperated pitch. "If Rob Arnold taught me anything besides that he is a huge asshole, it is that personality trumps good looks any day."

During their first year, Megan was borderline stalking Rob Arnold around campus and was often the subject of Nicole and Megan's late-night talks. Megan would drone on about being with him and everything she'd let him do to her— 'I want his lips everywhere!' That was until they finally met their junior year and hooked up. It wasn't nearly the romance novel love story that Megan had dreamt about. She was devastated.

"I haven't heard that name in like a year," Nicole said, cautiously stepping off the icy curb.

Megan grunted. "I saw him at the bar earlier. Did you hear that he broke into one of his brother's rooms at the fraternity house, stole his weed, and then sold it to a townie?"

"Really? Who told you that?" Nicole asked as they passed the last of the dimmed downtown storefronts.

"One of the frat guys."

"Hm. Feels like a rumor."

"Yeah, well. He's pretty shady. I wouldn't put it past him," Megan said. "Speaking of losers, what did Matty want?"

"Sex." Nicole fake gagged. "When I said no, he turned nasty. It kind of took me by surprise. Thank God Jesse was there to save me."

"Ooooo . . . what about Jesse? He's got that swimmer body," Megan urged. "It's funny. I always thought you two would hook up. The few times I saw you together, he always stared at you with those googly eyes."

Nicole wrinkled her brow. "Eww. That would be like hooking up with my brother."

"Your *hot* brother." Megan chuckled. "Whatever. You need to do something. Otherwise, you're going to become one of those cat ladies."

"I need to get settled in my new apartment, start my job, and then I'll think about going out and meeting guys," she said, counting on her fingers. "Got to get into a new rhythm first."

"Oh, I know about your rhythms. I lived with you for two years, remember? There was no talking to you if you got up late or didn't wash your face before bed."

"There is nothing wrong with having a daily routine."

Nicole caught Megan's ridiculed look as they passed underneath a streetlamp. "You are the only college student I know who voluntarily gets up before eight, even on weekends. You are so rigid."

"How did we get to talking about my daily habits?" Nicole deflected.

For the next couple of streets, annoyed silence floated between them. Nicole's shoulders rounded at the cold when they hit Pine Avenue, the last stretch before campus and home to most off-campus housing. With the majority of students already gone for the summer, there was no life.

"It's so creepy out here without all the people," Megan whispered.

"And so dark," Nicole said. The cold seeped in through the collar of her shirt, sending a chill down her back.

* * *

The metal side door of Megan's dorm clinked shut at the same time Nicole pivoted on the ball of her foot and headed to her dorm across the driveway, the last in the row. Exhaustion filled her. If she was going to have any attention span to finish that *goddammed* paper, she needed sleep. "That paper. . .," she mumbled.

Aggravated, Nicole thrust her hands into the air and flipped off the Dr. Bernina image in her mind. "Screw you!" she shouted into the sky, laughing at the sound of her words echoing off the buildings. *Screw you . . . screw you . . . screw you . . .*

Nicole half attempted to jog up the driveway, hoping to get to her bed faster, but she only made it about thirty feet before her lack of athleticism overtook her brief surge of enthusiasm. Her legs and chest burned.

Resting her hands on her hips, standing on the sidewalk between the lawn and the driveway, she hinged at the waist to catch her breath. She looked around, noticing how dark it was despite the light emitting from the lamppost next to the fenced-off dumpsters. Panic stiffened her throbbing muscles, suddenly aware of how hidden she was at the bottom of the driveway.

A twig cracked in the distance. She froze, convinced there was something in the darkness that she could not yet see. "Hey—" she called out, realizing how quivery her voice was. No answer.

Since she had been at Wheeler, nothing more serious than students getting busted for drinking and weed had happened. The campus was safe. She knew that. *It must be the wind.* Then another twig cracked—closer that time.

Her heart hammered. Goosebumps pebbled her arms. And despite the cool temperatures outside, beads of sweat formed along her hairline.

She leaned forward at the chewing sound of gravel crunching under the quick patter of someone's feet. *Run!* she told herself, but she was glued to the spot where she stood, cemented in fear.

A heartbeat later, hands tackled her, sending her flying. She landed hard on her side on the frozen lawn, crushed with the weight of a body, gasping for air. They rolled her onto her back, but she couldn't see who it was through the darkness. Overcome with pain and disbelief, she blacked out.

* * *

Nicole woke, terrified and confused, recalling only blurred moments of struggling to sit up. A vague sense of pressure around her ankles and a floating feeling slowly surfaced. The distinct shushing of grass and the sharp grinding sound of a zipper followed.

Fully awake, she found *him* on top of her with one of her legs hitched under his arm. She had no leverage. He had already wrenched up her skirt around her waist and was working on ripping off her underwear with one hand, pushing the side of her face into the cold, wet pavement with his other.

Dim streaks of light from the lamppost filtered through the fence, reflecting lines on the green metal bin. Nicole tried to scream, but the weight of his body compressed her chest, keeping her silent. She futilely attempted to turn her head to see his face beyond her peripheral vision, but he was too strong. When she tried to buck him off, he just bore down harder.

Tears poured out of the corners of her eyes as helplessness hijacked her body. *Why aren't you fighting? What are you doing?*

Limp with disbelief, she stopped trying to fight. Instead, she stilled, closed her eyes, and prayed for it to end.

He forced his way inside her, stabbing at her erratically. The violent motion dug the gravel into her cheek, tearing away at her skin with every thrust. Seeping garbage water from the dumpster pooled around her face, making her gag. Seconds later, she threw up.

It didn't stop him from continuing to move with brutal force. The pain inside her was raw . . . burning . . . unbearable.

He leaned closer to her face. She felt his moist, hot breath get heavier and faster until he let out a quiet groan. "I've waited so long to be with you," he hissed in her ear.

Barely able to move, she let out a strangled cry and then blacked out again.

| 3 |

Nicole

Nicole had no idea how long she had been lying alone in the cold, quiet darkness before distant voices trickled into her ears, snapping her awake.

In seconds, the pressure and throbbing in her pelvis from the ruthless friction forced inside of her registered. A soft cry from the back of her throat dislodged as she sat up. Cautiously wiping away the embedded gravel from the side of her face, she winced at the tenderness in her arm.

Nicole held her breath and made her way onto her hands and knees, favoring the stronger side. Using the garbage bin for support, she unfurled to a wide stance, easing the burning sensation between her legs.

Terror settled in her chest. *I have to get out of here,* she thought, urgently pulling down her skirt. She took off her denim shirt and tied it around her waist to cover her backside, soaked in scum water, when a strong whiff of vomit pierced her nose, causing her dry heave. "Ahh," she cried, drawing in a sharp breath. The shooting pain burned through her groin, doubling her over.

Fighting through the agony, Nicole poked her head past the open gate, struggling to see the driveway through clouded tears. She turned her head a fraction as though straining to hear a song in the distance, terrified that he still lurked in the dark. Carefully, she tiptoed out of the enclosure, pausing to let the shiver trickle down her back, and then double-timed it up the driveway.

Nicole managed to avoid seeing anyone in the courtyard and the vestibule of her dorm. Her chest rose and fell, forcibly pulling in the cold air as she punched her code into the keypad by the front door. Her pulse quaked when the lock released with a *click*.

In a beat, she flung it open and banked left in the lobby, down the hallway to her room. Fortunately, she was the only one left on her floor, so she was unlikely to run into anyone.

With one hand on the doorknob, Nicole used the thumb of her other to hastily pound her 4-digit code into the pushbutton lock. She twisted the knob and shoved her whole body into the door, but it didn't open. *Oh god ... oh god ...* She tried again. 5—3—0—1, *twist*. Locked.

"Fucking open!" she yelled, yanking on the handle, frantically banging the door against the frame.

She removed her grip from the knob, taking a few seconds to shake out her hands. *Try again.*

Clearing the lock, she let out a sharp breath and attempted one more time. That time, more slowly and deliberately. 5 ... 3 ... 0 ... 1 ... "Please," she prayed.

Her pleas were answered when it opened. "Thank you," she whispered, slamming the door shut behind her.

With her back pressed against the wall, she felt around the corner for the switch and flicked on the overhead fluorescent lights. Relief washed over her when she saw that her room was exactly how she had left it—discarded potential outfits from earlier that night sprayed all over her rug and futon, a weighed-down bookbag hanging on the back of her desk chair, and stacks of paper precariously balancing on the edge of her desk next to the marketing textbook she needed for her paper she should have stayed home to write.

Screw you, Dr. Bernina, AND your report.

She darted across the room to the window in three bounds and yanked the knotted cord on the metal blinds. They rattled closed with a loud *swoosh,* shutting out the view of the driveway, the dumpsters, the world.

Her entire body trembled uncontrollably in the quiet of her room, catching herself on her futon when her legs buckled. Dazed in disbelief, she hugged her knees to her chest, trying to keep warm, but the pressure inside her pelvis was too much. Her feet fell to the floor, as her detached expression fixed on the Wheeler Warriors flag hung on the wall across the room.

The radiator ticked, bouncing her thoughts back and forth like a metronome—*Who would do this to me? What should I do?*

Left alone with her thoughts was her least favorite place to be. The silence was unnerving. Her teeth chattered as the taste of acid watered in her mouth. Her skin itched under her cold, damp clothes. She needed to keep busy. Nauseating odors radiated off of her, curling into her sinuses. She needed a shower.

Nicole carefully inched herself off the low platform cushion. She toed off her Doc Martens, biting through the radiating pain in her groin, and fought her way to her feet. Her arm pulsed as she unbuttoned her tartan plaid skirt. The last two buttons were missing from the front, but she didn't care. It wasn't like she would ever wear it again.

She threw it and the rest of her tattered clothes into a plastic Chinese takeout bag she found in her garbage can. She wasn't about to keep any remnants of her clothes or reminders of that night.

With her robe on and a towel thrown over her shoulder, she quietly unlocked her door, bracing herself on the doorframe, impaled by fear. She coached herself across the hall to the handicapped bathroom—the only bathroom with a lock.

Moments later, the scalding hot water sluiced down her back. The constant rain of water over her head slowed her buzzing thoughts as she scrubbed every inch of her body, desperate to reclaim it as hers. Her eyes burned as she foamed up her hair with shampoo over and over. *Lather, rinse, repeat,* she recited, scouring incessantly.

She waited for the water to turn ice cold before getting out of the shower. When she reached for the knob, she saw that her arm had started to turn varying shades of purple, but it was only badly bruised, not broken, as she had initially worried.

Water ran down her legs, puddling around her feet as she cautiously patted herself dry on the cool tile floor outside the shower. The skin of her cheek throbbed, pulling tighter as it dried. She hesitated to look in the mirror, dreading what she would see. Thankfully, when she finally glanced, she saw that the road rash was superficial and would heal with some Neosporin in a day or two.

Nicole barely tied her robe before sprinting across the hall on her tiptoes. Once inside her room, she threw on her pajamas—an oversized Wham T-shirt and a pair of men's plaid boxer shorts—and choked down a couple of ibuprofens. She had no water but would rather suffer than leave her room again.

After flicking off the lights, she hurdled herself across the room, using the glow of her alarm clock to light her path. In the safety of her bed, the thought of the paper returned for a split second. It didn't matter as much anymore—if at all. Either way, she'd deal with it in the morning after she slept off her night. The night she pledged never to think about it again.

| 4 |

Nicole

Nicole lay in bed the next day. Her eyes were swollen with insomnia and tears as she vacantly listened to her phone ring. It was the third time in the last ten minutes. She was tempted to ignore it again but worried that it was Megan. If she didn't pick up, Nicole knew Megan would show up on her doorstep any minute, and she definitely did not want that.

"Hello," Nicole said groggily into the receiver.

"Good morning, Sleepyhead! Actually, good afternoon!" Megan chirped into the phone.

"Hey."

"Why do you sound like you're still in bed? Wait, are you still in bed? It's after one o'clock in the afternoon. You never sleep in."

"I don't feel well." *Understatement of the year.* "Why are you up so early?" Nicole asked, rolling onto her side, wincing at the pain in her arm. The driveway flickered in her mind, making her entire body tense.

"Cottonmouth. I got up to get some water and couldn't get back to sleep. I'm so hungover. I can't wait for a huge stack of IHOP pancakes and a jumbo coffee. Wanna go?"

Nicole's pillow was humid on her cheek, still damp from her hair. The weight of her blanket was no longer comforting. It was suffocating, reminiscent of him lying on top of her. "Nah, I'm good. Go ahead without me," she said, kicking off her covers.

"You're saying no to IHOP?" Megan asked. "You really aren't feeling well."

"I've gotta call my sister to see if she can help me finish my paper for Dr. Bernina. I can't keep pushing it off."

I should be calling the police. But Nicole quickly dismissed the thought. No good would come from talking. She had watched enough *Law & Order* to know that she would be the one that ended up on trial, forced to relive that night. Her actions, or inactions in her case, would be scrutinized and judged by a crowd. And for what? The guy, if they found him, always walked away unscathed. It was the woman who was scarred for life, which was going to happen whether she talked or not. It was best to bury it deep and learn to move on.

"You can't spare an hour? C'mon, blueberry pancakes . . . bacon . . . maple syrup . . . mmmm. . . can't you smell it through the phone?" Megan asked.

Nicole's face heated. She wasn't interested in seeing Megan, let alone having breakfast with her. What she wanted to do was tell her off. *How dare you call me like nothing happened. If I had stayed home and worked on my paper last night like I was supposed to, I would be fine right now—just another Thursday morning. But instead, I had to babysit you after you guilted me into going out again, and now I am left to figure out how to move forward with my life. Alone.*

But Nicole didn't say any of those things to Megan. She never did. Instead, she drew in a frustrated breath and shoved her emotions into the filing cabinet locked in her chest with all the other words left unsaid.

"It's tempting, but I need to finish this paper. Sorry."

After they said goodbye, Nicole slid the receiver onto the base of the phone and lay in bed. Hot tears flooded her eyes.

Who hates me so much that they would do this to me?

Nicole cut her thoughts off and wiped her cheek with the corner of her sheet. "Nope, I'm not doing this. I've got too much to do," she said, swinging her legs onto the floor. She knew if she let her mind continue, she'd spend her day circling the drain and accomplish nothing.

Ten minutes and a few bites of cold Chinese food later, she twisted her damp hair in a clip, pulled out her notebook, and dialed Jamie's number.

| 5 |

Jamie

"Hello, Thoroughbred Title Company, Mr. Riley's office. This is Jamie. How may I help you?"

"Hey, Jamie, it's Nic."

Jamie smiled at the familiarity of Nicole's voice. "Hey! I was just thinking about you this morning," she said, swiveling her office chair back and forth with the tip of her Mary Jane pump.

The front door rattled open behind her when her boss, Paul Riley, stormed in. "Crap, hold on a second," she hushed into the phone, covering the receiver with her perfectly manicured hand.

"Hi, Paul. Did you forget something?" Jamie asked, craning her neck up to meet his glaring steel-gray eyes.

"The property survey isn't in the Cudney folder. I need it for their closing. Why isn't it here?" he growled, slapping the folder on her desk.

"Oh! That's weird," she said, jumping to attention. Jamie knew better than to make Paul wait. Fortunately, he liked her, but she knew that could change in a hot second. "It was in there earlier when we went through the final checklist. Maybe it got lost on your desk. Let me check your office," Jamie offered, putting down the phone. If Nicole hung up, she'd call her back after Paul left.

Even though Jamie graduated from college with a secondary education degree, she accepted an office job as Mr. Riley's executive assistant.

The dark, wood-paneled office walls were the farthest thing from being in a high school she could find. After her first week of student teaching, she knew she had made a colossal mistake. It turned out that being in the classroom full of teens reminded her of her teenage years—a time she hoped would fade.

Jamie hurried back to her desk with the missing folder in hand. "Here you go, Paul," she said, handing him the file. "It somehow found its way underneath your coffee cup. I clipped the final title report to the front cover and put flags on the side so you can easily find the signature pages, just the way you like it," she said, smiling. "Need anything else?"

Paul grumbled, shaking his head. "Nope, that's it. What would I do without you, Jamie?" he asked, pointing at her with the folder in his hand.

"Be an unorganized, miserable mess, I'm sure. Now, you need to leave. You're going to be late. And you know how much Mr. Tillman hates it when anyone is late." She shooed him out the door.

"Yeah, yeah. I'm going," Paul grumbled as he closed the door behind him.

Jamie waited to hear the latch click before she picked up the receiver from her desk. "Nic? You there?"

"Yup, I'm still here. Tell me, do you wash his hands for him, too?"

"What do you mean? He forgot a file, and I got it for him. It's my job."

"You sounded like a waitress. 'Can I get you anything else, Paul?'" Nicole mocked.

"Wait until you get into the corporate world. You'll make your fair share of coffee and bite your lip to keep your boss happy. You'll see."

"You know, when you're a teacher, you're the boss of the classroom."

Jamie wanted to jab herself with a pencil at the thought. "This job is perfect for me. Now that I'm engaged, it's game on for wedding planning. Do you have any idea how many decisions need to be made in the next month?"

"You just got engaged. Can't you enjoy the moment a little first?"

"Ha! This coming from the girl who has her next five years laid out in a PowerPoint presentation."

"There is nothing wrong with having some direction."

"Fine. I'll enjoy the moment after I've found a photographer, a florist, and a DJ. These people book up quickly. The good ones, anyway," Jamie said, holding out her left hand to admire her engagement ring—a near-perfect two-carat, brilliant-cut round diamond accented with tapered sapphire baguettes, set in a platinum band inlaid with diamonds. She had dropped enough hints over the months leading up to the proposal that it was hard for Randy to get it wrong.

"My point is, I don't have time to create lesson plans and deal with parents right now," Jamie said. *Or ever.*

"Uh-huh."

Jamie was fifteen when their dad died. As the oldest daughter, she was sandwiched between Nicole and their mother. On the one side, Jamie witnessed her mom spiral into depression, swirling with the pressure of raising two daughters alone, juggling the demands of a full-time job while desperately trying to keep a roof over their heads.

On the other side, Nicole was only twelve and needed someone to care for her in their mother's emotional absence. It was Jamie who made Nicole's school lunch in the morning, who helped Nicole when she got her first period, and who lay in bed with Nicole, rubbing her back until she fell asleep on the nights she couldn't bear to be alone. Those were hard years. Jamie earned the easier life Randy promised her. She deserved someone to take care of her for a while.

Nicole sighed. "Don't get me wrong, I love Randy. But I am worried that you're putting your life on hold for him. Aren't you afraid you'll lose yourself? Don't you want to have your own friends? Your own money? Look what happened to Mom."

"What happened to Mom will *not* happen to me. I know how to keep Randy happy. He's not going anywhere."

If an easier life meant she wouldn't have a career because she'd be too busy keeping a home and supporting Randy's success, so be it. She would have a life filled with love and security and never have to worry about money. Wasn't that better? What more did she need?

"I'm not in the mood to talk about your sex life right now," Nicole said sharply.

Jamie flared her nostrils. "Well, this has been fun."

"I'm sorry. I have a lot on my mind."

Jamie relaxed into her chair. "What's up? Ready for graduation?"

"More than ever, you have no idea. That's why I'm calling. I have to interview someone who works in an office about workplace conflict resolution."

"It's Thursday. You still have work to do? Aren't you graduating on Saturday?" Jamie asked.

Nicole growled. "Because my professor is an asshole and insists I do another interview and include it in my final paper. Without it, I won't graduate."

"Doesn't he know you already have an amazing job lined up after graduation, and it doesn't matter?"

"Jamie, I have been through all of that with him already. Can you help me or not?" Nicole snapped.

"Alright, let me think," she said, tapping her pencil on the desk. "Well, last week, Paul had to call Maria and Larry, the two underwriters, into his office because Larry accused Maria of killing his favorite jade plant. She swore she innocently watered it while he was out on vacation, but he insists she overwatered it on purpose because he got the better office."

"Was he for real? He couldn't possibly want his boss to mediate over a succulent. Was something else going on?"

"Rumor has it that Larry is hot for Maria, but she keeps turning him down."

"So instead of taking 'no' for an answer and moving on, he retaliated and went to his boss about a dead plant?"

"Pretty much."

"Real mature, Larry." Jamie could hear Nicole's pen writing feverishly. "Well, that sounds like a 'Personality-based Conflict.' So, the textbook says Paul should hit the conflict head-on as soon as Larry puts in the complaint. What did Paul do?"

"He summoned them both to his office."

"Good, he addressed the issue immediately. Check," Nicole said, then read something under her breath. "Okay, it also says that to get the best outcome, Paul should play the role of mediator and allow Larry and Maria to be heard. Did you know how their conversation went in Paul's office?" she asked.

"From what I could hear through the door, Paul told Maria to stay out of Larry's office unless invited, even if his thirsty plants were calling her name. Then he told Larry that since he liked plants so much, he should start by growing a set of balls. Once those come in, he should buy himself a new jade plant. And then he threw them out of his office."

"Wow. There are so many things wrong with that story. Let me get this straight . . . Not only did Maria have to put up with Larry's unwanted advances and tantrums, but she also got hauled into her boss' office and got in trouble? Fair to assume you don't have an HR department."

"Paul *is* the HR department."

"Of course he is," Nicole said. "Geez. I hope I never have to deal with any of that nonsense."

"Best advice . . . play nice, but don't offer to water anyone's plants." They both huffed a chuckle. "So, see you Saturday."

Jamie loved Nicole but was dreading the weekend—a long drive with her mother, schlepping Nicole's stuff, boring ceremony. Most importantly, she recently learned that her wedding planner was available the same weekend.

"Oh right, Saturday. Um . . . I was thinking . . . you know, it's a long drive. I'll be on the stage for, like, fifteen seconds. I don't think you and Mom should come. I'll see you on Sunday when I get home. It seems like a waste of your time to make the trip," Nicole said.

Something was off in Nicole's voice. Jamie could hear it. *Stress from the extra work, maybe?* She might have asked if she wasn't so excited about her weekend suddenly freeing up.

"Really? You'd be alright if we didn't go to your college graduation?" Jamie asked, trying to contain her enthusiasm.

"Yeah. It's silly for you to come all this way to sit through a three-hour ceremony, watching strangers cross the stage. Heck, now that I hear it out loud, I might skip it too," Nicole said with a single laugh.

"Your timing is perfect!" Jamie squealed.

"It is?"

"I am trying to find a day that works for Randy and me, Mom, and Randy's parents to meet with the wedding planner at The Sullivan. She had an opening this weekend, but I told her we weren't available. If you're sure about graduation, I'll call her back now!"

"The Sullivan? How can Mom afford that place?"

"She can't. That's why Randy's parents offered to pay for the wedding." Giddiness pulsed in Jamie's chest at the thought of having her wedding at such a swanky venue. She hadn't planned a single detail, and the event had already outshined her wildest dreams.

"Oh!"

"Randall Sr. and Karen, Randy's parents, know how special Lake George is for us, getting engaged there and all. So, Karen suggested I give The Sullivan a call. As luck would have it, they had a cancellation for the Fourth of July weekend next year. With his parents' support, we snagged it before someone else did. The timing is perfect! I can already envision the fireworks shooting over the lake in the background of our wedding photos. They'll be stunning." She let out an enthusiastic squeak.

Jamie would never admit it, but she also saw wedding planning as the best opportunity to win Karen over. Randy's family was important to him, which meant it needed to be important to Jamie if she would be a part of it. But breaking through their family bond was harder than Jamie expected, especially since Karen held the keys. Around Jamie, Karen was curt and cold, which drove Jamie to second-guess her worth and often get tongue-tied. It was a new feeling for Jamie, who was usually socially adept.

"You need to spend more time with her. You'll see what a loving person she is once you get to know her," Randy assured Jamie after she first met Karen. That was over a year ago, and Karen still hadn't thawed any.

Jamie was too embarrassed to admit her obsessive need for Karen's validation and an easier life to Nicole. On the surface, it fed right into her argument about the importance of Jamie having her own identity outside of Randy. But the day with the wedding planner was going to change everything. She was confident that Karen wouldn't be anything less than impressed with all the ideas she had already come up with, and in turn, Karen would deem her a worthy addition to their family. After that, there would be nothing to admit to Nicole because it would all be in the past.

"You should be excited. Sounds amazing!" Nicole said.

It has to be.

| 6 |

Nicole

Without hesitation, Nicole punched her mom's number into the phone. It was minutes after three o'clock, and Nicole knew that her mom would be walking in the door from work.

Nicole felt the moisture of her breath on the receiver as the phone rang in her ear. She hadn't considered seeing her mom and Jamie on Saturday until Jamie brought up graduation. She was not ready to face them. They would know something was wrong immediately and then wear her down with questions until she talked. And then they would insist she go to the police, tell the school, and try to fix what happened. But there was nothing to fix. It couldn't be undone.

Nicole was grateful that Jamie had plans for Saturday that included their mother. It would make convincing her mom not to come to Wheeler that much easier.

"Hello," her mom, Anne, said, winded.

"Hey, Mom."

"Oh, hi, sweetie. I just walked in the door. Give me a second to put my bag down." A few beats later, she was back. "This is a nice surprise. How are you?"

"Good, good. Trying to finish the last of my schoolwork so I can get on with my life."

"Oh, honey, don't force time. I know you're looking forward to starting your new job, but this is college. Enjoy your last couple of days. You've got a lifetime ahead of you in the real world."

"Yeah, well . . . Anyway, I talked to Jamie. The Sullivan, huh? That's exciting," Nicole said.

"Your sister's going to make such a beautiful bride. I get teary every time I think about her walking down the aisle. And Lake George, gosh, it's such a special place for them. Well, to all of us. Right?"

"Absolutely," Nicole agreed. An image of her mom and Jeanie, her mom's best friend, sitting at the kitchen table at the lake house flashed into her mind. It was the first summer they stayed with the Youngs. At that time, it had been close to six months since her dad died in the car accident, and Nicole remembered being struck by how long it had been since she had heard her mom laugh. Or seen her even crack a smile. With a change of scenery, her mom was a new person.

Nicole couldn't ignore the similarities. *Maybe when I leave Wheeler, I'll be fine too.*

"So, what's up, sweetie? I don't mean to cut this short, but I have to start dinner for Bill. He likes to eat early."

Nicole hadn't met Bill yet, but from what little Jamie told her, it wasn't flattering. "He likes to talk about himself—a lot," Jamie told Nicole. "He's in his fifties, has never been married, drives a flashy car, and throws his money around. Red flags galore," Jamie had concluded.

"Oh, sorry. I'll make it quick. So, I was thinking. Um . . . for graduation, I don't think you and Jamie should come. It's a long drive to see me for fifteen seconds, crossing the stage and shaking hands with someone we will never see again. I'll be home on Sunday. It's no big deal."

"Are you sure? You're graduating college! It's a big day for you."

If I graduate.

"Mom, it's fine, really. Besides, Jamie mentioned that the wedding planner is available on Saturday. You should go to that. It'll be way more fun," Nicole reassured her.

Her mom sighed. "Well, it does take a load off, for sure. Save me the gas and the hotel money, and I still haven't found anyone to dog sit. Then I could go with Jamie and Randy. Hmm . . . Jesse is graduating, too, so I know Jeanie and Jimmy will be there. They can take pictures of you for me."

Nicole's heart jumped. "See, it works out for everyone," she said.

"Jimmy got a new fancy camera, too. Jeanie said he's tired of taking pictures of birds in the backyard," she shared. "Geez, honey, are you sure? How will you get home?"

"Jesse was already taking my stuff home in the U-Haul. I'll just ask him for a ride."

"Well, if it's okay with you, then I guess it's okay with me. We can celebrate at the lake at Jeanie and Jimmy's Annual Fourth of July party. We'll make it a graduation party for you and Jesse, too. I'll call Jeanie later to work out all the details."

**

Nicole hung up the phone with her mother and stared down at the notes she had taken during her call with Jamie. Before she lost focus, she needed to get her thoughts in some sort of order, add them to the report, and be done with it all. But the words spiraled off the page as her mind went round and round, thinking about everything but her paper—not graduating, the driveway, his breath on her neck. She paced her room, scratching at her arms like an addict going through withdrawal.

Four hours later, the piles of clothes on her floor were folded and refolded dozens of times before being packed into her oversized duffle bag. Her closets were empty, her walls were bare, and her desk drawers were cleared out. She refused to stay at Wheeler a minute longer than she needed to. She couldn't. She was graduating on Saturday, even if it killed her.

It wasn't until after all the late-night talk shows were over that Nicole pulled out her desk chair and forced herself to sit and focus on her work. She kept the television on in the background to distract the unsettled part of her brain. Weariness blanketed her as she tried to concentrate while fighting against a new level of panic ramping up inside of her. She was running out of time.

At 3 a.m., with her lids held open by paperclips, she finally finished her paper. She knew it wasn't her best work, but it was done. And at that point, it was good enough.

It has to be.

| 7 |

Nicole

Knock, knock, knock. "Please be here," Nicole quietly pleaded as she stood outside Dr. Bernina's office door a few hours later. She felt a breeze on her neck as a pack of flannel-wearing, travel mug-toting students rushed past her, down the hallway to their finals.

It was unlike Nicole to make the trek across campus without confirming a professor's office hours, but she was so absorbed with being outside when the campus was most crowded that she didn't think to check—*safety in numbers.*

Waiting impatiently, Nicole bounced side to side, listening for signs of life on the other side of his door. *Come on. Come on.*

The door finally opened. "Well, Miss Doherty, you're up early. To what do I owe this pleasure?" Dr. Bernina asked. He smugly stood in the doorway in one of his ugly mosaic print sweaters, a steaming cup of tea in his hand.

Really? "Here you go, revised with your feedback," Nicole said, handing over her typed report.

He blew into his mug before taking a sip. "Shall I send a copy to your new employer, or will you take care of that?" he asked, raising a sarcastic eyebrow.

I deserved that. "That won't be necessary," Nicole conceded with a tight-lipped smile.

"Well then, congratulations," Dr. Bernina said, giving her a slight bow.

"Thank you. I think you'll enjoy the last interview. The boss is a real piece of work." She chuckled.

He walked a few steps into his office and dropped the report on top of a stack of old *Wall Street Journals* on his desk. "Oh, I don't need to read it. I have no doubt it's all there," he said.

"What do you mean you're not going to read it?" *Do you know what you put me through these last couple of days? How much I anguished over this? Worried I wasn't going to graduate? And despite what happened to me, what awful thing happened to me, I still got it done.* Her chest felt tight, like a pressure cooker about to explode.

"Miss Doherty, your paper was already good enough to pass the—" She cut him off.

"So why did you make me do extra work?" she snapped without thinking.

"Well, partly to teach you a lesson on respect." He sat back in his chair and studied her. "But more importantly, good enough doesn't cut it in the real world. Your success in life depends on your character. And your character depends on your willingness to step out of your comfort zone and challenge yourself. Do you want to move up the corporate ladder? Be successful? Grow?"

She nodded.

"Then you better learn to be comfortable with being uncomfortable. It's how it works. Think about it as part of your journey here," he advised, reaching over and patting her shoulder. She flinched back at the feel of his hand.

Tilting his head at her reaction, he asked quietly, "Are you all right?"

She felt the back of her throat begin to close at his question. He couldn't see her break down. She had to get out. Nicole drew herself up, swallowing. "Thanks for the feedback," she said and rushed out of his office.

* * *

Later that night, Nicole was still reeling from her meeting with Dr. Bernina when she walked into the main office in her dorm to start her last night of RA duty. "Hey, Emily," Nicole said to her fellow Resident Assistant.

Emily glanced up from her *Cosmo* magazine splayed open on the clunky aluminum desk in the middle of the room. Her hair was slicked back into a high ponytail, showing off her large hoop earrings. "Should be a quiet night for you. Aside from a couple of other RAs graduating tomorrow, most students are gone for the summer. Rounds should be quick."

Nicole's throat constricted. *Rounds.* She hadn't considered that she'd have to walk the empty halls alone every hour until three a.m.

Emily shot her a look. "You okay? You're white as a ghost."

Waving her off, Nicole said, "No, I'm good. So, what's left to get done?" she asked, changing the subject.

"Easy stuff. Clean out the bulletin board in the lobby and check the empty rooms on your floor for damage and inventory," Emily said, handing Nicole a clipboard. "Need anything else?"

"Nope. Don't think so. Have a good time tonight." She wanted to tell Emily to be careful but hesitated, worried Emily would see right through her and that she would somehow know Nicole's secret.

The door closed behind Emily, leaving Nicole alone in the office. A cascading spider plant and a few cacti in maroon and white pots lined the windowsill, giving life to the otherwise institutionally depressing room. Part of Nicole was happy to have something to keep her busy, even if it meant walking the halls late at night. It beat the alternative—sitting in her room alone, replaying her last three days on a do-while loop in her head, wishing Jamie was there to rub her back and console her until she fell asleep like she had done endless times when they were kids.

Nicole's bottom lip reflexively quivered at the memory. It was easy to see that she needed her big sister. The hard part would be telling Jamie why. She wasn't ready to talk about what happened—she wasn't sure if she ever would be.

Nicole rubbed her hands down her face. *I've got to get out of here.*

With staple remover in hand, Nicole moved to the lobby and started on the bulletin board by the front door, knowing she'd be done in no time and could check it off her list. She needed the boost that came with a sense of accomplishment, as slight as it might be. At that point, she'd take what she could get.

Nicole gently removed the pictures from the board and placed them in a pile to be added to the dorm archives kept in the office, slipping one of her and Megan from their freshman year into her pocket as a keepsake of better times.

As she peeled away the old flyers—where to buy graduation tickets, dates to resell textbooks at the bookstore, rideshares to the airport—Nicole uncovered a formal notice from the Department of Public Safety on Personal Security Tips. She had read it dozens of times. She had sat through dorm meetings about it, half listening with the rest of the group. Everyone knew they wouldn't need it because nothing ever happened at Wheeler. Until it did.

Personal Safety Tips

- Be aware of what's going on around you. Watch out for others.
- In remote areas, walk with a friend.
- Do not prop outside doors open.
- Do not let strangers tailgate into your building.
- At night, walk in well-lit areas of campus and try to avoid walking alone.
- If you don't feel comfortable, call the Department of Public Safety for an escort.
- Remember, alcohol and drugs can impair perceptions of and reactions to situations. Be especially careful if you drink.

- Trust your instincts. If you feel unsafe, get to a safe place and call for help.

Living safely in a community is a shared responsibility, but common sense and crime prevention strategies can help ensure the student's safety and security.

Wheeler College - Department of Public Safety
(518) WLR-SAFE
9-911 Campus Emergency Line

Reading down the bullet-point list, mental alarm bells went off at the same time something plummeted into the pit of Nicole's stomach. Shame? Embarrassment? There it was in black and white—*watch out for others, walk in well-lit areas, avoid walking alone*—pure common sense. But once the door shut behind Megan that night, Nicole was alone, distracted, and too comfortable. The thought of anything happening to her steps away from her room was the farthest thing from her mind.

As much as she wanted to blame someone else for what happened to her—Megan, Dr. Bernina—she could only blame herself.

| 8 |

Nicole

Nicole snapped the bulletin board case closed. The sense of accomplishment she hoped for didn't come. Or if it did, she never felt it. She was too numb with regret.

Leaning against the cool cinderblock wall helped soothe her persistent nausea and refocus. After a few long and frustrated breaths, Nicole was able to stoically file away her shame—behind humiliation and pain—and get back to the tasks at hand.

Nicole dropped the photos off in the office and grabbed the clipboard to start checking empty dorm rooms. She hoped it would be a good distraction and make the night go faster.

At almost eight o'clock, Nicole hesitantly entered the first room. The orange light from the late sunset poured through the double-wide window, breathing little life into the catatonic space. She flicked on the harsh overhead light. It was quiet. Too quiet.

Hugging the clipboard like a childhood teddy bear, Nicole's body tightened. "Okay, what's first?" she mumbled, prying the clipboard from her chest. "Furniture." She barely glanced up from the paper and assumed there were two of everything. *Check, check, check, check,* she marked. "Damage," she whispered, briefly sweeping the room again with her eyes, neglecting to note the spilled nail polish on the desk and the toothpaste-patched holes on the wall.

Nicole scribbled the room number at the top of the page and completed the form with an 'N/A' in the space reserved for any damages found. For the first time in her life, she was doing a half-assed job and couldn't have cared less. The overwhelming need to be safe in her room was getting to her. She checked her clipboard and counted—*only six more rooms.*

By the last room, Nicole had worked herself into a lather and was close to a sheer panic attack. Her skin was flushed, her muscles clenched. She needed to get to her room. Steadying herself with the grip of the doorknob, she wiped the slick of cold sweat from her brow and held her breath like it was her last before running out of a burning building.

Out in the corridor, less than ten steps away from her room, she heard the click of the metal fire door at the end of the hall, followed by sneakers chirping along the floor. The hair on the back of her neck stood at attention. The door slammed shut—*Bang!*—sending echoes through the otherwise empty hallway. A small cry escaped Nicole, hurrying her pace.

"Hey, Nic," a familiar male voice called from behind.

"Ah!" she yelped. Nicole reluctantly turned to find Rob Arnold coming into focus. It always grated on her that Rob called her 'Nic.' She preferred that people other than her close friends and family call her Nicole, but he had done it since the first day they met despite her politely correcting him several times.

Relieved it was only Rob, she blew a sigh from her lips. He strolled toward her, wearing a heather gray Wheeler T-shirt, worn-out jeans, high-watt smile, looking cocky as usual. "Hey, what's up?" she asked. Her eyes drifted down to her clipboard, pretending to be busy reading the papers.

Nicole and Rob had been friendly all year, keeping their conversation light—confined to hallway chatter and staff meetings. Out of loyalty to Megan, Nicole kept her distance from him since he was such a jerk to her the night they hooked up, but she felt obligated to be friendly since they worked together.

"Sorry! Didn't mean to startle you," he said.

Nicole glanced up at him. "No, no, it's fine. I wasn't expecting to see anyone. Guess I'm a little jumpy," she said, letting her shoulder muscles relax.

"Yeah, it's too quiet with no one here, right?" He made a spooky woo-woo sound, dancing his fingers in her face.

"That must be it," she agreed. "Well, don't let me keep you from wherever you were going."

"Oh. I'm just heading to the kitchen to make some food," he said, holding up his saucepan and two packages of ramen. "Can't wait for my parents to get here tomorrow. I asked my mom to make reservations at The Butcherblock for my graduation dinner. I can't remember the last time I had real food, let alone a steak dinner."

"That's the only good place around. I'm sure it'll be mobbed with protein-deficient graduates."

He chuckled and then tightened his gaze. "Ouch, what happened?" he asked, extending his hand near the side of her face.

"Oh. Um." Nicole touched her hand to her cheek. "It's nothing. Looks worse than it is. I'm fine." She waved him off politely.

"You sure? Want me to take a look? I took Advanced Wound Care this semester. I am dying to use my new skills." Rob was the only guy she knew who was graduating with a nursing degree.

Don't touch me. "No, really, I'm fine. Thank you," she said, stepping back.

He put his hands up. "No problem. Just wanted to help."

"I'm good," she said, taking another step.

"Hm. So, hey, I saw you the other night. Looked like you were having a good time."

She shot him a narrowed glare. "What do you mean? Where?"

"Wednesday night. At MacArthur's. You were doing shots with your friend at the bar."

"I don't remember seeing you." *Be especially careful if you drink . . . watch out for others.*

"Yeah, and then I saw you walking into our dorm a little later. I tried to catch up, but you were in a hurry. Late night, huh?" he asked, waggling his eyebrows suggestively. "Surprised you were alone. You know you shouldn't be walking by yourself at night . . . never know who's hanging around in the shadows."

At night, walk in well-lit areas of campus and try to avoid walking alone.

The more Rob said the increasingly uneasy Nicole got. Her initial relief in seeing that it was *just Rob* in the hall faded as fear slowly suffocated her. She felt her face redden, her body visibly trembling. *He was watching me. He knew I was alone.*

After a few blinks, Nicole refocused on Rob's hand waving in her face. "Hello? Nicole? Earth to Nicole . . . Hello?"

Nicole's breaths were short. "I forgot something in my room," she lied, retreating backward, creating as much distance from him as possible, never taking her eyes off him.

He watched her stumble to her door. His stare was locked on her, expressionless. "Wanna hang out?"

She recoiled at the thought.

Nicole knew that once she was inside the safety of her room, there was no way in hell she would come out again. "Um . . . I'm suddenly not feeling well. I'm sure it's nothing. Would you mind taking over rounds? I've done everything already. It should be an easy night."

"You sure you're all right? You seem a little on edge," he said.

"Just need to get some sleep. Been a long week. Thanks," she stammered, slamming the door tight behind her.

She stood still, with one hand over her mouth to quiet her sobs. She waited until his steps retreated down the hall before sliding her back against the door, slowly reaching the floor.

Was it Rob in the dark?

| 9 |

Nicole

On Saturday morning, the Empire Field House was standing room only when the graduation ceremony started. Guests and graduates fanned themselves with their programs, sweating through their clothes and robes on the unseasonably warm May morning in upstate New York.

In a crowd of a thousand people bursting with pride and celebration, Nicole felt alone. A flash of regret for telling her mom and Jamie to stay home passed through her, but then her mind retreated to her run-in with Rob in their dorm the night before, and everyone around her seemed to disappear.

Nicole couldn't reconcile Rob's concerned words— "Let me help you" and "You sure you're okay?"—with his eyes—dark and vacant. She anxiously bounced her knee as if tapping out distress signals with the heel of her shoe. Something wasn't sitting right with her.

And then, the night Megan finally met Rob a year ago popped into Nicole's head, and all the pieces fell into place.

*　*　*

"Oh. My. God. There he is! I can't believe he's here. I am here. He's here. It's fate," Megan squealed in Nicole's ear, bouncing on her toes. "He can't see me freaking out like this."

"Fate? Or maybe it's because we came to a party thrown by his fraternity, and chances were pretty high that he would be here," Nicole shouted over the music pumping from the DJ booth in the corner of the basement.

"Whatever . . . the point is that he and I are in the same room," Megan said, her voice buoyant.

Nicole watched Megan track him around the crowded room like a hunter in a tree stand, waiting for her moment. "I'm going to finally do it. I'm going to talk to him! He's just a guy, right? I can do this! God, I'm sweating. I need a drink," Megan said in a flustered tone, gulping her plastic cup of liquid courage.

Before Nicole could say anything else, Megan had squeezed herself between Rob and one of his frat brothers. Nicole was close enough to see Rob's tightened facial expression as he struggled to hear what Megan said. Just as the music quieted, Nicole heard Megan yell, "I said . . . I love you." *Yikes.*

A few drinks later, Megan reappeared next to Nicole long enough to tell her she was leaving with Rob. Her eyes were wild with anticipation.

"You sure about this?" Nicole asked, concerned.

"Ah, yeah . . . are you kidding? I can't believe this is happening right now. I gotta go!"

A few hours later, Megan showed up on Nicole's doorstep in tears and recounted her story. The night did not go as Megan had hoped. In all her dreams of being with Rob, his kisses were soft and tender, he was playful and flirty, and all of it turned into undeniable passion. "Movie shit," Megan called it. But the only thing that night turned into was a disaster. He was a sloppy drunk, pinning her on the bed and ignoring her when she asked him to slow down.

"Isn't this what you wanted? You're the one that came up to me, remember? I didn't know who you were until tonight. What did you think was going to happen?" Megan retold Rob's words in a mocking voice. It was as if he was an innocent bystander, and it was all on Megan.

***

The longer Nicole sat in her chair in the field house, thinking about Megan's story, the more she was convinced that Rob was the one who attacked her. He pinned Megan down. He didn't listen to her cries. He was rough. And it was hard to ignore his ability to flip his charming personality to a predatory one when he cast the blame on Megan.

Nicole was surprised when the graduation ceremony was over. She had gone through the motions but had no memory of it. Rob had consumed her mind. Taking her place in line, she shuffled with the pack of graduates toward the double doors at the end of the field house.

"Nic!" *Megan!*

Nicole looked up from her feet and saw Megan motioning to her above the sea of black gowns. "Excuse me, excuse me," Nicole repeated, leading with her hand to cut through the crowd. When she finally reached Megan, she jumped into her arms, choking back her tears thick with remorse. *I'm sorry I blamed you.*

"Hey!" Megan cried, hugging Nicole as tightly. "Nic, you better not be getting all emotional on me. You're going to make me ruin my makeup. We've got pictures to take."

"It's a big day!" Nicole tried to cover. "C'mon. Let's get outside. It's like a sauna in here," she said, fanning herself.

Holding hands, they merged into the crowd, funneling out the doors onto the lawn filled with anxiously waiting families, primed to congratulate their graduates with bundles of flowers, stuffed animals, and balloon bouquets.

Nicole paused to admire a young woman's bright green loose-fitting dress. She was jealous of how easily the air swished around the flirty babydoll style, unlike her black synthetic graduation gown that trapped the heat like a glass greenhouse. The woman held a plush teddy bear off to the side of her bulging midsection. Nicole's eyes shifted from the bear's graduation cap to the expectant mother's stare, whose aura glowed in the sun, shooting rays as sharp as spears at Nicole.

Nicole's knees buckled. Her skin was raw and hot, like a new blister. After all that had happened to her, Nicole had not once considered that she could be pregnant. Ever.

She grabbed Megan's arm when she began to go down. "Oh, my God, Nicole," Megan yelped, bracing her. "Are you okay?"

Nicole managed to stay on her feet. After a few counts, her eyes refocused, and she let go of the death grip she held on to Megan. "Yeah. Sorry. It's just so hot out here. Maybe I need some water," she said, fanning herself with her diploma binder.

"Let's go find your mom and sister and get you some. Where are you meeting them?"

"They couldn't make it. They're meeting with a wedding planner today."

Megan shot her a perplexed look underneath the tented hand she held across her forehead. "But it's your college graduation."

Nicole waved her off. "It's fine. I'll see them tomorrow when I get home—no big deal. Besides, you know I don't like to be the center of attention."

Megan's face hardened in disbelief. "Well, we need to get you some water. I'm supposed to meet my parents by the big oak tree in front of Hawkins. We'll get you something over there," Megan said, pointing towards the library.

"Okay."

Megan squinted her eyes, using her hand to shield them from the sun. "You okay to walk?" she asked. "Hey, wait, what happened to your cheek?"

Nicole touched the side of her face. "Oh, that. I had an allergic reaction to my new moisturizer, and I scratched it. Super annoying. But it's much better than it was. You should have seen it on Thursday. Much worse. I'm totally fine. Really. Let's go find your family," Nicole overexplained.

Megan shot her another look like she didn't believe Nicole's story but dropped it when she saw her mom. "Congratulations! I'm so proud of you! So amazing!" Megan's family cheered at her.

Nicole's heart panged watching Megan and her mom embrace. Maybe having a line of loved ones waiting to hug her wouldn't have been so bad after all.

When there was a break in the excitement, Nicole walked over to Megan to say goodbye. Thoughts of pregnancy cycloned in her gut, threatening to vent themselves all over the lawn if she didn't get out of there soon. "Hey," Nicole said, touching Megan's back to get her attention. "I'm going to head to my room. I need to finish packing," she lied.

"Really? Wait, you can't leave without pictures!" she said, turning to her dad.

"Can you take some pictures of Nicole and me, please?"

"Sure, sweetie."

As they wrapped their arms around each other, Nicole thought about their picture from the bulletin board. The image generated a genuine smile for the camera.

Better times.

| 10 |

Nicole

Nicole opened her door to the digital ringing of her push-button phone on the floor across the room. Paranoid she might not be alone, she scanned the area before stepping inside to answer. "It's Jesse," he said, not letting her get in a word. Background voices faded in and out.

"Hey," she said, cradling the receiver in the crook of her neck to unzip her gown. Pinpricks stabbed at the back of her eyes as she rubbed her hands along her stomach. *Could I really be pregnant?*

"My mom wants you to meet us over by the field house. She said something about taking pictures for your mom," he said coolly.

A pulse of heat coursed through her. She had forgotten about that part of the plan. She pushed her fists into her gut and doubled herself over, trying to squeeze any possibility of pregnancy out of her as if it would be that easy to make it go away. "Oh, right. Okay. I'll be right there." Her voice was tight.

Nicole stole a few extra minutes to muster up the energy before reluctantly going outside. The sun was at its peak, blazing onto the sidewalk. For the graduation ceremony, she had hoped to wear the cute maroon tank top dress and strappy sandals she bought a month ago but had to scrap the plan once she saw the bruise the color of Barney on her upper arm that morning. That left her only one choice—a brushed wool black mini she wore to her accounting honor society initiation ceremony last November. Between her long-sleeved dress and the polyester gown, it felt like she was wearing a parka in Hawaii.

She wiped away the glaze of sweat that dripped from the sides of her nose and down the back of her neck, making her way across campus. Cardinals and robins chirped in the shade of the trees lining the street, answering each other's calls. She wondered if they were complaining about the relentless humidity making her scalp tingle—a tell-tale sign that her hair was getting bigger and higher. The only blessing was that the more her hair expanded, the more it covered the scratches on her face, making them less visible when she saw Jesse's parents.

A few feet outside the field house, a woman called out Nicole's name. Looking up from the sidewalk, Nicole found Jeanie, Jesse's mom, enthusiastically waving her arms. Nicole hardly recognized her in the gauzy purple layered dress she was wearing. It contrasted the red, white, and blue striped tube top and short shorts Nicole was accustomed to seeing her in at their annual Fourth of July barbeque. "Nicole, hi!" Jeanie beamed.

"Hi, Jeanie! You look great. I love your dress," Nicole said with a wide smile. "Congratulations on Jesse's graduation."

Jeanie wrapped her arms around Nicole and pulled her in close. Nicole drank in the familiar smell of Jeanie's *Beautiful* perfume, burying her head in Jeanie's honey-blonde hair resting on her shoulder. Her hug felt like home. *Don't let go.*

"Oh, Nicole, I'm so happy to see you! Congratulations to *you*!" she said, pulling away.

"Jimmy! Jimmy! Look, Nicole's here!"

Nicole and Jimmy exchanged waves and smiles. He had a squatty build and wore a dress shirt barely long enough to make it around his gravity-defying beer belly.

"This is so exciting! I can't believe you and Jesse are college graduates. It went by so fast!"

"Some days were a little slower than others, but here we are!" Nicole chuckled.

"Oh honey, I'm so proud of you. I know your mom is too."

"Thank you," she said, choking on an emotional lump.

"It's your turn, kiddo," Jimmy said to Nicole, walking toward her. Nicole never liked having her picture taken on a good day. She was always self-conscious, pasting a fake smile to pose for the lens. But snapshots documenting the aftermath of her last few days took her uncomfortableness to another level.

"Smile, Nicole! No, a real smile! Let me see those teeth! I promised your mom lots of pictures. Jimmy, take some from over there," Jeanie directed, barking orders from behind him.

Nicole put up her hands to shield her face from the lens. Every inch of her skin crawled. She was overheated. She just wanted to be alone. "I think you got 'em all," she said.

When she brought her hands down, she saw that Jesse had joined his parents on the lawn. "Do you want me to take a few of you together?" Nicole pointed to the three of them, redirecting the spotlight away from her.

"That'd be great. Hold on. Jesse, jump in there with Nicole," Jeanie said, still directing. *Please, Jeanie. Just let me go home. Please.*

"I've gotta put my cap on. My hair must look ridiculous," he said, smoothing his wild curls. Each extra second outside ratcheted up Nicole's anxiety another notch.

"Okay, now get a little closer, like you guys have known each other since you were kids!" Jeanie ordered, lifting her heels.

They reluctantly shuffled closer. After a few snaps of the shutter, Jesse surprised Nicole when he wrapped his arm around her shoulder, landing his hand on her bruise. "Ow!" she winced, pulling away awkwardly. Her arm throbbed. "Sorry. It's a little sore," she said, rubbing it. "Must have slept on it wrong."

Jesse shrugged. "Whatever," he said and walked away from her. Nicole was used to his quiet tantrums growing up but wasn't used to having them directed at her. They were usually reserved for his dad or his brother after a bout of their relentless teasing. At the thought, Nicole quickly dismissed Jesse's chilly mood as having nothing to do with her. She assumed Jesse and his dad had a tiff earlier in the day that she hadn't witnessed. It was a common occurrence.

"I think I got 'em all," Jimmy said, giving them a thumbs up.

"Thanks for taking the pictures for my mom. I am sure she will appreciate it," Nicole said to Jimmy. She could finally go back to her room and stay there.

She turned to Jesse. "Hey. Is it okay if I ride home with you tomorrow in the U-Haul?"

His mouth was tight. "Sure."

Ignoring his tone, she was relieved he agreed to help her. She didn't have a backup plan. But she knew Jesse would be there for her. He always was. "Great. That's a huge help."

"I'll pick you up around nine," he said.

Nicole looked at her watch, mentally starting a countdown clock to escape her hell. "Works for me," she said, then pivoted to Jeanie for a hug goodbye. "It was so great seeing you."

"Where do you think you're going? You're not done with us yet. You're coming to dinner," Jeanie said.

"Oh, that's very nice, but I am sure you all want to be together as a family."

"Yes, we do, which includes you. Don't be so silly. I made a reservation at that nice steakhouse for the four of us. What's it called again, Jimmy?"

"The Butcherblock," he responded, fiddling with his camera lens.

Goosebumps darted up the sleeves of her graduation robe. *Rob.* "Thank you, really, but I've got to finish packing my stuff. I've got food in my fridge." Her voice was borderline shaky.

Jeanie pulled her head back with a raised eyebrow. "Leftovers on your last night at college? Now you're being ridiculous. You're going. Get in the car."

| 11 |

Jamie

"You excited?" Randy asked.

Jamie nodded absently. She was mesmerized by the fiery glitter from her engagement ring caught in the afternoon light dancing along the interior of Randy's new ascot green BMW M3. She had been in her head since she woke up that morning. That day was her big moment to impress her future mother-in-law, and the crater-sized pit opening in her middle wasn't helping her anxiety.

She used to be more confident but somehow started to lose her footing once she got engaged to Randy and began obsessing about Karen's approval. She hated her growing need for acceptance from his family so much that part of her would rather sit through Nicole's mind-numbing graduation ceremony instead of heading to The Sullivan that day. At least she would have the comfort of her sister.

Jamie picked a piece of lint from her linen pants. "Excited . . . and anxious . . . like I might throw up." She rolled the lint between her fingers before dropping it onto the floormat. "I'm worried I'll make a fool of myself," she admitted.

Randy wrapped his oven-mitt-sized hand around Jamie's, pulling it to his lips. "What are you worried about? You get along with everyone. People love you. More importantly . . . I love you," he said, giving her hand a soft kiss before letting go to downshift and pull into her mother's driveway.

She brushed her hand over the three-inch wedding planning binder resting on her lap. Since Randy proposed, she had been collecting magazine pages of gowns, flower arrangements, rings, and cakes, which she meticulously organized in her handcrafted white lace and tulle-adorned album. "It's a big day. I want everything to be perfect."

He put the car in park and leaned in. "Hon, look at me," he said. Jamie's eyes met his and immediately softened. He had that effect on her. "Everything is going to be fine. Besides, my mom will be there. She has a lot of experience putting on client events for the firm. She'll be a big help. Have fun with it."

She's the one I'm worried about!

Randy was built like a rock wall but was soft at heart and loved her in a way she didn't know was possible. Jamie's parents weren't good role models for love, but it was all she knew. Before Randy, she often found herself in relationships with men who treated her the way her father treated her mother—badly. She thought being with a guy who lied and cheated was part of being a couple. It beat being alone. Isn't that why her mom stayed all those years?

But Randy showed her a different kind of love. One that was chivalrous, which she welcomed. From their first night out together in college, he made her a priority, making her feel wanted and secure. It could be something as small as giving her his coat on a chilly night to surprising her with private tennis lessons to build her confidence after she told him how uncomfortable she felt at his country club. When he got down on one knee and asked her to be his wife, she wondered what she did to deserve him and vowed to do whatever was necessary to stay with him forever.

Her shoulders dropped a few inches. She knew he was right. Her mind was getting the best of her. Besides, Randy would be there too to keep her at ease. "It's nervous energy. Once we get there, I'll be better. I'm excited to share my vision for the wedding with your mom and Susan."

"Who?"

"Susan, the wedding planner. I told you about her."

"This is your department, hon. I'm just the driver." He smiled. Jamie's insides somersaulted. *What?*

"But you're supposed to be a part of the planning. It's our day. It should represent us." If she had any chance of winning over Karen, Randy had to be there to hold her hand and lend his credibility. *Please don't leave me.*

He didn't bite. "You're always so thoughtful about all the details. It's one of the reasons I love you. Whatever you decide, I know it will be perfect."

She pressed her mouth against his and gave it one last shot. "Are you trying to sweet talk me out of helping?"

Before he could answer her, Jamie heard the clomping of her mother's wooden bottom clogs on the driveway. Jamie pulled away in time to notice that her mother was dressed in her post-PTA night out with her fellow teacher's outfit—a brightly colored floral blouse tucked into her high-waisted belted jeans and a pair of large drop earrings.

"Hi, sweetie. Hi Randy," Anne said. The dozens of silver bangles jangled on her wrist as she pulled the car door closed.

"Hi, Mom," Jamie said, still processing her conversation with Randy. "Ready?"

They drove in silence until Anne perked up from the back. "Jamie, is this the style dress you were thinking about?" Anne asked, leaning into the front seat to show her pages in the *Bridal Guide* she had packed. The magazine was opened to a model in front of an old stone building wearing a white lace, fit-and-flair gown with a matching floor-length veil. "You have such a beautiful figure. I think that shape is perfect for you. Or there's this one on the other page with a sweetheart neckline." She pointed to it. "Chances are it will be sweltering hot in July, and you definitely don't want sleeves."

Jamie grabbed the magazine from her mother's hands. "Mom! Randy can't know anything about my dress!" she snapped, slamming it shut and throwing it into the backseat. Jamie knew her annoyance was misdirected at her mother, but she couldn't help herself. She was beginning to panic.

"Hon, I didn't see the pictures. And besides, I don't know the difference between a sweetheart neckline and a plunging V. Don't worry."

"Trust me. You'd know if you saw me in a plunging neckline. And you'd probably pick it," Jamie said, catching the end of his smile. She let out a big exhale and rolled her shoulders backward to ease the tension in the back of her neck. *Pull yourself together.*

Jamie half turned to the backseat and met her mother's eye. "Sorry, Mom." Anne extended her hand and squeezed Jamie's shoulder.

A half-hour later, Randy drove across the island bridge, exposing the enormous main house of the historic Sullivan Resort perched on the hill. The bright white, board and batten exterior, nestled among the Adirondacks and surrounded by the waters of Lake George, was a prime example of colonial revival architecture. It was almost too much to take in all at once.

"Wow," was all Jamie could get out before a laugh of disbelief sprang from her chest. At the sight of the resort, the giddiness she felt about having the wedding of her dreams flooded back, crushing any trepidations she had about the day.

Randy shined a grin at her.

"Oh, sweetie, it is absolutely gorgeous," Anne chirped from the backseat.

Jamie barely waited for Randy to put the car in park before she grabbed her bag, clutched her binder, and jumped out of the vehicle. "I'll meet you in the front," she yelled over her shoulder, running ahead.

She made a beeline for the massive wraparound front porch, passing by a young couple sharing a bottle of wine and playing a game of lawn checkers with game pieces the size of manhole covers. *That's going to be us!*

Jamie dashed up the staircase, her sandals shuffling on the wooden steps. From the top, she scooped up the generous view of the property, fantasizing about her wedding day. Caught in the moment, she twirled around like Julie Andrews at the foot of the Alps in *The Sound of Music*, holding the train of her imaginary wedding dress. Ribbons of purples and reds swirled in her vision as her eyes swept over the overflowing baskets filled with fuchsia, cascading geraniums, and verbena hanging above the railings. It was more beautiful than she had ever dreamed.

Randy and Anne eventually caught up to Jamie and stood at the base of the staircase. "Oh, Randy, it's so pretty here! I can already see myself getting out of a white limo right where you're standing in the circular drive, photographers over there, the lake, and the mountains in the background. It is going to be unforgettable!" Jamie beamed.

She was bubbling with excitement, needing to take another twirl. With her head tipped back, she lowered her lids and spun again.

Jamie would have stayed in her dreaminess longer if it hadn't been for her smacking into something, or worse, someone, mid-spin.

Her eyes flared wide when she found her future mother-in-law hunched over. "Karen!" she cried, stumbling to keep her balance. In her moment of bliss, Jamie missed seeing Karen and Randy Sr. walk out from inside the building onto the porch but quickly learned when she pirouetted her elbow into Karen's gut, practically knocking her over. Fortunately, Randy Sr. was standing next to Karen to catch her. *This can't be happening.*

"You really should be more careful, dear," Karen said, slowly uprighting herself. She clutched her pearls and glared at Jamie.

"I am really sorry. I guess I got caught up in the moment. Are you okay?" Jamie asked, watching Randy Sr. and Randy, who had run up the stairs to his mother's side.

"Mom, are you all right?" Randy asked. "Can I get you anything? Some water?"

"That's very kind. Thank you, sweetheart," Karen said to Randy, patting his hand.

Jamie's mouth dried up like a puddle in the desert as she watched Randy disappear inside the building.

Her gaze darted to Karen—all five feet ten of her willowy, intimidating frame. With her white bob pulled back with a gilded clip, Jamie could see the disdain in her expression.

Out of nowhere, Anne appeared next to Jamie. Amongst the embarrassing chaos, Jamie had forgotten she was there. Anne touched Jamie's lower back, a small but comforting gesture. "Hi, Karen. Randy Sr. It's nice to see you again," Anne said. She gave them her biggest smile and led their attention toward the water. "Wow, this place is stunning, huh? And such beautiful weather today." Jamie felt unexpectedly nurtured. *Thanks, Mom.*

"This is one of our favorite places to visit," Karen explained. She drew in a big inhale. "That crisp, clean air always transports me back to my childhood when my parents would bring us here to summer."

Since when is summer a verb?

Randy Sr. wasn't much of a talker but always a gentleman. "It's nice to see you again, Anne. Jamie," he said to the two women, offering a dry smile.

The uncomfortable air thinned when a petite blonde woman approached them with Randy in tow. "Hello, hello!" she bellowed. "Where is my bride?"

It was Susan, the planner. Jamie felt as though someone had pulled a relief valve from her chest. "That's me," Jamie said, stepping forward.

"Hi Jamie, I'm Susan. We spoke on the phone," she said, shaking Jamie's hand. Susan rocked a pixie cut and was smartly dressed in khaki-colored slim-cut Capri pants, a black double-breasted jacket, and leopard print flats. "I already met your handsome fiancé inside. Who else do we have here?"

Jamie drifted to Randy's side as she made all the introductions, giving him a tight-lipped smile before lowering her stare to the floor. Randy knotted his fingers through hers and gave her hand a few pumps, reassuring her that everything was okay.

"Well, it's wonderful to meet all of you! Welcome to The Sullivan!" Susan said, clapping the back of her clipboard. On any other day,

Susan's perkiness would have been contagious, but that day was beginning to feel like the tickle in the back of the throat before a strep diagnosis. "All right, so are we ready for the tour?"

Randy spoke up. "Actually, we're going to break away," motioning between him and his father. "We'll catch up with you at the end." He looked at Jamie with a glimmer of amusement. "Hey, hon, Dad and I are going to do some of our own research. Make sure the bartenders in this place know what they're doing. If you need us, we'll be right in there," he said, throwing a thumb over his shoulder toward the bar through the glass door.

Jamie gave a reluctant smile. "Randy," she said, starting to object but then catching the look on his face. It was the same disinterested look his father wore. Staring up at the men standing shoulder to shoulder, she had never noticed how much Randy looked like his father—the same brown, upturned eyes and fuller lips that blended into their strong chins. It was like Randy was standing next to his age-progressed self. She backed down. "Sure, Randy, have fun. I'll let you know what we decide."

Randy positioned himself in front of her and pulled her in for a hug. He whispered through his kiss on her forehead, "You're going to be fine. I promise."

She hoped he was right because her brief moment of confidence was lost after she gut-punched her future mother-in-law. After one final squeeze, he turned on his heel and left her to fend for herself. She couldn't breathe.

"Great. Tell Charlie, the bartender, that your drinks are on me," Susan peeped, excusing the men. "Ladies! Are we ready? I hope you've got your walking shoes on. We have a lot of ground to cover."

Jamie managed to swallow the suffocating goiter in her neck and paint a smile on her face. "I'm ready!"

For the next two hours, Susan led the women around the property. Jamie's pulse quickened with each passing ballroom, guest cottage, and portico. She tried to contain her enthusiasm to match Karen's stone face and collectiveness. It was proving more difficult as the tour went on, especially with Anne, who was never far from Jamie's side, 'oohing and ahhing and 'oh my gosh'ing at every turn.

Jamie thought she had seen all the beauty the resort offered until they entered the grand ballroom, and her mouth dropped open at its grandeur. "I always like to end the tour here," Susan said. "Save the best for last."

"I'd say," Jamie said, moving to the middle of the room. She had never seen such a contrast in style and was surprised at how well it worked. Its massive size somehow felt homey with its mix of formal luxury and rustic charm. Her eyes were drawn to the crystal chandeliers hanging from the exposed beams in the thirty-foot ceilings. Slowly rotating, Jamie dizzily counted three stone fireplaces, finally landing her sights on the wall of floor-to-ceiling windows that beckoned the native surroundings of the lake and the mountains inside. "Wow," she whispered to herself.

"The French doors on the ends open to the patio," Susan said, leading them to the covered stone terrace. "Many guests choose to have their cocktail hour out here."

Anne chimed in. "I can see why. My goodness, the view is breathtaking."

"How many guests are you expecting?" Susan asked Jamie.

"Three hundred plus," Karen said at the same time Jamie responded, "Maybe fifty to sixty, including friends."

Jamie's eyes grew wide. "Three hundred?" She gulped.

Anne let out a chuckle. "We don't know a hundred people, let alone three."

"Well, we do," Karen said dismissively. "Not only do we have our dear friends from the club, but we also need to invite Rand's business partners. And, of course, we can't forget his important clients—and potential ones, too. Jamie, dear, this event is as much your wedding as it is a business opportunity for the men to grow the firm. You need to think bigger."

Jamie felt small. Her face flushed as she turned to Susan with a meekish smile. She hoped her embarrassment didn't show. "Well, it sounds like we have a big event to plan," she said, letting out a laugh rippled with nerves. "I brought my binder to show you some of my ideas. I am so excited to get started with the planning. My mind is on warp speed."

Karen moved between Jamie and Susan. "Jamie. Please. Let me handle this," Karen said over her shoulder. Jamie wondered if she knew how to speak to people aside from down at them.

"Susan. Here is how I see this day going," Karen started. "Rehearsal dinner on the boat the night before the ceremony, wedding on the lawn with the lake as a backdrop, cocktail hour on the terrace while your people change out the chairs from the ceremony to tables for dinner, and then reception back on the lawn next to the lakeshore. Of course, the cocktail party will be an open bar and passed hors d'oeuvres. The reception will be buffet, with no assigned seating— we want to keep people mingling. I'll put you in contact with the manager of a lovely jazz ensemble we use at the club for our annual fundraiser."

Jazz? Buffet? What about my seating chart and handmade place cards? What about what I want?

Susan jotted notes on her clipboard. "Great choices," she agreed. "My team and I will work with Jamie to iron out all the details."

Karen waved her off. "No need to get Jamie involved. We're paying for the wedding, so I'll handle this. She can worry about getting into shape and finding her dress." Dismissing others so casually must be common among patrons who *summer* at The Sullivan because Susan didn't even flinch at Karen's harshness, unlike Anne and Jamie, whose jaws simultaneously went unhinged.

Get into shape? Fuck you, Karen!

Jamie couldn't silence the click of her sharp breath before she snapped her mouth closed and let Karen's words settle into every nook and cranny of insecurity Jamie hid inside. Quietly fidgeted with the lace and tulle on her binder, she wished she never brought her stupid book. She looked like a child eager to share her art project from school instead of a woman who knew what she wanted. It was just another sign that she was out of her league.

What am I getting myself into?

| 12 |

Nicole

It was already past four o'clock when Nicole slid into the booth beside Jesse at The Butcherblock. She couldn't help but think she'd be home safe and far away from Wheeler by the same time the following day. *Out of sight, out of mind.*

"This place is so nice," Jeanie said, peering over the top of her menu.

Nicole followed her eye into the dining room, scanning it for any sign of Rob, trying not to give away the anguish rolling inside her. The steakhouse was darkly lit, making it difficult for Nicole to spot Rob. But that didn't mean he wasn't there. *I saw you at MacArthur's . . . I saw you walking into our dorm.*

Nicole sipped her water and let the icy thought plunge down her back.

"I'm starving," Jimmy said, smoothing down his thick salt and pepper mustache while he scanned the specials.

"Me too," Jeanie said, putting on her glasses to read the menu.

Nicole looked over at Jesse, who could only nod in agreement with half a buttered roll stuffed in his cheeks.

"You're reminding me of that time you shoved a sleeve of mini powdered donuts in your mouth at the lake." Nicole guffawed.

Jesse swallowed his roll with a chuckle. "I didn't want Jeremy to get any of them, and then it became a challenge on how many I could fit in my mouth."

"I think you were up to five before you started choking."

"If I died, it still would have been worth it as long as he didn't get any."

Jeanie shook her head. "Always a competition with you and your brother."

The waiter stood at the end of the table and asked, "Would you like to start with drinks . . . or are you ready to order your entrees," eyeing the empty breadbasket in the middle of the table.

A moment after the waiter walked away with their orders, Jeanie popped up in her seat and called him back. "I think today calls for champagne!" she announced. "We're celebrating these two kids, and today, we're doing it in style! I'd like a bottle of Dom Perignon."

"Mom, that's crazy. It's way too expensive," Jesse insisted.

Nicole nodded. "I agree. I am fine with water."

"I didn't ask for your permission. I am insisting. But don't get used to it. Tomorrow, we're back to boxed Franzia Chardonnay," she said with a belly laugh.

Moments later, the waiter returned with a perfectly chilled bottle of Dom and poured four servings into the tall, skinny flutes. Jeanie was the first to grab hers. "I'd like to make a toast," she said, holding up her glass and clanking it quietly with her fork.

"Mom . . ." Jesse said.

"Oh, hush you," Jeanie said, swatting him away. "It isn't every day my son graduates from college." She held up her glass and started again. "To Jesse and Nicole, congratulations on getting through the easiest part of life." She cackled.

Jeanie elbowed Jimmy with raised eyebrows. Nicole caught Jesse's eye roll and gave him a soft smile. "Seriously," Jeanie said, holding her eyes on Nicole and Jesse. "To Jesse and Nicole, a big congratulations to you today! We are very proud of you both, and we know that life has many more wonderful things in store for you." *More?* Nicole wasn't greedy. She'd take one. "Love you both so very much. Cheers!"

"Cheers!" they all echoed, clinking their glasses.

After a few sips of her champagne and devouring her house salad, Nicole felt her body relax into her chair.

Jeanie put down her salad fork and her elbows on the table, leaning in. "On our drive here this morning, Jimmy and I were remembering how much fun it was watching you kids grow up together. Nicole, do you remember the first time we all met? Summer of '85, I think," she said with a knowing smile.

"How could I forget? It was the day after my mom told us she had to sell our house. We packed whatever could fit her beat-up Civic wagon and moved into your basement."

Jeanie's smile faded. "Your mom had some stuff she needed to sort out, true. But I remember how adorable you were walking into the kitchen with your arms wrapped tight around your Garfield stuffed animal."

Nicole let out a half-hearted chuckle. 'Sort out' was Jeanie's nice way of saying that when Nicole's drunk, cheating father wrapped his car around a tree after a night out, enjoying both of his vices, he left her mom with no money and a pile of unpaid bills, leaving them homeless.

"You were so nice to let us take over the bottom floor of your house. Not sure I'd be able to let a family move into my house for an *entire* summer," Nicole reflected.

"Are you kidding? I was so happy to have you all there. When I was a kid, we would spend the summer at the lake, and my parents' friends would vacation there with their kids for weeks at a time. I have such cherished memories and wanted to give my kids that same experience. It was a no-brainer when you all needed a place to stay."

"You're a good friend," Nicole said as the waiter delivered their dinner to the table.

"Yeah, well, your mom didn't have it so easy raising you girls alone, and I was dealing with my own grief after my mom died, so it was an opportunity for us to support each other. That first summer was the seed that blossomed into this beautiful annual tradition."

Digging into their main courses, Nicole thought about how right Jeanie was. After a couple of awkward days that first year—getting to know Jesse, sharing a bathroom with strangers, sitting as a big family every night for dinner—they had settled into a routine. Their house felt like a real home, one she craved for herself. By Labor Day, Nicole was already excited for the following year.

"I remember that first summer like it was yesterday. I was so scared to go in the lake because I couldn't see the bottom," Nicole said.

Jesse interjected, "You used to freak out whenever something brushed up against you." Nicole wiped away the phantom lakeweed from her leg underneath the table at his words.

"True. But then you and I started swimming out to the floating dock, and it became a competition, so I got over my fear pretty quickly."

The memories were so vivid for Nicole. Suddenly, she was twelve years old, hair wet and tangled, wrinkled fingers, a towel draped over her shoulders, sitting next to Jesse on the dock with their legs dangling off the edge, eating Italian ice after a day in the water.

Jimmy chimed in, "Remember that time Nicole beat Jesse in the swim race we organized for all you kids? Boy, Jesse, were you mad. 'I slipped! She got a head start! It's not fair! We need a do-over! Do over!'" Jimmy mocked. His extended belly bounced with his loud, raspy laugh.

Jesse huffed.

"That was almost as funny as when Nicole beat Jesse at miniature golf," Jeanie howled. "You swung your putter at that lobster claw on the Maine hole so hard that the head snapped right off. We were worried we'd have to buy a new club. What a temper you had."

"Around the U.S. in 18 Holes, I used to love that place. I earned my bragging rights that year, didn't I?" Nicole teased. But her amusement was stifled when Jesse's jaw tightened.

"Wow, it's like Jeremy is here," Jesse said, downing the last of his champagne. Nicole exchanged a look with Jeanie. They had hit a nerve.

When Nicole first met Jeremy, Jesse's older brother, she thought she had met her future husband. Any time she saw him around the lake, it felt like she had a kaleidoscope of butterflies fluttering in her stomach, and she'd get a tingle between her legs. He reminded her of Jason Bateman, Ricky Schroders' friend on *Silver Spoons*—dark hair, freckles, quick wit, and a little mischievous. But after she saw Jeremy repeatedly torment Jesse, usually in front of a crowd, and how hurt Jesse would get, the tingles went away, and Jeremy's luster wore off. He made being an ass look like a sport.

"Oh, Jesse. Don't be such a little girl," Jimmy said. "You're always so sensitive."

Now I know where Jeremy gets it from.

After they finished their meals, the waiter reappeared. "Anyone save room for dessert?" he asked, breaking the silence. "Unfortunately, we are out of the cheesecake before you answer."

Nicole felt Jesse's eyes on her when she let out a disappointing sigh. "I'm fine with coffee, thank you," Nicole said.

With their orders in, Jeanie spoke up. Nicole sensed she was trying to change the mood. "Gosh, how many times did your mother and I take you kids to see *Footloose* that first summer?" She chuckled.

"Any time it rained," Jesse complained. "And if I remember, it was a very wet year."

"What did you expect from us? You kids were going stir-crazy in the house, and it was a cheap option. *Footloose* was playing at the dollar theatre. Don't you remember, we used to pack a huge beach tote and sneak in sodas, Ziploc bags of homemade popcorn, and a box of gummy bears for each of you? And then we'd let you guys sit a few rows ahead of us—close enough to keep an eye on you but far enough away that you couldn't see us sipping our airplane-size bottles of Sutter Home White Zin while we shared our bag of popcorn."

"No wonder you wanted to go so often!" Nicole teased. "You kept us distracted with the candy and the movie while you were busy day drinking."

Jeanie let out a cackle. "You make us out to be terrible mothers. I'd like to think we were resourceful."

"The snacks were the only part that made it bearable," Jesse said dryly.

"Oh, stop, it wasn't that bad," Jeanie shot back. "And besides, being uncomfortable builds character, which is good."

Nicole cringed at Jeanie's words, reminding her of Dr. Bernina. *'Your success in life depends on your character. And your character depends on your willingness to step out of your comfort zone and challenge yourself.'*

Jesse questioned his mother's logic. "You're seriously arguing that *Footloose* has made me a better person?" His tone was unreadable.

Nicole turned in Jesse's direction and was happy to see his face was showing signs of softening. "I'll give it to her. In the end, we did have fun. Remember the recital we put on for everyone at the end of the season when we reenacted the final prom scene from the movie? I can still see you flying down the basement stairs as Ren and me pretending to be Ariel, throwing a handful of glitter in the air for your grand entrance," Nicole said.

"I do!" Jeanie said. "I'm still finding it in the dryer lint catcher. Glitter never dies," she said, pumping her fist in Nicole's direction.

Nicole met Jesse's expression and pushed her leg against his, telling him to lighten up. She loved being around Jesse's relaxed and fun side, and by the slight crinkle in the corner of his eye, he was back. While they enjoyed their last drops of coffee, Jimmy settled the check.

"Thank you so much for including me," Nicole said to Jimmy as he held the door open, motioning for the people waiting outside to come in first. And then, there he was.

Horror sinched around Nicole's chest. She couldn't breathe. "Oh, hey, Nic! Funny seeing you here," Rob said, standing in the doorway behind a woman with his same jet-black hair and ice-blue eyes. "Feeling better? I saw you earlier and wanted to check on you, but you were with a group of people taking pictures. I didn't want to bother you."

She ducked her head to avoid showing the color bottom out of her face. *"I saw you earlier . . ."* He was taunting her, making sure she knew he was watching her. Her pulse was thready. She felt faint. She needed air.

"Yup, I'm fine. Sorry, we were leaving," Nicole said hurriedly. She ran out of the restaurant, practically knocking over another family walking inside.

Nicole stood in the sun on the sidewalk, rubbing her clammy palms on the front of her dress. Sweat dotted along her forehead. She needed to get to her room. *Safe and alone.* Thankfully, Jimmy had let the crowd of new customers into the restaurant before leading Jeanie and Jesse outside. It gave Nicole a few seconds to shake her nerves.

"Friend of yours?" Jeanie asked.

"No!" she cried. Jesse's head popped up. Her adamant response seemed to catch his attention. "Sorry. We work together. We're both RAs in the same building," she said in a less defensive tone.

"Oh. I thought something was wrong. The way you ran out of there."

"Nope. All good," Nicole assured her.

And I'll be even better tomorrow with Wheeler in the rearview mirror.

| 13 |

Nicole

Sunday morning arrived, and Nicole could practically taste her freedom. Leaving Wheeler was her first big hurdle to moving on. The thought of her next obstacle was locked away in a 'can't deal with this right now' mental compartment. Terrified at the possibility of being pregnant, she decided to wait until she was in the comfort of her home before taking a test.

"C'mon, Jesse . . . where are you?" she said under her breath. It was a 9:01 a.m. One minute past her breaking point. Her teeth chattered nervously. She was on the verge of a meltdown. *What if he got into an accident? What if he forgot about me? What if he's already halfway home? How would I get in touch with him?*

Her catastrophic spiraling thoughts were interrupted at 9:04 a.m. when the phone rang. She pounced on it. "Hello!" she said eagerly.

"You ready?" Jesse asked. *Jesse!* His voice physically affected her—her chest drummed, her pulse raced.

"I will be by the time you get here. Just finishing up packing my clothes," she lied. Nicole had been packed for almost two days. "Thank you again for doing this. Really. Thank you. Thank you," she sputtered, bouncing on her toes.

"No problem. I'll park in the driveway next to your building. Meet me out there." Her heels dropped to the floor, her systems halted—*the driveway.*

Saliva pooled in her mouth like she was about to vomit. "Um, would you mind coming in? I need help carrying my stuff." She'd never admit it, but her arm still hurt, and she couldn't manage anything heavy.

"A real damsel in distress," he deadpanned.

Nicole winced at his comment, taking her need for help as a sign of weakness. She would rather suffer in silence. "Never mind. I'll figure it out."

"It's fine. I'll come in." She heard him smile. "See you in ten."

With nothing left to do except wait, Nicole paced around her room. Closet, bed, window, desk . . . closet, bed, window, desk . . . jitters building with every step.

While she accrued endless laps, Nicole's mind toggled between her self-image of being a victim and starting her new life as a briefcase-toting, confident professional woman. She was mentally and physically exhausted from carrying the shame. Her body was healing, but her mind was still held hostage by the memories. As long as she was at Wheeler, there was no way she could escape the constant reminders—the driveway, the dumpster, Rob. She was more than ready to leave the panic-stricken and humiliated Nicole behind and knew a change of scenery would be a great start.

At the rhythmic patter of footsteps in the hallway, Nicole threw herself against the door, pressing her eye to the peephole. Her heart did a cartwheel at the sight of Jesse and his worn-out Yankees hat. His dark, curly locks rested along the collar of his Wheeler Swim Team pullover.

Before he could knock, Nicole grabbed the handle and swung open the door. "Hi!"

His eyebrows shot up, disappearing under his hat. "Whoa, hey."

From the hallway, his presence was like a beam of light cutting through her darkness. "Sorry, I didn't mean to startle you," she said, stepping aside to let him in.

"You are *way* too peppy for a Sunday morning," he said wryly, sidling by her. "I forgot you were a morning person."

"I probably had one too many cups of coffee." More lies.

"Just one?" he quipped, scanning the room. "This everything?" He pointed to the overstuffed bags of clothes and the small stack of milk crates filled with accounting textbooks. "What about the futon?"

"Yes, to the pile, no to the futon. Leaving it to be donated." Nicole refused to bring any reminders of Wheeler into her new life.

He loaded up his arms, she carried a small bag, and they headed outside. Passing by the budding trees that lined the courtyard, Nicole's limbs felt lighter at the sign of spring—rebirth, renewal, regaining control of her life.

Nicole drew a breath and held it as she turned right and started down the driveway to where she thought Jesse had parked.

"Hey, this way," he said, nodding to the left toward the main road. Giddy relief shot through her like a flash of lightning when she saw the hazards blinking on the truck parked in front of her dorm. *I love you, Jesse Young.* "I figured everyone was gone. I could park here. No one should bother us. We won't be long."

When Jesse pushed open the tailgate, Nicole was struck by how full the trailer was. "Wow, you have so much more stuff than I thought you would. This is all yours?"

His eyes pinched. "What do you mean? I have a whole apartment to bring home," he snapped.

"I assumed guys brought a couple of towels, their favorite pillow, and their CD collection to college. I wasn't expecting all this," she said, taking in all the furniture, boxes, bags of winter coats, and laundry baskets filled to the top with neatly folded clothes.

"I like to feel at home, not like I'm living in someone else's house."

"I respect that," she said, stepping into the truck and dropping her bag in an empty corner. A sour odor hit high in her nose. *Hurk!* She gagged. "What is *that* smell? Oh, God, I think it's that." She pointed to the lopsided plaid couch. "Actually, I take it back. I don't respect anyone who wants to keep that."

"What do you mean? I love that couch."

"Obviously. But let me do you a favor and help you bring it to the curb. You can leave it here with my futon."

"It's not that bad. It's just a little loved."

"You call that love? It has burn holes on the arm, stains from I don't want to know, and that stench," she said, holding her hand to her nose. "C'mon, you take that side. I'll get this one." Nicole squatted, pretending to pick up the end of the couch.

He took a few sniffs. "I don't smell anything."

"Really? I don't think I can un-smell it," she teased.

He jumped down from the truck. "The couch is staying."

"Your choice, but don't be surprised if the health department shows up at your house one day. And don't say I didn't try to warn you."

Jesse was barely listening to Nicole's mocking. He was ten steps ahead of her, heading back inside to get the last of her stuff.

When she got to her room, he was standing in the middle, holding the last crate. "This it?"

"Looks like it," Nicole said, taking one last sweep of the room, her gaze stopping at the garbage can. She saw the sleeve of her denim shirt from the other night jutting out of the plastic Chinese takeout bag. Shame flamed her cheeks. "Let's get out of here," she insisted, shutting the door behind her forever.

Nicole practically floated down the hallway, held up by the feeling of being released from prison for a crime she didn't commit. Her eyes burned at the sentiment, but she managed to will her tears away before they surfaced.

That was until they got into the truck, and reality hit. *It's over.*

With little time to react, tears raged down her cheeks. Mortified, she scrambled to find a napkin in her bag to mop them up before Jesse noticed, but then she began to laugh. Hard. She was caught between laughing *and* crying and couldn't stop. Her whole body shook as emotions raced through her veins looking for an out. She had lost complete control.

"Jesus. What's the matter?" Jesse asked, panicked.

"Nothing. I'm fine. Really," she said. Her nose dripped down her top lip into her mouth.

"Really? You don't look like it."

Nicole couldn't speak. She tried to use her hands to tell him she needed a tissue, but he had no idea what she was doing.

"Two words? TV show? What?" he guessed and then threw up his hands, which only sent Nicole further into hysterics.

Five minutes and a few convulsions later, Nicole finally caught her breath. Through the haze of tears, she found a few old tissues in her purse. After she blew her nose and wiped her puffy eyes, she finally said, "Despite what you witnessed, I'm fine. We can go now."

"Are you sure? Shouldn't we talk about the exorcism first?"

Whatever you want to call it, it was cathartic.

Nicole's head was clear, and she was happy to spend a few mindless hours on the road. "I'm sorry. I am not sure what happened." Nicole let out an uncomfortable chuckle.

"Maybe you should lay off the caffeine."

"I'll think about it." She smiled. "Ready?"

"You sure you're okay?" he asked.

"Honestly, I'm good." Nicole turned toward the passenger window, trying to compose herself. Embarrassment seared her skin like a third-degree burn. She wasn't used to being emotional in front of others. Certainly not Jesse.

Nicole could feel his stare. She wiped her face with her sleeve and turned to him. Under the shadow of the brim of his baseball hat, his hazel eyes were filled with concern, making her feel even more vulnerable. Nicole didn't like anyone worrying about her. She didn't want his sympathy or his pity. "You know how to drive this big rig?" she asked, diverting his attention.

"I just need to turn around, and then it should be smooth sailing from there."

"Famous last words." She watched Jesse do a perfect three-point turn, backing into the driveway.

"Can you tilt the mirror more towards you so I can see the back corner of the truck?" Jesse asked.

Nicole rolled down the window and pulled the clipboard-size mirror towards her. "Sure. Like this?"

"Perfect."

Nicole caught her reflection in the mirror alongside the green dumpsters in the distance and immediately clamped her eyes shut. She was done with Wheeler. She wanted out. She needed out. She needed to move on.

Out of sight, out of mind, she recited as Jesse pulled away from campus.

* * *

Not long into their ride home, Jesse's stomach rumbled like he hadn't eaten in days.

"Hungry?" she asked. They had close to three hours before they were home, and there were limited rest stops once they were driving through the Adirondacks.

Jesse glanced at Nicole through his Maui Jim's before turning his eyes back to the road. "What makes you think that?" Jesse cleared his throat. "Sorry, I guess I forgot to eat this morning."

"Who forgets to eat? I am already planning what I am going to have for dinner."

"I guess I got caught up loading the truck and getting to you on time."

"Well, feeding you is the least I can do. Take this exit," Nicole said, pointing to the right. "I think I saw 'food' on the blue sign back there. We need to feed the rabid beast growing inside you."

They came to a lone stop sign at the end of the exit ramp. In both directions, the single-lane road disappeared into dense woods—no houses, cars, or signs of life.

"If we ever needed to dump a body, we know where to go," Nicole decided.

"Are you sure this is right?" Jesse asked, with doubt in his voice.

"I think so. Look," Nicole said, pointing to a column of roadside signs promising food and gas one mile to the left. "At a minimum, we should be able to find you an old cup of coffee and a package of Drake's Coffee Cakes at a gas station."

"I may get that even if there are other choices. That's one of my top three gas station snacks."

A line formed between her brows. "You have a list?" Nicole asked, intrigued. "What are your other two?"

"Easy. Cup Noodles or a two-pack of Slim Jims." He shrugged. "What about you?"

"Slim Jims? I've always wondered if there is actual meat in those," she said, genuinely curious. "Every time I see them sticking out of that red box at the register, I can only think of the bully sticks my mom gives her dogs. Those are made from dried bull penis." Nicole blushed. She couldn't believe the words came out of her mouth.

Jesse's eyebrows raised in amusement. "Wow, this conversation took an unexpected turn."

Nicole giggled, waving her hand, trying to erase the words lingering in the air. "Okay, okay, I'll go. I need to get the image out of my mind." Nicole tapped her finger against her chin. "I've never been able to say no to a bag of Fritos, so that would be on the top of the list. I guess a close second would be Fig Newtons. The problem is that I can't eat just two or three of them."

Jesse scoffed. "Fig Newtons? Oh, God, I can't eat one. They're too cakey, and the seeds always get stuck in my teeth."

"Too cakey, says the guy who eats Donettes by the sleeve," Nicole rebutted as the forest opened to a four-lane highway lined with every fast-food restaurant and gas station one could imagine. Jutting from the horizon, the mid-morning sun hovered above the shoulders of the snowcapped mountains, providing a picturesque background from the otherwise eyesore.

"Well, I guess we found food," Jesse said. "What are you in the mood for?"

"How about Dunkin' Donuts? I could use a coffee."

"You're cut off from caffeine for the rest of the ride."

Nicole laughed. "Probably best."

Twenty minutes later, with their coffers full of their favorite roadside snacks and a few sodas, they headed back toward the highway. Jesse skillfully maneuvered the truck around the newborn potholes birthed over the bitter winter.

"Unless there is a corn chip emergency and we need to stop, we should be home in less than three hours," Jesse calculated, turning onto the Northway.

"Great," Nicole said. She settled into her *People*, ready to lose herself in the cover story about what made Keanu Reeves so cool and mysterious, as the headline suggested. But by the second page, she was bored with Keanu. She was more interested in watching the maple trees flicker past the truck window as they worked their way south through the Adirondacks and talking to Jesse.

She had laughed and had more fun with him in the last hour than she could recall in the last year at Wheeler. Most things were better than crushing amounts of schoolwork and the pressure of building a resume that stood out from all other accounting majors, but this felt different. Easy. And for the first time that week, her thoughts weren't consumed by *that* night.

He always had that effect on her. Maybe it was from all their time together at the lake, where they had little real responsibilities or stress, or perhaps because she never felt like she had to be anyone else but herself around him.

"Isn't it weird that we never hung out in college?" she asked.

Jesse shrugged. "We fell into different crowds freshman year. I guess it stuck," he suggested. "Maybe without our families around to bother us, we didn't feel like we needed to huddle together to survive, like at the lake."

"I guess." Her voice dragged out as she thought more about it. Maybe it wasn't anything more than a friendship borne from convenience. They only hung out because they were stuck together with no other options. Her heart hurt a little at the revelation.

Nicole's thoughts were interrupted by the grinding of the downshifting gears as the road started a long ascent to the top of a peak. At their slow speed, Nicole could see the seasonal waterfalls created by the melting snowcaps gently running down the steep rock faces along the shoulder.

Resting her elbow on the windowsill, Nicole turned to Jesse, who was concentrating on the road. She watched as he tapped his hand against the steering wheel to the beat of the rock station playing on the radio.

He drew a slight smile. "What?"

She jutted her chin at him. "What's your handle?"

"Handle?"

"Yeah. Your call sign for the CB radio. You know . . . what you would want your fellow truckers to call you. You can't go by Jesse. That'd be boring."

"Ah. Hm . . . I never needed one before." He sat for a second. "How about Jesse James?"

Nicole burst out laughing. "Like the outlaw, Jesse James?"

"Is it so unbelievable?" he defended. "I could be a train robber. I have a bad-boy side. You've just never seen it."

"*Bad boy* is not a phrase I would use to describe you," she balked. *White knight, maybe.* "I hate to break it to you, but you're one of those nice guys."

He winced. "Just what every man wants to be called."

"I could add competitive, and maybe even anal retentive and neat freak to the list seeing as how you packed the truck, if you thought that would help tarnish your good guy reputation." She snickered. "But, sorry, *bad boy* is a stretch."

The radio went from sporadic to complete static high up in the mountains. "Got any CDs in the cab, or are they all packed?" Nicole asked.

"Behind the seat."

Nicole reached around to find the black nylon album on the floor. "What do you want to listen to?"

"I'll get it," he insisted, flipping the plastic sleeves filled with colorful discs using one hand and driving with the other.

Nicole tried to see over his arm. "What are you going to put on?"

"It's a surprise," he said. In one motion, he put his finger in the center of a CD, slid it out of the case, and popped it in the dash before Nicole could see the label. He hit play and settled back into his seat.

After the first two notes, Nicole recognized the unmistakable opening drum solo to *Footloose* and immediately cranked up the dial. Before the guitar riff kicked in, they were already dancing in their seats like nobody was watching. And for the next three minutes and forty-seven seconds, they sang into their thumbs at the top of their lungs like they wrote the song.

Energy blossomed throughout her body. "God, that was awesome! I had no idea how much I needed that," she sighed. Then she remembered their conversation at dinner. "Wait. Last night, you said you hated that movie!"

He shot her a sinister smile. "I didn't want to give my mom the satisfaction."

"You're evil," she said, examining him.

Jesse's cheeks raised with delight. "Secretly, I listen to the entire CD when I need a good pick-me-up. Reminds me of fun times."

"I never pegged you as the sentimental type," she said, nudging his elbow. "You've always been more of a cynic."

His mouth curved up. "There's a lot you don't know about me."

It was true, and she could say the same. Sadly, she knew Jesse used to cry when his brother relentlessly teased him but didn't know simple things like his favorite color. It was no different from Jesse knowing that Nicole resented her mother for emotionally abandoning her and

Jamie but not knowing why Italian cheesecake was her favorite dessert. For two people who spent so many summers together, often with a front-row seat to the other person being smothered by their family dynamics, they didn't know each other at all.

"What I do know is that we're going to have to add sentimental and nostalgic to your profile, and those aren't going to bode well on your bad boy resume."

He swung his head from side to side. "You're relentless."

For the next couple hours, they snaked their way through the mountains, driving past forests crammed with pine trees and the occasional boulder outcroppings, swapping stories, laughing, and sharing their life plans now that they were officially adults with college educations—Nicole was heading into public accounting and moving to a new apartment outside Albany. Jesse had joined the engineering firm he interned at the previous summer and was moving downstairs to the basement of the lake house where Nicole and her sister used to sleep.

With less than twenty minutes from Nicole's house, their collective energy was fading. It had been a long day, and it wasn't even two in the afternoon. The radio had come back and was playing quietly in the background. "So, how's Sarah? Do you think you'll see her again?" Nicole asked.

Hesitancy flitted across his face. "Who?"

"Sarah, the one from the other night at MacArthur's."

He shifted in his seat. "Oh, right. Sarah. Yeah, no."

"Why not?"

"She left with that mess of an ex-boyfriend of yours," he said briskly.

"Matty?" Nicole let out a breath. That meant that if Matty was with Sarah, he couldn't have been with Nicole on the driveway. *Stop thinking about it.* "Oh, geez. I'm sorry. I didn't know. Obviously," Nicole said, embarrassed.

And with that one innocent question, Jesse shut down quicker than a blown fuse. Nicole's chest deflated when she tried to talk to him again, and he turned up the radio. She ached to end their trip on a high note, like when they were blasting movie anthems and laughing so hard they had to stop at a rest area to pee—an ounce of joy in her otherwise heavy and painful week.

When they arrived at her mom's house, Nicole was relieved to see an empty driveway. Her mom would have too many questions and want too many details about graduation that Nicole was not in the mood to give. Her emotions were sparking like a live wire. All she wanted to do was find her pillow and blanket, crawl into bed, and shut her door to the world.

Nicole groaned as she got out of the truck, unfolding herself upright. Jesse wasted no time flipping over the latch on the tailgate. By the time Nicole walked to the back of the U-Haul, Jesse had already thrown her duffle bags on the driveway and held a crate in his hands.

After several trips inside, he said, "I think this is the last of it," dropping a box on her bedroom floor.

He radiated annoyance. That wasn't how she wanted to end her time with him, but she didn't know how to fix it. "I think it is," Nicole said, glancing around her room. She stopped at the Garfield stuffed animal sitting on her bed. "Probably time to get rid of him," she said, motioning to the orange cat. It was her last attempt at breaking the chill in the air.

"Yeah, maybe," he said, turning with a quick snap of his broad shoulders, leaving her room like he was running from the law.

She followed his hurried pace to the front door. "I can't thank you enough for letting me catch a ride. It was so much . . ." was all she got out before he walked out the door.

Fun. It was so much fun, Jesse . . . James.

PART 2

| 14 |

Nicole

Nicole awoke to the early summer morning light pouring through her bedroom window. For the first time in four weeks, she opened her eyes and knew exactly where she was—in the bedroom of her new apartment. S*afe. Home.* And with some certainty of her future—*not pregnant.*

Relief continued to flow from her body ever since she saw the streak of blood on the toilet paper the night before. Even after seven negative home pregnancy tests, getting her period was the only evidence she trusted. She wouldn't have to decide and would never have to tell.

Stretching her arms and legs, she nearly touched the four corners of her bed before her muscles recoiled, rolling her onto her side like an expended rubber band. A smile bloomed inside her chest, almost as bright as the sunbeam that drenched her face. She slipped her hands under her pillow and soaked up her new surroundings—tranquil green walls, white-washed bedroom furniture, tufted headboard, and a woven seagrass area rug on the floor. The gentle hum of the oscillating fan, the only noise in the whisper-quiet room, blew a slow breeze over her, completing the coastal feel.

Before Nicole moved into her apartment, she never thought twice about throw pillows or side tables. She was only concerned if there was a place to put down her soda and if there was a TV in the room. But then, she had her own space to decorate.

After countless hours of combing through catalogs, watching home improvement shows, searching for inspiration, Nicole had her vision—bright, light, airy, relaxed, *comfortable*—akin to how she wanted to feel when she was home.

But it was one thing to have a dream. It was another to execute it. Lying in bed, she chuckled, recalling the first three times she went to her local hardware store, leaving empty-handed each time. She would make it as far as the power tool aisle and then chicken out when she started to agonize over being judged by the man working behind the counter with his receding gray hairline and self-assured canvas apron. She assumed he would be annoyed with her basic questions—*What's the difference between a Phillips head and a flat head? Is there a noticeable difference between Chantilly Lace and Decorators White?*—because, of course, everyone except Nicole, who walked into the store, already knew which screwdriver and paint color they wanted.

On her fourth trip, though, she finally rallied enough courage to ask for help. The need to transform her apartment into her haven and the excitement of doing it on her own outweighed her fear of the apron-clad elder behind the counter.

I need this for me.

When she first started her DIY projects, some days made her dizzy with frustration, like when she was assembling furniture with only a tiny Allen wrench and following instructions in hieroglyphics. But as her space transformed, so did her conviction in her work and her choices. Imperceptible at first, like when the late spring air shifts to the first days of summer, but as it all came together, her confidence was palpable.

Nicole glanced at the alarm clock on the glass bedside table. It wasn't quite eight in the morning. Her head hadn't hit the pillow until 2 a.m., shortly after she finished painting the kitchen ceiling. But the long hours were worth it. The apartment was finally done, and she loved it.

The sun had been out for a while, which meant Nicole needed to start her day. She sat up with a groan, feeling every ache and pain, even in places she didn't know were possible. She felt like she had gone to battle, but this time she had won.

Smiling to herself, Nicole rolled her shoulders, easing the soreness in her neck, when she noticed the white paint speckling her wrist and gunk clogged underneath the few nails she had left. *Manicure?*

Then she thought better. She had to stretch her savings and the signing bonus from Graham Partners until she started her job in mid-August. She had no room in her budget to be frivolous, and besides, who would notice her hands anyway? She barely left her apartment, except for her morning routine, when most neighbors hadn't made it outside yet.

Dressed in her favorite high-waisted jean shorts and a plain white T-shirt tucked in the front, Nicole grabbed her house key, slid on her flip-flops, and stepped onto the wooden landing outside her front door. A warm, gentle breeze glided across her face as the melodic songs of birds soared through her ears. Sweet-scented air wafted up from the nearby rose blooms, filling her nose. She closed her eyes and took a moment to drink in the natural mosaic enveloping her.

With each passing day, Nicole's muscles clenched a little less, which she read as a good sign. The repetition of her morning routine was dulling her sensitivity to being in a new area and helping her blend into her community.

A cloud drifted in front of the sun, waking Nicole from her quiet bliss and prompting her to start her safety protocol. Despite her landlady Claire's assurance that the neighborhood was safe, "Just a bunch of geezers around here. Nothing to worry about," Nicole had developed a regular process, starting with surveying the street from her perch at the top of the stairs. She scoured the landscape for anyone suspicious, like an unwelcomed solicitor looking for donations, and for signs that something was out of place, like a man she didn't recognize sitting in his car a little too long.

That morning, the neighborhood was exactly as it had been since she moved in—neatly manicured lawns, cars expertly parked in driveways, no bustle of traffic in any direction, only the sound of a little league game playing at the park nearby.

Comfortably in the clear, Nicole slipped her house key between her index and middle fingers, plunged down the stairs, and powerwalked to the deli to start her morning.

* * *

The bell chimed above Nicole's head when she pushed open the glass door to Zuke's Italian Deli. The air conditioning felt cool against her skin, which had heated up during the short walk from her apartment.

Nicole had become accustomed to the irresistible sensation that hit her every time she entered the storefront. Even at eight-thirty in the morning, when she historically craved pancakes slathered in maple syrup and smokey bacon, her salivary glands watered at the pungent bite of sharp cheeses, fragrant cured meats, and enough garlic in the air to ward off a throng of vampires. Not that she had ever tasted any of it. Nicole wasn't adventurous when it came to food and wasn't about to try months-old sausage that hung from the ceiling like a meat chandelier. She was admittedly a diner or mini-mart kind of girl.

"Mornin' Nicole," Zuke chirped from behind the counter. Nicole pegged Zuke to be in his late twenties with the onset of fine lines around his mouth and eyes and a few grays emerging along his temples in his overly gelled dark hair that he meticulously styled with a front flip. He gave her an easy grin, his teeth strikingly white against his olive skin. "The usual?" he asked, reaching for the sleeve of to-go cups next to the coffee machine.

Warmth percolated in Nicole's chest, hearing that she had a *usual*. "Yes, please," she said too excitedly. It was a simple question, but it was an acknowledgment that some part of Nicole's new community had accepted her as one of them.

She glanced over her shoulder at the wall of brightly lit built-in coolers to hide her blush from Zuke. The well-stocked refrigerators were next to an exposed brick wall decorated with framed black-and-white vintage photos.

From a distance, she could see old Italian men playing cards, a large family sitting around a dinner table, a grandmother in the kitchen stirring the contents of a large metal pot, children covered in flour kneading pasta dough, and a row of women holding babies on their hips. The last picture was of a man and a woman sitting at a small café table underneath a scalloped awning that read Zuccarello Trattoria. There were some subtle resemblances to Zuke's big, deep-set eyes and round face, but with one distinct difference—their expressions were guarded and small. Zuke had a naturally captivating way about him, starting with the broad and inviting smile that took over his face.

"Going to be gorgeous today. Any big plans?" Zuke asked.

Nicole turned back to him. "Not today," she said, covering the massive yawn with the back of her hand. "Oh, God, I'm sorry. That was so rude."

Zuke handed Nicole her usual—dark roast with a splash of whole milk—with a smile. "Looks like you need this. Late night?"

She nodded her head. "Lots of them," she said, peeling back the plastic tab of her lid. She lowered her nose into the steam rising from her cup. "I've been staying up way past my bedtime working on my apartment these past weeks. It was pretty rough in the beginning, but I'm proud to say it's all done." She beamed, taking a sip. The coffee felt like a warm hug caressing her insides.

"Congrats!" he cheered with his demitasse coffee mug that was cartoonishly small against his massive arms.

"Thanks."

"I've always found that home improvement work is harder and takes longer than you think." He eased against the counter behind him, crossing one ankle over the other. Nicole glanced around the deli as Zuke spoke. "I gutted this place when I bought the building. I did all the work myself, but it took about three months longer than I had budgeted. I didn't factor in all the trips back and forth to the lumber yard . . . and the ER." He held up his stubby index finger. "Cut the tip right off."

Her eyes winced shut. "Ouch! They never talk about blood and stitches on HGTV."

"You never realize how much you use the tip of your finger until it's gone."

"See, this is why I am an accountant. The only digits I need to worry about losing are numbers on a balance sheet." She surprised herself by giggling. His mouth split wide, but Nicole couldn't tell if Zuke was laughing with her or at her. "Well, the place looks great," she said.

"Thanks. I am happy with how it turned out." He glanced at Nicole, smiling. "It's funny, my dad used to say, 'The harder the job, the sweeter the success.' After this project, I finally appreciate what he meant."

"I know exactly what you mean. At two o'clock this morning, when I was cleaning paintbrushes, half asleep, I couldn't help but think about how much more I loved my apartment because the work was hard." Nicole fished her money from her pocket to pay. "What did you do before you opened the deli?"

"I worked for the highway department for almost eight years. Started right out of school. It was a good job. It came with union benefits, which were important at the time. I was all set to get married and settle down. I thought I knew where my life was going." *Me too.*

She knew something horrible had happened by the change in his tone and the way his eyes shifted downward. Her face must have said what she was afraid to ask.

"And then one morning, almost two years ago, my fiancé, Gianna, was killed in a car accident on her way to work. My life blew up in my face. Just like that," he said, snapping his fingers.

"Oh my God, Zuke," she startled. "I am so sorry."

"Thank you." He exhaled. "So . . . after the accident, I tried to go back to work, but it was just a job. I needed something that got me out of bed in the morning. Growing up, between my Nonna and my dad, I had always been around food, and I wanted to do something where I could be my own boss. So, I decided to put it all together. And here I am—Zuke's Deli." His lips slid into a gradual smile.

"That's amazing, Zuke. Takes a lot of insight to realize that about yourself and to take that kind of chance." Nicole returned the expression. "Do you have anyone working for you?"

"My sister Annamarie helps me out if I need to take care of something during the week, but otherwise, she only stops by for an espresso and cornetto if she's in the area. I mostly see her and my nephew for Sunday dinner at their house," he said, clapping his cup down in the miniature saucer. "Gotta keep the family traditions alive."

Nicole's heart stung. She missed Jamie and their closeness. They used to be sisters in arms, surviving their childhood as a team, but as they got older, when the battle wasn't as intense and they didn't need each other the same way, they drifted apart. When Wheeler happened, and Nicole needed Jamie more than ever, she couldn't bring herself to ask for help.

Zuke interrupted Nicole's thoughts. "Not gonna lie, it's also nice to have someone else cook occasionally."

"Occasionally? It's nice to have someone else cook all the time," she said. "Wait, but then that means you never get a day off. It must be exhausting."

"It's fine . . . for now. I'm still establishing myself. Besides, I live upstairs. I wouldn't be able to stay away if I tried. I like things done my way—the right way." He chuckled. Nicole knew that to be true just by how he professionally dressed—a smooth black T-shirt with Zuke's Deli logo embroidered over his heart, black and white houndstooth chef pants, crisp white bib apron. Even the freshly baked loaves of crusty bread were neatly stacked high on the shelves above his head.

"Well, I'll let you get back to work." Nicole worried she had overstayed her welcome. "I'll take a loaf of bread and the coffee."

"I just pulled two frittatas out of the oven," Zuke said, thumbing over his shoulder toward the kitchen. "I've got porcini and potato or spicy sausage and scamorza—my personal favorite."

Nicole was too embarrassed to admit she had no idea what he offered her. Whatever it was, it was definitely more exotic than she was used to and way out of her culinary league. She chewed at the inside of her cheek as her chest filled with the same pressure she felt in the hardware store—expecting to know everything.

"Um . . . no, thank you. I already ate breakfast," she lied. Nicole felt her cheeks heat up. It was too much pressure to try something new, especially with the person who made it standing there watching her reaction.

He gave her a small smile, reading her thoughts. "I tell you what. You try them both at home when you're hungry—on the house. When you're ready, let me know which one is your favorite. It will be our little experiment," he said, neatly wrapping up two pieces and packing them with her bread.

Here was a guy that, if Nicole didn't know him and saw him in an alley, would make her sprint the other way—burly, exuding masculinity, intimidating. But that day, she learned that he confidently knew how to make a frittata, that family and tradition were important to him, and that he somehow figured out how to thrive after the impossible.

Maybe people aren't always as they seem.

| 15 |

Nicole

Nicole exited the deli, her hands filled with her *usual* coffee and mysterious frittatas. Her legs were heavy with exhaustion, feeling like she was swimming in lead pants, but she had a daily walk around the neighborhood routine and was committed to sticking to it.

A half-hour later, Nicole arrived home just as Claire was squatting to grab her newspaper from the front lawn of their apartment building. "Hi, Claire," Nicole said with a wave. Claire wore her silver hair short, accessorized with a white sweatband. She looked like an aged Olivia Newton-John from the "Let's Get Physical" video in her fuchsia-colored leggings and a full face of makeup. "You're out early."

Claire straightened herself. "Only got so much time left on this earth. I'll have plenty of time to sleep when I'm dead."

Nicole gave her a wordless smile, letting the awkwardness linger for a beat. "Well, enjoy your day," Nicole said politely, squaring her body toward the stairs leading up to her front door.

"Oh, before you go, I've got mail for you. The mailman screwed up again," Claire said, disappearing into her apartment on the first floor. The duplex was an exceptionally tall, two-story colonial with light blue aluminum siding. The oversized windows on the top floor where Nicole lived made the house appear top-heavy.

Uneasiness melted over Nicole as she waited for Claire on the sidewalk in the warm June sun. When she walked the neighborhood, she felt invisible, but standing out there alone, tapping her foot impatiently, she had an unnerving feeling of being watched. She needed to get inside the protective cocoon of her four walls.

Claire finally reappeared with a small stack of envelopes, catalogs, and that week's *People*. "Thanks!" Nicole said hurriedly, snatching the mail from Claire and bolting up the stairs, ignoring the weighty sandbag feeling in her legs.

Safely inside, Nicole sighed a flutter of relief as she dropped her bags on the kitchen table. She tried to convince herself that her jitters and paranoia were from sleep deprivation and copious amounts of dark roast on an empty stomach, but she wasn't a fool. *What if he's out there?*

Nicole cradled her mail in one arm, shuffling through it as she paced her tiny kitchen, expending energy. A pink envelope with the words 'PHOTOS DO NOT BEND' in Megan's loopy handwriting caught her attention. Nicole lit up. It was as if Megan had reached through a portal into Nicole's apartment with a reassuring hug. *Graduation pictures—this should be fun.*

With no cross ventilation in the kitchen, the room filled with the heavy scent of fresh bread and smokey cheese emanating from the bag. A low rumble gurgled from her stomach in response. *My goodness, I guess I'm hungry.*

Nicole ripped off the heel of the long loaf of Italian bread and shoved it in her mouth. Still struggling to chew her bite, she remembered the frittatas Zuke packed her and ruthlessly tore the side of the bag like a black bear invading a campsite. There sat two beautifully sliced pieces of crustless quiche. She was suddenly ravenous. And without an audience, she didn't hesitate to try the breakfast pies.

After one taste, she decided that whoever first thought to put scamorza, which she deciphered was cheese, and crumbled sausage in an Italian breakfast pie was a culinary genius. Her eyes practically rolled into the back of her head. With each mouthful of the fluffy, creamy goodness, her hunger and caffeine shakes subsided, and her appreciation for Zuke skyrocketed. *That man can cook!*

Nicole felt the color return to her face as her blood sugar restored to normal levels after a few more bites. Even her paranoia dissipated. *No one is watching you from the shrubs. Stop being ridiculous.*

Nicole lumbered to the living room to read Megan's card, plunking herself onto the loveseat. *Crack!*

"Ah!" Nicole yelped, springing to her feet, worried the sofa was about to buckle under her weight. *Maybe I shouldn't have eaten the entire loaf of bread.*

She shook her head, chuckling, as she pushed on the cushion a few times before cautiously lowering herself back onto the couch. Her self-esteem was restored when the frame silently held up, but the feeling was short-lived. When she put her feet on the coffee table, it swayed like a boat in the water. Her furniture had become a metaphor for her life—on the outside, it looked put together and stable, but with one tiny push, it was on the verge of collapsing.

She let it go for the moment, knowing she had nothing but time to fix it later, and settled on the couch with Megan's card. With a smile glued to her face, she ran her thumb under the envelope flap and found a handmade card with a moose silhouette on the front, wearing a plaid bathing suit. *Ha!* Nicole flipped open the card, catching the stack of four-by-six-sized photos sandwiched inside.

> *Nicole!*
>
> *Greetings from beautiful Saranac Lake—Recently ranked #1 among small towns in New York State! (It's the reporter in me. I can't help myself) How are you??? I miss you so much! It's been too long since we've talked. Call me when you get this. We need to catch up!*
>
> *XOXOXO!*
>
> *Megan*
>
> *PS – See if you can spot the loser in the photo. Call me!*

Nicole set the card beside her on the couch and flipped through the pictures, trying her best to ignore the unresolved feelings stirring inside from seeing herself on graduation day, *that night* still raw.

She stopped at a picture of Megan, smiling from ear to ear, standing in front of a small brown log cabin, wearing cutoff jean shorts, an oversized t-shirt, and hiking boots. *Awwww . . . that must be her new place. She looks so happy.*

Nicole considered sending Megan pictures of her apartment. *She'll never believe I did all this myself.* But she thought twice when she caught the leaning coffee table in her view. *Or maybe she will.*

Continuing through the remaining photos from graduation—an action shot of Megan and Nicole tossing their caps in the air, the two of them in front of the Hawkins Library fountain, Megan squeezing Nicole so hard she almost passed out—Nicole's eyes prickled at the sight of them together. *We used to be so close. We really did have so much fun together.*

Alone on her couch, she suddenly didn't feel so lonely. Part of her wished Megan lived closer than a two-hour drive away. But then her short-term memory was overshadowed by her remembrance of what it was like to be Megan's friend—and babysitter— toward the end of school and erased the thought. She reasoned it was better to keep Megan's friendship at a controlled distance while she struggled to manage her own life.

At the end of the pile, Nicole still hadn't found the 'loser' Megan called out in her note, assuming it was Matty. Still curious, she started from the beginning, scrutinizing each picture. She almost made it through the stack again without detecting *him*, but there he was, lurking in plain sight in the last picture. *Rob.* Nicole's chest caved in. She thought she was going to be sick.

While Nicole and Megan beamed for the camera, Rob photobombed their shot in the distance, flashing a big toothy smile and the 'W' hand signal for Wheeler at the camera as if he belonged there. If Megan hadn't mentioned it, Nicole never would have caught the miniature Rob in his Wayfarers in the background who, given the perspective, appeared to be standing on Megan's shoulder—the devil himself.

I moved over two hundred miles from Wheeler, from you, and somehow, you found a way inside my home.

| 16 |

Nicole

It was almost afternoon on Sunday, and Nicole had done nothing except fuss over and fall in love with the new kittens she adopted from the litter Zuke found in the alley behind his store. "I'll take two," she had said, smiling so hard a crowbar couldn't pry the grin off her face. She had read that animals can reduce a person's stress levels and boost their mood and knew they would help cure her loneliness.

Back at her apartment, with the cats snuggled on her lap, Nicole wanted to share her news with someone, anyone, and decided to call Megan. At a minimum, she owed her a phone call after she sent the card.

"Hello," Megan whispered into the phone.

"Hey! It's Nic!"

Megan quietly shrieked. "Hi!"

"How are you? I got your card. We've got so much to catch up on!" Nicole responded in a mocking whisper. "Why are we talking like this?"

"Wait, let me move." Nicole could hear a door unlatching through the phone, then the creaking of a spring-loaded screen door. "I'm back. How are *you*?" Megan said in her normal voice.

"Someone there? I can call you later if you're busy."

"No, all good. Tom's still sleeping. I didn't want to wake him."

"Oh . . . who's Tom?" Nicole asked in a cheerful voice.

"Nothing serious. We just started hanging out."

"What's he like? How'd you meet him?" Nicole pressed. She hoped Megan had finally found a guy who was more than a one-night stand.

"Geez . . . I thought I was the reporter," Megan quipped.

"Oh."

"Sorry. Haven't had coffee yet," Megan laughed. "He's pretty cute—outdoorsy. He likes to hike a lot. I'm so happy to hear your voice. How are you?"

"I don't start my job until August, so I have been busy decorating my apartment. You should see it—I have end tables, curtains, plates, real utensils. I'm like an adult."

"Stop it! Send pictures. I've gotta see!"

"I will. And I'll send you pictures of my new kittens," she said, feeling their weight on her legs.

"What? Did you say kittens? Plural?" Megan's voice got louder.

"Yup! Corn Chip, well, CC for short, and Noodle. They're so cute! CC is an orange and white tabby, the color of a Frito. And Noodle is a calico with a freakishly long, skinny tail, like a piece of spaghetti."

"Clever."

Ignoring Megan's disinterested tone, Nicole said, "Thanks. I was pretty proud of myself for coming up with their names."

"Nic, I warned you about becoming one of those crazy cat ladies if you didn't get out more. It took, what, six weeks? I wouldn't even have taken those odds."

Nicole rubbed Noodle behind his ears. "I couldn't resist. Zuke had a box of them at the deli this morning. He found them abandoned in the alley behind his building. They were too cute to pass up. Besides, they'll be good for me. Keep me company."

"Or you could go out and meet people. They're good at keeping you company, too," she challenged. Nicole was suddenly embarrassed by her admission of loneliness. She sounded pathetic to someone on the outside. "Who's this Zuke guy? Is he hot? Single?"

"He owns the deli down the road. Good looking, yes. Single, I think so. But it doesn't matter. I'm not his type."

"How do you know that?"

"He's a family guy. Traditional. He wouldn't want to be with someone with my dysfunctional baggage. He wouldn't understand. I need someone jaded and scarred like me." Nicole chuckled. "And more importantly, he's also the guy who knows how to make my coffee exactly how I like it. I don't want to jeopardize my relationship with the guy that makes a perfect cup. They're hard to find."

Megan let out a strangled breath. "Coffee and cats. Got it."

"What?"

"Nothing."

"Why the sigh?"

"Cats aren't the only thing that will keep you warm at night, Nic."

"My goodness, are you in heat or something? Sheesh! Down, girl, down."

Megan didn't laugh. "I think you should get out and live a little, that's all. You're turning into a spinster and not even twenty-three."

Nicole was beginning to second-guess her decision to call Megan that morning. "Ouch."

"Sorry, that came out harsher than I meant."

"There is nothing wrong with having a life plan that doesn't put having a boyfriend at the top," Nicole said, annoyed.

"Who's talking about boyfriends? I'm talking sex." Nicole heard the snap of the screen door through the phone.

"Hold on a second," Megan said. The phone went quiet.

"Hey, I'm back," Megan chirped a minute later. Nicole knew her well enough to know she was putting on an act.

"Everything all right? You sound off."

"Yeah. Sure. Just saying goodbye to Troy."

"Tom," Nicole corrected.

"Right. Tom."

"Think you'll see him again?"

"Not sure. Maybe."

Nicole had a feeling that their conversation was about to turn. "Why do you feel like you have to lie to me?"

"About what?" Megan's voice was littered with irritation.

"You clearly don't know the guy who just left your apartment. It's fine."

"Is it, though?"

"What do you mean?"

"Well, maybe I was trying to avoid your lecture about who I can and can't sleep with. I already have a mom. And besides, what do you expect me to do? Go on dates, rent rom-coms from Blockbuster, and make sure he loves me before I sleep with him, like you? How boring."

"Wow. Tell me how you really feel."

Megan let out a "ha," but Nicole could hear sniffling.

Nicole was confused. "You and I have always had different views on this. It isn't a new thing. Why are you so upset all of a sudden?"

Silence.

"Megan, what's going on?"

"Fine. You want to know why?" Megan cried.

"I do. That's why I asked. If I've done something to upset you, I want to know."

And then Megan exploded like an ice cube dropped in hot liquid. "Because for the past four years, I have thought about no one but Rob *Fucking* Arnold—either wanting to be with him or desperately trying to get over him. And then, during our last week at school, I found out that he liked *you* out of all the people in this world."

Rob? "What are you talking about? Where is this coming from? Whe . . . when did you ever talk to Rob about me?" Nicole asked, nervously rubbing her hand over her mouth.

"That last night when we went out to MacArthur's. He stopped to talk to me when I was in the bathroom line. I stupidly thought maybe he would apologize or something for how he treated me." Megan raised her voice. "He didn't remember we were together. All he wanted was to know where he could find *you.*" *MacArthur's? Find me?* Nicole's stomach dropped through the couch cushions.

"What? Why didn't you tell me?" Nicole pleaded. *I could have been smarter, more aware, on the lookout.* Black spots zipped around in her clouded vision. *Maybe it wouldn't have happened!*

"Why do you care so much? You going to call him up or something?" Megan sneered.

Nicole yelled into the phone. "You have no idea what you're talking about."

"Please, enlighten me then." Nicole could hear Megan's stuttered breaths through the receiver. "Oh, wait. Let me guess. You already hooked up with him."

Nicole couldn't believe what she was hearing. "Do you know me? Do you really think I would do something like that?"

"I don't know what to think."

Nicole paused. The only possible way to make Megan understand her reaction would be to confide in her, which she might have considered years ago, but their relationship had become toxic, and Nicole didn't trust her with such a personal admission. It was obvious that Megan didn't respect her, and Nicole had no room for that in her life—not then, not ever. "Well, let me help you. I don't think we need to be friends anymore. I don't need your drama. I have enough of my own." And with that, Nicole hung up.

| 17 |

Nicole

An early July stormy wind billowed the sheer curtains around a potted ficus in the corner of Nicole's living room, wafting in the scent of impending rain. Nicole bustled around her apartment, fluffing the yellow accent pillows on the couch, and even made her bed while she waited excitedly for Jamie—her first guest—to arrive.

It had been years since they hung out together, just the two of them. She missed how close they used to be when they were kids. A bond between sisters was one thing, but living through their childhood brought a vulnerability they only allowed each other to see. They were each other's emotional support system and the only person each could entirely rely on as they navigated their teenage years.

As a latchkey kid, Nicole remembered being most anxious when she was alone in the house after school. She obsessively worried if her mother would make it home from work until her mom walked in the front door. Sensitive to Nicole's anxiety, Jamie quit the yearbook club and the field hockey team to be with Nicole.

But they naturally drifted apart as they got older and Jamie left for college. With Jamie gone, Nicole spent her days reading teen magazines and watching mindless television. Their daily phone calls became every few days and then weeks on end without talking. Now that they lived closer, Nicole hoped the void in her life without Jamie by her side would start to fill in. She needed her more than ever.

At a little past noon, Nicole was straightening the framed pop art print of Marilyn Monroe hanging above the couch when her ears tuned into the *shushing* of Jamie's feet shuffling up the wooden stairs outside.

Nicole checked her fuchsia lipstick in the small mirror above the side table before swinging open the door. "Hi!" she said, startling Jamie, who had her fist in the knock position.

"Hi!" Jamie said with a face-splitting grin.

"Come in. Come in," Nicole said, grabbing Jamie's hand and pulling her inside.

Jamie put down a small, handled bag on the entrance table and flipped her hood back, revealing her beautifully tanned skin. "Look at this place!" Jamie cried, scanning the living room, smoothing the back of her hair.

Unlike Nicole's uncontrollable frizz, Jamie had shiny brown, professionally layered locks with wispy bangs that perfectly framed her face. Jamie shrugged off her rain jacket and handed it to Nicole, who draped it around one of the nearby kitchen chairs.

"Thanks. I love your outfit!" Nicole said. Jamie looked like she stepped out of the pages of Country Club Digest in her soft pink cami, pastel plaid skort, and pristine white Keds. "I am so happy to see you." Nicole lunged at Jamie with open arms.

"Me too!" Jamie said, wrapping her arms around Nicole. Her hug was comforting, like a warm cup of morning coffee. Spontaneous tears sprang from Nicole's eyes, rolling down her cheeks before she could stop them.

Jamie must have felt the wetness on her shoulder and pulled back. "Why the tears?"

Nicole ran her fingertips along the rims of her eyes. "They're happy tears, I promise. It's been so long. I've missed you."

"Aww."

Nicole grabbed Jamie again. She wasn't ready to let go so soon. And call it sisters' intuition, but Nicole could tell that Jamie needed their embrace as much as she did. It felt like they both had untold stories clinging to her insides, clawing to get out.

When they finally let go, they were both in tears. "We're a mess," Jamie said, shaking her head.

"I guess this means we shouldn't wait so long to see each other." They both chuckled.

"Wait here," Jamie said, retrieving the bag she left by the front door. "Here, this is for you. Happy housewarming. Larry told me they're good luck."

"Oh, Larry. How is the office botanist these days?" Nicole asked, pulling a jade plant out of the bag.

Jamie waved her hand. "He's gone. Maria filed a sexual harassment case against him. Too much drama for Paul. He fired him a month ago."

"There is justice in this world."

"Yeah, but I don't want to talk about office drama right now because . . . look at this place," she said, pushing Nicole aside to get a better view of the apartment. "Oh . . . my . . . God! It's beautiful! Even with the gloominess outside, it feels so light and bright in here."

"Thank you. Lots of late nights, but I'm happy with how it turned out."

"I mean . . . everything is so coordinated. And it's modern. No, not modern, contemporary. *Ouch!*" Jamie stopped in her tracks. "What the . . ." Jamie was startled to find an orange kitten climbing her bare leg.

"Oh, geez, I'm sorry! CC, no!" Nicole said, grabbing the kitten around her belly and unhooking her from Jamie's leg.

"You have a cat? When did that happen?"

"Two, actually. I got them a few weeks ago. Noodle is around here somewhere. Probably curled up on my bed."

"You have two cats and a beautifully decorated apartment? Fess up. Whose place is this? Where are the cameras?"

"Oh, stop it. I couldn't resist their little faces," Nicole said, kissing CC on the nose before putting her on her shoulder.

"Do they have their shots? I don't have time for rabies. I've got a lot on my plate with all the wedding planning," Jamie said, rubbing her wrinkled nose.

"I'll put her in the bedroom," Nicole said, turning away.

"Who did all of this?" Jamie called out.

Nicole reappeared in the kitchen. "I think there's a compliment in there somewhere."

"What do you mean? Wait, *you* did this?" Jamie said, surprised.

Nicole held out her palms, smiling. "I did. Look, I have the callouses to prove it."

"I had no idea you had this in you. And to think all these years, I thought I was the creative one," Jamie said sarcastically. "You're still an accountant, right?"

"I am. I can show you my expense ledger where I tracked all my spending if you'd like," she said.

"I mean, wow! I'm so impressed. I mean . . . no offense."

"None taken. I impressed myself, too." Nicole beamed. Jamie's gushing was exactly the validation she needed.

"I might need to hire you to decorate my apartment."

"Yeah," Nicole huffed, "I wouldn't take that job if you paid me. I love you, but you'd be brutal to work for."

"What do you mean? I'm lovely," she said, gripping her heart, feigning her offense.

"Let's just say I feel sorry for that wedding planner you hired."

Jamie's smile faded. "Ha. Ha. Let me see the bedroom."

"There's a pair of starving tigers in there. You sure?" Nicole teased.

"Oh, stop it." Jamie opened the door enough to poke her head into the bedroom. "You made your bed?"

"Only because you were coming. I never make my bed. That hasn't changed. Don't worry. I haven't completely grown up."

"Phew."

"So that's the tour. Small, but mine. I love it here."

Jamie's smile was genuine. "It's awesome, just like you, Nic."

It felt good to turn Jamie's underestimation of her into respect. "Want something to drink? I have iced tea and Diet Pepsi. I also have a few Zima's if you want to get saucy."

"No, I'm good. I brought my lunch," Jamie said, pulling a SlimFast shake out of her bag. The liquid gurgled as she shook the can.

"I don't know how you drink that stuff. It's so gritty and thick. It's like wet cement." Nicole poured herself a Diet Pepsi from the fridge and led Jamie to the couch in the living room.

"I've got some weight to lose."

Before Nicole could retort, a strong gust blew in through the open window and knocked over a metal vase, startling her to her feet. Closing the window, she asked Jamie, "What time are you going to Jeanie and Jimmy's Fourth of July barbeque on Tuesday? Mom asked me to come early to help set up, and I need a buffer." She picked up the vase and placed it on the end table.

"We're not going this year. Randy and I need to scout out engagement picture locations, and then we're meeting his parents at the club. Won't Jesse be there?"

Nicole skirted the Jesse question. Usually, she would hang out with him, but she didn't know what to expect since he left her house in such a huff the day he dropped her off from school.

"Ew . . . the creepy couple pictures you see in the newspaper," Nicole said, scrunching her nose. "That's the picture they always show on the news when the husband kills the wife, and the reporter is commenting on how happy the couple looked." Nicole chuckled.

Jamie gave a half-hearted shrug. "Karen is insisting that we have them taken. Whatever."

Nicole raised an eyebrow. "Whatever? How is wedding planning going? How was The Sullivan? You never gave me the scoop," Nicole said, gingerly sitting on the cushion next to Jamie, half expecting it to screech under the weight of two people.

"It's good. Busy, busy. You know. Lots to do," she said. She let out a small, off-pitch laugh with a smile that didn't quite reach her eyes.

"You had Mom and Karen at The Sullivan, and all you have to say is, 'It's good.' That has all the makings of a bad situation. What's going on?"

Jamie pinched her lips, unsuccessfully keeping them from quivering. "It's fine. It's great," she said, her voice breaking.

"I can definitely tell that it's not fine."

Jamie tilted her head back toward the ceiling. As kids, Nicole was the one to talk about her feelings. Jamie was more tight-lipped, so Nicole was surprised when Jamie said, "I just need to say it." She paused. "Karen blindsided me the day we met at The Sullivan. And if that wasn't bad enough, Mom witnessed the whole thing. I felt like an idiot. I am an idiot," she exclaimed, burying her face in her hands.

"Wait. Slow down." Nicole offered her a box of tissues.

Jamie exhaled. "I thought Randy's parents offered to pay for our wedding because they were happy for us and wanted us to have the wedding of our dreams. Well, my dreams. Randy doesn't care about the wedding planning. Typical guy. But that's a different story." Jamie dabbed at her nose. "Anyway, I thought *I* was going to plan this spectacular wedding, and then in front of Mom and Susan, the wedding planner, Karen told me how naïve I was."

"What? Why?" Nicole was confused.

"Karen told me that the wedding was just as much for Randy and me as it was a way to bring more business to the law firm. She's planning on inviting all their business partners and clients, and I needed to think bigger. 'More strategic.'"

Nicole slapped her hand over her mouth, not before a gasp tumbled out.

"She told me my job was to find a dress and, I quote, 'Get into wedding shape,' and that she'd be taking care of the rest," Jamie said, neatly folding the mascara-smeared tissue disintegrating in her hands.

Nicole gasped again. She couldn't help it. "What a bitch!"

"Yeah. And to make it worse, I was holding this stupid, ruffled binder full of all my *grand ideas*," Jamie said in her adopted snooty

Karen voice. "I looked like a kid holding my new Trapper Keeper on the first day of school. I was mortified."

"Oh, geez, Jamie. That's awful. What did you do?"

"What did I do? What could I do? She has the money. She has all the power, which she also told me. So, I cowered and said, 'Okay,' and then went to the bar and had a vodka soda with Randy and his dad," she said, wiping her nose.

"What did Randy say when you told him?"

"I didn't tell Randy. It's his mother. I can't rag on her to him. He'll take her side. Besides, he has too much stress already, with law school and all. He doesn't need this. He'd think I was being petty. I can't risk it."

Nicole squeezed her hand. "Jamie. He loves you. If he sees how hurt you are, he'll listen. He'll try to help. He adores you. You know that. He won't want to see you this upset." Jamie gave her a flat smile. "I'm so sorry. Is there anything I can do to help?"

"Yeah, you can be my maid of honor and live through this shit show with me."

A giddy blend of love and excitement pulled inside Nicole. "You want me to be your maid of honor?"

Jamie's smile brightened. "Of course I do. I wouldn't have it any other way."

And just like that, Nicole and Jamie fell in lockstep like no time had passed, exactly how Nicole had hoped—side-by-side, sisters in arms.

| 18 |

Jesse

Standing at the workbench in the garage at the lake house, Jesse drilled a screw into the handle of the kayak paddle that he had cracked against a tree after a recent argument with Jeremy. The vibration in his hands throbbed with dread. That afternoon, his parents were hosting their annual Fourth of July barbeque, and he was in no mood for a party that included an opportunity for Jeremy to embarrass him in front of a crowd. He would have skipped it altogether if Nic wasn't going to be there.

Acid agitated his gut every time he thought about what a complete dick he was to her when she innocently asked him about Sarah on their ride home from Wheeler. He was kicking himself for falling into his usual quiet rage of embarrassment, leaving Nicole on her mother's doorstep, confused about what she did to make him leave so abruptly.

He later acknowledged to himself that he should have told her the truth—he was having so much fun on their road trip that Sarah was the farthest thing from his mind, and he would choose to be with Nicole any day. Nicole deserved it, but sometimes, he couldn't help himself until it was too late.

With the repaired paddle, Jesse walked out the garage door, ducking to avoid hitting his head on the Texas-size flag that jutted from the front porch roof. He thought Jeanie went a little overboard with the decorations that year. Between the American flag wreath hung on the front door and the half-round red, white, and blue flag buntings hanging from the railings, it was like five pounds of America shoved into a one-pound bag. *We get it. It's July Fourth.*

The sun was already high in the sky at ten in the morning and beating down on him. With the paddle back in the shed, Jesse pulled his baseball hat from his back pocket when he heard Jimmy yell from his perch on the second-floor deck. "Hey, Jesse! Where have you been? Your mother gave us a list, and we've got a lot of work to do."

We? More like I'll do all the work while you sit on your ass and watch. "Be right there, Dad."

Jesse meandered up the exterior staircase, taking time to notice the terra-cotta pots filled with cascading red geraniums and white super bells that his mom had arranged along the stairs earlier that morning. At the top, Jesse found Jimmy sipping his coffee, talking to a man he didn't recognize. He had white hair, a walrus mustache, and a pitted red nose the size of an apple. "Hey, Dad."

"Finally," Jimmy clapped with annoyance. "You met Bill before? He's Anne's friend." Bill stood to greet Jesse.

"No, I haven't. Nice to meet you," he said, shaking Bill's hand.

"Where've you been? Tinkering in the garage again? This kid is always building something," Jimmy huffed, turning to Bill.

"I had to fix one of the kayak paddles."

Jimmy flipped up his clip-on sunglasses and gave Jesse a demanding glare. "Need you to start setting up the tables on the lawn."

"You a Yankee fan?" Bill asked Jesse, motioning to his baseball hat. *No, I'm a Sox fan. I wear it to be ironic. What kind of question is that?*

"Yeah."

"Did you see that new kid, Jeter, they brought up from the minors? The one from Kalamazoo. He looked pretty good out there. Scored a couple of runs his second day."

"They already sent him back to the minors. He was only hitting two-fifty and had two errors in thirteen games," Jesse retorted. "They said he needs more time to simmer. May never see him again."

Bill nodded his head once. "You seem to know a lot about baseball. You play?"

"Just a fan. I swam in college," Jesse said while shaking his head.

Jimmy chimed in. "You want to see a real athlete? You need to meet my son Jeremy. He's the star of the family—football, baseball. You name it."

Last I checked, swimming was a sport.

"Can't wait to meet him," Bill replied.

"It'll have to be another day. He's over at a buddy's party across the lake."

Jesse bit back a smile at the news. *No Jeremy!*

"Next time, then," Bill said, turning his attention back to Jesse. "So, I believe congratulations are in order. Graduated college. That must be a big load off your shoulders."

"Feels pretty good," he said humbly.

"Got a job lined up yet?"

"Yeah. At an engineering firm in Clifton Park. Working in their marine division."

"Engineering's a great field. I guess that explains the tinkering that your dad mentioned."

Jimmy interjected before Jesse could reply. "It also explains why he's never satisfied with a simple answer. Real pain in the ass growing up. He always needed to know the details. I remember one time he asked me how a car worked. So, I told him—put gas in it, turn the key, and it goes. Right?" Jimmy shrugged. "But he kept asking more and more questions. He wanted to know from beginning to end. Next thing you know, I'm having a conversation with a six-year-old about internal combustion engines, power trains, and how the drive shaft brings power to the engine."

Jesse coughed into his fist. "The drive shaft carries the power from the transmission to the axle, which connects the wheels. It has nothing to do with bringing power to the engine."

Jimmy shot Jesse a heated look.

"You want to talk about power. Let me tell you about my new Dodge Viper I'm picking up next week," Bill boasted. "Oooo-weee! She's got a V-ten under the hood with six hundred forty-five horsepower. Cherry red. She's a real smoke show." He pulled his hand back as if he had just touched a hot engine.

Jesse forged his excitement. "Awesome. I can't wait to see it next time. Well, nice to meet you, Bill. I'll catch up with you later. Need to set up for the party," he said, freeing himself from the conversation.

Jimmy glanced at his watch and said, "Oh, Jesse, let me help you. Looks like we don't have much time."

Jesse knew his dad would only offer to help if he was trying to avoid doing something else. He could only assume his dad wanted out of his conversation with Bill, which pleased Jesse.

"What are you talking about, Dad? We've got like three hours. You stay here with Bill and talk more about his new car." Jimmy shot daggers at Jesse, giving him a slash of a smile. "I'll take care of it," Jesse said, dashing down the stairs before his dad could see the smug look on his face.

* * *

A half hour had passed since Jesse left his dad with Bill and his insufferable stories, and he was still snickering about it. He was rolling the last of the tables onto the lawn when he heard the sliding door open from behind. "Need some help?"

His heart stopped. *Nic.*

Jesse turned toward Nicole's hesitant voice and found her standing on the flagstone patio outside his makeshift basement apartment. She was holding a red Solo cup, chewing on her bottom lip. His chest fluttered like a panicky butterfly trapped in a mason jar at the sight of her in a pair of white cut-off jean shorts, a red tank top, and a pair of navy blue flip-flops. *How festive. How beautiful.*

Jesse gave her an unsure smile. "Hey, Nic," he said. Her roaming, blank eyes gave nothing away in the shadow of the upper deck. Nervousness forced his apologetic view downward. He removed his hat and ran his hand through his curls, releasing the trapped heat as he held his breath and squirmed in the silence.

Ice rattled in her cup as she casually sipped her drink. He braved a glance toward her when she spoke. "I see the couch survived the trip." She hitched her thumb in the direction of the slider. "It goes perfectly with the wood paneling and drop ceiling. Very seventies chic." Her voice was unemotional, but then her stoic façade cracked, and she hurled a smart-ass grin his way.

An involuntary smile sprang across his face as relief revived the butterflies suffocating in his core. All it took was her joke about his foul-smelling couch, and Nic single-handedly dissolved any lingering tension between them like nothing had ever happened. It was like she had a flywheel stored with positive energy that she could tap into whenever she needed to move past an uncomfortable situation.

She took a few steps toward him.

"What are you drinking?" he asked. She was close enough for him to draw in the sweet essence of lavender and summer, draining all strength in his legs. He had been thinking about seeing her all morning. If she didn't say something soon, he feared he would try and kiss her right there.

She peered into her cup. "Vodka," she said lightheartedly.

"That explains your compliments about my beloved couch," he bantered, still wearing his stupid grin.

She laughed. All seemed forgiven.

"Lake looks beautiful. So calm," she said, scanning the water quietly kissing the shoreline.

"For now. The yahoos next door must not be up yet," he said, moving on to burying bottles of beer at the bottom of a cooler. "Wait until later when they start speeding through here. They completely ignore the 'no wake zone' sign. Bounces the boats all over the place. Not to mention the noise."

"Wow. Okay, Dad." She laughed again.

Her happiness coasted over him, smoothing out his ruffled feathers. "Can you start putting the chairs around the tables?"

"Sure!" she said, jumping into action.

The warm sun baked down on them as they worked together, draping the tables with patriotic cloths and filling the rest of the coolers.

Nicole ran her palm over one of the tablecloths. "So, hey, I had a thought on my way here this morning," she started. "What do you say we commit to having fun today?"

"You want to make a fun pact?"

The amber splashes in her eyes glistened with excitement. "Exactly! No getting wrapped up in family bullshit . . . or annoying neighbors." A grin curled her lips. "We graduated college. We have beautiful weather and this gorgeous view." She gestured her arms wide toward the lake and the mirror images of towering pine trees reflecting in the clear, still water. "We've got each other to hang out with. It will be like old times. Let's enjoy the day."

He squinted. "How many cups of coffee have you had today?"

"One too many?"

He smiled wide. "Here we go again."

| 19 |

Nicole

"This really is unnecessary, Mom," Nicole said, looking at the Italian cheesecake with the words 'You Did It!' piped in black icing underneath a fondant graduation cap and a scroll.

"We know you two don't like to be the center of attention, so we're celebrating now before the barbeque starts," Jeanie said, standing next to Jimmy and Bill. She motioned for Nicole and Jesse to stand closer together. "Let's take a few pictures, and then we have a surprise for you!"

While they waited for Anne to light the candles on the cake, Jesse shuffled closer to Nicole. He was in perfect casual summer attire—navy blue T-shirt, khaki shorts with embroidered whales, barefoot.

"First, you have to make a wish," Jeanie said, holding her digital camera at the ready.

Wish. The word twisted like a corkscrew into Nicole's heart. She'd dropped the word from her vocabulary the night she wished for a man to stop hurting her. A wish is filled with hope, but if anything, that night left her feeling hopeless.

"I think that's only for your birthday," Jesse said.

"Oh, hush. Now, blow out the candles on the count of three."

Nicole shot Jesse a wide-eyed face, telepathically reminding him of their pact. He gave Nicole a tiny nod. "Fine," he said to his mom. "I've got my wish."

"Great! Here we go." Jeanie clapped. Nicole and Jesse leaned over the cake and blew out the candles while the parents yelled, "Three!"

Everyone cheered, "Yah!" as the candle smoke carried Jesse's wish into the cloudless sky.

"Who's ready for the surprise?" Anne asked giddily.

Nicole hated surprises. Her gut was telling her that whatever was leaning against the easel would be particularly awful, and something terrible was about to happen. And boy was her gut right.

Anne lifted the curtain in one motion, unveiling a posterboard covered in pictures of Nicole and Jesse from childhood through graduation. At first, Nicole was flooded with warm memories of summers at the lake with Jesse—the two of them diving off the floating dock, a close-up of their smiling, sun-freckled faces trying to keep up with the drippings from their ice cream cones, watching sparklers slowly burn out in their hands.

But the warmth went cold when she saw the pictures of just her—struggling to hoist herself onto the dock with her bathing suit half up her butt, posing in an ill-fitted two-piece with her pudgy midsection bulging out, standing next to a ten-speed bike with her sweaty, frizzy curls stuck to her forehead. The more she looked, the worse they got. Nicole's limbs were heavy with embarrassment.

Anne must have seen Nicole's bottom jaw drop to the floor. "Oh, honey, you were so cute. I love those pictures," she said.

"I'm glad one of us does," Nicole countered.

"Hey, Jesse, do you remember this day?" Jimmy asked, pointing to a picture of Jesse and his brother, with matching mullets, sitting on the front bumper of a pickup truck.

Jesse's nostrils flared. "How could I forget?"

Jimmy elbowed Bill. "Get this one. Jeanie and I got Jeremy this awesome truck for his high school graduation. He was so excited to take it out for a spin that he didn't notice Jesse's bike behind it. He gunned it down the road, leaving the bike crushed like a bug in the driveway. You should have seen the tears falling from this kid's face," Jimmy howled.

Jesse's face was hardened, unyielding. "Or maybe I was upset because Jeremy is my brother, and I am stuck with that asshole for the rest of my life," he snapped.

"Jesse, language!" Jeanie yelled.

Nicole downcast her eyes to the floor, waiting for the tension to dissolve. *Jesus, Jimmy. No wonder Jeremy treats Jesse the way he does. He learned it from you.*

No one said a word until Bill perked up. "Nicole. Did your mom tell you I had one of the pictures Jimmy took of you at graduation blown up and framed for her? It looks great in the living room," he said, puffing out his chest.

Nicole pulled back the corners of her mouth into a tight smile. She might have been fine if he had stopped there, but he didn't.

"Anne, you must be so proud. You did such a great job raising her on your own. Look at her—she graduated college with honors, has a great job lined up, and can afford her own apartment. Cheers to you, Anne!" he said, raising his cup.

"Oh, Bill. Thank you for saying that." Anne blushed, patting his knee.

Nicole's words were stacking up in her throat like a pile of unread papers... *And... And... That's it? Aren't you going to say, 'But I can't take any credit. Nicole put herself through school and figured out how to make all those things happen on her own.' When will you tell him he has it all wrong? You were never there for me, which is why I didn't bother calling you when I needed a mom the most.*

Nicole's gut tightened, forcing all the air out of her lungs and leaving her mouth dry. "You always seem to know the right thing to say, Bill," Nicole said, forging a smile and meeting his cup in the air with hers.

A hand warmed Nicole's shoulder. She started to shrug it away until she realized it belonged to Jesse. She met his 'Let's get out of here' look. "Wanna go kayaking?"

"Absolutely." Anything was better than being on that deck with their families a second longer.

Moments later, they were down on the lawn, dragging the boats from the shed to the shoreline. "Do you think I need my suit? I don't feel like changing," Nicole whined.

"Not unless you plan on going in."

"Not planning on it," she said, kicking off her, sandals.

"You good?"

"Sure. You?"

He blew a laugh from his nose. "Sure." Jesse put his boat in the shallowest part of the water. "Need help getting in?"

Nicole jerked her head no. "I may need help getting out, though."

"We'll worry about that later. Right now, we're trying to get away." He smiled, dropping his butt into the seat of the kayak before floating away.

A chuckle rumbled from her as she pulled her boat into the water next to her before getting in. "Right."

They paddled along the shallow shoreline for the next hour, bobbing in the wake of the speed boats zigzagging across the lake, dragging skiers and tubers behind them.

Nicole drew in the landscape just past Jesse. "Nice job back there," she said, sliding her eyes to his.

His hazel eyes twinkled from the sun's reflection in the water. "Just living up to my part of our deal." Their gazes tangled together. There was a connectedness between them that she had never felt before. *What is going on here?*

Blushing, Nicole dropped her view to her lap, where a pair of small, beady eyes stared back at her from the darkness of the boat's hull. "Oh my god, what is THAT?" Her voice got progressively louder until she was full-on screaming. "Jesse, help me! Get over here! Help me!"

"What? What is it?" His voice was just as panicked as hers when he swiftly paddled over to her. "I'm coming. What does it look like?"

Her entire body broke out into a sweat. "I don't know! It has eyes. Nothing in here should have eyes except me. Stop asking questions. Just get over here," she demanded, shoving one end of her paddle into the kayak, attempting to keep whatever it was away from her. "Oh my god, I don't have any shoes on," she realized, pulling her feet in closer.

"What color is it?" he asked, floating up beside her. He peered into the darkness of her boat.

"Too many questions!" Her nerves swam through her like a school of startled fish. With Jesse's head in the way, she couldn't see anything until she saw *it* scurry past her leg, under her seat. "Oh my God, get me out of here. Get me out of here. What are you doing? Jesse, help me!"

Jesse couldn't help her. He was too far gone in his laughing fit, almost convulsing, watching Nicole thrash around in the boat. The kayak tipped side-to-side, knocking her off balance, finally tossing her into the water. *Splash!*

"Nicole!" Jesse yelled through his mix of concern and amusement. "Nic!"

She surfaced with a hair flip. "Seriously?" she said, sputtering water from her lips, plucking at her tank top that had suctioned to her torso like a wetsuit. Goosebumps rippled across her body. Self-consciously, she crossed her arms over her chest to shield her tightened nipples that had grown to the size of olives.

His laughter settled. "Are you okay?" he asked with more concern than amusement.

"I'll live," she said, trying to play it cool. But her mild annoyance lasted for about six seconds before her bare feet sank into the spongy lake bottom, and she was back to screaming. She pulled her knees into her chest and tread water. "What do I do? What do I do?" she cried.

He pressed his mouth into a straight line, stifling the visible laughter ready to erupt from his chest. "You're not drowning. Just swim to the big rock over there, and you can get back into your kayak."

Nicole hoisted herself onto the boulder, watching impatiently as Jesse seized through his second round of chortling while she shuddered through a case of the heebie-jeebies.

"Holy shit, I haven't laughed like that in years," he said, wiping his tears away with the heels of his hands.

"Glad I could help. Now give me your kayak."

"What do you mean?"

Nicole made an exasperated noise. "I *mean*, I am not riding back in this kayak with whatever that was."

"Wait, let me see if I can find him." Jesse glided Nicole's boat toward him using his paddle and snapped the seatback forward to reveal a black salamander hiding behind the chair. "Oh, he's a little guy. He's probably more scared of you."

"Doubt it," she said, chewing at the corner of her mouth. "Now get him out of there."

"Their skin is poisonous. I can't just grab him with my bare hands. Hold on. I'll use my shirt."

Nicole watched Jesse pull his T-shirt over his head like a snake shedding its skin, exposing his bare chest. Her whole body felt light and jittery at the sight of the small patch of hair trailing past his toned washboard abs, disappearing into the front of his shorts. Her head didn't know what to think.

Jesse?

She counted a ten-pack from her vantage, which she didn't know was physically possible. "Looks like you got quite a workout with all that laughing at my expense," she said, skipping a flushed glance his way. *What am I saying?*

A grin bloomed from his mouth as he balled up his shirt and gently scooped the black lizard in it.

"What are you going to do with it?" she asked as a shiver wriggled down her back.

"I'm going to release him into the water," he said, teasingly lowering his shirt to the surface beside her.

"Like hell you are! Jesse, stop it!" She laughed nervously, bobbing on the balls of her feet.

"You're no fun," he said, paddling to the shore. A sting burned in her chest.

After releasing the salamander into the woods, he floated toward Nicole. "He's gone. You're safe to get back in the boat."

"I'm *not* getting in there," she told him, vehemently shaking her head. "What if he has a friend in the shadows of the hull, waiting to pounce?" She paused at her words. *Stop it. You're having fun. Don't ruin it.* "Seriously, please, trade with me. I am totally freaked out."

He half groaned, half laughed. "Fine.

My hero . . . again.

* * *

Hours later, Nicole snuck away from the party. She had her fill of family and small talk for the night. Out on the front porch, she reveled at how the fireflies gracefully floated in the air like untethered helium balloons, twinkling in the darkness just past the reach of the porch lights.

Lost in the blinking lights, she was confused when her pulse shifted into overdrive. The low, closing-in sound of footsteps on the gravel driveway disrupted the distant chatter of the party. She silenced her breath as she pulled her knees into her chest, hoping the bunting draped from the railing gave her enough coverage.

Rob?

Her body clenched.

Who's there?

She began to tremble.

Please don't hurt me.

"Fireworks should be starting soon," Jesse said, emerging from the night.

Her chest exploded like a firecracker. "Jesse! Jesus Christ!" she cried, slapping her hand over her heart. "Don't you know you're not supposed to sneak up on people like that!"

She gulped at the air, catching her breath. *When will this stop?*

"Sorry. Just thought you could use a beer," he said, offering her a long-neck bottle with a lime slice wedged into the top. She could hardly hear what he said over her heart pounding in her ears but understood his gesture.

Her breath still vibrated. "Please!" She scooted over on the step, leaving enough room for Jesse. "Wanna sit?" she asked, turning away to wipe the tears from the rims of her eyes with her thumb and index finger.

"Sure. Thanks," he said, dropping down next to her. He was so close she could feel the heat radiating from his body.

"You didn't happen to bring a piece of our graduation cake, did you?"

He shook his head. "Sorry."

"It's fine. I can't remember the last time I had cheesecake. I probably don't even like it anymore."

Jesse chuckled. "I don't think it's possible to outgrow a love of cheesecake."

"No, probably not. Maybe next time." She shrugged.

They sat in silence, watching the final minutes of the day disappear behind the treetops as the murmur of the party drifted in the background. "Well, we survived another barbeque," she said, picking at the corner of her beer label.

"Um, hmm. If that's what you want to call it," Jesse grumbled, taking a pull of his bottle. His shirt sleeve rose when he rested his elbows on his thighs, revealing his hardened triceps. A distinct flutter loosened in her belly as she recalled the image of a shirtless Jesse earlier that day. *I really should have gone to more swim meets in college.*

"Well, I had enough sense to bring a spare set of clothes in case I got wet. And we stuck with our fun pact. I'd say, mission accomplished." She left out the part about how nice it was to be with him.

"Where do you get all this positive energy?"

"Years of practice, I guess." She took a sip. "I realized a long time ago that I am a happier person when I focus on the plus side of things and not the shitty side, which is usually out of my control. Trust me. I am not saying it's always easy." She let out a short laugh. "Like today, when my head almost popped off listening to my mother's distorted retelling of my *happy* childhood and her taking all the credit for my success at school.

"If I take my mother out of it, I'm proud to say that I pretty much stay away from the dark side. You should try it sometime," she teased.

"Right," he said sarcastically, turning to face her. He gave her a light bump on her knee. "Hey. I wanted to say I'm sorry."

She squinted at him. "Sorry? For what?"

"For being such a jerk to you when I dropped you off from school."

Wow. She never remembered a time when someone had apologized to her. She was usually the one to say sorry—mainly to avoid conflict. By the tinge of remorse in his voice, she believed he was being sincere.

"Don't worry about it," she said, clinking his bottle with hers. Jesse's stare lingered. With the glow of the porch light overhead, she watched his eyes dip to her mouth. She mirrored him, hoping he couldn't see her heart thumping inside her chest.

There were less than two inches between their faces when a flash appeared overhead. Nicole jolted at the screaming whistle of a sky-rocket shooting through the air and pulled away from Jesse.

"I love fireworks!" she squealed with her head tilted back. The faint tail of the comet raced high above their heads, exploding with a thunderous bang. Her core was still vibrating when a pinpoint of light burst into red, white, and blue streaks, raining and crackling until finally disappearing behind the tree line.

In the glow of the lit-up sky, Nicole glanced at Jesse through the corner of her eye, catching the lift in his cheeks as he watched the show. Something new was happening inside of her. Interest and temptation were scrambling around her intense fear of being touched by a man. She had no idea how her body would react, and kissing Jesse would be complicated. She wasn't ready for either.

Not tonight, anyway.

| 20 |

Nicole

"What are you wearing for your first day of work?" Jamie asked Nicole on the other end of the phone. Nicole held the receiver in one hand as she half-turned her body toward the full-length mirror on the back of her bedroom door, checking for visible panty lines that Jamie warned her about.

"I went with the black peplum jacket with a white shell underneath, black pencil skirt, nude pantyhose, and black pumps. I look like I'm going to a funeral."

"You can't go wrong with black, ever. So how do you feel?"

"Like an imposter. Like I am in over my head. Like I am one pair of sneakers short of Melanie Griffith in *Working Girl*," Nicole confessed, assessing her reflection up and down.

"Listen to me. Nobody handed you this job. You earned it, and a thousand percent deserve it. Remember that!"

"I know, I know."

"And if there is one piece of advice I can give you, don't ever take your heels off until you are done with them for the day. Your feet will swell like sausages, especially in this heat, and you'll never get them back on again."

"Geez . . . good to know. Honestly, I am convinced men came up with all this corporate gear to torture women for taking their jobs."

"Ha! I gotta go and take a shower. Get ready for work. Call me when you get home. I can't wait to hear all about your day!"

"Love you."

Since the two of them went suit shopping together a few weeks ago, Jamie called Nicole every morning to check in when she got home from the gym. Nicole liked the company. But more importantly, she was grateful that she and Jamie had reconnected—it was everything.

With one final look in the mirror, Nicole felt strong. Jamie was right. Nicole had earned every bit of her job on her own. With her hands on her hips, Nicole studied herself. She didn't fully recognize her reflection, but that was the clothes. In her eyes, she saw herself completely. *You've been through a lot worse. You can make it through a day with a bunch of accountants.*

"You got this!"

* * *

Nicole inched her car through the unfamiliar traffic-filled streets of Downtown Albany, navigating her way to the parking garage closest to her office building, incessantly glancing at the printed-out directions plastered to her steering wheel.

After a few wrong turns onto poorly marked side streets, Nicole found the garage. Her anxiety mounted as she eased into the windowless concrete cave that supported the five-story building above it.

She slowly crept up the ramp on high alert, worried she would take out one of the briefcase-toting professionals who kept darting out from between the cars neatly parked between the painted yellow lines. On the third floor, she found a few open spots and purposely chose the one a few spaces away from other cars so she could take the moment she needed to organize herself without someone noticing her.

Nicole's skin tingled with emotion, ping-ponging between excitement and nervousness. She wanted to walk through the lobby confidently, like she knew where she was going, not like the first-timer she was. Before she pulled the car handle open, she checked her makeup one last time in the review mirror, swiping her tongue over the fronts of her teeth to remove lipstick residue. *You got this!*

Once out on the sidewalk, she merged with the rest of the crowd of powerwalking professionals into her office building toward the elevator bank. She moved purposefully, doing her best to ignore the raw pain from the blister forming on the back of her heel.

When the elevator doors opened on her floor, Nicole was met with a wall of glass doors etched with Graham Partners. She let out one last breath and walked inside. Standing in the formal lobby, her new corporate life became a reality, and imposter syndrome crept back into her psyche. But before Nicole could spiral too far, she was greeted by the receptionist.

"Hi," the receptionist chirped. "You must be part of the junior class. Name?"

"Hi. Yes. My name is Nicole Doherty," she said politely. Nicole wiped the beads of sweat from her upper lip just as the receptionist looked up from her desk. "Sorry. First day."

"Nice to meet you, Nicole," she said reassuringly. Nicole watched the receptionist's bright red acrylic nail slide down the paperwork, landing on her name. "Here we are." She made an exaggerated checkmark with a pink highlighter beside Nicole's name and stood. "Follow me, please. I'll give you a quick tour and then bring you to the boardroom with the other newbies."

Nicole followed her through the dark wood paneled door down a long, green-carpeted hallway lit with fluorescent overhead lights and stodgy brass wall sconces. "Kitchenette on the right," she said over her shoulder. Nicole limped on her blistered feet, admiring how the receptionist effortlessly walked in her heels but thought the black piping trailing down the back of her stockings was a little too risqué for a stuffy accounting office.

"Coffee is made fresh throughout the day. Fridges are filled with non-fat milk, creamers, and various yogurt flavors. Cabinets are stocked with granola bars, microwave popcorn, and packets of soups," she rattled off.

"Wow, fully stocked kitchen. Wasn't expecting that."

"Trust me. You'll appreciate it come busy season when you're starving in the office at two a.m.," she quipped.

Nicole nodded.

The receptionist walked backward, motioning for Nicole to follow her. She put her finger to her lips, pointing out the partner's offices, silently telling Nicole to remain quiet.

Nicole collected mental notes along the way—stocked kitchenette, two a.m., keep mouth shut outside partner office.

Once around the corner and in the clear, the receptionist motioned to Nicole's feet. "New shoes?"

"How'd you know?"

"Well, the pained look on your face, for starters. And now I can see the blood seeping into your stockings," she said, pulling Nicole into the ladies' room. Inside, she swung open the metal door to the first aid kit hanging on the wall. "Here, these should work."

Nicole accepted the two Post-it note-sized bandages from the receptionist, opening her tote to drop them inside.

"No, no. Go into the stall, put these under your stockings."

"I don't have time. I need to get to the group. I'll wait for a break."

"No, you're good. You have a few minutes. Everyone is still milling around, eating breakfast, and having coffee."

Nicole wasn't a strong believer in faith but was starting to think angels were in their mid-forties, had long blonde teased locks, inch-long red nails, and oozed confidence in their black patent leather stiletto heels.

***

After a full day of onboarding at Graham Partners—leadership introductions, company history lesson, benefits paperwork, setting up her company-issued laptop—Nicole and her fellow newbies were excused for the day. Her mind was on overload.

Once outside, Nicole headed toward the parking garage. Her aching feet pillowed out of her shoes like a pair of twice-baked potatoes. She waited until she was a safe distance from the office before kicking off her pumps and walking in her stocking feet, retracting any ill feelings she had toward Melanie Griffin and her sneakers. *I get it.*

She didn't get much farther before she stripped off her suit jacket, threading it through the handles of her tote. She was suffocating in the late summer humidity. Her arms seemed to float without the synthetic fabric and plastic lining against her skin.

The sun was still above the edges of the trees, but it might as well have been midnight once she entered the parking terminal at six-fifteen. There was no natural light, and most spots were empty. The heat rose inside her, and she suddenly felt confined and vulnerable. *Where is everybody?* A car alarm beeped, echoing off the cement walls. She slowed her walk to listen for footsteps, which never came.

Hiking back to her car, the rough pavement poked the bottom of her bare feet. She kept her head down, avoiding the oil stains and puddles of brown water collecting in the corners as she rounded the turns.

By the time Nicole strolled past the column labeled 'C2,' she was panting and red faced but coached herself to keep moving. With the amber lights flickering overhead and no one in sight, her mind was getting the best of her, and staying calm was becoming increasingly difficult.

A few heartbeats later, a metal stairwell door screamed open in the distance, ringing through the garage. The little hairs on the back of her neck stood while the rest of her body froze, listening to the footsteps that followed getting faster, growing louder. The door slammed like a gunshot, the sound piercing her gut, sending an avalanche of uncontrollable shivers and memories of that night on the driveway, her dorm room within reach . . . the moment before he tackled her.

She looked behind her but didn't see anyone coming. She whipped her head around the other way. Nothing except the distorted footsteps bouncing around the windowless garage like a pinball, making it impossible to know where they came from.

The thought of that night, of him, jolted her into a sprint for the last hundred feet to her car. Anxiety sputtered through her as the footsteps closed in.

"Nicole!" the voice yelled.

Nicole? What? No one knows me here, she reasoned. *Keep going!* she ordered.

"Nicole!"

There it was again—a woman's voice. *Don't stop! It's a trick.*

Nicole was in full panic mode when she rounded the trunk of her car to the driver's side door, throwing her shoes on the ground. Her feet were burning. Her throat was burning. Her whole body jerked uncontrollably as if she was on fire.

She ripped her suit jacket from the tote handles and threw it to the ground beside her pumps as she frantically bounced her bag, listening for the familiar jingle of her keys. She heard nothing but the thumping of reams of first-day paperwork and some loose change. "Where are they?" she screamed, burying her head inside.

"Hey, Nicole!" the woman said in a friendly, breathless tone. "Over here."

Nicole warily looked up, her heart beating behind her eyes. Her mind reeled with confusion. The receptionist from the office was standing before her, waving with a toothy smile.

"Hi! Sorry. Didn't mean to sneak up on you like that. I saw you running. Wanted you to know it was me and not some wacko." She laughed. "This place can get a little spooky at night. I don't usually park in here for that reason. There is an open lot around the corner on Washington. Much safer."

Nicole nodded wordlessly.

"Goodness. It looks like I scared the bejesus out of you. You okay?"

Nicole gave her a pained smile and nodded again.

"Good. I am running to meet my husband for dinner. I was supposed to be there fifteen minutes ago. Get home safe!" she said before jumping into her car and speeding away.

Nicole threw her bag to the ground and paced in small circles, raking her hands through her hair, mumbling words she didn't even understand. After a few beats, she crouched next to her purse and pulled everything out to reveal her keys tucked quietly in the corner. "I fucking hate big bags," she murmured. Hot tears burned hollows into her cheeks as she accepted defeat from the tote.

Still squatting, barefoot, she gathered all her belongings—papers, shoes, jacket— that were strewn on the ground like it was her bedroom. She fought to her feet and struggled to find the keyhole in the car door through her blurred vision.

Finally locked safely inside her car, she allowed herself to sob all the shame-filled tears that she had been accumulating for months. "I can't live like this. I . . . can't . . . live like this!" she screamed, pounding her fist on the passenger seat. She was furious at her vulnerability and her lack of control. "I had a God damn plan!"

Minutes ticked by as desperation and loneliness dripped from every pore in her body. She had painted herself into a corner of helplessness by keeping her secret. The weight of her pounding head dropped into her hands, shaking a quiet, clear moment out of her.

This is not me. I want my life back. I need my life back.

| 21 |

Nicole

Nicole had read somewhere that 'The secret to your future is hidden in your daily routine.' On her Saturday morning walk to Zuke's for her usual coffee, Nicole wondered when her future self would be able to look back and say, "See, it was because you stuck to your routine that you were able to stop spinning out of control."

She hoped it was soon because a new wave of dizziness was overtaking her mind after her first two weeks at Graham Partners. No one told her that when she started in public accounting, it would feel like a never-ending game of dodgeball, except in her version, the higher-ups in the office were her opponents. They threw debits and credits, detailed processes, high expectations, and a low tolerance for error, not to mention the panic the receptionist hurled at her when she unintentionally snuck up on her in the parking garage, driving Nicole further into isolation.

The air was perfumed with the last summer rose blooms on the bushes lining the uneven sidewalk. Nicole slid her sunglasses on her head and tilted her face toward the late August sun like a flower relaxing open its petals. Usually, her walk cleared away the cotton clouding her mind, but that morning, she couldn't see a way to make her life stop spiraling. The only credit Nicole could give to her routine was that if it weren't for it and the primal need for coffee and food, she'd probably never leave her apartment.

She dragged in a breath as deep as the hole she was trying to climb out of, pulled down her sunglasses, and pushed in the door to Zuke's. She was relieved to see that Zuke was busy with another customer. It gave her time to fix a smile.

But Zuke being Zuke, looked up at the sound of the chime over her head and cheerfully greeted her. "Morning, Nicole!"

She gave Zuke a small wave and quietly returned his smile. "Hey," she said, almost to herself.

She wandered down one of the aisles, waiting for her turn.

"Nic?" a man's voice said, stopping her cold. *Nic?* No one in her new neighborhood was familiar enough to call her that.

She glanced over the neatly shelved jars of sun-dried tomatoes, marinated artichokes, and dried pasta. His baby blue one-pocket tee and khaki shorts emphasized his caramel-tanned skin. She recognized his worn-out Yankee hat immediately. "Jesse? Wha . . . what are you doing here?" she stammered.

"Hey, I thought that was you," he said, his eyes smiling. "Well, this a coincidence."

Nicole rounded the endcap and made her way to him by the counter. "I'd say. I'm so confused," she said, flinching her head back. "Did you know I lived around here?"

The sunlight streamed through the large plate glass windows, illuminating his hazel eyes into a brilliant green. "You mentioned you got an apartment near Albany, but I had no idea it was here. Like here, here," he said, pointing to the ground.

She had the urge to hug him but stopped herself. *Do I hug Jesse? Have I ever hugged him? Do I shake his hand? Why am I overthinking this?* Nicole glanced away when she realized she was staring. Her cheeks burned as snapshots of the July Fourth barbeque, the last time they saw each other, flashed in her mind—his bare chest in the kayak, the moment they almost kissed, the moment she pulled away.

"Almost a half hour from your house is kinda far to drive for coffee, no? Although Zuke does make a mean dark roast, so I wouldn't be surprised if word got around," she said, smiling at Zuke. She was babbling but couldn't stop the nervous energy fluttering inside her.

"I'm taking a scuba class at the Y not far from here, but the class doesn't start until ten. I was killing time and saw the sandwich board sign promising hot coffee and egg sandwiches out front. I couldn't resist."

"Scuba? That's cool. Searching for lost treasure at the bottom of the lake?" She cringed at her words. *Why are you making stupid jokes?*

"Umm . . . maybe, hadn't thought about that. I'm working to get certified for my job."

Nicole narrowed her eyes. "I must have missed a step. I thought you were an engineer."

"I am. I'm part of the special team that inspects bridges, the New York State Canal System—really any infrastructure that comes in contact with water. Right now, I'm spending all my time analyzing the data outside the water, but I want to be on the diving team that collects the data in the water. Inspecting for corrosion, deterioration, that sort of stuff," he said, cutting himself off. His face flushed. "Dorky, I know."

"You're talking to an accountant. The only bigger dorks than accountants are actuaries. You're safe here."

"Phew," he said, pretending to wipe his brow.

She caught a glimpse of his smile. They hadn't seen each other in a few months, but that didn't stop them from falling back into their playful razzing. It felt so natural. Well, except for the unexpected nerves zinging through her insides.

"What'll it be today, Nicole? The usual?" Zuke interrupted. For a moment, she forgot where she was, lost in her conversation with Jesse.

"Um," she said, her eyes lingering a little too long on Jesse before turning her attention to Zuke. "This may surprise you, but I am going with an iced coffee today. Large. And a slice of your delicious frittata." She beamed, winking at him. *Did I just wink? Am I having a stroke?*

Zuke looked at her with disbelief. "Wow, keeping me on my toes. What's the occasion?" he asked, sliding open the glass display case where the prepared food was kept.

"I've got to run to the dry cleaner, and it's already starting to boil outside. My car's A/C is acting up again, so I'm thinking iced is a better option."

"It may just need some refrigerant. I can look at it when you're back if you'd like," Zuke offered, handing her the coffee.

"That's sweet of you, thank you. But honestly, I don't want to know what's wrong with it. I'd feel compelled to fix it with the money I don't have right now. It's cheaper to ignore the problem and drink iced coffee instead."

"Here when you need me," Zuke said.

She smiled. "Every morning." Nicole liked having Zuke looking out for her. It was partly by design. She felt safer believing that if she didn't show up for her coffee, hot or iced, Zuke would wonder where she was. She was confident he would get concerned and check in on her if it went on too long. He was that kind of guy.

"All set," Zuke said, putting a small bag and a foil-wrapped sandwich on the counter next to Jesse's untouched cup of coffee. "Together or separate?"

"Together," Jesse said.

"Separate," Nicole said at the same time.

Jesse handed Zuke a twenty he had pulled from his wallet before Nicole could get her money out of her pocket. "I got it. No problem."

Nicole's cheeks twitched in embarrassment. She was uncomfortable with Jesse paying for her breakfast.

"Well, thank you. Next time is on me," she said, grabbing the bag's handles and putting it in her canvas tote.

"I'm gonna hold you to it." The warmth of his smile echoed in his voice. "You walking out?"

Nicole nodded at Jesse and then waved goodbye to Zuke. "Thanks, Zuke. I'll see you tomorrow."

He flashed her one of his Zuke smiles and wiped down the counter by the register. "Looking forward to it."

Nicole clicked the door open when Jesse reached over her head and held it for her. "Thanks, man," Jesse said, jutting his chin at Zuke.

Out on the sidewalk, a small pickup truck sputtered down the road past Jesse and Nicole. "Well, it was great to see you," Nicole said, fiddling with her straw. She was having a hard time downplaying her giddiness. "Thanks again for breakfast. Sorry Zuke put you on the spot in there."

Jesse shook his head. "He didn't. I was happy to do it. It was great to see you, too."

Nicole pulled her sunglasses down and secretly admired Jesse's preppy nautical look. He looked laid-back, as usual, but the confidence was new. Or maybe she had never noticed it before. Nicole sipped her iced coffee to loosen her suddenly dry mouth. "Yeah, great to see you too." *You already said that.* Her eyes flashed wide behind her dark lenses.

She pointed to the blue sedan parked out front of the deli. "This you here?" she asked, diverting his attention away from her nervous bumbling.

"It is. Where's your car?"

"Back at my apartment. I walked here. I only live a block away."

"Want a ride?"

"Oh, no thanks. I've got a little routine going," she admitted. "I'll walk."

Jesse checked his watch. "I've got some time before my class starts. Want some company?"

"Sure!" she said a little too enthusiastically.

Moments later, they were plodding side-by-side down the sidewalk, sipping their coffees and catching up like two old friends. It felt different to share her morning—in a good way. Having someone with her was a nice change.

"Sounds like you've been spending a lot of time outside. Explains the fantastic tan. So jealous."

"Yeah. And this is with SPF 50 and wearing long-sleeved T-shirts most days. The sun is brutal by the water."

"The only color I get is from the copy machine in my office." She laughed. "My job is more of an indoor thing."

"So, what's happening with you and the deli guy?" Jesse asked.

Nicole's eyes pinched together, confused by his sudden change of subject. "Who? Zuke?" She threw a thumb over her shoulder. "He's my deli guy. Doesn't everyone have one?"

"Well, for starters, you have *a usual*. And then he offered to fix your car. He likes you."

"No, he does not! That's how he is with everyone," she insisted, turning her body toward Jesse.

"Um, hmm. Just be careful."

Be careful?

"You've got him all wrong. He's friendly like that with everyone. He's building his business," she said, not realizing that the sidewalk was heaved until it was too late. She tripped and tumbled to the ground, sending her iced coffee and tote flying onto a nearby patch of grass.

"Nic!" Jesse cried. "Oh my God, are you okay?" he asked, threading his arm under hers. Nicole scrambled to her feet, wondering which hurt more, the burning pain shooting through her knee or her pride.

"I'm fine," she said, rubbing the dirt off her hands. "Mortified. But going to live."

"We need to get you home and clean your knee," Jesse said, pointing to the blood trickling down her shin.

If he had not been there, Nicole might have cried. "Jesus Christ," she said, blowing out her breath. "Good news, that's me right there. The blue one. My apartment is on the top floor." She pointed to the two-story duplex next door to where she flopped.

He studied the building. "It looks nice. Neighborhood too. Feels very homey."

"Thanks, I really like it here."

"I can see why," he agreed. "Well, let's get you inside and clean you up."

"Great. Claire's outside," Nicole whispered, catching a glimpse of her weeding the flower bed on the side of the house. "Just what I need."

Jesse recovered Nicole's bag and drink from the lawn. "Who's Claire?"

"She's my landlord."

Claire must have overheard them and pushed herself to a stand. "Hi, Nicole." She blinked down to Nicole's bloody leg. "What happened to you?"

Nicole waved. "Hi, Claire. Oh, it's nothing. I'm fine."

Claire barely noticed Nicole once she saw Jesse. "And who's this tall drink of handsomeness? New boyfriend?"

Nicole felt a flash of alarm in her chest. "No, no, no," she said, shaking her head. "This is Jesse. He's a friend of mine. We grew up together."

"Nice to meet you," Jesse said, smiling boyishly. "Sorry, I'd shake your hand, but . . ." He finished his sentence by gesturing at the breakfast and cups in his hands.

Claire gave a quick nod. "I like this one, Nicole," she said, talking to Nicole like he wasn't standing right in front of her. Nicole's cheeks seared with humiliation.

"You should take her out more. She doesn't leave her apartment very often. You kids are young. Enjoy it while you can," she told him in a whisper loud enough for Nicole to hear.

Jesse chuckled politely. Nicole's chest caved in, listening to Claire speak about Nicole's comings and goings. She felt naked when Claire told the truth.

"Oh, my. Well, it was good to see you, Claire," Nicole said. "Sorry to cut this short, but I need to get a towel before I bleed out on the sidewalk. Jesse, do you want to check out my apartment?" Nicole asked.

"Ah, sure. It was nice meeting you, Claire."

"Nice to meet you, Jesse. I hope to see you around more often." Nicole wanted to crawl into a hole. "You kids go have fun now," Claire said with a wave.

Nicole ignored her knee and hurried up the stairs, waiting to speak until they were safely inside her apartment. "That was awful. I am so sorry."

"She seems harmless. Just looking out for you."

"Since when are you the rosy, tolerant one?"

He shrugged. "What can I say? I have a soft spot for old ladies. She reminds me of my grandmother—she tells it like it is. No filter."

"That's Claire for sure," she said, hobbling into the kitchen to get a wet paper towel.

Jesse followed her, emptying his hands on the table. "Here, let me help you," he said, taking the towel from her. He squatted next to her leg, which she was thankful was recently shaved. She should have been more worried about Claire exposing her hermit-like tendencies to Jesse, but her mind was distracted by his gentle touch and clean, woodsy scent.

She sucked in her teeth when he dabbed the cold towel along her raw skin. "You don't have to do this," she said, her voice pained.

"I want to. I like helping you," he said, unphased. It was unlike Nicole to let someone help her in such a way, but she rested against the counter, closed her eyes, and let him. It was a nice change.

"And who's this?"

Nicole's eyes sprung open to find one of her cats rubbing against the side of Jesse's leg. "Oh, that's CC. Noodle should be around here somewhere," she said, scanning the room. "There she is." She pointed to the calico curled up underneath the kitchen table.

"CC?" he asked.

"That's her nickname. Her real name is Corn Chip. Her coloring reminded me of Fritos." She shrugged. "I thought it was clever."

"You realize you named your cats after our favorite mini-mart snacks?"

"Ha! I guess I did. Must have been subconscious. They should be flattered that they were named after such iconic road snacks. You know, as much as cats are impressed by anything." She chucked.

Jesse stood up. His closeness was warm. "I think it's clean." He smiled. Her pulse quickened.

"I think so too. Thank you." Nicole diverted her eyes to the bright yellow wall clock in the kitchen. "Oh, geez. It's already nine-thirty. You're going to be late for your class! You need to go," she said, rushing him to the door.

Seconds later, they stood in awkward silence on the landing outside her apartment. She sucked in a lungful watching him study her face like an open book. She didn't know how to say goodbye. *Wave? Hug? Punch in the arm?* The best she could come up with was, "Watch your head on your way down the stairs." She motioned to the cascading philodendron over his shoulder.

He gave a slight nod with a grin, his eyes still locked on hers. "I'm happy I ran into you this morning. It was a nice surprise."

"I hate surprises," she blurted, ignoring how his gaze heated her skin. His smile dropped to a straight line. "Sorry." *Shit!* "Sorry. I didn't mean this was a bad surprise. I was just saying that, in general, I hate surprises. All the pretending to be having fun." He tilted his head. "Oh, geez. That's not what I meant. I'm not talking about . . . You know what? I'm going to stop talking," she said, self-consciously crossing her arms over her chest.

He matched her nervous laugh. "Well, I better go."

She chewed at the corner of her lip. "It was great to see you, Jesse. Thanks again for your help. Be careful on your way back to your car. Sidewalk's a killer."

"I'll keep that in mind," he said, tipping forward and pulling her into a hug. She slid her arms around his back and hooked her chin on his shoulder, letting him take the lead on how long to hang on and how hard to squeeze. His soft, cotton T-shirt was warm and pillowlike, emitting a citrusy scent as if it was dried in the summer sun by the lake. Her mind buzzed with his broad shoulders and hard stomach pressed against her.

Jesse eased his hold, and she pulled away with a start like he had just told her he was covered in poison ivy. "Bye," they said in one voice as he disappeared down the stairs.

Had she imagined the lingering smiles? The flirty glances?

Is this the moment I realized my daily routine revealed the secret to my future?

| 22 |

Jamie

A brisk fall breeze pushed open the front door of the two-bedroom apartment Jamie shared with Randy. Sunburst-colored leaves tumbled behind, following her inside. "Randy?" she yelled, hanging her barn jacket on the hook in the foyer.

"In the kitchen," Randy shouted.

Gloom pulsed when she remembered it was Sunday, which meant brunch with her future in-laws in a few hours.

When Randy announced they were moving in together shortly after getting engaged, Karen asked Jamie, "Living in sin before the wedding . . . what will people think?" At the time, Jamie thought she was kidding and laughed it off, but since their recent interactions, Jamie realized there was nothing funny about Karen.

Jamie closed her eyes and put her palms together in front of her chest—*I won't let Karen ruin my day today.* She repeated her daily mantra three times before heading into the kitchen.

Clad in her sweaty workout clothes, she found Randy sitting at the table drinking his coffee, reading the sports section of the *Times Union* newspaper in an old college T-shirt and basketball shorts. "Hi, Randy," she said, kissing him good morning. "Any coffee left?"

"Should be enough for a cup." Jamie heard the crinkle of the newspaper behind her. "Well, aren't you a filthy little thing? And I mean that in the hottest way possible," he purred, smacking her on the tush.

She made a face. "Oh, God, you do not want this. I have sweat in places I didn't know could sweat."

"Are you trying to turn me on?" he asked, peering over the rim of his mug.

"You're so fresh," she said, swatting him away with a dishtowel. Jamie could feel the weight of Randy's flirty attention as she worked her way around the kitchen, making her coffee. Given his mood, she thought it would be a good time to tell him about her idea for their wedding. "So . . ." she started.

"Uh-oh. I don't like where this is going. You always start conversations like this when you want me to do something."

"No. No. It's not bad. Hear me out." Jamie gave a reassuring smile.

That morning at the gym, Jamie remembered her conversation with Nicole about how supportive Randy was of Jamie. "He loves you. If he knows how much Karen hurts you, he'll listen. He'll try to help. He adores you. You know that." Considering her words, Jamie decided to take Nicole's advice and talk to Randy about the wedding. Karen wasn't getting any better. If anything, she was getting worse, and it was wearing on Jamie. It had been months since she had a full night's sleep.

But, if she had any shot of making her idea work, Jamie couldn't let Randy know that her change of heart about the wedding had anything to do with his mother. He would shut her down immediately.

Mug in hand, she stood next to Randy, stroking the back of his neck. "When I was on the treadmill this morning, I got to thinking . . . what if we eloped? It would be *so* romantic. And such a great story for our kids. Imagine . . . their parents were so in love that they couldn't wait for a big wedding. They ran to Town Hall and got married in their gym clothes." She swooned, laying it on thick.

He put his cup down and tilted his head up at her with squinted eyes. "What are you talking about? You've been planning this wedding for months. You were so excited about The Sullivan. What happened?"

She snapped at his questions. "Correction. Your mother has been planning this wedding for months. It's becoming more about her showing off in front of her club friends and PR for the firm and less about us. Do you know what she told me the other day?"

So much for not making it about Karen.

"Hm," he grunted listlessly, going back to his paper.

Jamie paced the kitchen. "She told me I needed to find four bridesmaids. Having only Nic up there with me will make it look like I have no friends. Randy, I don't know four other women I would want to stand up with me. It would be such a charade. I just want the big dress, the pictures, and the party. Not a corporate boondoggle."

Randy stood up from the table and corralled her in his towering frame. "Hon, my mom is just trying to help. She doesn't want you to get stressed out," he said, kissing her forehead. "I think you're misunderstanding her intentions. She loves you."

Jamie clasped her mug in front of his chest, searching his expression for any signs of support. "We could go to Town Hall in Saratoga. I could wear my dress, take pictures in Congress Park, and then we'll have a small reception at the club with just family and close friends. It would be so much more intimate."

He lifted the mug from her hands and set it on the counter. "Hon. You don't mean that. You're just overwhelmed," he said, pressing his body against hers.

She spread her feet, making room for him to move in closer. When he dipped his head, she softly kissed the small birthmark just below his ear, breathing in a trace of his spicy citrus cologne leftover from the day before.

He groaned. "You taste salty. How about we head upstairs to the shower, and you let me release some of that wedding tension? We've got time before we need to get to the club." She melted into him. "My parents can wait a few extra minutes for us."

The thought of Randy's parents, of Karen, was Jamie's arousal kill switch. "You're thinking about your parents right now? Seriously? Totally ruined the moment," she said, slinking out from his embrace.

He threw his arms out playfully. "Wait, that's it?" he asked, mouth open.

"That's it, Randy." The phone rang. "Saved by the bell." She laughed, walking over to the receiver hanging on the wall. "Now go take a cold shower and think about what you did. You should be ashamed of yourself."

"Hello," Jamie said into the telephone.

"Hi, Jamie, it's Nic."

"Hey, Nic!" Randy planted his mouth on Jamie's collarbone. "Can you hold on a second," she said, pressing the receiver into her T-shirt.

"I love you. Now go," she said, sending him off with a quick kiss.

Randy may have blown off her eloping idea, but Jamie wasn't done yet. She meant what she said. Once Karen commandeered their wedding, Jamie wanted to run away with him. But Karen had a firm hold on Randy, and Jamie didn't want to risk losing him in the process.

Jamie put the phone back up to her ear. "I'm back."

"Busy? I can call you back."

Jamie opened the refrigerator door and grabbed a can of SlimFast. "No. No. Now's good. What's going on?" she asked, sitting in the kitchen chair, still warm from Randy.

"Did you know that Jesse Young was charming and hot?"

"Jesse? As in Jeremy's little brother? Isn't he like twelve?"

"Yeah, like ten years ago."

"Well, this got interesting fast. What happened with Jesse Young?" Jamie asked, perking up in her seat.

"I ran into him at the deli around the corner from my house yesterday. I am pretty sure he was flirting with me. And the worst part was that I was such a bumbling dork, making stupid jokes like my mouth was having a seizure."

"So, you were being yourself?"

"Good one," she deadpanned.

Jamie stifled her fun. "I remember him being pretty intense. Not really a smiler."

"That was just around Jeremy. We always had a good time when we hung out," Nicole said, jumping to his defense.

"You'd know better than me. You spent way more time with him than I did. I was busy sneaking beers from Jimmy's garage fridge with Jeremy and his friends." Jamie laughed, sipping her shake.

"It's funny, in all the years I have known him, I never saw him other than a family friend, more like a brother. Then, all of a sudden, he's all tan and confident with these ridiculously hard abs. He's got a good job. He's driven. He bought my breakfast. And now I can't stop thinking about him."

"When did you see his abs?"

"Is that all you heard?"

"Kinda."

"I'm serious, Jamie. Has he always been all those things, and I never noticed it right in front of my face?"

"Ooo . . . you like him. Are you going to go out with him?"

"No! I'm sure I'm reading too much into it. Besides, I don't have time for dating. I have a new job."

Jamie scoffed into the phone. "You and your routines and life plans. You can have a career and a love life. Not everything has to be so linear, Nic. Geez, sometimes you are so rigid."

"My schedule is unpredictable."

"Excuses, excuses. What are you really afraid of?"

There was silence on the other end of the phone. Even though the sisters had become closer since Nicole graduated, Jamie still felt a wall between them.

"Nic? Hello?"

"Yeah, I'm here."

"I wish you saw how amazing you are."

"I'll see what happens the next time I see him. How's that?"

"So next time you happen to run into each other in a random deli?"

"If it was meant to be, it will be. Isn't that what they say?"

"Yes, but others say, 'Some people want it to happen, some wish it would happen, others make it happen.' If you want it, make it happen," she retorted. *Maybe I should listen to my own advice.*

"When did you become an inspirational poster?"

"I love you and want you to be happy."

"I am," Nicole said. "I promise."

Something in Nicole's voice wasn't convincing. More walls. "People that have to tell you they are a certain way usually aren't. Everything okay?"

"Yup. I just wanted you to know that Jesse had turned into a hottie. That was it," she said.

Jamie still wasn't convinced but gave her a pass. "All right, I gotta go. I need to mentally prepare to see Karen at the club, and I need a shower. I am still in my workout clothes. Which reminds me . . . I joined a new all-women's gym in Cohoes, and I want you to come with me."

"Not for me."

"C'mon. I need an accountability partner. It will be fun. The step classes really work your ass. I'm already sore from this morning."

"You're not a very good salesperson."

"I got you a coupon book for five free classes. I'll even pick you up. You don't have any excuses. You're going. We start next Saturday."

"Sorry, busy. That's the day I bathe the cats," she joked.

"Well, if that's true, you definitely need to get out more. I'll be at your house at nine. Love you."

| 23 |

Nicole

Nicole and Jamie ambled their way toward the lobby of the women's gym as the stench of sweat and chemical disinfectant floated over the blaring pop music in the air. "I'll meet you upfront in a minute. Need to run to the ladies' room," Jamie said, wiping her brow with the towel hanging around her neck.

Nicole's T-shirt was soaked from front to back, and her wet curls stuck to her neck. It had been nearly two months since she started going to step aerobics class with Jamie. She had resigned herself to the fact that it might never get easier, but Nicole had a standing weekly date with her sister, which was worth the embarrassment of her clumsy display.

Standing in the front of the studio, Nicole glazed over the notices tacked to the bulletin board—gym membership specials, nutrition expert contact information, local real estate listings, inspirational messages—and was about to pivot on her cross trainers toward the water fountain when a flyer in the bottom corner caught her attention.

Model Mugging read across the top in bold lettering, right above an image of a woman in a tank top and yoga pants, jaw clenched, kneeing an ominous character, donning an oversized helmet, in the gut.

She read on. *Empowerment-based self-defense training class.* Her belly fluttered. She touched the paper, half expecting it to dissolve in her hands. *Is this for real? Can't be . . . But what if it is? What if this is exactly what I've been looking for?* She quickly ripped one of the paper piano key tabs at the bottom of the page and shoved it into her bag before Jamie reappeared.

* * *

Later that afternoon, Nicole was watching an HGTV marathon in her living room when her phone rang, startling her from her cable coma.

"Hi. This is Leia from Model Mugging. I got your message that you would like more information about our self-defense program. How can I help?"

Nicole hesitated to take a breath. "I saw your flyer at the gym. It said something about self-defense, overcoming personal fears, and confidence-building. I don't know exactly what to ask. I just know I want it all. I *need* it all," Nicole said without thinking.

Her admission surprised her. It turned out that blurting out her fears to a stranger on the phone was easier than looking in a mirror or even thinking about admitting it to a loved one. "How on earth is there a class for all these things? It sounds too good to be true."

Nicole could hear Leia smile on the other end of the phone. "I completely understand your reaction. I felt the same way when I first learned about the program. Most women do. In a nutshell, Model Mugging aims to teach women how to turn the adrenaline rush in a realistic assault situation from a fear response to an active response. We achieve this through full contact simulated attacks where you learn how to effectively channel your fears into energy used to incapacitate an assailant." *Full contact? Incapacitate an assailant?*

"Do I need to know karate or something already?"

"No advanced martial arts training is required. In fact, you don't even have to be particularly athletic."

Nicole let out a chuckle. "Well, that's a relief. I am not very coordinated."

After a few more minutes of Leia answering Nicole's questions, Leia suggested, "I'll tell you what, our next three-day session starts this Friday. How about you come by and check it out for yourself? There is absolutely no pressure. Just come down, observe, and then we'll go from there."

Nicole knew that if she didn't commit then, she'd spend her week deliberating with herself and may end up chickening out. She couldn't take that risk. She needed to act. She needed to *make it happen*. "I don't need more time. I'm in."

She didn't know exactly what she had signed herself up for, but anything was better than treading idly, wishing for things to change.

| 24 |

Nicole

Nicole thundered up the crumbling front stairs of the YMCA and approached the makeshift front desk—three metal desks shoved together in a U-shape. Behind it, she found a skinny teenage boy wearing a black Stone Temple Pilots T-shirt with his eyes closed tight. His whole body was wed to the music coming through his Walkman, and based on his hand gestures, he appeared to be in the middle of a drum solo.

After a few beats, Nicole knocked lightly on the desk to get his attention. His eyes opened with surprise. "Oh, hey. Sorry." He chuckled. "Can I help you?" he asked, sliding his headphones around his neck. The green lights from the small fake Christmas tree on top of the desk shined on his pimply face, making him look sickly.

"Hi, yes, can you please tell me where I can find the Model Mugging class?" she asked, nervously hovering over the desk.

"Ah, sure," he said. While Nicole impatiently waited for the boy to flip through the clipboard of papers, she re-inventoried her tote to make sure nothing magically fell out of it between her car and the lobby. In the distance, chirping sneakers, screaming kids, and bouncing balls echoed from the nearby gym.

"It's downstairs in the basement," the little drummer boy finally said, sliding his headphones over his ears before she could ask him how to get there. *Never mind, I'll figure it out.*

She hurried down the hallway to find a set of stairs next to the glass wall displaying the pool area. A faint chemical smell drifted into the corridor. *Chlorine. Swimming. Jesse!*

A shiver ripped through her when she remembered that he was taking scuba classes at the Y. *Crap. What if we ran into each other? How would I explain why I'm here?*

She had already lied to Jamie when she canceled their Saturday step class, telling her she had to work, too ashamed to tell her sister she was learning to 'channel her fears.' If she ran into Jesse, she'd have no choice but to lie to him too.

Down in the basement, the long passage was poorly lit. Dim fluorescent lights flickered overhead. All doors along the wall were closed. There was no movement—just emptiness and silence. The little hairs on the back of her neck stood at full attention. It was the parking garage all over again.

Nicole trickled down the hallway like a slow leak, dragging her fingertips along the cinderblock wall, wondering if she was undergoing her first Model Mugging test. The chill of the foundation grounded her as adrenaline battered her interior. With each step, her knees became rubberier. *If this is supposed to simulate a dark alley, they've nailed it.*

Halfway down the hall, she heard the faint cry of a woman. "Eyes!" *Eyes?*

More yelling. "No! . . . No! . . . No!" Followed by a heavy *thud*.

"What is going on?" she muttered, scrambling around the corner toward the commotion, worried the woman needed help.

Nicole almost tripped over the leg of the easel that held a large white poster board outside an open classroom door that read *Welcome to Model Mugging* in green block letters. In the shadows of the artificial light of the classroom, Nicole paused to consider the use of 'welcome' and 'mugging' in the same salutation. Nowhere else would such a sign exist.

In the doorway of the windowless room, Nicole allowed her eyes to adjust to the bright light before going inside. She swallowed hard when she found a woman, no taller than five feet, standing over someone wearing an alien-like helmet similar to the one she saw in the flyer, splayed out on their back.

When the woman saw Nicole, she marched over to her, appearing unfazed that she had just assaulted someone. "Hi! I'm Leia. Are you here for Model Mugging?"

"Um." Nicole's mind changed focus. "Sorry. Yes. Yes, I am."

"No apologies. Come on in. You're in the right place. I'll be one of your instructors this weekend. What's your name?" Her voice was gruff.

Nicole took a few hesitant steps into the room. "Ah . . . Nicole. Doherty. We spoke on the phone a few days ago."

"We sure did. Hi Nicole." Her fair skin and warm smile juxtaposed the persona she emitted when paired with her dyed jet-black long shag—a borderline mullet—heavy black eyeliner and piercings up to the curve of her ear.

"Nice to put a face with a voice," Leia said, reassuring Nicole. "You can change in the small bathroom at the back of the room." She pointed over the heads of the women sitting on the mat. "When you're ready, come back to me to get a nametag and a set of elbow and knee pads." *Gulp.*

A few minutes later, Nicole joined the other women on the edge of the mat with her 'Hello My Name Is' sticker on her shirt and equipment in hand. Everyone's darting glances and fidgeting hands told Nicole that she wasn't the only one questioning whether she had made the right decision to join the class. Nicole waited silently, picking at the edges of her French-manicured acrylic nails, senselessly wondering if they would last through the night.

"Looks like we have everyone," Leia boomed from the front of the room. She paused to scan the circle quietly, undeterred by the flustered expressions of the fifteen women surrounding her. A slightly-framed man about the size of a jockey joined her. "For those of you I haven't met, my name is Leia. I am one of your instructors for the weekend. And this is Jose," she said, turning toward him.

"Good evening." He smiled with a wave at the group. "As Leia said, my name is Jose. In addition to being your male instructor this weekend, I also play a second role in the class—attacker." Nicole's chest seized at the word. "When I have on the protective suit and mask you saw earlier, I am no longer Jose. I am Blade. We will get more into this shortly, but essentially, Blade's job is to take on the characteristics and actions of an aggressor to help you learn hands-on how to defend yourself."

Jose's words rolled around in Nicole's head. She never envisioned a scenario where she exchanged pleasantries with someone who introduced himself as an 'attacker,' but there he was, waving to the group and flashing an easy smile.

Nicole realized that he must have been the person in the alien head who crawled off the mat when she initially walked into the room. Given his stature, it made sense how Leia effortlessly got him to the ground.

"We are already so proud of you for taking the gigantic step of coming here," Leia said. "I know you're all wondering what will happen tonight, especially since I told you to wear protective gear. My best advice is to trust the process. You're in a safe place. I promise, if you do that, you will be amazed at your transformation by Sunday."

Relief softened the innate tension in the room, but only for a moment.

"Everybody up," Leia commanded, leading the anxious room to stand. "We're going to get started with warmups to get loose, and then we're going to jump right into it." They started with 'centering' themselves, the basis for every defensive move they would be taught in the course. Nicole was sweating through her clothes. With her knees bent, elbows in, hands up, and weight on the balls of her feet, Nicole watched herself repeatedly practice the move in the wall-mounted mirrors. She worried she looked ridiculous but caught glimpses of others in the class shadow crouching, too. She wasn't alone.

After some time, they moved on to learning their first defensive moves—the elbow strike, the eye strike, and the knee to the groin.

Blade emerged from the back, wearing loose-fitted coveralls layered over full protective pads. A large helmet covered in layers of duct tape designed with impassable screens for the eyes and mouth protected his head. At first, he looked like a child in a homemade costume on Halloween night, but as he menacingly strolled past the women in the room, the wimpy Jose transformed into a horror movie monster. A mist of cold dew surfaced on Nicole's skin.

The instructors stood in the front of the room to demonstrate. Because Blade was padded from head to toe, Leia could deliver full-force blows. "It helps with muscle memory and achieving the full experience," she explained.

For the first role play, Leia pretended to wait at a bus stop reading a book when Blade casually walked near her and then unexpectedly grabbed her from behind. "Oh, God!" One woman cried, covering her gaping mouth.

"Center!" Leia shouted, dropping to her ready stance. "Elbow!" Sweat slicked Nicole's palms in anticipation of his next move.

With Blade still holding Leia, she bent forward, putting all her weight on her front foot, appearing to retrieve something near her instep, knocking him off balance. Nicole held her breath, anticipating Leia's next move, then watched her fly up to a standing position in one swift motion, throwing her bent elbow over her shoulder and striking Blade in the nose. "No!"

Nicole felt a flash of alarm, watching Blade land flat on his back. *How did she do that?*

Leia stood cold as Blade bounced back up like a Weeble Wobble, ready to take his next punch. She told the group, "It's important to yell with each move. Not only will it make your strikes more powerful, but it will keep you from holding your breath. Believe it or not, breathing helps to keep you calm, even when your adrenaline is rushing through your veins."

For the following demo, Blade was face-to-face with Leia, pretending to be drunk. Stumbling down the sidewalk toward her, he started whistling, catcalling, and getting uncomfortably close. "Tonight might be my lucky night," he snarled.

"Center!" Leia commanded. "Eyes!"

Leia pressed her fingertips together into a point as if she were making alligator shadow puppets with each hand. When he touched her, she thrust her fingertips forward and poked Blade in the eyes. "No!" His head flipped backward, which left him wide open for the next move.

"Knee!" Leia shouted.

With a look of determination and focus, Leia delivered a powerful knee to his groin three times, shouting "No!" each time.

Blade dropped to the ground, and Leia got away.

"Holy shit," Kristen said, echoing Nicole's thoughts.

Nicole was pretty sure she couldn't do what Leia just did. She didn't have that kind of strength. And even if she did, she didn't think she had the mindset to hurt someone physically. It wasn't in her DNA. If it were, she wouldn't have stopped fighting that night.

"There is something we call a 'Winner's Mindset' that you will all develop this weekend. It's a fighting spirit that says, 'I will not stop until I win,'" Leia said. "And what's so powerful and beautiful in having it inside of you during an attack is that unlike pepper spray or a stun gun, which could be swatted away or dropped during an attack, leaving you vulnerable and more likely to become a victim, your 'will to win' can never be taken from you."

Nicole thought about how she carried her keys laced between her fingers whenever she left her apartment and how much faith she put in them to protect her. It never dawned on her that the attacker could knock her keys from her hand, removing all her defenses and rendering her helpless. *I really am naïve.*

Judging by the stillness around the room, Leia's words hit everyone. Hard. "Let's take a break and sit in a circle," Leia said calmly, gathering the class on the large blue mat. She passed around water bottles and said, "Supporting each other is a big part of making this class a safe environment—where all of us feel comfortable being vulnerable while we learn, transform, and recognize that everyone here is on their own journey. As a start, I'd like to go around and have each of you introduce yourself, and only if you're comfortable, tell us what made you decide to join Model Mugging."

Nicole stared at the open space in front of her lap, motionless. She hoped she'd be able to remain anonymous, stay in the back of the room, and figure it out on her own like she always did when bad things came her way. She gnawed away at her bottom lip. Her mind raced to come up with a plausible story. *Or maybe I just won't say anything.*

Leia offered to go first. "When I was in college, I was in a physically abusive relationship," she said very matter-of-factly. "In the beginning, he was loving and attentive. We were inseparable. I truly thought I had found my husband. But then he started showing a different side of himself. The first time he hit me, we were both surprised. He apologized for a week, said all the right things, brought me lots of flowers. Soon, we were back to Leia and Kyle, everyone's favorite couple. But then it started happening more often. When he got frustrated . . . or jealous . . . or had a few too many beers . . . And then one night, he hit me so hard that I ended up in the ER with a broken jaw."

In succession, the women flinched like the wave going around a stadium.

"Thankfully, with the help of a few of my close friends, I left him that night. But the fear that he would find me and hurt me again never disappeared. Even when we lived hundreds of miles apart, I lived like a prisoner in my home, constantly worried he was in the shadows."

It was as if Leia was reading Nicole's mind burning with the image of Rob in the graduation pictures Megan had sent her.

"And if it wasn't him out there, I worried somebody else was hiding, ready to pounce. As if bad guys in my neighborhood got some sort of secret memo letting them know I was an easy target."

Leia took a sip from her water bottle. "That was until my therapist taught me that if I continued to stay inside, locked in my house, I wasn't helping myself. I was actually hurting myself. I was the one that was reinforcing my victimhood. I was the one giving Kyle, and everyone else I was afraid of, the power. So, when I was ready, she encouraged me to take this class. And three years later, I am proud to say that I now know I can take care of myself. That I am safe to leave my house. That I can live my life the way I want to." Her smile was broad, strong, unapologetic—inspiring.

The next few women introduced themselves but didn't share any details as to why they were there that weekend. Nicole's eyes roamed the circle, searching for judgmental looks, but found none. There was no pressure to talk.

Next was Kristen, with her beautiful pale blue eyes, feathered back dirty blonde hair, and athletic build. Nicole gathered that she was in her mid-thirties based on her 80s style alone.

During the summer between her senior year in high school and college, she worked as a waitress in Saratoga. "At the end of the night, when we were cleaning up, drinks would flow, we'd hang out, sometimes hook up—mostly kissing. Nothing serious. We were having fun." Her shoulders bobbed. "But then, one night, my boss asked for help in his office. As soon as I walked in, he locked the door behind him." She didn't speak for a few moments. "That's where he raped me. I begged him to stop, but he kept telling me what a tease I was and that it was his turn to be with me. When I threatened to tell everyone that worked at the restaurant, he told me not to bother because 'Who would believe a *whore?*' So, I didn't. I pretended like it didn't happen. I thought he was right. Who would believe me? I kissed a lot of guys that year." She shrugged again, smiling apologetically.

As the introductions continued, nervous energy flickered inside Nicole. She knew she didn't have to talk, but part of her wanted to. She had been carrying around the weight of *that night* alone. Maybe if she shared, it would somehow lessen the burden. Maybe.

Nicole wrapped her arms tight around her knees, listening to Donna and Amanda, a mother-daughter team, speak. Donna looked like Howard Stern's sister, with gold aviator-framed glasses and layered shoulder-length permed hair. For Amanda's high school graduation gift, Donna paid for them to take the class together. She worried about her daughter leaving for college but also thought it would be a fun bonding experience. *Fun?*

Nicole didn't know any of these women's addresses or if they preferred their coffee black or with milk and sugar, but she knew their most intimate secrets. Her eyes slipped in and out of focus, weighing what she would share. After a few moments of silence, Nicole realized Donna had passed the floor to her.

"Oh, sorry," Nicole said, embarrassed. Before she could overthink her story, words fell out of her mouth like a line of dominos. "Honestly, I was going to make up some BS story. I've never told anyone what happened to me. I keep it locked away inside like it never happened. But you have all shared so much of yourselves. You're all so brave. So, I'm going to try." More silence.

Donna took her hand while Kristen said softly, "If you want to talk, we're here to listen. This is your story. We'll believe anything you say."

Nicole dragged out a long breath, lowering her shoulders into place. And then, she spoke, sharing her story about the night she was raped. Nicole's gut tightened as she relived the trauma, pushing the words out with force. "I didn't do anything to help myself. I just froze and let it happen, helplessly wishing for it to end. That's all I did—I wished."

She brought her knees down and sat with her legs crossed, picking at her nails. She lifted her head, finding Leia with her eyes. "I am so tired of being afraid. I am tired of being alone. I want my life back," she cried, letting the tears burn down her cheeks like wax on a candle.

Leia got up, kneeled in front of her, and hugged her. "I know this is difficult," she said. "Many women in the same situation say they were frozen. It is a natural reaction. You can't judge yourself for your body's natural reaction." She gently placed her palms over Nicole's shoulders. "You did the best you could at the time. If you could have stopped him, you would have."

Nicole uncinched her lips. "Thank you," was all she could say.

Donna slid a box of tissues to Nicole, who plucked several and then wiped her nose, giving Donna a nod.

The air in the room was heavy, with everyone retreating inward again. Quiet. Nicole stared at the blue mat, her body tremoring with embarrassment at her confession, unsure of what to do next. A quiet applause woke her from her thoughts. Glancing up, she found Jose as the source.

After a few rounds of soft claps, Leia joined him, pushing to her feet. "I love it, Jose. Everyone here absolutely deserves to be celebrated and honored. You are all inspiring and brave," she said, intentionally making eye contact with everyone in the circle.

Nicole watched Kristen rise to her feet, joining Leia and Jose. She sensed the energy shift in the room. One by one, each woman stood, applauding. A smile crossed Nicole's face when she got to her feet, and the knot in her stomach loosened. Before she knew it, the entire room had erupted into cheering.

The healing has begun.

* * *

After introductions, they got a fifteen-minute break. Not knowing what to do with herself, Nicole sat next to Kristen. Seeing the pained look in Kristen's eyes was like holding up a mirror. Nicole spontaneously put her hand on top of Kristen's and squeezed it. "I'm hopeful for both of us." Kristen squeezed back.

When the break was over, Leia faced the group. "So now we're going to start the next phase—confrontations." An icy chill ripped up Nicole's spine at the sight of Blade threateningly reappearing in full alien gear at the front of the room. Horror music played in her head. Observing and cheering for others was one thing, but being center stage with nowhere to hide made Nicole sweat.

Her nerves settled when Blade removed his helmet, and she could see Jose's kind-spirited face again. "Before we start, there is one fundamental rule you need to understand. When I have the mask off, like now, I am Jose." He slapped his hand against the outer layer of his hard hat. "You can ask me anything. We can practice. Whatever you need. Just don't hurt me," he joked.

Laughter sprinkled the room.

Jose put the giant padded cover back on. "But when I have it on . . . I am Blade," he said in a measured and calculated tone filtered through gritted teeth. "I am not your instructor. I will not help you. Only Leia and your classmates can do that."

The horror music blasted in Nicole's head, her pulse racing like a caged animal. She believed every word Blade said, and she was terrified.

"I can visibly see the adrenaline ripping through all of you," Leia said empathically. "Don't worry, that's the point. We want it to be as realistic as possible here, so you can get all your anxieties out on the mat while we teach your mind and body how to redirect that energy away from a fear response to an active one without a second thought."

With Leia's lead, they started with verbal interactions. "Not all confrontations have to become physical. Your voice is also a weapon. Saying things like 'Stop!' or 'Get away from me!'" she shouted, jarring Nicole, "you can diffuse the situation. The goal is to get away as quickly and safely as possible."

"Nicole, why don't you go first?" Leia suggested. *Shit.*

Nicole stood at the opposite end of the mat from Blade in a face-off. There was no sign of Jose. His mask was emotionless and cold, like a predator. A knot pulled tight through her center. Her feelings were beyond performance anxiety.

Blade crept near her, but Nicole didn't move. Her heart thumped against her chest. Her legs were heavy. Her mind was blank. Leia lightly touched Nicole's arm, waking her from her trance and leading her down the mat toward Blade before breaking off.

"Center!" Leia yelled.

Nicole reflexively pulled her elbows in and put her hands up, showing Blade she was in ready mode. Her lip trembled.

Blade continued to slink closer until Nicole finally whimpered, "Stop."

"Again!" Leia commanded.

"Again!" the sidelines echoed.

"Stop!" Nicole cried. Her voice was thick. "Back off!" she said more assertively.

He continued to walk toward her, ignoring her command. "I said, back off!" Nicole held her ground.

Blade paused, then nodded and walked away.

Nicole froze on the mat, hoping, *wishing* it was over.

At the sound of Leia's whistle, a sound Nicole would soon grow to love, the role play was over.

"Yay!" Leia shouted, giving Nicole a rib-punishing squeeze. "Very convincing!"

Nicole admitted that her performance wasn't perfect, but it was good enough to make Blade walk away. That was enough to lift Nicole's confidence and float to the back of the line.

After a few more verbal standoffs, Leia told them they were ready for their first physical attacks. Nicole thought *ready* was a bit presumptuous. Her entire body quaked, despite knowing the attacks would be choreographed and she would know what was coming.

Nicole was the last to go, which meant she got a front-row seat to each woman's face—filled with angst, shock, and fear—when Blade grabbed these women from behind. Distress pricked Nicole's scalp as she watched. Choreographed or not, it was terrifying.

Nicole stood on the mat with her back to Blade. With little warning, he slithered up behind her. Her whole frame hardened at the humidity of his breath on her neck. With her eyes squeezed shut, waiting for him to attack, the sight of her dorm room window flashed behind her lids. Then, her body hit the ground.

Leia's earlier words drifted around Nicole as she lay face down with Blade on her back, working to flip her over. "Learning to fight while on the ground is critical. That's where rape victims usually end up." *I remember.*

The 'No!' Nicole was supposed to yell clawed at her throat. She scrambled underneath him, forgetting everything she was taught to do. "Help!"

"Elbow!" Leia barked.

Leia's voice snapped Nicole out of her spell. Still face down, Nicole swallowed her fear and let her training take over. Propping herself on one forearm, Nicole cocked her other arm and threw it back, striking Blade in the face— "Elbow!" she roared. The adrenaline in her veins turned into controlled rage as he hit the mat.

At the same time she scrambled to her feet, Blade rolled to a stand, reaching for her. Instinctively, she glued her fingertips together and lunged at him. "Eyes!"

He stumbled.

"Knee!" shouted Leia, but Nicole was already winding up, knowing what to do.

"No!" she cursed, kneeing him in the groin.

"Again!"

Nicole kneed him three more times. "No! No! No!"

The noise in the room was deafening. Nicole's classmates were yelling. Leia was shouting. Blade staggered back with his hands up. Leia blew the whistle, signaling that Nicole had knocked him out and the role play was over.

Nicole rested her hands on her knees and sobbed. Her entire body shivered as a cold wave of emotion washed over her.

Leia crouched beside Nicole with her gentle and consoling hand on Nicole's back and asked, "You okay?"

Nicole couldn't explain why, but the sight of Leia transformed her sobs into a fit of inappropriate giggles. Her abs contracted, doubling her over. Her laugh became inaudible. She was delirious but in the best possible way.

I did it.

| 25 |

Nicole

Nicole tried to scream, but the weight of his faceless body compressed her lungs, leaving her gasping for air. Tears poured out of the corners of her eyes. She strained to scream again. Silence.

Her chest . . . deflated. Her breath . . . short. Her brain . . . foggy. Helplessness won over her body. *Why aren't you fighting? What are you doing?* she screamed inside. Against her will, her body had gone limp. She laid still, closed her eyes, and wished for it to end. *Again.*

He leaned in closer to her face. Nicole felt his moist, hot breath get heavier and faster until he released, groaning quietly. "I've waited so long to be with you," he whispered in her ear.

"No!" she yelled breathlessly. "Get off me!" He settled in like a dead weight, solid and square on her chest. Her body wilted with defeat, like a flower with no water.

They lay like that for what felt like hours. Then, out of the quiet darkness, there was a faint hum, vibration pulsating between them. Pinpricks pierced her flesh. The humming got precipitously louder. The pinpricks became increasingly painful.

He shifted his weight, giving her a moment of salvation when her lungs reinflated. She sucked in the air greedily. Her body, once numb, was coming alive.

"Eyes!" A woman screamed.

Leia?

"Again!"

Why are you here?

"Again!"

Her heart tripled in speed. *Where am I?*

Nicole startled awake, eyes popping open, gasping on his whisper, "I've waited so long to be with you . . ."

After a few blinks, Nicole saw glimmers of sunrise peeking through her curtains, dimly lighting up her apartment bedroom. *Home.* The relief was intense and immediate, like jumping into a lake on a blistering hot day.

"Holy shit," she murmured, startled to find Noodle standing on her chest, purring loudly, finding a place to settle. He kneaded his paws, piercing and retracting his nails into her skin, just before he plopped down and wrapped himself into a ball.

She drew a deep breath through her nose and watched an unphased Noodle rise with her expanding chest. Slowly exhaling the air out, she sank into the warmth of her bed, giving in to Noodle's weight.

When will this stop?

| 26 |

Jesse

Jesse was on the verge of mastering buoyancy control in the deep end of the pool—a requirement for certification and critical to becoming a member of the marine inspection team—when he was jolted to a halt by the lifeguard's whistle. He had been in the pool for less than fifteen minutes before one of his scuba classmates, Phil, threw up, forcing everyone to evacuate.

The water boiled with Jesse's heated temper when he emerged into a puff of cloudy brown bits floating around him. "What the fuck, dude?" he howled, swimming over to Phil. Jesse could feel the blood pumping through his body as he splashed the puke water at Phil, who was being towed to the pool's edge by their diving instructor. "You couldn't just get out of the pool? It's not that hard, asshole." His words ricocheted off the tiled walls.

Jesse swam to the ladder and was met by a lifeguard on the pool deck. "Sir, I have to ask you to keep your voice down. You're scaring the children."

"Me? He's the dick that puked," Jesse said, pointing to Phil, who was still dry heaving across the water.

"Sir," he said, touching Jesse's arm.

Jesse swatted the lifeguard's hand away. "I'm going." Jesse stomped on the pool deck as much as he could in flippers and went to the bleachers to find his towel. "I just need my fucking CPE hours. I don't need to deal with this shit," he said through a clenched jaw.

Parents cautiously steered their children away from him as he shoved his gear into his backpack. "Why was that man yelling?" Jesse overheard one of the little girls ask her mom as she skipped by in her pink swimcap.

After a long shower, Jesse funneled into the main hallway of the Y with a few other people evacuated from the pool. The cool water from his wet hair ran down his neck, absorbing into his hooded sweatshirt. "Such bullshit," he mumbled.

His internal rant ceased when he spotted Nicole walking swiftly toward him in the hallway. His face split open with a grin as he slowed. *Holy shit. My morning just got a hell of a lot better.*

He could tell she was lost in thought, with her eyebrows knitted together and her mouth pressed closed in determination as she checked her watch. She wore black leggings, an oversized hot pink sweatshirt, and sneakers. A large bag was draped over her shoulder.

"Hey," he said softly, trying not to startle her.

She stared right through him, giving him a second to admire her before he tried to catch her attention again. Her hair was different from when he saw her at the end of the summer—shorter and darker with blonde streaks but still wavy and somewhat uncontrollable—*Nic*. In three short months, she seemed older. More mature. Less college student-*ish. Beautiful as ever.*

"Nic?" he said quietly, giving her a small wave.

"Huh?" she grunted, lifting her head to meet his gaze. Two lines formed between her eyebrows. His heart was pounding when she stopped inches from him. "Jesse?" She looked disoriented. "Oh my, God —Jesse! Hi!"

He melted when he saw her face rearrange into a full-watt smile. "Hey! I thought that was you." The glass door to the pool thudded closed behind him.

He leaned in for a hug, which she quickly accepted. Her head tucked perfectly underneath his chin, giving him the chance to drink in her scent. *Lavender.* It was only the second time he had hugged her, and his heart whirled with a need for more.

"Hey! Sorry. I didn't expect to see you here," she said, stepping back. "Took me a minute to realize it was you."

"We need to stop meeting like this. Maybe we should make actual plans instead." He gave the Zuke's Deli cup she was holding a once over. "If I remember correctly, I believe you still owe me a coffee," he said, motioning to the container.

"I thought I was the auditor," she bantered, skirting his offer to go out.

Jesse's insides curled at the thought of Nicole being with someone else. *Maybe they're already together. That Zuke guy was way too attentive not to be into her.*

"Did he end up fixing your air conditioner?" Jesse asked. His tone came out green.

She grimaced. "Who?"

"Never mind. It's not important," he said, shaking his head. He switched his backpack to his other shoulder. *Shut up, dude. What are you doing?*

Jesse was happy when she changed the subject. "How's scuba going?" she asked, motioning to the large black flippers sticking out of his bag.

He let out a half laugh. "It's taking a little longer than I thought. A guy threw up in the pool this morning, so we had to cut class short," he said, feigning his mirth.

"That's repulsive." She cringed. "Were you near him when it happened?"

"Near him? I was right next to him. F'in gross."

Disgust curled her lip. "And you hugged me?"

He felt his face and neck flush. "I showered! What kind of a person do you think I am?"

A laugh ripped all the way up from her toes. "I'm sorry, it's probably not funny to you yet."

"I'm glad my suffering amuses you," he said, allowing a drop of a laugh to sneak out.

"It does a little," she said, coughing behind a lingering giggle. "Payback for the salamander."

He caught her glance at her watch again. "I'm sorry, are you late for a class or something? I don't want to keep you."

"Um. Yeah. Aerobics. I mean, step. It's only my second class. I don't want to be late." He studied her for a few seconds, watching her bite her lip like she used to when they were kids. *She's nervous.* "I've never worked out before. Jamie talked me into it. She needed someone to go with her. She's crazed about getting into shape for her wedding."

"You're a good sister."

Jesse caught Phil walking by him out of the corner of his eye. "Hey, man, hope you feel better," he said, giving him a light pat on the back. Jesse's concern was about as hollow as an empty box, but he was working to impress Nicole.

He hoped Nicole didn't see the scowl Phil gave him when he walked by. "That's the poor guy," he whispered, puffing his cheeks with his lips closed tight. "He's gotta feel awful. So embarrassing."

Nicole raised her eyebrows. "No one wants to be known as the guy that threw up in the pool."

"Yeah, well. I'm not sure I want to be the guy that swam into it either."

"We need to stop talking about puke."

The laughter in her eyes made him chuckle aloud. "Deal. Well, I don't want to hold you up. What time is your class over?"

"Um . . ." she said, adjusting her view downward.

His eyes searched the ground to try and find what had Nicole's attention. "I was serious about getting coffee. Or an early lunch. I can stick around until you're done with aerobics. I mean, if you're interested." He moved his hands into the back pockets of his jeans.

She looked up with the corners of her mouth turned. "Unfortunately, I have to go into the office later. Otherwise, I would love to. We have a tight deadline. Gotta get everything done before the client shuts down for Christmas." Her voice faded, and she was back to biting her lip.

He didn't believe she had to work. "Oh. No problem. Maybe another time." *Fuck. She has a boyfriend.*

She rummaged through her canvas bag and pulled out an old, crumpled receipt and a ballpoint pen. She clicked it open. "How about you give me your number, and we'll make plans when we're both free?"

He could feel the shit-eating grin on his face. "That works," he said, reaching for the pen and paper.

Jesse bent forward, using his thigh to write his number. He sensed her presence over his shoulder. "I already know your name," she teased, pointing to *Jesse* that he had written on the receipt.

He flashed her a playful grin and then continued to write. "Wanted to make sure you had the correct spelling."

Jesse stood and rolled his shoulders back, filling up with happiness. "Here you go."

He held on to it when she tried to take it from him. When he finally let go, his hand brushed against hers, sending a ripple of excited heat up his arm. He watched her cheeks flush. *I saw that.*

"I'll call you," she said, checking her watch again.

"I hope so," he said, swiveling on his heel and heading for the front door. "I don't want to keep leaving it to chance."

| 27 |

Nicole

Nicole felt a cold gust of December air whip through her thin cotton leggings as she lingered in the hallway, watching Jesse disappear out the front door of the YMCA. Her whole body tingled with pins and needles. She couldn't remember the last time it did that. If ever. *Jesse? Really?*

She hummed along to "All I Want for Christmas Is You," playing from the boombox on the front desk, filing through her memories from that morning. She couldn't deny the sparks igniting in her chest at the prospect of being with Jesse. But two seconds before she ran into him, she was running from her early morning nightmare, reliving her attack, to a class where she would learn how to kick the shit out of a man in a padded suit.

Her heart wanted to say yes to Jesse. Heck, if he kissed her right in the hallway, she wasn't sure she would have stopped him. He was the only guy she could unapologetically be herself around, and it was becoming more apparent that he liked her. But it was her mind that put on the brakes. *You're not ready for a boyfriend. You have no idea how your body will react when he touches you. You've got more work to do.*

She had a plan, and it was working. She could feel it. She just needed more time.

***

Nicole was still swirling from her chance meeting with Jesse when she dropped her tote along the wall with the others' stuff and plopped herself on the edge of the mat next to Kristen. "Hey!" Nicole said, patting Kristen's arm.

Kristen looked at her with a half-smile. "Hey. Why are you so giddy?"

Nicole shifted her seat. "Nervous to get started again."

"Hmm... Does it have anything to do with the guy you were talking to in the hall upstairs?" Kristen's lips pursed with suspicion.

Nicole smiled shyly. "Maybe that, too."

"Boyfriend?" she asked, leaning on her elbows.

"No. He's just a good friend. It's complicated."

"Aren't all relationships complicated?"

"I am hoping to have one that isn't."

"Is he a jerk?"

She leaned her head to the side. "No, not at all. He's actually a nice guy."

"Are you related?"

"No!" Nicole barked.

"Do you like him?"

"Kinda," Nicole said, picking at her cuticles.

"Then I would strongly advise you to figure it out because he's obviously smitten with you. Did you see the way he looked at you?"

Her face burned, remembering the ring of iron circling his hazel eyes. "I'm trying." She sucked in a big breath. "That's why I am here. I . . ." Her voice broke off at the same time her giddiness vanished.

Kristen gave her a reassuring squeeze on her forearm.

"I just want to be confident and know, without hesitation, that I can be with someone," Nicole said as an exhale hissed out of her. "Does it get any easier after . . . you know?"

"It does when it's the right person. Communication is key."

Nicole had no intention of telling Jesse about what had happened to her. It was her baggage to deal with and hers alone.

"A good vibrator helps, too." Kristen chuckled.

Embarrassment burned Nicole's face like the strike of a match.

"It's perfectly natural in any circumstance, but I found it to be a safe way to test myself for any triggers without my boyfriend there to watch in case I had a meltdown. The more I did it, the more desensitized I got."

Nicole appreciated Kristen's honesty. "Thanks."

"A word from the wise, though," Kristen said just above a whisper. "Make sure you always have batteries on hand! Nothing worse than being halfway to O, and the damn thing dies on you!"

Nicole laughed along with Kristen, but that kind of self-care never rose to the top of her list of priorities. The closest she'd ever been to a vibrator was the extra one Jamie got from a friend's Bachelorette party and gave to Nicole. It was still in the box in the top drawer of her dresser.

"Good morning!" Leia smiled. "Lots of good energy in the room. I love it. Welcome to day two. How'd everyone sleep last night?" Leia shifted to the front of the room. Jose joined her as she pulled her hair back using the red scrunchie on her wrist.

"Like a baby," Donna shared. "Totally exhausted."

Kristen pumped her fist. "Like I could take on the world."

Nicole fell into a pit of silence. She had almost forgotten about waking up in a pool of sweat, paralyzed from her nightmare earlier that morning, until Leia reminded her. She was so tired of giving her baggage so much attention. It felt good to dream about kissing Jesse, to laugh with Kristen. Thinking about her nightmare, it felt like a bucket of ice water had been thrown over her good mood.

"How about you, Nicole? How are you doing today?"

"Great!" Her voice came out two octaves higher than usual. *Come on, Nic. You're here for a reason. Remember your plan. You know you'll feel better if you talk.* She recalled how she had felt the day before. *Remember when you realized that you weren't alone? Remember when you told your story and felt a little less shame? It's progress, Nic. Be kind to yourself.*

Despite her pep talk, she ate her trembling words and decided not to share. She was committed to moving forward and wanted to get to the next lesson in class.

* * *

Two hours later, they had learned and practiced several new strikes—the palm heel, aimed at the chin and nose, the heel kick to the shin for when being attacked from behind, and Leia's favorite, the elbow strike, for all the power it delivers but with minimal risk of personal injury.

At that point in the day, Leia assured the class they were ready to put their arsenal of techniques to work. It was time to go through an open attack with Blade. An open attack meant they wouldn't know what was coming. Nicole chewed the inside of her mouth at the news. She hated surprises. But at least for once, she wouldn't have to pretend to be having fun.

An anxious knot twisted in Nicole's chest when it was her turn. The anticipation of each role-play hadn't gotten any easier. *It doesn't have to be perfect. You just need to get to safety.*

Blade menacingly walked toward her on the mat. It was hard to move, let alone get to safety, with her legs limp like a strand of overcooked spaghetti. "Stop!" Her voice was weak.

He paused for a beat, then resumed his steps toward her.

Instinctually, her body dropped into her centering stance—hands up, elbows in. Her legs steadied. "Stop right there! Go away!"

He paused again, then walked around her.

Was that it? Did I do it?

Wait, there was no whistle. Shit.

Halfway through her exhale, Blade lunged at Nicole, grabbing her ponytail.

She leaned back, unsteady on her feet. "No!"

He latched onto her right arm, leaving her left arm free. She saw her opening. Without hesitation, she cocked her hand back, exposing her palm, and drove it as hard as she could into his chin. He stumbled backward and fell to the ground.

Leia blew the whistle to end the attack. Nicole had knocked him out.

"High-five, Nicole!" Kristen yelled, jumping on the mat to slap her hand.

"High-five!" Nicole repeated, catching her breath. A ribbon of pride pirouetted her to the back of the line.

* * *

"Ladies! We have an assignment for all of you during our lunch break, which will lead us into the last half of the day," Leia informed the class. For a woman of such small stature, she had a firm hold on the room. She carried herself in a way that exuded confidence but not in an aggressive way that turned people off. If anything, it endeared her more to Nicole.

The assignment—write about an emotional or physical situation that left them hurt or powerless. Nicole's insides knotted up like a pretzel at the thought of putting her story on paper. She wanted to move on, not keep reliving it.

To make it more real for each of them, Blade would include aspects of their personal experience in their final simulation of the day. Nicole's mouth twisted to one side at the word "simulation." *Tell my heart, jackhammering my ribs, that this isn't real.*

"Confronting the situation in a supportive classroom environment will help you come to terms with how you originally responded. In these reenactments, *you* have the power," Leia said, spinning around the circle with her finger pointing at each of them. "*You* have the control."

An hour later, they assembled on the mat again. "Shit. I'm not ready for this," Kristen said under her breath while chewing on her cuticles.

Examining Kristen's face, Nicole recognized the look of defeat. She had seen it on her own face before. But here was their chance, their moment, to take back control. She held Kristen's shoulders and met her stare. "We can't let them win." Nicole tried to convince Kristen as much as she was trying to convince herself. *I can't let him win.*

Kristen cracked a weak smile, then went back to gnawing her nails.

At the start of each woman's scenario, Leia read the victim's statement aloud to the group. Blade was there as their attacker but also the vessel of their pain. Nicole witnessed women yelling and kicking and elbowing their abusive boyfriends, their alcoholic mothers, their rapists. Even Donna, the mom from the mother-daughter *fun* duo, flew at Blade like a scalded cat, attacking her cheating ex-husband. "You lying piece of crap," she yelled. "I hope you rot in hell!" Her eyes swelled. Her chest heaved. She was freed.

One by one, Nicole watched in awe as each woman ahead of her metamorphosized from a self-conscious, humiliated, powerless victim, working to make themselves smaller and smaller as Leia read their story aloud, to becoming a confident, gloriously empowered victor, shedding all the pain and guilt and shame that had been holding them down.

"Nicole? You ready?" Leia asked. *Does anyone ever say yes?*

As Nicole lay on the mat, her eyes closed, listening to Leia read her words, brilliant pinpoints of light glimmered behind her lids like the night sky. She was calm when Blade shook her awake, grabbing her foot and dragging her across the mat. The vinyl shushing mimicked the vibration of the thick lawn against her body. There was peace in the darkness and the familiarity of the situation. Warmth blanketed her as he laid on top of her, compressing her chest. It had replayed so many times in her head that it felt almost comforting.

But then Blade started talking. "Oooo . . . you're one of those good girls. I *like* good girls," he said, gritting in her ear. "You don't fight. You do what you're told."

And a switch went off in Nicole. *I can't let him win.*

She squirmed underneath him. "I do fight. You can't hurt me anymore," she screamed. She saw an opening— "Eyes!" sending him swimming back.

"What the FUCK do you think you're doing?" he seethed.

She exploded with fury, screaming her words. "I am fighting for myself. I don't deserve to be treated this way. You can't hurt me anymore." The adrenaline zigzagged through her veins as she endured the fight.

They were still on the ground when Blade grabbed her left ankle, pulling her toward him. He reached for the top of her pants. His head was down.

With her right leg free, she lifted it over his head and dropped her heel in the nape of Blade's neck, landing her ax-kick perfectly. He collapsed onto her left leg, groaning loudly as he rolled to his side.

"No! No! No!" she shouted, kicking Blade in the groin.

Leia blew the whistle, letting everyone know that Nicole had knocked him out. But for Nicole, it was so much more. It meant her transformation was complete—she felt it deep in her core. *He can't hurt me anymore.*

***

That night, in her apartment, Nicole sat on the couch with her hands cupped around a warm mug of chamomile. The steam from her tea cleared her mind like the morning fog burning off a still lake. Over the last two days, she had developed a strong connection with the women in class because they were all willing to be vulnerable. But sitting at home alone, she felt isolated and closed off from the most important women in her life. Her next move was obvious. *I don't want to be alone.*

She picked up the phone and dialed. "Hi. It's me. Can you come over? I need you. It can't wait."

Twenty minutes later, Jamie was at her door.

| 28 |

Jamie

Jamie knew something was seriously wrong by Nicole's hollow tone on the phone. *Guy trouble? Maybe she lost her job.* But when she took one look at her sister in the doorway, startled by her swollen eyes, red face, and quivering chin, she knew it was bigger than a bad date.

She wrapped her arms around Nicole and dragged her into a hug. "Nic, what's going on? You're scaring me. Are you okay?" she asked into her shoulder.

Nicole drew back, adjusting her view downward to the crumpled tissue in her hands.

"Nic, it's okay. I'm here," Jamie said. She shrugged off her coat and threw it on the couch. She was wearing a black cocktail dress and snakeskin pumps. When her sister called, she was on her way out the door for dinner at the club with Randy and his parents.

Nicole noticed Jamie's clothes. "I'm sorry I interrupted your plans. You look like you were on your way somewhere."

"Absolutely not. If anything, you're saving me from another night out with Karen," she said, kicking off her heels. "Let's sit." Jamie clasped Nicole's hand, leading her to the couch. She couldn't remember a time she saw Nicole so upset and did not know what it was about.

After a few quiet minutes, Nicole let out a breath. "It's bad."

Jamie sat upright and rigid, bracing herself for whatever Nicole was about to tell her. "It's okay. I'm here. Whatever it is, we'll get through it together."

Nicole paused, reading Jamie's face. "A few days before I graduated at Wheeler . . ." she began. As Nicole recounted the night she was raped, Jamie sat silently and listened. On the inside, Jamie's heart splintered with every detail, finally shattering into infinite pieces when Nicole admitted that for the last seven months, with Jamie living only a few miles away, she had never felt so helpless, alone, and scared in all her life.

When Nicole was done, she looked at Jamie expectantly. Her body went cold. She wasn't prepared. She didn't know what to say. Who would? Despite knowing the statistics—one in four women are sexually assaulted during their time in college—she couldn't believe it. *This can't be real. Rape doesn't happen to women like us. We know better.*

"Why didn't you call me?" Jamie was frustrated, borderline angry. But as soon as the words left her mouth, she regretted them. She didn't want to upset Nicole. "Never mind. I'm sorry."

But Nicole answered her. "What would you have done? You couldn't take it back."

"I could have taken you to get help," she countered. "Did you report it?"

"No," she said softly, shaking her head. "I couldn't bring myself to be interrogated by a campus rent-a-cop. 'Were you drinking? Were you alone in the dark? What were you wearing?' I was already beating myself up for being so stupid. I didn't need someone else to point it out," she cried. "I just needed to keep it together long enough to get out of there. I barely made it home without having a breakdown."

"It's killing me to hear that you were here all this time suffering in silence. Why didn't you tell me sooner? I could have been there for you."

"Killing you?" Nicole mocked.

"I'm sorry. It's not about me. I'm sorry."

"I know," Nicole said, closing her eyes. She fought to keep her voice from breaking when she opened them again. "I was too ashamed to tell anyone. I thought it would just go away with time, and I'd never have to. A few times, I thought about talking to you, but you're always so stressed about the wedding, and then you told me about Karen, and I didn't want to add more drama to your plate."

Jamie was consumed with guilt. She was so self-absorbed in planning her wedding and fitting in with Randy's family that she wasn't there for Nicole when Nicole needed her the most. *Where are my priorities?*

Tears slipped down Jamie's cheeks. "Is that why you didn't want Mom and me to come to your graduation?"

Nicole nodded.

"You know it's not your fault, right?"

"I do now. At least I am working on believing it's not. I should have known better. I did know better. Either way, it doesn't give him the right to do what he did to me," she said, ripping at her tissue.

"Do you have any idea who did it?" Jamie whispered, not wanting to press.

"Not a hundred percent. But I have my suspicions. There was an RA that I worked with that was kind of creepy—Rob. He always seemed to appear out of nowhere. He had made some comments about seeing me that night," Nicole said, shrugging. "Megan had a run-in with him junior year, too. He's not a good guy. I don't know. I guess I'll never know. I can't keep dwelling on it. I'm trying to focus on the future as much as possible."

"It's not too late. We can go to the police. Go after him."

"Are you listening to me?" Nicole said in a raised voice. "I just told you I'm trying to move on. Going to the police would only set me back."

"Okay. I'm sorry," she said.

In the low light of the table lamp, dark purple circles rimmed Nicole's eyes—one of the many clues the toll her attack had taken on her and how much pain she had been carrying by herself. *How did I not see it?*

She pulled Nicole into her arms. "I'm glad you told me," she said, giving Nicole a motherly kiss on the side of her head.

"Me too," Nicole said, wrapping her arms tightly around her. The warmth of their embrace gave Jamie some solace.

"Is there anything I can do to help?"

"Don't leave me here alone tonight."

"I'm not going anywhere."

* * *

The following morning, Jamie woke up in Nicole's bed with a start. The first rays of morning filtered through the curtains. Her eyes zoomed around Nicole's bedroom, searching for her sister. Jamie was alone.

Nic? Where's Nic?

She called out to her. "Nic?"

She listened for movement, but the apartment was uncomfortably quiet. *Where is she?*

"Nic?" she said a little louder. Her voice grew more panicked. "Nic?" Still nothing. "Nic!"

She was in a cold sweat. Frantic, Jamie flipped the covers off and scooted herself out of bed when she found a golden yellow Post-it stuck to the pillow with a handwritten note.

Morning!

Went to Zuke's to get us coffee and breakfast. Be right back.

Love,

Nic

Relief swaddled her nerves.

Still numb from the night before, Jamie barely felt her feet touch the floor.

She wrapped a small blanket around her from the foot of the bed and padded into the kitchen. Two steps in, the apartment door opened and closed.

"I've got coffee!" Nicole bellowed, rounding the half wall. She held two giant cups and a paper bag freckled with dark brown grease stains.

Jamie practically tackled Nicole. "I got scared when you weren't here this morning."

"I'm here," Nicole said, still holding their breakfast. Nicole looked bright and refreshed in the morning light streaming through the kitchen window when they broke away.

Jamie held Nicole's face in both of her hands. "I love you."

"I love you too. Now, you have to try one of these croissants. They. Are. Amazing," she said, emphasizing each word."

"No pastries for me. Go right from my mouth to my thighs." Nicole arched her brow at her. "Why don't you get a coffee maker like everyone else?" Jamie asked, taking her cup from Nicole.

"No reason to. I get my coffee at the deli down the road every morning. I've got it all planned out. If I didn't show up one day, Zuke would be the first to know something was wrong," Nicole said, digging into the bag.

Jamie ripped the plastic tab off her lid. "Does he know he's part of your security plan? Does he know he's supposed to do that?" she pressed, sipping her cup.

Nicole shrugged. "No. He doesn't need to. He's just the kind of person that would do something like that. He's like a neighborhood watch."

"You're putting a lot of trust in this deli guy."

"What are you trying to say?" Nicole asked with her hand on her hip.

"How do you know he won't try to . . ." The words died on Jamie's tongue. "I'm just worried about you." *Worried you're putting yourself at risk again. Your security plan is about as foolproof as putting a deadbolt on a cardboard door.* "This is all new information for me. I am still trying to process it."

Jamie watched Nicole tear off a piece of her croissant. She wanted to protect her baby sister and take all her hurt away like she used to. "How are you doing?" Jamie asked cautiously.

Nicole let her arm fall to her side. "Kind of amazing," she admitted, slurping her first taste of coffee. "I practically floated down the sidewalk this morning."

"I can see it in your face." Jamie smiled lightly. "I'm so proud of you for telling me."

"Thanks. I'm proud of me for telling you, too." Nicole took in a deep breath. "So, do you have plans for today? I have something I want you to come to with me," she said, leaning the small of her back against the kitchen counter.

"I'm all yours," Jamie said. "More shopping?"

"Not exactly. I have a graduation this morning."

Jamie shot her a look of confusion. "Graduation?"

That was when Nicole told Jamie about the Model Mugging class. The more Nicole shared, the more excited she got, and the more nervous Jamie got. Like her deli guy plan, she worried it was feeding into Nicole's false sense of security. *How would a man in a padded suit help her learn how to defend herself? How could Nicole take down an attacker in the heat of the moment? It's not real life.*

"Is this why you blew me off yesterday? You didn't have to work, did you?"

Nicole chewed at her bottom lip. "No. I'm sorry. I didn't want to lie to you. I needed to see what it was about on my own. If it were a joke, I never would have said anything."

"Are you sure about this?"

"With all my being."

"It sounds like a man-hating rage room to me."

Nicole's brow lowered. "I don't hate men, Jamie. I hate unnecessary violence. Big difference!" Her voice grew louder. "You want to know what else I hate? Cowering in my apartment alone, terrified that I'd be attacked every time I step out of it. Worrying that if it did happen again, I wouldn't be able to defend myself—again. What the hell, Jamie?"

Jamie jumped to Nicole's side and grabbed her hands. "I'm sorry. I just don't want you to let your guard down and get hurt again."

"Me either! If anything, I am more aware than I was before," Nicole said, giving Jamie a thoughtful look. Her voice was calmer. "You're the one that told me to stop wishing for something to happen, that I needed to make it happen. That's what I'm doing. I'm taking back control of my life. Come with me. You'll see. It's not what you think. It's not a bunch of women sitting around, crying and bashing men." Nicole let out a small laugh. "Well, we cry, but I'm serious. It has changed my life."

Jamie let out a concerned sigh. "I love you so much. It's just . . . after what happened, I'm worried about you. You have to understand that."

"I do. That's why I want you to come with me. I want you to see what I can do."

Jamie looked at her watch, shaking her head. She gave Nicole a half smile. "Well, we better get ready then. You've got an ass to kick in about an hour."

* * *

Walking into the classroom, Jamie was transported back to gymnastics class in the makeshift studio when she was a little girl—the bright lights humming overhead, no windows, wall-to-wall tumble mats, and floor-to-ceiling mirrors. Even the trapped tang of foot odor was the same.

Nicole hugged Jamie and then left her with all the other friends and family sitting in the chairs lining the back wall. Jamie swallowed hard. She felt like she was there to watch some illegal women's fight club.

She untied her scarf and slid off her coat, draping them over the back of her seat, and sat upright, her hands folded on her lap and her legs crossed at her ankles. The cold from the metal folding chair seeped through her jeans, giving her a chill.

In her peripheral vision, Jamie saw the pants of the woman sitting next to her were covered in white cat hair, making her lip curl in disgust. Sensing the woman saw her repulsed reaction, Jamie straightened her gaze to the front of the room. Unfortunately, they found each other's reflections in the front mirror. The woman gave her a crooked smile. *Busted!*

A few long minutes later, a petite woman stepped onto the mat facing the audience, her expression erupting into a toothy smile. "Good morning, everyone. Thank you for coming to this exciting day," she said, clapping her hands together. "I'm Leia, one of the instructors." Jamie calculated that she was no taller than a sixth grader. In her all-gray sweatsuit and choppy black layered haircut, she looked as if Joan Jett and Rocky had a baby.

"And next to me is Jose, my co-instructor."

"Good morning, everyone." He greeted the audience with a wave.

That's the attacker? Jamie expected to see a professional wrestler, not the water boy. *No wonder Nicole can get away. He's tiny. Oh, Nic...*

"So, I can promise you, this will not be like any other graduation ceremony you have ever attended. For the next hour or so, you will watch your loved ones be confronted and attempted to be assaulted." The room flinched. "But you will also see something so beautiful—strength, courage, transformation," she said, counting with her fingers.

Leia paced in front of the audience. "But let's take a step back. Let's talk about why we're here first." She smiled. "You're probably asking yourself, why would anyone *choose* to take a class where they subject themselves to mock attacks? It won't ever happen to me. Why do I need to worry about it?"

Leia paused and shifted her body toward the audience. "And this is what I would tell you . . . every sixty-eight seconds, an American is sexually assaulted. And one in three women will experience sexual violence in their lifetime," she said, pointing to the audience as if counting them off by threes. Leia's eyes flared. "That is a staggering rate."

Jamie shifted her weight, recrossing her ankles. Her chin trembled at the thought of Nicole.

"You also might say, 'But I live in a good neighborhood. There aren't bad guys in ski masks waiting in the bushes outside my house. I'm safe. I don't need to worry about all of this,'" she said, waving off the group. "Well, statistically, about seventy-five percent of sexual predators are either acquaintances, family, or romantic partners. Not the man in the bushes.

"We also know that trauma from the event isn't over when the assault is over. Not everyone can return to their daily lives like it never happened. There are long-term effects, like potential suicide, where nearly a third of women who have been raped consider it. Their daily lives are also dramatically impacted. Many experience PTSD and intense emotional distress, making relationships difficult."

Jamie recoiled in her seat. *Geez . . . a little heavy for eleven in the morning, no?*

"Now, I'm not suggesting that you are in imminent danger. I am simply sharing these alarming facts because one of the ways we can help change behaviors and cultivate a society where sexual assault is never appropriate is through awareness. The first step—stop blaming victims for putting themselves in the situation. 'What were you wearing? Were you alone?' Instead, let's focus on holding the assailant accountable for their actions. That's number one," she said, holding up her index finger.

"Amen!" a woman behind Jamie hollered.

Leia held up a second finger. "The next way is to empower women to learn how to help themselves if they are ever faced with a situation, which brings us to today. The women here with me, your loved ones, have taken a courageous step. Over the last two days, they have voluntarily immersed themselves in this unique self-defense class, where they learned how to defend themselves when faced with an aggressive masked attacker." Leia smiled. "I know. Just thinking about it gives you an adrenaline rush, right?

"And that's exactly what happens to them in class—that rush." Leia slapped the back of her hand into her palm. Jamie jumped in her seat. "That's the point. We want to simulate a situation as realistically as possible, including their emotional reaction. Doing this forces the woman to deal with those rubbery knees and pounding hearts in the classroom, minimizing the chance she will freeze during a real assault. God forbid she's in the situation."

Jamie spun her engagement ring around her finger, becoming increasingly antsy in her seat.

Leia let out a quick exhale. "I understand this is not something you want to think about, especially on a Sunday morning when most of us are usually home sipping coffee and reading the morning paper." She put her hand on her chest. "But from the bottom of my heart, thank you for being here today to support these incredible women on their journeys. And to all of you," Leia said, facing her class, "thank you for being so brave. You are all nothing short of amazing."

Jamie caught Nicole's eye, meeting the beginning of a smile tipping the corners of her mouth. Jamie gave her a quick wink, sending her love across the room. An unshed tear resting on Jamie's lid unexpectedly fell to her cheek, which she quickly wiped away before anyone could see. Or so she thought.

A tissue appeared in her line of sight. It was from the cat lady sitting next to her. Jamie turned to her. "I have extras. I think we're going to need them," the woman said, smiling empathetically.

"Thanks," she said quietly.

Leia cleared off the mat. "Nicole. How about you start?" Leia suggested.

Nicole stood, brushing off her butt. Jamie felt a jolt of panic. "Come on, Nic. You can do this," she murmured into her fingers resting on her mouth. *I hope.*

Nicole positioned herself at one end of the mat while Jose put on his enormous, padded mask, transforming into Blade. Jamie wasn't expecting the conversion to be so dramatic. He was undeniably scary.

With every step Blade heaved toward Nicole, Jamie scooted one inch closer to the edge of her seat. Impatiently, she watched the situation unfold. She saw Nicole focus intently on Blade, tracking his steps, moving out of his way. Her hands were up, elbows pulled into her sides, knees slightly bent.

Blade crept closer to Nicole. "Stop!" Nicole said firmly.

Jamie felt her thighs tighten. She wasn't expecting Nicole's voice to be so assertive.

"Again!" Leia commanded.

"Again!" the sidelines echoed.

"Stop!" Nicole yelled. "Back off! I said, back off!"

Blade walked past Nicole, nodding, and then Leia blew her whistle. Jamie was confused. *That's it?*

"Thank you, Nicole, awesome job," Leia said, giving Nicole a high-five.

Leia faced the audience. "As the class has learned, not all confrontations need to end in violence. Often, your voice is enough to diffuse the situation. Remember, your goal is to get away quickly and safely."

"Donna, it's your turn," Leia said, waving her onto the mat.

"C'mon, Mom, you got this!" A young woman whooped.

Donna approached the edge of the mat. She resembled a typical middle-aged mom to Jamie—out of shape, pudgy around the middle. She was certain Blade would go easy on her but quickly realized he had no mercy. Jamie's eyes grew larger at the sight of Blade charging at Donna. *Oh my God! Stop! You're going to hurt her.*

But Donna didn't need him to go easy on her. "Eyes!" Donna yelled over the crowd of classmates cheering her on, poking him in his sockets.

Jamie's mouth gaped open when Blade stumbled a few steps backward. It lingered open when she watched him come back at Donna, and Donna kneed him in the groin, roaring, "Knee!" When he fell to the ground, holding his crotch, Donna ran to safety, and then Leia blew her whistle, ending the attack.

For the next hour, Jamie sat on the edge of her seat with her elbows resting on her knees, bobbing like pistons, observing, in mesmerized disbelief, woman after woman confidently take down Blade. Then Leia called Nicole to the mat, and Jamie's hammering heart thrust her to her feet.

Anxiously shifting her weight back and forth, she listened to Nicole try to diffuse the situation with her voice like the first time, but it only seemed to antagonize him. "Shut up, bitch," he snarled under his breath, snaking his way forward. *It's not over.*

He was a step past her, and then, without warning, he grabbed Nicole by the shoulder and spun her around. She arched her knee without hesitation and stomped on his foot. "No!"

Jamie couldn't contain herself. "Come on, Nic!" she hollered, clapping her hands like a coach on the sidelines. "You got this!" Jamie pushed up her sleeves. She was breaking out into a sweat watching her sister fight for her life.

Blade reactively bent forward toward the pain. At the same time, Nicole stretched her arms out straight, hands clasped together, and delivered a volleyball serve right underneath his chin, sending him staggering back. Nicole lost her balance and ended up on the ground.

"Get up!" the crowd screamed.

But Blade quickly recovered from the crack and scrambled on the mat to grab Nicole's right leg before she could get to her feet. "C'mere, you bitch," he growled.

Jamie clapped her hands to her mouth. Angst pricked at her skin. It all felt so real. She watched Nicole instinctually flip onto her right side, the same side as the leg Blade was holding. She propped herself onto her elbow and cocked her left leg back until her knee practically touched her shoulder and then delivered the final blow—a thrusting sidekick—to Blade's head with awesome force.

Jamie jumped up and down when the whistle blew, screaming with the rest of the class. "Yes!" With tears streaming down Jamie's face, she turned to the cat lady and high-fived her. The cat hair didn't seem so important anymore.

When the graduation was over, Jamie ran to her sister's side and grabbed her into a hug. "Seriously, Nic? I thought I was proud of you last night. Honestly, I am at a loss for words," she cried.

"That's a first," Nicole bantered. "I tried to tell you."

"You. Are. Amazing. I love you so much."

"I love you too," Nicole said. Her voice was muffled in Jamie's shirt. "So, when are you going to take the class? You can take all your Karen aggression out on Blade."

Jamie drew back and met Nicole's glittering eyes.

"I couldn't do what you just did. Besides, Karen isn't *physically* attacking me."

"No, not physically, but she is abusing you. You know that."

Jamie felt the truth of the jab in her gut. But admitting it meant she'd have to confront it, and she didn't know if she had her sister's courage to take on a force as big as Karen. She couldn't risk losing Randy. "Tempting."

| 29 |

Nicole

"Good Lord, this day can't be over soon enough, and it's only eight-fifteen in the morning," Christy, one of Nicole's managers, said to her as she flew into the conference room like a tornado. Nicole caught a whiff of fury, masked only slightly by the sweetened vanilla latte Christy was holding.

Nicole stiffened upright in her chair. *Uh-oh.*

"I am so ready to start my vacation," Christy huffed.

Nicole scrambled to her feet. "Can I help?"

"Can't even put my bag down before I get accosted at the door," Christy grumbled as she threw her Coach briefcase on the floor. "I know what I need to do, *Dave*," she muttered.

Christy had warned Nicole earlier that week that the last day before the office shuts down for the holidays was always hectic. "Everyone wants to tie up loose ends and then not think about work for the entire week between Christmas and New Year's. We'll see each other plenty during the upcoming busy season starting in January."

"Hey. Sorry," Christy said. She gave Nicole a thin smile as she unbuttoned her double-breasted overcoat. It was unusual to see Christy frazzled, but as usual, she looked and dressed like the anti-accountant. She wore a bright red Merino wool turtleneck that perfectly matched her ruby red lipstick. Black and white Glen check pants and skinny-heeled black leather boots completed her outfit. Nicole smoothed out the cream-colored satin shell she wore underneath her fuddy black blazer.

"Can you please bring the Callahan debt file to Dave? He needs it *right away*," she said mockingly. "He should be in his office down the hall." Dave was one of the reviewing managers on the Callahan job.

"Knock, knock," Dave thundered at the same time he rapped his knuckle against the open conference room door. "Did I catch one of you ladies talking about me?"

Both women startled. With his slicked-back brown hair, Dave could have been Charlie Sheen's stunt double in *Wall Street*. He was as cocky as him, too, strolling into the room, not bothering to wait for an invitation to enter. He was on the tall side of six feet with bulging muscles that noticeably filled out his crisply ironed windowpane oxford shirt, which he accessorized with a green paisley tie and gold cuff links.

"I told you I would bring the file in a minute. Can I at least take my coat off?" Christy said to Dave. "Geez."

He ignored her words and dropped a box of donuts in the middle of the conference room table. *Thump.* "Want one?" he asked Christy, picking up a frosted strawberry topped with rainbow sprinkles.

Dave made himself at home with the two women, casually sitting on the table's edge close to Christy as he bit off half of his donut. Nicole chuckled soundlessly when she spotted colored sprinkles lodged in the corner of his mouth.

"Hey, watch my latte," Christy said, grabbing her cup. "You almost knocked it over."

"Donut would be good with that," he said. His voice was garbled with food.

Christy rolled her chair away from the table, creating space between her and Dave. Nicole watched his eyes drift up and down Christy, analyzing her like an income statement. *Pig.*

"You're really pushing 'em. Not like you to be such a nice guy," Christy said. "What's the occasion? Or better question . . . what'd you put in them?"

He took another bite. "Just fulfilling my obligation as a team member."

"Obligation?"

"Oh, come on," he said between the loud lip-smacking of his chews. "You know the rule—when you get laid, you bring donuts for everyone on the team the next day."

Nicole shifted in her seat, opening a file, pretending to be busy. As Dave and Christy's conversation continued, Nicole's armpits became increasingly sticky.

Christy rolled her eyes. "You're a jackass."

He ignored her insult. "How come you never play along?" he asked as a sprinkle sputtered out his mouth. "Or are you like every other married woman in this world?" He held up his left hand and wiggled his ring finger. "Once you got the big rock, you stop putting out. Until you want kids anyway." He roared at his own joke.

Christy glared at him, jerking herself to her feet. "I'm ignoring you," she said with hooded eyes and pursed lips. Standing, she reached across the table and grabbed the debt file from the stack of manilla folders in front of Nicole. "Here. Take the file," she said, jamming it into Dave's gut. "And your donuts."

"Okay, okay." Dave stood, half laughing, with his hands up as if to say, 'Don't shoot.' Nicole wouldn't have blamed Christy if she had shot him. But that would have been too easy. Watching Christy knock him down with nothing but confidence was way more entertaining.

When Dave turned to grab the box on the table, Nicole dropped her head, avoiding his eye. *Please go.*

Nicole felt the weight of his stare on the top of her head. She held her breath, her body rigid. "Hey." He snapped his fingers. "Hey, newbie." He snapped again.

She lifted her head, silently meeting his eyes with a white-lipped smile.

His face split open into an arrogant grin. He jutted his chin at her and asked, "What about you? When are you going to bring in treats for the team?"

With his gaze tight on her, uneasiness swelled the back of Nicole's tongue. Watching his eyes flip down to her chest, her gut wrenched, sending a sputter of uncomfortable laughter out of her.

Nicole scrambled to pull up one of Leia's avoiding conflict lessons in her mind, but the situation was unlike anything she had practiced. Nicole was in a prestigious accounting firm's office in a safe, brightly sunlit, glass-enclosed conference room. There was another woman with her. They had complimentary French roast coffee in the kitchenette, free tampons, and Static Guard in the ladies' room. She wasn't alone on the street, and Dave wasn't some derelict man in a dark alley next to a dumpster. He was quite the opposite. He was a leader in her office. A man who had power over her career. She couldn't shout, "No! Get back! Go away!" as much as she would have liked. Instead, she sat wordlessly and wished it to be over. *Again.*

His smile was so vast that Nicole could count all his teeth. "You know, I could arrange for the both of us to have a reason to bring in pastries," he said, motioning to the box in his hands, giving her a wink.

Nicole was struck by how sure of himself he was. So confident that somehow what he was saying was acceptable. She hoped her face didn't betray her, giving away how her insides were churning with disgust.

"Oh, shit. You're not one of those *good girls* who run to HR, are you?" His eyes popped.

The same switch that flipped in Nicole when Blade called her a 'good girl' when she didn't fight for herself went off in the conference room, unleashing her inhibitions. *I can't let him win.*

Nicole looked at Dave evenly and said, "I walk to HR. I don't run, scared." Her eyes widened. *Oh, my God. I can't believe I said that.*

He let out an awkward laugh. "Hey. I was just having a little fun. Don't worry. You're too inexperienced for me—*Newbie.*"

"Don't you have somewhere to be?" Christy asked him. She tipped back, arching her stare at him. "Thought you had to review the Callahan file *ASAP.*"

"I'm going, I'm going," he said. At the same time Dave reached the doorway, Danielle, the office staffing coordinator, walked by. He stopped, giving her the right of way. "Good morning, Danielle. How's my girl?" he asked. He stuck the box he was holding out into the hallway to stop her. "Donut?"

Pig.

"Thanks!" She accepted. "What's the occasion?"

"Just spreading some holiday cheer," he gleamed.

"Awww, Dave. You're so good to us." Through the glass wall, Nicole could see that Danielle delighted in Dave's attention.

"And while I have you," he said with his fake smile still plastered on his face. "For busy season, make sure you get Miss Newbie over there on one of my jobs." He tossed his thumb over his shoulder. "I've heard good things about her, and Christy is hogging her all to herself."

"I'm on it!" She said, parting ways with Dave.

Nicole fought to swallow the regret-sized lump lodged in her throat. Dave wasn't done with her. *There was no whistle.*

| 30 |

Nicole

It was almost six o'clock that night when Nicole stepped inside her apartment. Her break between Christmas and New Year's had officially begun. She drew a deep breath, inhaling the scent of cedar and pine from the dried potpourri on the coffee table.

The outdoor holiday aromas reminded her of their annual family tradition of cutting down their Christmas tree at a farm outside Saratoga. After they picked out the perfect one, she and Jamie would stand off to the side in knee-high snow, drinking the hot cocoa their mom had brought for them while her dad lay on the ground and sawed away.

A warm smile played across her face, remembering the last year they went together as a family. She and Jamie attempted to make a popcorn garland, but after about two feet of struggling to thread the needle through the kernels and drawing blood from several fingers, they both got so bored that they ate the rest of the popcorn and listened to John Denver and the Muppets instead.

Nicole dropped her apartment keys in the bowl by the door. Still singing the last verse of "12 Days of Christmas," she kicked off her sneakers and pushed play on her blinking answering machine.

"Hey, Nic, it's Megan!"

Nicole's back muscles tightened. *What do you want?*

After her shitty day in the office, she was in no mood to stir up memories of Megan or anything else that Nicole associated with her—Wheeler, Rob, *that night.*

"Haven't talked to you in a while. I hope that means you've been too busy shacking up with the cute deli guy to call me." Megan giggled. Nicole was annoyed. "Just kidding. Well, not really, but . . ." Nicole's finger hovered over the erase button. "I just wanted to call and say I'm sorry for what I said the last time we talked. I miss you." There was a long pause. "Merry Christmas, Nic! Bye." The message ended with the smack of a kiss blown into the phone.

Nicole had made peace with letting go of Megan a long time ago. Too much time had passed, and she didn't see any reason to open any of the old wounds. Nicole blew a kiss into the air, sending Megan love for all the good times they had together, and then hit the delete button on the answering machine. *Bye.*

With an audible exhale, Nicole strode in her stocking feet into her kitchen and flipped on the overhead light. On the table was a bottle of wine she had bought for Zuke for the holidays—a small token of her appreciation for making her feel so welcome in the neighborhood.

The baseboard heat knocked, ushering Nicole to debate leaving the coziness of her apartment to deliver the wine. It was below freezing outside and was only going to get colder the later it got. On the other hand, if she stayed home, she would be kept company by the endless replaying of Dave and his donuts looping through her mind. *Wine it is!*

***

Donning her black peacoat and duck boots, Nicole tucked the bottle wrapped in silver mylar under her arm. As she approached the last step outside, the noise of the crinkling foil was overpowered by the click of Claire's car door opening.

Nicole wasn't in the mood for another interrogation from her about Jesse, like the one she gave her a few days earlier— "Where's that handsome boy I met? It's about time he got you out of that apartment." Nicole stepped back into the shadows and waited until she drove away.

For the first time in a long time, Nicole felt her life was getting back on track. She had a steady routine, she and Jamie were as close as ever, and she was doing well at work. She didn't want to go backward, not even an inch.

If she went out with Jesse, there was no guarantee she would keep her momentum going. Even if they both wanted to explore their relationship beyond being 'summer siblings,' the truth was, she was terrified. What if she flinched or cried, or worse, got sick when he touched her? Jesse wasn't someone she could walk away from without telling him why. They had too much history. But the thought of telling him strengthened all the shame and embarrassment she was still working through.

It was easy to say, "You've got to learn to be comfortable with being uncomfortable," like many in her life had advised, but it was another to put it into practice.

Practice.

Nicole chuckled at the idea of finding a tester friend, akin to the sample-sized lotions at Bath & Body Works. A tester would allow her to see how her body reacted to the touch and feel on her skin before committing to the bigger bottle—Jesse.

Nicole watched Claire's taillights disappear down the road as she folded the thought of Jesse to the back of her mind and pulled a flashlight from her jacket pocket.

With every disappearing breath, she felt more alive as the cold, crisp winter air filled her lungs. Something was different in the quiet and peaceful dark—her shoulders weren't in her ears, she wasn't chewing at her lip, and her fists weren't clenched in her gloves. Her feet were firmly planted on the ground when she made the shocking realization—*I'm not afraid!*

Everything around her suddenly seemed brighter, like she had taken the light filter off the end of her camera lens. The Christmas decorations along her path were vibrant enough to send signals to space, and the white string lights on the hedges radiated through the thin blanket of freshly fallen snow like disco balls. Nicole was giddy at the sight of the two life-size plastic nutcracker soldiers standing guard outside Zuke's front door at the end of the block.

When she reached the step, Zuke was standing on the other side of the door, about to turn the dangling sign in the window to *closed*. Nicole caught his eye and gave him a small wave. His face lit up like a tree topper when he recognized her. The lock clicked, and the door swung open. "Hey, Nicole," Zuke said, standing in the doorway.

He didn't look as perky and put together as Nicole was used to seeing him in the morning—bright-eyed, clean-shaven, not a hair out of place. His freshly dry-cleaned apron had been replaced with an unbuttoned flannel worn over his black Zuke's Deli T-shirt. His shoulders had a slouch to them, he had dark circles under his eyes, needed a shave, and the cowlick on the top of his head was roaming free.

"Hi! Sorry, I don't mean to bother you. I can come back another time," she said, batting her flashlight hand toward him. "I don't want to keep you from closing. I'm sure you want to leave for the night."

"No worries at all. Come in, come in. It's cold out there." He ushered her inside. "Truthfully, you're giving me an excuse to walk away from my paperwork," he said, pointing at the piles on the counter next to the register. "My bookkeeper had a heart attack the other day."

"Oh no!"

"Mild. Thank God," he said, raising his hand to the sky. "But it means I have to do my books for a while. Food is my specialty, not numbers. Unless I can cook them, I'm at a loss."

"As a public accountant, I feel compelled to inform you that most government agencies frown upon people who cook their books." Nicole chuckled at her joke.

Zuke laughed, too. "Good one."

Nicole noticed Zuke squinting his eyes. He held up his hand to block the light she was pointing directly into his face. "Do you mind turning that off?"

"Oh!" She fumbled to click off the flashlight. "I'm so sorry!"

He rubbed his eyes. "Ahhh . . . that's better." He closed the door behind her. "Surprised to see you. A little late for coffee, no?"

"Wanted to bring you a present. My way of saying thank you for being such a huge help to me since I moved here," she said, handing him the bottle of wine. "Merry Christmas, Zuke."

"You didn't have to do that. I am always happy to help you. That's what friends do. But thank you, it's very sweet of you." he said, pulling her into a hug before she could mentally prepare.

He was only a few inches taller, so she didn't have to reach up when she hugged him back. Surprised at how good his firm hold felt, she found herself melting into his arms, holding on a little too long. A flash of embarrassment shocked her cold when she realized how much she was enjoying it.

"Well, I should go. I don't want to keep you," she babbled, pushing away from him. The heat was rising in her cheeks, and she worried her face was tattling on her.

"You're not keeping me from anything." His eyes lit up. "Hey, I just pulled a fresh batch of meatballs out of the oven. Have you eaten yet?"

At the mention of food, Nicole's stomach growled. "I actually haven't had anything since breakfast. That was my next stop."

"I have a better idea. It's Friday night. How about you stay? I'll make us some dinner. We can even open the wine if you'd like."

The thought of spending another night alone in her apartment made Nicole's heart hurt. She was tired of being lonely. And she knew she could trust Zuke. "You know what? I think I will."

His smile grew. "Great!"

Nicole followed him further into the store. He darted a few steps ahead and pulled a stool from behind the counter for her to sit on. "Have a seat here," he said, lightly patting the vinyl cushion. The deadening sound was reminiscent of the blue mats at the Y. "I'll grab the corkscrew."

Nicole slipped her coat off and laid it on the stool while he opened the bottle. She noticed the folders on the counter, swelling open with receipts. "If you need help with your books, let me know," she said, sitting down.

His expression brightened. "I may take you up on that. I think I am in over my head."

"I'd be happy to. That's what friends do, right?" She perked up. "Besides, I like projects like that. They're fun."

"Fun is not a word I would use for accounting." He handed her a coffee cup. "Sorry, I don't have stemware down here. I am embarrassed to serve you wine in a paper cup. My father is probably rolling over in his grave right now."

Zuke poured himself a cup and raised it in the air. "Sorry, Dad!" he said, breathing off an easy laugh.

The corners of her mouth quirked into a light smile. "No judgment from me. Truthfully, the paper is probably more my speed."

"Regardless of the vessel, cheers to friendship!" he said, bumping her cup.

"Cheers to that," she said, mirroring his grin before taking a sip. "Geez . . . I didn't realize how much I needed that. I had such a shitty day today." She put her palm to her forehead, attempting to push the image of Dave away.

His eyebrows shot up. "What happened?"

"Oh, you don't want to hear about it. Boring office stuff," she said, giving him a dismissive wave.

"I wouldn't have asked if I didn't want to hear about it." Nicole liked how his eyes crinkled when he smiled. "Besides, I find it's usually better to get it out of your system. Easier to move on. Otherwise, it festers right here," he said, motioning to the middle of his chest.

Nicole bobbed her head. She recalled how unleashed she felt when she told her truth at Model Mugging. And then again with Jamie. So, she told Zuke about Dave and the donuts, including how uncomfortable she was when Dave asked Danielle to put her on one of his upcoming engagements. "What can I do? He's my manager, right?" She shrugged, using her cup to cover the embarrassment on her face. As the words left her mouth, she worried that she may have shared too much.

"That's awful. I can understand why you'd be upset by that. I can't believe people talk like that in business. I always thought when someone worked in an office, they had more couth."

"Yeah, well, I guess pigs are everywhere. Even in accounting firms." She paused. "It's funny. Back in college, I had a professor tell me that to be successful, I needed to learn to be comfortable with being uncomfortable, that it builds character. At my current rate of uncomfortableness, I will be the most successful person you know." She chuckled nervously.

"I'm sorry you had to go through that."

"Thank you for saying that," she said, finishing the last of her wine.

"Oh! Let me get the food. I don't want you to have too much to drink on an empty stomach. Make yourself comfortable. I'll be right back."

A few minutes later, Zuke appeared from the kitchen. Somewhere along the way, he had lost his flannel. She pretended to take a sip from her empty cup to hide her gaze, quietly admiring how his fitted black T-shirt showcased his broad upper body. He proudly carried two white plates in her direction while her eyes traced the vein popping from the front of his bicep to the Italy-shaped tattoo on his forearm.

"Real plates?" she teased when he presented her with gourmet-looking dishes filled with mouthwatering homemade meatballs drowned in the perfect amount of red sauce.

"I promise you, I would serve my Nonna's meatballs out of my bare hands before I served them on paper plates. It would be disrespectful to the meatball," he said, chuckling. He pulled two neatly wrapped sets of silverware from the front pocket of his crisp white apron and set them on the counter next to their dinner. Nicole admired his quiet confidence.

The smells of sweet basil and garlic coated the inside of her nose, and her eyes fell to her plate. "Wow, I sure picked the right night to bring your present."

"Parmigiano?" he asked, holding out a block and a small grater.

"Please!"

After Zuke generously blanketed her meal with flakes of cheese, like freshly fallen snow, Nicole ate her first bite. "My God! How on earth do you make a meatball light? Or moist, for that matter," she said, her mouth still full.

"That's the panade."

"Is that another one of those fancy Italian cheeses?"

He shook his head. "No. It's a paste made from stale bread soaked in milk. You mix it in with all the other ingredients—ground beef, pork, veal, garlic, fresh herbs, egg, etcetera. The paste expands as the meatballs cook, keeping them from drying out and hardening up like a golf ball," he explained.

"I can't believe you made these."

"I make probably three to four batches a week. The lunch crowd goes wild for them." He leaned against the counter, tucking one leg under him. "This batch, though, I made purely out of procrastination from working on my taxes. Cooking relaxes me. Kind of like how you said numbers relax you."

She cut off another piece with the side of her fork. "Where did you learn?"

"My Nonna Zuke. She used to put my sister and me to work in her kitchen every Sunday rolling meatballs while she made the gravy," he said, smiling at the memory. "Then my dad owned a classic Italian restaurant in downtown Schenectady. As soon as I could reach the counter, he put me to work, starting in the kitchen. He'd easily go through four to five hundred meatballs on a Saturday night. At this point, I can make them in my sleep," he said, rubbing his palms together in a circle.

Nicole refilled her paper cup and raised it. "Well, cheers to Nonna Zuke and . . . sorry, what's your dad's name?"

Zuke met her cup in the air. "Francesco Zuccarello," he said proudly. "But everyone called him Frankie."

"Wait. Are you a Frankie junior?"

"I am, but my mom called me her little Zukie instead of Frankie," he blushed. "Probably so when she yelled at us, we knew which of us was in trouble. It just stuck." His smile reached clear to his heart.

"Awww, Zukie . . . I love that. Okay, let me start again." She inhaled. "Cheers to Nonna Zuke and Frankie Zuccarello for this Italian festival in my mouth. Quite possibly the best meal I have ever had."

"Salute!" he cheered.

"Salute!" she repeated, taking a sip. "It's like my senses are more alive. I think the wine even tastes better."

He put his hand on his chest. "Hearing that warms my heart. Food was such a big part of how I grew up. It's how we show love and friendship and connect." His eyes danced. "Late nights at the restaurant, when all the customers cleared out, my family and I would sit and have a full meal together. It could be eleven o'clock at night. It didn't matter. It was our time to check in with each other. Food has a funny way of opening the door. Of course, there was also a lot of Italian passion at the table, so sometimes you wanted to close that door, too," he chuckled. "Speaking of . . . I've done all the talking. It's your turn. Tell me about you. What's your family like?"

She was embarrassed to share too much about her family. They were so different in that regard. "Not much to tell. My friends call me Nic. I come from a small family. My dad died when I was twelve. I'm close to my sister, Jamie. Not so much with my mom." She shrugged. "That's kinda it."

"Nic. I like it. My aunt's name is Nicole, too. Did you know that it means *victory?*"

"I didn't. First, the panade, and now this. You're quite the wealth of information tonight," she teased.

His mouth turned down. "I am sorry to hear about your parents."

"Thank you. I appreciate you saying that, but honestly, there's no pity party here. Yes, I had to grow up quicker than most. But it forced me to figure things out on my own. If anything, my childhood made me stronger," she admitted.

"Victorious. Like your name. Maybe your parents knew your resilience when they named you."

"I'm not declaring victory yet," she laughed as she stood, "and I am certainly not giving my parents that kind of credit."

He put his leg down and pushed off the counter to his feet. "Well then, you should at least give yourself credit. It doesn't sound like it was an easy time in your life."

"Maybe one day," she said, yawning. "Oh, geez. I'm sorry. I think my day is catching up to me. Let me help you clean," she offered, picking up her empty plate.

"Please," he said, taking it from her, "I'll do it later. Let me walk you home."

"Oh, you don't have to do that. I'm just down the road," she said, putting on her coat.

"It's dark outside. It's not safe. Let me grab my jacket," he insisted. She stopped him.

"Honestly, Zuke. Look at me." She tilted her chin up to him. "There are Christmas lights, and I have my flashlight, remember?" She flicked it on and shined it in his face.

That got a chuckle out of him.

"It was already dark when I walked here. It's only nine o'clock. Honestly, I'll be fine," she said, slipping the light back into her coat pocket. A surge of pride warmed her. She truly believed it.

"Do you at least have pepper spray?"

She gave him a proud smile. "I have something better. I have a *winner's spirit*," she said with an inflection in her voice. He tilted his head. "It means you don't have to worry about me." *It's part of me now. No one can take it away from me.*

His arms fell to his sides. "I don't like it, but okay." He followed her to the front door.

"Well, this has been wonderful. Thank you so much." Nicole pushed her thumb down on the handle, but it didn't open. Zuke reached across her to unlock it. He smelled of vanilla and musk and maybe a sprinkle of sharp cheese.

Her gaze followed his hand pulling the door open, then drifted upward just as his espresso-colored eyes cut to her. Specks of gold traced his iris, adding depth and comfort. Heat flared up her neck, reaching her cheeks as they stood close, sharing the same breath. He moved in an inch closer, his mouth lingering around hers, sending tingles dancing along her skin.

Maybe it was the wine or the romantic dinner, or she wanted to test herself. Whatever it was, after a flicker of apprehension, she gave in and kissed him. The touch of his lips on hers sent an unexpected wave of want down her spine.

His kiss was gentle, like a whisper, brushing across her lips. The caress of his mouth and the strokes of his tongue, still tasting like the sweet cherry notes in the wine, narrowed her thoughts only to that moment— a delicious sensation.

She wrapped her hands around his neck as he slipped his hands around her back, bringing her closer. She pulled away for a split second, met his stare, and kissed him again—deeper and more hungrily that time. She was surprised at her willing response to his touch, far from uncomfortable.

They leaned against the doorframe as one, immune to the cold winter night drifting over them through the wide-open door. Losing herself with him was exhilarating. She couldn't get enough. And then, in a split second, a knot of guilt filled her rib cage and began to suffocate her.

She broke the kiss with a sharp gasp, her mouth filling with shame. She was using Zuke to test herself to see if she could stand to be kissed. He didn't deserve to be her practice kisser, unknowingly. If Nicole's heart was with Jesse—*It was, wasn't it?*—then he was the person she should be kissing. *Right?*

Nicole pulled away from Zuke. His eyes searched her face. "I'm so sorry," she whispered, covering her eyes. "I shouldn't have done that."

He lifted her chin. "Hey," he said, gently moving her hands away. "Nic, it's okay." His voice was tender, almost a murmur.

She turned away from the attention. "Please don't take this the wrong way." She was fighting back tears. "I had so much fun with you tonight. I don't want to take anything away from that. I'm going through some stuff right now. I can't do this. I'm so sorry." Her voice cracked.

"It's fine. Honestly," he sighed. Nicole let him pull her into a hug. She pressed her face against his shirt. "I just want to make sure you're okay."

"I will be . . . victorious, right?" She gave a single laugh.

"Exactly." He held her awhile longer. "Can I ask you a question?"

She nodded, pulling away.

"Was it because I served you wine in a paper cup?"

The awkwardness in the room fell like a loaf of day-old bread. Her frown stretched into a smile, and they quickly fell into hysterics.

After her giggles wound down, she tilted her head up. "Can we stick to coffee for now?"

His face softened. "Of course." As awkward as their exchange was, she didn't feel self-conscious around him.

"And your books. My offer still stands."

"I'm holding you to it," he said before their final goodbyes.

Out on the sidewalk, with her back to the door, she waited to hear the lock click before she let out a relieved breath. For the umpteenth time, she considered her next move. Her mind was stuck like her cemented feet. *What if, what if, what if . . .*

But after her day, her month, her year, she realized that she couldn't stand to be in her self-imposed purgatory anymore. She wanted out and was the only one with the power to do it. With her renewed confidence, her legs propelled forward.

I'm calling Jesse. I'm making us happen.

PART 3

| 31 |

Jesse

"Here you are, sir," the maître d' said to Jesse, pulling out his chair. Jesse felt underdressed in his blue mock turtleneck sweater and black jeans next to the host, dressed in a full tuxedo. "Would you like to start with a complimentary aperitivo while you wait for the rest of your party? It's included in our New Year's Eve special."

"Just water for now. Thanks, man," Jesse said, sitting at the white-clothed table in the back of the restaurant. Jesse saw the host snap his fingers at someone across the bustling dining room, and seconds later, a waiter dressed in a crisp white dress shirt and black vest, matched with a sparkly sequin bowtie, appeared with a pitcher. Jesse held the bottom of the glass, impatiently watching the ice cubes tumble out of the pitcher, splashing cool droplets onto his hand as nerves clawed at his chest.

Jesse gulped his water, quietly panting, when he noticed the old wicker-wrapped bottle of chianti turned candle in the center of the table. "Actually, can I get a bottle of red wine? It's a special night," he told the waiter.

"Of course, sir. House?"

"Please."

"Right away."

Jesse had almost lost all hope of Nicole ever calling him. He was no stranger to the crushing disappointment of the two of them never being more than friends. But ever since their almost kiss on the Fourth of July and chance run-ins, keeping the embers of hope in his chest from igniting was becoming increasingly harder.

The waiter returned with the wine and went to work on uncorking the bottle while Jesse thought more about Nicole. When she finally called, she was as spirited as he felt. They shared a good laugh when she recommended the local mini-mart for their first date, but he insisted on New Year's Eve dinner at Giancarlo's, one of the best Italian restaurants in the area. He only had one chance to impress her. If he crashed and burned, that was it. But, if all went well, he might finally get the kiss he had been craving. He couldn't think of a better way to start the new year. Dinner had to be perfect.

Jesse kept one eye on the door, nervously fidgeting with the champagne bottle-shaped confetti scattered over the table. The air was thick with the aroma of fresh bread and garlic, the ringing of clinking glasses, and loud cheers from large tables filled with overly primped partygoers.

The heavy velvet drapes by the front door billowed into the restaurant, retreating to reveal Nicole. His heart jumped like a swimmer on the starting blocks just after the gun went off at the sight of her beside the hostess podium. He could tell she was uncomfortably cold, with her shoulders hovering around her ears and hands tucked tightly in her pockets.

His eyes were glued to her as the maître d' checked her coat, then led her through an archway of black and silver balloons draped with a banner that read *Felice Anno Nuovo*. A blend of performance anxiety and excitement swirled Jesse's insides. *One chance.*

Nicole kept her head down as she walked through the bustling restaurant. She wore snug black jeans that showed off her beautifully curvy silhouette and a fitted black wool turtleneck. Her hair, normally curly and unpredictable, was uncharacteristically smooth but still happily bounced with every step. Jesse couldn't help but notice her nipples poking through her sweater—a wonderfully unexpected byproduct of the cold weather outside.

He wiped the sweat from his palms on the dinner napkin resting on his lap before standing to greet her. When she stopped inches from him, he hoped his big idiot grin distracted her from seeing him flinch at the flames roaring inside him.

"Bella," the maître d' said, flipping his wrist toward Jesse with a slight bow, "your table."

Her eyes were wide with the half laugh that came with nerves. "Hey," Jesse choked out, leaning down to give her a hug and a quick kiss on her cheek. Every cell in his body tingled at the smell of her lavender scent.

Nicole stepped back, looking a little lost as to what to do next when the waiter finally interrupted. "Bella?" he said with his palms resting on the back of her chair, prompting her to sit.

She tittered, taking her seat. "Oh! Right."

The waiter snapped open the silver pyramid-folded napkin on her plate and handed it to her while he filled her water glass. "I'll give you a few minutes to enjoy your wine," the waiter said before disappearing into the kitchen.

"I hope you don't mind. I ordered a bottle for us to share. Do you drink red?" Jesse asked.

She shrugged blankly. "I'm not picky."

His eyebrow raised a fraction. "Good to know," he replied with a chuckle. "Did you find the restaurant okay? I could have picked you up. It wasn't a problem."

"It was out of your way. Besides, I should have my car in case this doesn't go so well."

Jesse's eyes widened at her bluntness.

"Oh, my God. Did that sound as bad as I think it did?" she asked, covering her mouth.

Jesse nodded. "It did."

"I swear it was funnier in my head," she blushed.

Jesse picked up his wine glass. Nicole followed. "Well, here's to hoping the night, and the jokes, get better. Cheers!"

She giggled. "Salute! To good health."

"Listen to you," he teased just before they both took a sip.

Nicole hitched up one shoulder then put her glass down. "I'm working on being more cultured," she said, slipping her hand under her leg.

"Are you cold? Want me to have the waiter bring your coat?"

She waved him off. "I'll be fine in a minute. The wine will help."

The waiter reappeared. "Would you like to hear about our menu this evening?"

"Yes, please," Nicole responded.

As the waiter rattled off the chef's specials for the night, Jesse watched Nicole read along on the chalkboard menu hung close by, admiring the dusting of faded freckles across the bridge of her nose—a small reminder of all the summers they had spent together.

And her lips—the perfect shade of dark red gloss. He desperately wanted to kiss her.

When the waiter left them to decide on their order, she told Jesse, "If I get nothing else, I am getting the cheesecake. I've been dreaming about it since I missed out on it at our graduation party."

"Is there a story behind your love of cheesecake, or is it simply the anticipation of your biochemical reaction seeping into your subconscious?" He chuckled.

Her expression flattened. "My dad used to buy me an Italian cheesecake for my birthday every year from this bakery near his office in downtown Schenectady. It was my favorite. After he died, I didn't want it anymore. It was too painful of a reminder. But when I graduated from college, I knew he'd be proud of me, so I wanted to celebrate with him in a way, I guess." She looked away. "Sounds ridiculous when I say it out loud."

"Not at all," Jesse said, reaching for her hand. "Should we start with dessert?"

Her eyes brightened. "I've waited this long. I think I can make it through dinner."

"Nic, you're freezing." He pulled her closer and blew his warm breath into their cupped hands.

With her hand still nestled inside his, her eyes drifted over Jesse's shoulder. "Did you know sunflowers are my favorite?" Nicole jutted her chin at the oil painting hanging behind him. He turned to look. "Over the summer, I always had a vase of them on my kitchen counter. They have this ability to brighten my mood. Even a rainy day feels sunny when they're around."

Just like you. "Sounds familiar."

"Wow, you are definitely not the Jesse Young I grew up with," she teased. Her lids dipped down. "That Jesse put disgusting nightcrawlers on my fishing hook and saved me from the scary salamander in my kayak." His gaze lingered on the fringe of her lashes until her eyes lifted, glittering in the tealight on the table.

"When you're an awkward thirteen-year-old boy, helping a pretty girl bait her hook is equivalent to holding her hand."

A flash of humor crossed her face. "The salamander was this past summer, and you were twenty-two."

"If I had the chance to hold your hand that day, I would have," he said, lacing his fingers through hers as naturally as tying his shoes.

From there, their conversation flowed easily for the next couple of hours, finally ordering dinner on the waiter's third drive-by to their table. "I think he's trying to move us along," she leaned in and whispered after he left.

Jesse had been waiting for that night for over a decade, and he was going to stretch it out as long as he could. "I'm not leaving until you tell me it's time to go."

A waitress decorated in a silver and black Happy New Year tiara approached their table and asked, "You guys want glasses and noisemakers? The Ball is dropping soon." She motioned to the basket of celebratory novelties she was carrying.

"Of course!" Nicole exclaimed before Jesse could turn the waitress away.

"We have to play along. It's New Year's, Jesse!" she insisted, showing off her new glasses. Her smiling eyes glimmered through the nines of the silly 1996 frames as her lips curled open.

"Nicole?" a woman's voice emerged out of nowhere.

Nicole pulled her glasses off and jumped to her feet like a spring. "Kristen!" Nicole chirped, "Hi!"

Jesse stood to meet the woman. "Kristen, this is my friend, Jesse," Nicole said. Jesse noticed the subtle eye exchange between the two of them.

"Nice to meet you." He smiled. She looked significantly older than Nicole with her leathery fake tan and teased hairstyle. He was trying to imagine a scenario where they would know each other. She didn't look like an accountant. "Do you work together?"

Nicole was quick to respond. "No. We met at the gym."

"What are you doing here?" Nicole asked her. He took note of her changing the subject.

"They throw a great New Year's Eve party in the bar," Kristen said.

"Maybe we'll see you over there later for the countdown," Nicole said, giving her another hug goodbye. Jesse overheard Nicole and Kristen whispering to each other like giddy schoolgirls but couldn't quite make out what they said over the sounds of the restaurant.

Jesse and Nicole sat back down. "Well, that was unexpected," she said, pulling her mouth to one side.

"So, did I pass the test?"

"Perhaps," she said coyly. Nicole rested her chin on her fist and leaned on her elbow, reading him.

"If I had to pick one woman in this place you'd be friends with, I would never pick her in a million years."

Nicole tilted her head, squinting. "Why?"

"Seems a lot older than you, still single, hanging out at bars. Doesn't seem like your type."

"She and I have more in common than you'd think."

"Well, she's clearly on the hunt for a good time in that outfit," he chuckled. "And if she's not, you should warn her."

Nicole's face crumpled. "What do you mean?"

He huffed out a laugh. "She's alone at a bar in a skin-tight cat-suit and thigh-high boots. She's asking for trouble. Guys are going to make some assumptions about her. She needs to be smarter about it, that's all."

Once full of glitter, her eyes were suddenly blazing balls of fire. "First of all, Kristen can take care of herself just fine. And two, let me be very clear when I say," she gritted, pointing her index finger in his face, "she's not asking for *anything* unless it comes out of her mouth. She should be able to sit at the bar naked, for Christ's sake, and not be in any danger."

Nicole's fiery reaction took him aback. "Nic, please don't be upset. I'm sorry. I am not trying to attack her. It's just reality. Guys don't always have an off button. They can't always control themselves."

Nicole scowled at him. "And isn't *that* the problem? Not what she was wearing!"

Dude, shut the fuck up. You're going to ruin this.

"Nic." He extended his hand across the table like an olive branch. "I'm not excusing it. Some guys are scum. That's all I was trying to say." He was losing her. He could see it in her face. His chest constricted. "Please."

Their conversation was reaching boiling temperature when the waiter appeared with their food. "Here we are," he said in his sing-song voice, putting their plates down. "Need anything else?"

"No," Jesse said. His voice was curt. She said nothing.

"Well then, buon appetito!" The waiter blew them a chef kiss and disappeared.

They sat in silence while the clanking of silverware, the hiss of the espresso machine, and the buzzing energy of the people carried on around them. Jesse took a half bite of the arugula salad they ordered to share but lost his appetite watching Nicole push her pasta around her plate.

It wasn't long after that when Jesse's ears honed in on her quiet sniffles. He pivoted his gaze toward her and caught her dabbing her nose with her napkin. She met his stare through her wet lashes and shook her head. "I think I should go." The chair legs scraping against the tiled floor were like nails on a chalkboard. *Fuck!*

He scrambled to stand, trying to catch her hand when she walked by his side of the table. "Nic . . ." His voice faded.

What did you do, asshole? You had one chance! He curled his hand into a fist and pounded the table so hard the silverware leaped, falling with a *clang*. A hefty middle-aged woman sitting nearby let out a startled screech.

Jesse barely heard the waiter approach him over the blood rushing in his ears. "Everything all right, sir?"

"Fine," Jesse spat out, clenching his jaw.

The waiter fixed his smile. "Then can you please keep it down, sir? I don't want to disturb the other guests."

Jesse glared at the woman sitting at the table beside him who was giving him a side eye while whispering to her dinner companion. Jesse pulled enough cash from his wallet to cover the bill, grabbed his jacket from the coat check room, and ran out the door after Nicole.

Outside in the parking lot, lit by faux vintage streetlamps reminiscent of those found along cobble paths in the Italian countryside, he scanned the lot, desperately searching for Nicole. In the distance, he saw her silhouette and sprinted toward her. "Nic!"

He caught up to her just as she was about to get into her car. She put her hand up. "Jesse, please. I'm just gonna go." Her voice was thick.

"Nic, I'm sorry. You know I didn't mean to upset you," he pleaded, hoping she saw the remorse written in his eyes. "Please don't leave."

"This was a bad idea. We should just be friends." Her breath caught.

"Nic. Look at me." She shot him a glare. Her face was blotchy from crying. *Shit! Shit! Shit!* "Nic. I'm sorry. I should never have said that about your friend. It's none of my business." He was still panting from his dash across the lot.

She stared at him blankly, chewing the inside of her cheek.

"Come on, Nic. We were having fun until I put my size twelve foot in my mouth like a real jerk." He plowed his hands through his hair. He was dying inside.

"You got that right."

"Which part?"

"That you were a jerk." She leaned against the driver side door, shoving her hands into her pockets. "And that we were having fun." Her voice drifted off.

"I'm sorry," he said quietly.

Her expression was softer than when her finger was jammed in his face at the table. "I'm sorry, too." She blew out a breath through her teeth. "I overreacted. I guess it's a hot button for me."

"You have nothing to apologize for. I shouldn't have said anything in the first place." Jesse reached for Nicole's hand, but she kept her hands in her pockets.

"Thank you. But I still think I should go."

One chance. "You can't go. The ball is about to drop."

"I can't go back inside after I made this big dramatic exit."

In the distance, cheers flowed out of the restaurant. "10...9...8..." With each tick down, Jesse's heartrate sped up. "7...6...5...4...3...2...1. Happy New Year!" the crowd hollered seconds before "Auld Lang Syne" started playing.

"I guess it's midnight," she said.

He nodded in agreement, desperate for her to stay. "Can we go back to having fun? I don't want our night to end like this."

Nicole reached into her bag and pulled out the New Year's novelties. The corners of his mouth quirked as she appeared stone-faced, with a metallic horn hanging out of her mouth like a cigarette and wearing the glittered glasses from earlier. "How's this?" she asked, tilting her chin."

He stepped closer to her and pushed the silly glasses to the top of her head, revealing her damp eyes and winter-pink cheeks. He needed to kiss her. He reached for the horn dangling between her teeth, but before his hand could get there, she blew a flirty honk of the paper noisemaker right into his face. He flinched, scrunching his eyes closed as if she squirted him with a water gun.

"Before we go any further, I am going to take this away so that you are never tempted to do that again," he deadpanned, slipping the horn into his back pocket.

"It's probably best for everyone's sake," she agreed.

He moved in closer. "I'm really sorry, Nic."

"I know." She looked at her feet.

"Like, *really* sorry," he said, cupping her face.

She bit the corner of her lip, locking eyes with him.

"Happy New Year," he hushed into her breath.

She released a visible exhale. "Happy New Year, Jesse."

His pulse fluttered. "Are we doing this?" he asked softly, searching her expression for signs of hesitation.

She nodded once. "I think we are."

He slowly lowered his mouth, touching hers in a featherlike motion. Her lips were salty from her tears. He wanted more but was giving her one last chance to pull away. To his surprise, she ran her hand along the back of his arm and pulled him closer.

Taking her lead, his kiss built in intensity. He parted her lips with his tongue. She opened her mouth, and he slid inside. A surge of energy rippled through him as he tasted her for the first time—sweet and buttery. It was better than he could have ever imagined.

She pulled away, tenderly wiping her lipstick from his mouth with her thumb. *What happened? Why'd she stop?*

"Hey," he said quietly. His mouth went dry, worried she had a change of heart. He ran his finger under her chin and gently tilted it to see her face. "You all right?"

She nodded and shifted her eyes to a couple getting into their car nearby. After the doors clinked shut and the car started, Nicole opened her mouth to say something but held off.

"What?"

"It's just . . . I'm not the girl who makes out with a random guy in a parking lot with an audience," she whispered. "That was Megan. That's not me."

A tease squinted his eyes. "Random guy?"

"Oh, stop it." She playfully swatted at him. "That's not my point, and you know it. I just thought I owed you an explanation for cutting you off. I don't like to be on display."

He opened the front of his coat and wrapped it around her like a warm blanket. "I don't want you to do anything that makes you uncomfortable." He waited until the car pulled away and then stole a kiss from her lips.

She rested her cheek on his chest. He loved how she fit perfectly under his chin. "Thank you," she said.

"What are you doing tomorrow?" he asked. "Well, I guess at this point, later today."

"Laundry."

"Need some help?"

She scoffed in his chest. "You want to go to the laundromat with me?"

"I haven't stopped thinking about you since the Fourth of July," he admitted, watching his breath fade into the cool air. "I'd take any chance to spend more time with you. So, yes, even doing laundry."

She laughed. "As odd as this may sound, I might have more fun doing that with you."

His eyebrows inched together.

"Can I be honest?" she asked.

"Always."

"I'm worried about what this will do to us. You've been such an important person in my life in so many ways. If it doesn't work out, that's it. There's no going back. We're done. Forever." Her voice was brittle. She shifted on her feet. "Do you know how hard it is to find someone to make a 'fun pact' with me?" He smiled to himself, listening, holding her in his arms.

She went on. "And the pressure for tonight to be perfect was overwhelming. First date . . . with *you* . . . fancy restaurant . . . New Year's Eve. It's a lot." *Epic fail!* "You saw what happened. One misstep and I assumed the universe was telling me we were a bad idea. And then I ran. If this is right, I should have stayed and talked to you, not run away. It's just . . . I've had so many hard relationships in my life. I want ours to be easy. Fun. Uncomplicated."

We are right together. I promise.

She cut herself off. "I'm babbling, and you've said nothing." She pulled away to see his face.

Delight pulled the corners of his eyes.

"Did I say something funny?"

"Sorry. But . . . you said relationship."

"I'm not looking for casual, Jesse. We can end this now if that's all you want. That's not me."

He grinned, not taking his eyes off her. "Me either." He held the side of her face, tracing his thumb along the delicate softness of her lower lip. She turned into his palm and nuzzled it. "How about we have a redo and start with laundry? I'll teach you my trick on how to fold a fitted sheet."

She tightened her look. "You fold your sheets?"

"You don't? Well, that may be the deal breaker right there," he teased. The need to taste her again was becoming unbearable. "So, where do you stand on kissing a not-so-random guy outside an Italian restaurant in an empty parking lot?"

She tipped a shoulder. "No crowd. No issues."

The corners of Jesse's mouth turned upward as he leaned into her, pressing her against the car with his hips. He bent down toward her mouth and playfully grazed his tongue along her top lip. She released a soft gasp and relaxed her body into his, kicking Jesse's heart into high gear. He moved his mouth to hers, devouring its softness. Her fingers curled into the back of his sweater as she curved into him, sliding her velvety tongue against his. His hands tangled into her hair, helping him angle her face to kiss her deeper. An embarrassing low groan rumbled out of him like a distant summer night storm. He didn't care, he was finally kissing Nic.

Jesse brought them up for air, leaving his mouth hovering over hers. He could see her short breaths mixing with his in the cold air. "You okay?" he whispered.

She nodded, closing the gap between their lips. "Better than okay, but I should probably go."

"You sure?" he asked, slowly planting taunting little kisses on her bottom lip.

She smiled at his efforts, giving him another kiss. "No." A rush of want plummeted to his pulsating groin. He thought he might lose his mind. "If I don't go now, I may never leave," she said, sliding her hands into his.

"I don't want you to leave." He gave an amused hum, stroking his thumbs across her wrists. "Nic, I'm crazy about you. About us." Their foreheads pressed together, her lavender scent exciting him more.

"Me too," she said, leaning in and giving him one last kiss. "Happy New Year, Jesse." ...*James.*

| 32 |

Nicole

"Thanks for carrying my laundry for me. You didn't have to do that," Nicole said, holding open the glass door to Sudsy's Laundromat the following afternoon.

"You don't need to thank me. I offered," he said, trailing her inside.

"I'm not used to someone doing things for me."

"Well, get used to it. I like doing things for you," he said. He swung her duffle bag, bulging with a month's worth of dirty clothes, off his shoulder, dropping it on the floor with a *thud*. His hazel eyes, grayer than green in the shadow of his NY Yankee baseball hat, smiled at her.

Nicole had spent all morning anxiously trying to anticipate how they'd act around each other after the night they had—Awkward? Self-conscious? Searching for things to talk about? Avoiding eye contact? —But from the moment he picked her up, they settled into each other like they'd been together for months, fading her fears about them being together.

The familiar scent of laundry detergent and warm clothes charged her nose. "Ever been to a laundromat before?"

Jesse laughed. "First time."

"Well, let me be the first to welcome you to Sudsy's." She expanded her arms to the room, like Vanna White introducing the next puzzle.

She shrugged off her coat and balled it up, tossing it on one of the orange molded plastic chairs lining the wall.

"You come here alone?" he asked, scanning the room with a wrinkled nose. "This place is kind of a dump."

A sting of defensiveness pulsed in her chest. Nicole would admit that at first glance, it was about as welcoming as a visitation room in prison, with its institutionally green-painted cinderblock walls and excessively bright overhead lights. But it was *her* laundromat.

Nicole could barely hear herself think over the Rose Bowl Parade commentators blasting through the TV bolted to the wall. "Oh look, it's our Grand Marshal, Kermit the Frog," one of them reported as she walked toward the box hanging high in the corner. When she reached up to adjust the volume, she saw flowers thrown at Kermit as he was chauffeured down Colorado Boulevard in Pasadena in an old convertible Lincoln Continental.

"It's not so bad," she shot back, ignoring the spilled detergent pooled on the linoleum floor and the clumps of dryer lint floating along the baseboards like tumbleweeds. "I find the white noise of the machines relaxing. I sit and read my *People* and chill."

At that exact moment, a dark-haired toddler shrieked from the back of the room, "Mommy! Mommy! It's Kermie! It's Kermie!" startling Nicole. He wildly pointed at the television while sitting in one of the wheely wire laundry baskets, still in his footie pajamas.

"Uh huh," the mom said, barely paying attention. "Where's your brother?" she shouted over her shoulder as she wrangled a comforter from one of the industrial-sized dryers.

"Over here!" a second boy screamed, running out from behind a folding table at warp speed toward the boy in the basket, shoving the cart and slamming it against the cement walls. It halted with a *crash*, sending both boys erupting into howling laughter.

"Do it again!" the boy in the basket cried.

Jesse shot Nicole a look. "This is relaxing?" His face was flat.

"I'm just thankful they're not mine," Nicole mumbled as she walked by him to find a cart.

A minute later, Nicole wheeled two baskets from across the room to where Jesse had dropped her bag. He was quiet, hands shoved in his front pockets, chin sagging on his chest—all the usual signs of Jesse's annoyance. A look she knew well after spending so much time with him around Jeremy over the past decade of summers. It was one of the benefits of being with someone whose moods and reactions she already knew. After a few minutes, she knew he would be fine.

Nicole focused on sorting her lights and darks into the baskets. As the minutes ticked and his silence persisted, heaviness circled her chest. She was becoming more aggravated that Jesse couldn't rise above the minor irritations of kids yelling and dirty floors and just be happy being there with her.

The door rattled closed behind the mom, dragging her boys out in a huff, leaving Jesse and Nicole alone. Aside from the muffled TV, the only noise in the laundromat was Nicole turning her jeans inside out and the buzz of the fluorescent lights overhead.

"You can relax now. The animals are gone," Nicole said to break the quiet.

He faced the front door. "Yeah," he said.

She pulled out the last of her clothes from the bag. "Are you seriously annoyed about a couple of kids running around, making noise?" She couldn't take it anymore. "You can be such a curmudgeon sometimes."

He turned toward her, cracking his knuckles. A habit that had always grated on her. "No, it's not that. Seeing them triggered something from . . ." he began to say but stopped short. His expression brightened. "Umm. Never mind. I've lost my train of thought."

"What?" Nicole followed his line of sight to the black lace bra dangling from her hand, sending a brushfire of embarrassment to her face. "Oh!" she yelped, quickly burying it underneath a pair of jeans in the pile. "Maybe I didn't think a trip to the laundromat together all the way through."

A laugh escaped from his chest, visibly relaxing his frame.

"You started to say . . .?" Nicole said, bringing the conversation back to Jesse.

His shoulder bobbed. "It's not a big deal."

"Get it off your chest. I promise you'll feel better."

"It's going to sound so stupid."

"Try me," she said, loading her clothes into the machine.

Jesse leaned his shoulder against a washer near her, his arms crossed over his chest. "Those two little boys got to me." He blew out his cheeks.

"I know. I'm sorry about that. Sometimes parents let their kids run wild around here."

"No, that wasn't it. When I saw them having so much fun together, it hit me that I never had that kind of relationship with Jeremy growing up. Instead, he takes his father's lead and makes me look stupid any chance he can get."

Nicole laughed tenderly. "His father? I know you don't always like your dad, but he's your father, too."

He wagged his head slowly. "My whole life, the two of them have made me feel like an outcast, and my dad punishes me because I'm not his."

"His . . . what?"

"His." He hesitated. "His son," he said, his voice annoyed.

"What do you mean? Jimmy isn't your . . ." Her voice stalled. "What are you saying?"

"I'm saying Jimmy isn't my real father," he blurted out.

Her eyes widened. "What?"

"Yup," he said, dipping his chin.

Nicole's bottom lip hit the floor. "Oh, my God. I had no idea."

"I don't think many people do."

"Does Jeremy know?"

"I don't think so. If he did, he'd have a field day with me."

"I have always thought of your parents' relationship as the crown jewel of marriages." She had a million questions. "Did your mom tell you?"

He cracked his knuckles restlessly. *Pop. Pop. Pop.* "I overheard them fighting in the kitchen one night when I was like ten. They thought I was outside by the water, but I had come in through the basement sliders to get a towel. My dad was yelling at my mom about me doing something stupid. I remember my mom defending me, 'Oh, stop, he's a good kid, and you know it,' she yelled. And his response to her was, 'Don't turn this on me, Jeanie. I have always treated him like he was mine, but we both know he's not.'"

"Jesse! I'm so sorry." She grabbed his hand. "Do you have any idea who your father is?"

His eyes, rimmed with red, had a distant look to them.

"You never asked?"

He blinked several times before speaking. "My parents don't know that I know. And how would that go anyway? 'Hey, Mom, can you pass the syrup? Oh, and did you cheat on Dad?'"

Nicole could hear the agitation building in his voice, but she couldn't help herself. "Is Jeremy . . . theirs?" She regretted it as soon as she asked.

"Oh, he's theirs, all right. That's why he's the golden child. I'm the mistake." He blinked hard.

Nicole frowned as her heart sank. "There is nothing about you that is a mistake, Jesse." She watched him pace the floor. She wanted to drape over him like a weighted blanket, hugging his entire being. "Your father and . . ." she rephrased, "Jimmy and your brother are two of the most insecure people I know. It's like they have you on a perpetual teeter-totter, continuously putting you down to ensure they stay up. The problem for them is that for those paying attention, they're the ones who look like jerks. Not you. Not ever."

He released a sharp sigh, moving his vantage toward the ceiling, trying not to blink. "Why are families so difficult?"

"You wanna know what I think?"

"Sure."

"We're stronger people for it. I mean, who'd want a drama-free childhood with devoted parents who spoiled them with love and attention? We'd be so basic. So boring." She breathed off an easy laugh, moving closer to him.

He smiled a lopsided grin at her.

"And think about it. We'd never have met if it weren't for our dysfunctional families. So, some good came out of it."

She wrapped her arms around his waist and pulled him in tight. With her ear resting on his chest, she felt his heartbeat begin to regulate. "Thank you," he whispered, relaxing his arms on her shoulders and kissing her temple.

Then, a crazy idea popped into her head. "Get in the cart."

"What?"

"What part don't you understand?"

"The part where you told me to get into the cart."

"Just do it." She huffed. "You're going to have fun today, dammit."

He reluctantly walked over to the cart and straddled it like he was getting into a kayak. He plunked his butt inside it, leaving his legs hung over the sides.

"I can't believe I am doing this." His face was pained. "Now what?"

"Tuck your legs in."

He did as he was told and balled himself inside the cart. He looked ridiculous, but she would never tell him that. Once she was situated behind him, she gripped her hands on the rim of the basket and bent her legs in a runner's position. "Ready?"

He clutched the front of the cart, bracing himself. "Do I need a helmet?"

"You're giving me too much credit. I'm not that fast, don't worry," she said, cracking up. "You should be fine."

"*Should* . . ." he said just before she hauled off down the stretch of the laundromat. "Shit!"

Their giggles bounced off the metal machines as she hugged the first turn around the folding tables, roaring down the other side. But when they rounded the second turn, she got too cocky and took it too fast. The cart tipped onto two wheels, and she couldn't recover it. "Hold on!" she yelled as the cart and Jesse flipped. *Crash!*

"Jesse!" she screamed, dropping to her knees. He was lying on his side, his back to her, half in the cart. She hovered over him, "Jesse!" His body was shaking, but he didn't say anything. *Oh, my God. He's hurt!* "Jesse! Jesse!" She bridged her hands by his head, bracing herself not to put any of her weight on him. She didn't know if he was in pain. "Jesse! Say something."

Then she saw his bright red face, eyes squinted closed, mouth gaping open. "You're such a jerk!" she cried, pushing his side. His fit of laughter was so intense he was silent.

"I thought you were hurt," Nicole said, sitting back on her heels, relieved.

After a minute or so, he kicked out of the cart and worked his way over to her side. "Do it again," he said, echoing the little boy from earlier, sending himself into another fit.

Nicole joined him. Soon, tears were sliding off her chin, and she was snorting along. She never remembered a time when she saw Jesse laugh like that—except maybe when she was held hostage by a salamander. Seeing him clutch his sides with pure joy made her deliriously happy. Her cheeks hurt from smiling. *I did that.*

He used the heels of his hands to wipe the tears from the corners of his eyes. "Holy shit, that was amazing," he recovered, letting out a long breath. A wide grin spread across his face when he tapped her leg. "Look at you, being all crazy and fun."

No one in Nicole's life had ever called her fun. The word usually came in the form of a question— "Do you ever have fun?" or as a demand— "How about you lighten up and have some fun." She was different when she was with Jesse— she was unapologetically Nicole— who *was* fun.

He got to his knees and scooted himself in front of her. His eyes—a cheerful green—lowered to hers. "Thank you for that," he said, rubbing his hand over hers.

Her pulse fluttered under his touch. "Anytime," was all she could get out. Her brain struggled to compose a coherent sentence when he tilted her head to his face. He was close enough that she could smell hints of peppermint on his breath. The tips of her ears reddened with anticipation. She wanted to taste the candy cane flavor in his mouth. Their eyes, his locked, hers flirty, intertwined with each other and then jumped in tandem at the jarring buzz of the washing machine.

"Laundry's done," he said, moistening his lips.

"Yeah," she breathed.

He teased her with a kiss on the end of her nose. "I have a surprise."

"You know I hate surprises."

"Don't worry. You won't have to pretend to like this one. I am pretty sure it's a guarantee." He gave her a reassuring smile. "I didn't want you to miss another Italian cheesecake. Since we didn't have dessert last night, I went back inside the restaurant after you left and got some for us to have today."

"Jesse!" she squealed. "That is so sweet!" No guy had ever done anything like that for her. Although, in hindsight, the bar was pretty low. After a year with Matty, she was confident he didn't know her eye color, let alone her favorite dessert.

He pinched his lips shut. "Why the look?" she asked.

"I don't think I can bring myself to eat anything in this place."

She glanced around. "I'll give you that. How about we finish my laundry and then hang out at my place? Not much else open on New Year's Day."

"I like your thinking." He stood and reached for her hand, helping her to a stand. "How much do I owe you for the laundromat therapy session?"

"Initial consultation is free."

***

Jesse casually rested his hand on the gearshift and brushed his pinky against Nicole's hand to get her attention. His touch sent a ripple of excitement up her arm. "You've been awfully quiet since we left the laundromat. What's going on in that pretty head of yours over there?"

he asked, glancing at her before turning his attention back to the road. It had started to flurry, and a thin coating of snow covered the streets.

Nicole wouldn't dare admit to him that her mind was caught in a loop, repeatedly replaying their kiss, the best kiss of her life, as pleasure pulsed between her thighs.

"So, when do you find out about the engineering diving team?" she asked, diverting her attention.

"I should know by late spring. I still have more diving hours to complete, but the marine team doesn't start the scheduled inspections until May. So, I've got some time."

"I'm excited for you." She pulled the visor down to block the lowering sun bouncing off the falling flakes. "I can tell that it's something you want."

"I don't want to get my hopes up, but I've had a few conversations with my boss. He told me I have a pretty good chance," he said humbly, with a half-shrug. "If I make the team, I'd be the youngest member. That'd be kinda cool."

"Kinda? That would be awesome!" Nicole loved his ambition. It made him more attractive—hotter. She had always envisioned herself with someone like her—goal-oriented, knew where his next paycheck was coming from, and when he kissed her, it meant more than just a kiss. She couldn't believe he had been there the whole time.

"My sister will lose her mind when I tell her we went on a date." Nicole leaned her head back against the seat. She couldn't contain her smile.

"You didn't tell her? I thought you told her everything."

"I do . . . eventually. I told her I had a date but didn't tell her it was with you. She was already firing a ton of questions at me. If I told her it was you, it would have been a complete interrogation— 'Jesse? Like Jesse, Jesse? When did that happen? How did that happen? What are you wearing? Have you kissed him yet? What time is he picking you up? Where are you going?' I was already on the verge of throwing up the entire time I was getting ready. She would have put me over the edge."

He arched a questioning eyebrow in her direction. "The thought of going out with me made you want to throw up?"

"Lately, yes," she nodded, chuckling. She was surprised by her admission.

His lips quirked. "Don't feel bad. I popped a couple of Tums before I got in the car last night," he admitted. "I know my mom will be ecstatic. I can't tell you how many times she has said to me, 'What about you and Nic? Why don't you ask her out?'"

"What? Jeanie?" Love and acceptance filled her.

"She told me that my personality changes when you're around. That I'm a different person—happy."

"How does that make you feel?"

"She's not wrong," he said truthfully. "You're like those sunflowers in your kitchen. You make the day brighter just by being there."

"Have you been spending time at the Hallmark store?" she deflected.

"It wasn't nearly as cheesy in my head."

Nicole watched Jesse wither. She never could take a compliment but didn't intend to make him feel self-conscious. "Well, if it makes you feel any better, I thought it was a brie-utiful sentiment."

"Not really. That was a horrible pun."

"But now you feel better about your sunflower comment." She grinned.

Jesse rolled his hand under Nicole's and curled his fingers through hers. "I am crazy about you, Nic."

"Is it because of my cheese jokes?"

"They help."

"You must know, I'm nacho ordinary girl."

The corner of his mouth pulled up. "Is this over yet?"

"The gouda news is that the longer this goes on, the cheddar the jokes get." His smile turned into a full-fledged grin, and then the two of them erupted.

"Sorry. Sorry." She cleared her throat. "You were being serious. I think you were saying something about being crazy about me before I rudely interrupted you," she said, struggling to hold in her giggles.

He turned left into Nicole's neighborhood, palming the steering wheel with one hand, leaving his other in hers. The road was home to large colonial houses tucked back from the curb, partially hidden behind mature pine and maple trees.

"I don't want to play around. I want you to be my girl." He squeezed her hand.

Her heart tripped over itself. Suddenly, being in a relationship with Jesse became real.

She opened her mouth to speak, pausing to think for a minute. "Did you take Psych 101 at Wheeler?"

Jesse shot her a confused look. "Yeah. Like four years ago. Why?"

"Do you remember Maslow's Hierarchy of Needs?"

"Vaguely."

She was quiet again.

According to Maslow's Hierarchy, a person's need for safety must be satisfied before moving up to the next rung on the pyramid—love. She had a job, her own money, and was in good health, but she questioned her confidence in her personal security.

How did she know, with complete conviction, that the foundation she had spent the last seven months building wasn't on a bed of sand like the Leaning Tower of Pisa? Would she notice if she started to fall back before it was too late?

Or maybe she was just stalling.

"We're here," Jesse said, startling Nicole from her distant thoughts.

Nicole squinted out the window, surprised to see her apartment. She had no memory of the second half of the drive. She was too focused on deciding how she would answer Jesse. If she couldn't find a way to get past her fear of intimacy, they didn't have a future, and she'd have to tell him that.

He gave her hand a small kiss before letting go. "I've got a little something for you in the back."

"You've done enough already today," she said. *And I don't like surprises!*

"Well, hopefully, it will keep you from continuing to psychoanalyze us." He chuckled and then got out of the car.

She jokingly sighed loud enough for him to hear.

"Can you please let me do something for you without you putting up a fight? Sheesh," he said, closing the trunk. He met her on the sidewalk and handed her a large box wrapped in green and red striped wrapping paper. "Here, you take this, and I'll grab your clothes and the dessert." He pulled a handled bag from the cooler on the floor of his car and hoisted her laundry bag over his shoulder. "After you, my dear," he said, motioning to the stairs.

"What's in the box?" she asked. Curiosity was killing her.

"If I told you, it wouldn't be much of a present, would it?"

"True. But why are you buying me presents anyway?" she asked, unlocking her door.

They stomped and wiped the snow off their shoes on the welcome mat before walking inside. "I bought it after we ran into each other at the Y. I hoped I'd see you before Christmas so you could open it that morning."

She flicked on the ceiling lights in her apartment and headed toward the kitchen table, setting the box down. "Now you're making me feel bad for not calling you sooner."

"Then my plan is working."

She shucked off her coat and threw it on the chair. "Can I open it?"

"Of course." Her bag slid off his shoulder and thumped like a dead body onto the floor. "But now I'm worried you'll be disappointed when you see what it is."

She tore through the wrapping like a kid on Christmas morning. "A coffee maker?"

"I know how much you like your coffee, so I wanted to make sure you were never without it."

"You have got to be one of the most thoughtful people I have ever met." Her chest caved in. "First, the cheesecake, and now this. Thank you."

"I'm glad you like it."

"I love it!" she said too enthusiastically.

"I'll use it for my three o'clock caffeine fix on the weekends once I figure out how to use it. I have never made coffee in my life."

He turned the box to show her the features. "It has a timer, so you can have your coffee ready when you wake up every day, not just on the weekends."

"Oh. But I get my morning coffee at Zuke's."

Nicole watched the muscles in his jaw flex, leaving her to wonder what sore spot she had just poked. "Right." He dropped the box on the table. His face had disappointment written all over it. "What's up with you and that guy?"

"Jesse, I told you before, he's a nice guy who makes great coffee." His posture was hunched over one of the kitchen chairs as if she had punched him in the gut. Guilt kneaded her core thinking about the night she kissed Zuke. She wouldn't dare admit it to Jesse. "That's it."

"Um-hum."

Her eyebrows pulled together. "Wait. Is that why you bought this for me? Because you don't want me around Zuke?"

"I bought it to remind you of when we ran into each other at the deli, and I bought you your coffee," he explained.

"Jesse Young, you're not getting jealous on me, are you?"

His chin slumped with his shoulders. "I saw how he looked at you that day." His hands were halfway into his front pockets.

Nicole walked over to him. "He's a good friend. That's it. I promise." She rested her chin on his chest. His eyes were hardened. She smiled at him reassuringly, hooking her finger around his pinky. "I'm here with you, right?"

Jesse slipped his hand into hers. His cemented face eased when she squeezed it, conveying her choice to be with him.

"Good. That's settled." She walked to the kitchen drawer and grabbed two forks. "How about some cheesecake?"

"The reviews say it's the best in the county."

Nicole popped open the container and stared at two precisely cut slices of creamy cheesecake resting on a bed of graham cracker crust, drenched in a bright red raspberry compote flowing down the sides.

With her fork, she pierced the tip of one of the pieces, making sure to get a gooey raspberry in her bite. "I'll be the judge of that." Her eyes grew wide as the dessert melted on her tongue. "Oh God, this is amazing. Italian cheesecake usually isn't this creamy," she garbled, shielding her mouth with her hand.

His smile broadened with approval. "I'm glad you like it."

She cut off a taste for him. "Here, you have to try this. I think there's lemon in there," she said, offering to feed him.

"Ooh!" he howled at the taste, sucking in his cheeks. "That's really tart. Too tart for me. It's all yours," he chuckled, pushing the container closer to her.

"Fine by me." She gladly took another bite, angling herself against the counter, savoring the dessert. And Jesse.

Glancing up, she caught his eye. A flicker of pleasure played across his lips as she slowly pulled the fork from her mouth. "You never answered my question," he reminded her.

"Which was?" she asked, trying to buy more time.

He walked the few steps over to her. "I want us to be together. I want you to be my girlfriend."

"I'm scared," she blurted.

"I know. Me too." He pushed a loose strand of hair away from her face, exposing her worried look. His nearness overwhelmed her, sending her thoughts rolling around in her conscience. He leaned in and dropped his voice to a murmur, heat pumped from his skin. "But I'm more happy than scared, and I think you have a lot of good things running through your head when you think about us, too."

She felt herself dissolving as she drew in his woodsy essence, tangled with the clean scent of soap radiating from his neck. "Oh, yeah. Like what?"

He skimmed his hands down her sides, grazing them along her hips until he straightened up, effortlessly hoisting her onto the counter.

"Oh!" she let out a nervous cry. "I wasn't expecting that."

She saw his eyes slowly scan her face like he was gathering data. "I think you're intrigued about us."

She grinned. "Who's psychoanalyzing who now?" Her thighs settled loosely around his hips as he moved in, closing the space between them.

"I think you wonder what we could be," he said, flipping his baseball hat backward.

With her legs straddled around him, she was acutely aware of the heaviness building between her thighs.

"I think when you let yourself imagine us together, you get excited. That we feel right." Goosebumps ran up her arms.

Without the cap's brim casting a shadow on his face, his hazel eyes shined a bold emerald color. He leaned closer, bracing himself on the counter. She ran the tip of her tongue nervously along her bottom lip, her throat working hard to swallow.

"I think you like it when I tease you." His mouth hovered over hers. "And you wonder why we waited so long."

Her breath was shallow. She was getting flustered.

"How am I doing so far?" he asked, seemingly tracking her thoughts. He ran his thumb along her lip, still wet from her tongue.

Her eyes fluttered shut, she let out a small breath. "Not bad," she said quietly, sliding her arms around his neck. She waited for her body to recoil, but it didn't. She was okay. She was better than okay. *I can do this!*

With his hands on her hips, he pulled her to the edge of the counter, crushing his body and lips to hers. Nothing could have prepared her for the explosion of his kiss, full of intensity and need. His arms slid up her back, snaking around her possessively. She gave into him, wrapping her legs around him, their hips drawing together like magnets. Her eagerness to feel his thickness through her flimsy leggings surprised her.

He ran his tongue along the seam of her lips, cueing her to open her mouth. She loved the silky feel of his tongue rubbing against hers, completely consuming her as he angled her mouth and kissed her deeper. The tartness of the raspberries and lemons still lingered. She clung to him, losing herself, never wanting the kiss to end.

He pulled back and gave her bottom lip a playful bite before his mouth trailed along her neck, sending a tickle down her spine. Slowly, he kissed his way up from the hollow of her collarbone—his breath warm and close to her ear. She bit her lip to quiet a moan.

And then, like a sucker punch, the intensity triggered her. A warning shot fired off in her head, commanding her to slow down. It was too much, too fast. She needed to stop.

"Wait," she said reluctantly.

He froze. "I'm sorry, I didn't mean to . . . I'm sorry."

"No. No. No," she whispered into his opened lips. "You didn't do anything wrong." She silenced his apology with a tender kiss.

"Are you sure?"

Nicole fanned herself. Her swollen lips stung from his stubble. In a good way. "Yeah. I just need to take a break. Getting hot in here." She smiled.

He drew her into his arms. With her chin resting on his shoulder, she felt his face crack into a grin. "So, is that a yes?"

She pulled away to see his face, sliding her hands onto his chest. "I can't argue with anything you said. When I overthink us, I worry we're making a mistake. But when I shut off my mind, I want this. Us."

If she didn't take the chance, wasn't she still giving her power to someone else, continuing to stoke the victim flame? There were no guarantees, but if she was going to take the risk and move up a rung on Maslow's pyramid, she wanted it to be with the one person who made her feel the most secure—Jesse. She owed it to herself to try.

"I want to say yes." Embarrassment and excitement pulled at her insides. "But if I told you that we need to take it slow, like at a snail's pace, would you still want to be with me?" She felt guilty for having to ask for his patience without giving him an explanation. But it was going to have to be enough for him.

He didn't waver for a second. "I don't care. If it means I get to spend more time with you and have days like today, I'm in."

"So, if I'm your girlfriend . . . I think that makes you my boyfriend." Her voice was calculated like she was working through a math problem.

The corner of his mouth ticked up. "I'm pretty sure that's how it works."

She leaned into him and smiled against his mouth. "I like it." She gave him a peck. "A lot."

| 33 |

Jesse

With his hands full, Jesse used his hip to close his car door, setting off a lone dog yapping in the distance. Glancing up at the front of Nicole's apartment, he was excited to see her that afternoon. The early spring sky was overcast, turning everything gray except his mood. It had been over a week since she had left for a business trip with her team to London and the same number of days since he had spoken to her. He was so proud of her for being handpicked by one of the partners at the firm for the engagement, but the time difference and their busy schedules had kept them apart, and it was wearing on him.

Jesse walked toward the stairs, his mind adrift with the feelings of Nicole in his arms and the intoxicating thought of their bodies pressed together. His daydream vanished when Claire appeared in a dark purple tracksuit powerwalking on the sidewalk toward him. "Hi, Claire," he said, flipping his hand up, trying not to drop his tool bag.

Claire stopped in front of him, continuing to walk in place, pumping her arms. "Hi Jesse!" she shouted over the *shushing* noise of her windbreaker. "What brings you by? I don't think Nicole is coming home until later today."

"She doesn't. I came by early to fix some things upstairs before she got here. And, of course, to feed the caaa . . . Nicole." *Shit! Claire doesn't know about Noodle and CC.* "Going to bring in some dinner. I know she'll be tired and in no mood to go out."

"Aww. That explains the wine and sunflowers, then." She wagged her finger at him. "I knew you were a keeper the first day I met you."

He politely smiled. "She doesn't know I'm here. It's our three-month anniversary today. Want to surprise her."

"You've been spending a lot of time here lately. I may have to start charging you rent." Jesse let out an uncomfortable laugh. "I could use the extra cash. Millie has been on a winning streak down at the senior center. My poker funds are running low."

"Maybe you need to learn when to fold 'em."

Clair wasn't nearly as amused as Jesse was with himself. "Well, you kids have fun tonight. I've got to finish my walk, and you have a couple of felines to feed." She winked at Jesse and powerwalked away.

Once inside, he put his things on the table, including his newly minted key to Nicole's apartment that she gave him before she left. He rubbed his thumb over the engraving on the silver heart-shaped key chain—*Jesse & Nic 01.01.1996.*

He heard the weight of the cats jumping off the bed. "Hey guys," he said, greeting them in the kitchen. CC slinked in a figure-eight around Jesse's legs while Noodle strutted over to the empty food dish, only to turn back and give him a shameful look. "What's the matter, Noodle? Hungry?"

While Jesse put out the fresh food and water for the cats, he stirred, thinking about how unfulfilled his days were when he wasn't with Nicole. Being in her apartment alone only made it worse. Her personality and personal touches were everywhere, but it was missing her beautiful face and her positive energy that somehow reached every corner of the room when she was there. It was like he could see her, but she was just past his reach.

He knew she would be home in no time if he kept himself preoccupied with his projects. "CC, where do you think Nic keeps that metal vase she uses for fresh flowers?" he asked, searching the cabinet under the sink. "Found it!" He found some tea lights, too. "These will be perfect for dinner."

A few minutes later, pleased with his arrangement, he placed the vase filled with a dozen coaster-sized sunny yellow blooms in the middle of the table, reminiscent of their first date at Giancarlo's.

Plodding around the kitchen, cleaning up the flower ends and paper cellophane wrapping, he recognized his bold script on the crumpled receipt, tacked to the refrigerator by an oversized sunflower magnet. His heart waxed remembering the day he gave her his phone number.

Next to the receipt were two pictures. The first was a yellowed Polaroid of Nic and Jamie in their bathing suits, wet hair slicked back into hardened candy-like shells, with their arms clinched around each other so tight it was like they were holding on to each other for dear life. Metaphorically, they probably were. Jesse recognized the lake house shoreline in the backdrop and gathered it was the first summer they had stayed with his family after their father died.

The second photo was of Jesse and Nicole, huddled together on a cow print painted swing outside Nicole's favorite ice cream shop in Saratoga. It was taken a few days before Valentine's Day earlier that year. Their smiles were so big they barely fit in the frame.

He had offered to take her out to eat for Valentine's Day, but she insisted, "No more fancy dinners. I want a gigantic waffle cone full of coffee ice cream topped with chocolate sprinkles and to be with you." They had joked about her order of importance.

In the picture, he saw the silver bracelet he had given her that day during their stroll through Congress Park. He had two charms added to get her started—a heart for Valentine's Day and a horseshoe representing Saratoga, one of their favorite towns to visit for its downtown vibe and historical equestrian charm. His heart pulsed, thinking about how her face shined when the bracelet first jingled on her wrist. "When you hear the chime, that means I'm thinking about you," he told her.

"Been spending more time at the Hallmark store?" she teased with a kiss.

Jesse smiled at the memory. "Next project, Noodle—living room furniture. We want to make sure Nic doesn't crash to the floor one of these days." He grabbed his tool bag and got to work, drilling pilot holes in the coffee table.

The minutes waiting for Nicole felt like hours ticking by, unlike the lightning speed of their last three months together—the best three months of his life. Jesse couldn't remember another time when he felt loved, accepted, or wanted.

As Jesse and Nicole predicted, his mother was thrilled about the news of the two of them— "Finally!" she cheered. And Jamie had a ton of questions— "When? How? I need details!"

Nicole admitted to Jesse that Jamie was initially skeptical and, therefore, suggested the two couples go to dinner to ease Jamie's concerns. For Jesse, the dinner was more like a cross-examination. Before they ordered drinks, Jamie had dived into her prepared list of questions. "What was your relationship like with your last girlfriend? Why did you guys break up? What do you like most about Nicole?"

It was her parting words that stuck with him the most. "I like you two together. You have my permission to date my sister. But be sure, if you hurt her . . ." She shot him a scowl. "I will hunt you down and kill you." Jesse looked to Randy and Nicole for confirmation and found both nodding.

Jesse's thoughts were interrupted by the sound of the coffee table legs hitting the floor. He gave a slight push to the tabletop to test his handy work. It didn't move. *Perfect.* He gave a little bounce on the couch with his seat, and the creaking was gone, too. *Nice.* Proud of his work, he collected his tools and returned to the kitchen to wash his hands.

Next to the sink was the coffeemaker, prominently displayed on the counter. His blooming smile quickly faded when he noticed the packing tape on the handle of the carafe, suggesting that it had been barely used—if at all. When he flipped open the water tank lid, he found a chunk of white Styrofoam still inside. A stabbing sensation punctured his chest.

"How's the coffeemaker working out? You like it?" he had asked Nicole a few weeks ago.

"I'm still trying to figure out the right number of scoops. It's either too weak or strong enough to grow hair on my chest," she joked. *She lied to me?*

All the warmth and love he felt earlier quickly repackaged itself into hurt and anger. *Fucking Zuke.* Without thinking, he grabbed his apartment key and walked out the door. Clouds darkened the sky as he headed down the sidewalk to pay Zuke a visit.

* * *

The bell chimed over Jesse's head when he pushed open the door to the deli. It was lunchtime, and the place was buzzing. With his hands coiled into tight balls, he found a spot in line behind a group of construction workers wearing the same energy company logos on their jackets. His temper burned like a fire under his skin as he sized up Zuke, who was bustling behind the counter. To Jesse, he appeared to be average at best. He wasn't particularly tall. Brown hair, brown eyes—ordinary. *He's such a douche.*

Jesse believed his own bullshit as long as he ignored the fact that Zuke was a relatively young guy, running a successful business, seamlessly conversing with his customers, not to mention his chiseled arms and chest that looked like he bench-pressed refrigerator at night.

By the time it was Jesse's turn, he was practically foaming at the mouth. "Hey man, what can I get for you?" Zuke asked, wiping his hands on the towel hanging from his apron.

Jesse jammed his fists in his front pockets and jerked his chin toward the sleeve of paper cups. "I'll start with a coffee."

"How do you like it?"

"I'll take Nicole's usual. You know what that is, right?"

Zuke narrowed his eyes. "Nicole? You a friend of hers?" he asked. There was a tightness in his features.

Jesse lets out a sarcastic chuckle. "Yeah, boyfriend."

"Ah," Zuke said, adding a splash of whole milk to the cup. "Funny. Nicole never mentioned she had a boyfriend."

"Probably doesn't come up when she pops in."

Zuke shrugged. "Maybe. But she didn't mention it when she was here helping me with my books a few weeks ago, either."

Jesse felt an invisible punch to the gut. *Books?* "It's obvious you want more than coffee with her. She probably didn't want to hurt your feelings. She's good like that."

"She said that?"

"No, but you and I know." Jesse wagged his finger between the two of them. "Don't worry. It will be our little secret." He paused. "It's ironic how you're hot for her, but she fell for me in your deli last summer."

Zuke shrugged. "Well, it has been great catching up. Anything else? I've got a line of customers to get to."

"Yeah." Jesse bent down to get a better view of the prepared food displayed in the clear case. "Nicole comes home today, and I've got a special night planned for us," Jesse said, dragging his fingers along the pristine glass, deliberately leaving smudge marks. "I'll take four of those meatballs and a container of the mixed green salad." He stood upright and noticed the Italian bread in the wire baskets along the wall. "And a seeded loaf."

"My meatballs are one of Nic's favorites. Good choice."

Nic? One of her favorites? What the fuck? Flashes of green clouded Jesse's vision, bitterness relentlessly tearing at him like mosquitoes on a humid summer night.

Jesse glared up at Zuke to get his total but instead found Zuke curling his index finger, beckoning Jesse closer. Jesse leaned in. "You know, if you pissed a circle around her, guys would know to stay away. It'd be a lot less embarrassing for you," Zuke whispered in a voice loud enough for others in the deli to hear.

The construction workers openly snickered. Rage singed Jesse's face, his neck, his heart. He threw two twenties on the counter and grabbed the bag. "Fuck you, pal," he said, slamming the door behind him.

***

Jesse paced the apartment, boiling over into a sweat. *Nic is your girlfriend. Nothing is going on with that guy. He's fucking with you. It's Nic. She wouldn't do that.* With a trembling hand, Jesse picked up the glass coffee carafe and smashed it against the wall, shattering it and all the feelings that had been building inside him.

Regretful tears pricked his eyelids. Nicole would be home in less than a half hour, and he didn't want her to see the evidence of his outburst. *Shit! Shit! Shit!*

He scrambled around, searching the closets for something to clean up the glass. He found a small broom and dustpan under the sink and frantically swept up his mess. Shards were everywhere—on the counter, the table, the cats' food bowl. *Pull your shit together. She can't come home to this.*

Once he was sure he found every sliver, he got to work setting the table. CC emerged from the bedroom, crisscrossing between his legs as he lit the tealights. "I'm sorry, CC, I didn't mean to scare you earlier," he said, scratching her under the chin. "Sometimes, I can't control my temper. It happens." He could feel the vibration of a low purr building inside of her. He took it as acceptance of his apology.

Moments later, there was a click of a car door opening outside, rocketing him to his feet. "I think she's home, CC!" He ran to the living room window, pulling back the sheers. His heartbeat pounded. "It's her!" he yelled in a loud whisper, watching her lift herself out of the cab. He dimmed the lights to the apartment on his way out the door.

Running down the stairs two at a time, he made it to the sidewalk in seconds. "Thank you," he heard her say to the cab driver, who was getting back into his car. Jesse's eyes were glued to Nicole, watching her swing her tote bag onto her shoulder and telescope her suitcase handle. He was expecting to see her in more casual clothes, yoga pants maybe, but was struck by how professional and mature she looked all dressed up—long cardigan sweater and houndstooth stirrup pants with ballet flats. It was a side of her he hadn't seen before. A jealous pang knocked, leaving him wondering if Zuke saw her that way every morning.

She was moving tiredly when Jesse approached her from behind. "I can help you with that," he said, startling her.

Nicole turned with surprise on her face. "Jesse!" she cried, letting go of her suitcase handle and jumping into his arms. "You scared me. I didn't know you were here!"

"I couldn't wait to see you," he said, ratcheting his hold around her. "I hope it's okay that I am here."

"It's more than okay." He felt her heart fluttering against his chest. She missed him, too.

Jesse lifted her from her tiptoes to his lips. "Can we talk while I kiss you? It's all I wanted to do for the last week," he whispered into her mouth. His soul slowly reinflated at her taste, her touch, her scent. She was no longer out of reach.

The dark clouds overhead finally gave way, and fat drops the size of nickels started raining on them. Nicole slid down Jesse to her feet. He groaned inwardly at the feel of her body moving against his. "Yuck. More rain. That's all it did in London. It's like it followed me home," she said.

"Let's get you inside. I've got a surprise for you that should brighten you up," he said.

She grinned. "You and your surprises."

He gave her a peck on the lips, then ran behind her up the stairs with her suitcase in hand. She hesitated to open the door. "Can I go in?"

He pushed the door open for her. "After you." He smiled.

Two steps into the apartment, and she *gasped*. Her hands covered her mouth. "Jesse!"

He was so focused on preparing dinner after wasting time cleaning up his mess that he never got to admire the table. Seeing it from Nicole's point of view, he impressed himself. The dozens of tealights illuminated the table, and the two wine glasses filled, ready to be sipped. The table was set for a proper meal, with napkins, silverware, and real plates. But the best part was the vase of sunflowers standing tall in the middle with their faces pointing toward Nicole as if she were the sun.

From behind, Jesse circled his arms around her and kissed the side of her face. "Happy anniversary," he hummed.

"You did all this for me?"

He let out a huff. "It certainly wasn't for me."

She pulled away, dropping her tote. "I've got to get a closer look. Did you cook? It smells amazing in here," she said, dashing into the kitchen. "I haven't had a real meal in over a week. The food in London was horrible. I'm still not sure what toad in the hole is."

He followed her. "I take no credit for the food. I got us takeout."

She lingered over the table and inhaled. "Meatballs. Yum."

"Zuke told me they were your favorite. With that kind of endorsement, how could I not get them for you?"

She hesitated, still hunched over the plates. "You went to Zuke's?"

He shrugged. "I had time to kill before you got home, so I went for a coffee. I don't remember it being so great, but you always rave about it, so I thought I'd give it another try," he said, feigning innocence. "I happened to mention your name to him, and then we got to chatting. That's when he told me about the meatballs." Heat burned down his back like a lit fuse. *Dude, shut up.*

She stood up, avoiding eye contact. "Oh."

He swallowed hard against his restlessness. "And the coffee," he paused, "I can see why you don't bother making your own."

You couldn't help yourself, could you? You're such an asshole.

His throat worked to swallow again, following her eyes to the coffeemaker on the counter. "Where's the coffeepot?"

"I'm sorry, I was moving it, and it cracked. Does it matter, anyway?" Nicole squared her shoulders and crossed her arms. "I'm getting the sense that this has nothing to do with coffee." He could tell she was pissed.

"Why'd you lie to me?" His voice got louder. "You told me that you had tried the machine. And not just once. A few times."

Her gaze dropped to the floor.

He continued. "This afternoon, I was going to make a pot for when you got home, thinking you might be tired." His voice raised. "But when I opened the top, there was still packaging inside. What the hell, Nic?" A strangled noise came from him.

"Jesse . . . I'm so sorry. I wasn't trying to hurt you. It's just . . ." She hesitated. "I've been working like crazy and never know my schedule. My morning routine is the only thing I have control over in my life right now. It wasn't about you. I'm sorry."

"You say you're so busy yet have time to help *him* with his books?"

The color drained out of her face. He watched her chew at her bottom lip.

"Is something going on with you two?" Venom snaked up his throat. "Just tell me."

"Honestly?"

"No, please lie to me again," he shot back.

She blew out a breath. "We kissed once."

The words shredded his heart. "I fucking knew it," he said through gritted teeth. "Since we've been together?"

"Jesse! Of course not. Do you know me *at all*?" She reached for his hand. "Let me explain."

His hand hung by his side like a dead fish. He refused to hold hers.

"As it was happening, it didn't make sense why I was there with him because all I wanted was to be with you. Right after it happened, I ran home and called you."

"And since then?"

"Since then, yes, I have helped him with his books—his accountant had a heart attack, and he needed help for a couple of days. I worked at the counter, in plain sight. I promise you, since that night, it has been strictly coffee and taxes. He's a friend. That's it. I didn't want to tell you about the kiss because it didn't mean anything to me, and I knew all it would do was upset you." Her expression was heavy with remorse.

Jesse considered her long and hard. She stopped biting her lip and looked him in the eye. "If I wanted to be with him, I'd be with him. But I don't. I want to be here with you." He believed her.

"I never want you to feel like you need to lie to me. You can tell me anything." He wasn't expecting to say the words, but they flowed out of his mouth. "I love you."

"Did you hear yourself?"

He couldn't remember a time when he didn't love her. "I did, and I'll say it again. I love you, Nic."

She smiled up at him. "Well, that's a relief because I love you, too, Jesse," she said, moving in closer and kissing him. "I'm sorry."

"Next time, take the Styrofoam out. I would have at least thought you tried." He cradled her head in his hands. "I am sorry that I got nasty with you. I was upset. I'm sure the last thing you wanted today was to come home and fight with me."

"No, no. This has been great."

He threaded his fingers through her hair, pushing it away from her face. The amber flecks rimming her brown eyes caught the light of the candle. "It kills me thinking about you kissing someone else."

"Well, stop thinking about someone else and kiss me yourself." His jealousy cooled.

Her mouth opened to his. He didn't tease her for it. He devoured her lips into his, lightly at first, pulling away, then slipping his tongue into her mouth, wrapping it around hers. *Mine.*

Nicole drew back from his lips, catching her breath as his mouth strayed. He didn't know how long he would only be able to kiss her. "I fucking love everything about you," he rasped into the hollow of her neck.

"C'mere," she whispered, asking for his lips to be back on hers. Their mouths moved in tandem, tongues sliding against each other in long strokes. Jesse's hands traveled up her curves, grazing his thumb along her nipple. She sucked in her teeth, her hand pulling at his fleece, bringing him closer. His shaft pulsated against his zipper at her purring.

Nicole moved her hands to his lower back, sliding them underneath his shirt and finding his bare skin. He flinched at her touch. "Your hands are cold," he said, softly chuckling without breaking their kiss.

"Sorry. Is this better?" she asked, pressing her palms flush against his torso.

His skin came alive. "You're evil!"

"Just having fun," she said, stifling a yawn. "Oh, geez. I'm sorry," she said, clapping the back of her hand up to her mouth.

"You've had a long day, babe. Let me show you my other surprises before you pass out," he said, grabbing her hand and leading her into the living room.

"Babe?" Amusement puckered her lips. "I like it."

He gave her a quick kiss. "Have a seat. Put your feet up on the table."

She did as she was told. "Now what?"

"Did you hear anything?"

Her eyebrows jumped. "No squeak!" She shifted the weight of her legs, trying to sway the coffee table. "It doesn't move! You fixed it! You did all this for me?"

Her joy made him feel needed. He glowed proudly. "I told you, I love doing things for you. I love you. Get used to it." He gave her knee a loving nudge. "Are you hungry?"

She kicked off her shoes and pulled her feet under her. "Not yet. How about you bring the wine over? Come sit with me."

He grabbed the glasses and met her on the couch.

She leaned in and gave him a soft kiss. "To us," she said, clinking his glass. After one sip, she put her wine on the table and grabbed the TV remote. "Here, you pick something. I'm going to take a quick cat nap. Wake me in twenty minutes."

Nicole cushioned her head with her hands and rested it on his lap. She was asleep faster than he could click the power button.

He pulled a soft knit blanket from the top of the couch and gently draped it over her, careful not to wake her. In the light of the TV, he noticed a shimmer of silver on her wrist—her charm bracelet. He softly batted the heart, listening to it quietly jingle against the horseshoe. *She loves me.* He forced the rising lump back down his throat. *And I almost fucked it all up.*

"Sweet dreams, babe. I love you."

| 34 |

Nicole

"You're here early," Danielle, the staffing coordinator and office busybody, told Nicole, looking at her watch. "Gosh, I feel like we haven't chatted since you returned from London. You've been so busy. How was it?"

Nicole shot her a nasty look at the same time she yanked her chair out from underneath the desk in the cubicle next to Danielle's, throwing her tote bag on the floor with a *clonk*. She was in no mood for chit-chat that morning, especially with Danielle, who only ever wanted to *chat* when she was about to spring an unexpected client engagement on her. Nicole had worked nonstop for the past five months, including late nights and weekends, and needed a break. "Fine," Nicole said, her voice spiked with irritation.

Danielle stopped typing and peered over her red-rimmed glasses at Nicole. "I'd love to go there one day. I've barely left Albany. My uncle went there once. He swore he saw the Queen at the supermarket."

Doubtful.

"Sounds like he had an eventful trip," Nicole said, disinterested.

Nicole plunked down in her seat. After a few silent moments, she took a long, regretful breath. She knew Danielle wasn't her problem. Nicole's annoyance had been building for the last four weeks since she and Jesse fought about Zuke. While Jesse didn't outright ask Nicole to find a new place to get her caffeine fix, he didn't leave her much choice either. That morning had been her third try at a new deli in as many weeks, and all their coffee tasted the same—like pond water. She could buy a replacement coffeemaker, but out of principle, she wasn't about to buy something she didn't want in the first place.

She loved Jesse, and spending time with Zuke made him uncomfortable, but her beloved routine was out of sorts, which didn't sit well with her. She didn't like someone else controlling her morning—intentionally or not. It made her feel unnecessarily uncomfortable. Zuke was a good friend—who happened to make fantastic coffee—that was it.

"London wasn't as glamorous as you might think. I spent eight days in a windowless conference room working until one a.m. every night," Nicole said. "I might've forgotten I was in the U.K. if it weren't for the British accents and everyone drinking tea."

Maybe Nicole should consider tea to solve her caffeine problem.

Nicole began to untie her sneakers and change into her heels when Danielle said, "So . . ." *I knew it.* "You've been assigned to the Capital Transportation job. You start Monday."

"Seriously?" Nicole groaned. "I just planned a spa day with my sister next week. Is there any possibility that someone else could take it?" Nicole loved her job but was burned out and needed some well-deserved downtime.

"Nope. Besides, it wouldn't matter anyway. Dave specifically requested you." Nicole knew it would happen sooner or later. He didn't seem like the type to give her a pass. If anything, he enjoyed the power.

"Anyone else on the engagement with us?" Nicole held her breath, waiting for the answer.

"No. It's a small job. Just the two of you."

Nicole sigh-laughed when an image of Dave flashed in her mind. He was in his usual crisp button-down and cuff links, except his slicked-back hair was replaced with Blade's helmet. A mischievous smile made her mouth twitch. *Bring it on, Dave. I'm not afraid of you and your donuts.*

"Great."

Nicole's chest felt lighter. Confidence carried less weight than the annoyance of the morning. Out the large office window, a thick, fluffy cloud drifted across the bright blue sky. The office suddenly felt stuffy. Still chuckling to herself, Nicole stood up sharply. "You know what, it's still early. I'm going for a walk outside. I'll be back in a little while," she informed Danielle.

"Oh, good. I'll go with you. I have to drop my bills off at the post office."

Nicole was hoping to rejoice in her tiny victory alone. "Um. Well, I'm leaving now," she said, hoping Danielle would tell her to go ahead without her.

"I'm ready. Let's go," Danielle said, standing up with a stack of envelopes in her hand.

* * *

Nicole and Danielle walked side-by-side on the gravel pathway in the park across the street from their office building, meandering through the pristinely manicured lawns. Nicole tuned out Danielle, who was busy rattling off all the office gossip she missed while away.

It was early May, one of Nicole's favorite months. The tree buds began taking shape, and the bulbs were blooming. As cliché as 'Every cloud has a silver lining,' spring signified revival and growth—very representative of her life over the past year.

Along the path, they passed the tens of thousands of vibrant colored tulips, standing at attention, cordoned off by decorative black iron chains. Her nose was stunned by the sweetly potent scent of the purple hyacinth.

But Nicole was robbed of her moment when they crested a small knoll near the pond in the middle of the park, and she was faced with a man in a business suit charging her on his bike, forcing her to jump onto the lawn to avoid being taken out by him. "Gee-zus!" she shouted.

"Get out of the way!" he roared back.

Nicole's face flamed when Danielle snickered next to her. "What happened to people driving to work?" Nicole asked, shaking her head.

Back on the path, she noticed a shirtless runner approaching them. "Like, check out this guy, running in his scrubs," she said, motioning toward him with her chin.

"Maybe there's an emergency," Danielle guessed.

Nicole scoffed. "Or he's super insecure and is starving for attention."

"He certainly has mine," Danielle said, tongue wagging. She fanned her face with the envelopes as he ran by them. "Holy smokes, that man is H. O. T!"

"He can hear you," Nicole said without moving her lips.

He flashed a smile mostly seen in toothpaste ads. "Nic?"

Danielle elbowed her when she didn't respond. "He's talking to you," Danielle whispered out of the side of her mouth.

Nicole shielded the sun from her squinted eyes with her hand. She didn't recognize him at first—polarized wrap-around sunglasses, manscaped chest hair. But once he pushed his glasses onto the top of his head, everything fell into place in rapid succession—jet-black wavy mane that made JFK Jr look like he was going bald, ice blue eyes sharp enough to cut glass, and a cocky smile like he owned the park. *That's no doctor. That's Rob Fucking Arnold.*

He gave Nicole a million-dollar smile. "Nic. It's me, Rob. From Wheeler," he said, putting his hands on his chest.

I know exactly who you are. Her head felt light like someone had opened a trapdoor in her neck, draining all the blood from it.

Danielle leaned into Nicole. "Whoa. You know him?"

A massive groundswell of nausea crashed over Nicole, forcing a stuttered gasp. She worried he could see her chest heaving in and out when he stepped closer. Danielle's eyes drilled into the side of Nicole's head, watching her every move with bated breath. Imaginary walls were shifting closer, boxing Nicole in.

She flipped her gaze between Rob and Danielle, paralyzed with a decision. She couldn't confront Rob in front of Danielle for fear it would get back to the office within minutes and could be a career-ending move. But how could she let Rob stand there and act like it was a small-world coincidence that they ran into each other like a couple of old college buddies?

"What are you doing here?" Nicole growled with her jaw clenched so tight, it hurt.

Rob casually crossed his arms and relaxed his stance, appearing unphased by Nicole's tone. "I'm a nurse over at Albany Med," he said, jerking his thumb over his shoulder, beaming at her. "I just got off the night shift. It's a beautiful morning, so I thought I'd get my run in before I go home and sleep." He nudged his head toward Nicole. "What about you? What are you doing here? This is so wild. I can't believe you're here." He gently tapped her on the arm.

Danielle interjected. "I'll let you two catch up. Nicole, I'll see you back at the office," she said before hurrying away.

With Danielle gone, Nicole was alone with Rob. The sidewalk, suddenly free of any people, swayed under her feet. "Don't you dare touch me," Nicole demanded. Her eyes crinkled to slits. "Are you following me? How'd you know I was here?" Nicole's knees began to bend. At first, she worried they were giving out, but then she realized her body naturally fell into a defensive stance. *Center!*

His face twisted into confusion. "What? How would I know where you were?"

"I don't know. How did you find me that night at school?" she retorted. Her elbows were bent, her hands up. "Back off."

His eyebrows knitted together. "Are you feeling all right?"

Adrenaline rushed through her in waves. "I'm fine," she said calmly, her eyes locked on him. "I know it was you."

"Nic," he said, putting his hands up, mirroring hers. "What are you talking about?"

"You know what I am talking about."

He let out a small laugh through his nose. "I really don't."

"When you raped me. Outside our dorm. You left me by the dumpster like a piece of garbage." Her voice quivered. "Or was that just another Thursday night for you?"

Rob's eyebrows shot up with alarm. "What are you talking about? Nic, I, I didn't," he stuttered. "My God, I would never. Where is this coming from?"

"Men like you are all the same. Thinking you can go around and assault women like you'll never get caught," she said, her voice growing louder. "First, you hurt Megan, and then you attacked me. How many other women have you done this to?"

"Nicole." He took a few steps backward. "I honestly don't know what you're talking about."

She was about to reply, but Leia came to mind. *Don't engage. Just get to safety.*

"Huh. And to think, I was going to ask you out." He dropped his sunglasses back on his face. "I hope you get the help you need, Nic. You really do have it all wrong," he said quietly, turning around and jogging back the way he came.

Nicole stood on the path, pressing her fist against her trembling lips. He was right. She did need help.

* * *

Nicole jumped out of the elevator and yanked open one of the glass office doors. Her chest was burning from running nonstop from the park. Fortunately, the waiting room was empty, and the receptionist was alone at the front desk.

She sprang from her chair when she saw Nicole. "Hey, sweetie. What's wrong?" she asked, looking alarmed. Nicole wasn't surprised by her expression. She had already seen her runny makeup collecting in black bags underneath her eyes in the mirrored elevator wall.

"I need a phone," she said, flapping her hands. Nicole was winded and panting, barely able to form a sentence. "Is there somewhere . . . private . . . I can go . . . and use the phone?" Her voice was shallow and tacky.

The receptionist waved her hand for Nicole to follow. "Come with me. You can use the small conference room."

With her head down, Nicole planned her escape from the office once she got ahold of Jamie and decided on a place to meet. She didn't want to be alone after seeing Rob.

"Dial nine first and then the number," the receptionist said before closing the door behind her.

Nicole waited a minute to compose herself. Her head felt like a concrete block resting on her shoulders. She let out one more sigh and picked up the phone.

"Thoroughbred Title Company, this is Gina. Can I help you?"

"May I please speak to Jamie?" Nicole asked. Her words came out shaky and clipped.

"I'm sorry, she ran out to grab breakfast for Mr. Riley. Can I take a message?"

"No, thank you. I'll try her later." *Shit!*

Nicole slammed down the phone. She was alone, hiding in a conference room like she used to hide in her apartment. *I'm not doing this again. He can't hurt me anymore. I won't let him.*

She reached for the phone again to call Jesse but hesitated mid-dial. She hadn't told him about the attack. It was a serious conversation to spring on him over the phone. But there was something else, something more significant, holding her back. Her thoughts filtered back to New Year's at Giancarlo's after he met Kristen. "She's clearly on the hunt for a good time in that outfit . . . Guys are going to make some assumptions about her . . . She's asking for trouble . . . She needs to be smarter." Nicole knew Jesse loved her but had no idea if he would want to be with her once he found out. *Would he think it was my fault? Would he blame me for being stupid?*

Nicole pushed the heels of her palms into her pounding forehead. Her mind was swirling, replaying Rob's final words. "Huh. And to think, I was going to ask you out." His comments, his demeanor, none of it made sense. *If it wasn't Rob, then who did this to me?*

***

Nicole was almost home, but without realizing it, she had pulled up in front of Zuke's instead. She sat in her car for a few minutes, vacantly staring out the windshield, fidgeting with her charm bracelet. The corners of her mouth dimpled when it jingled. *Jesse* ...

In her fantasy, she'd tell him everything, and at the end of her story, he'd love her more, not less. But a fantasy was like a wish, and she had no control over the outcome. She loved being in love with Jesse too much to risk losing it all.

A few minutes before ten, Nicole opened the door to Zuke's. Coffee-scented air filled the store. Other than a heavyset man leaning against the counter, feverishly rubbing a coin over a scratch-off lottery ticket, the deli was empty.

Zuke lifted his head at the door's chime, and his face perked up into a smile. "Hey, Nic. I haven't seen you in a while." His voice lit a fuse inside her. Her nose instantly burned, her eyes welled up. She covered her mouth to hide her quivering chin, but it was too late. His eyebrows collided together. "What's wrong?"

Nicole bowed her head slightly. "I'm sorry, I didn't know where else to go. I didn't want to be alone." She choked out a cry.

"Hey, hey, hey," he said, racing over to her. "Nic! You can always come here." Nicole let him pull her in for a hug. His arms felt protective. She covered her face with her hands and buried them in his chest as he rubbed circles on her back.

Nicole felt Zuke swivel his head toward the scratch-off guy. "Hey, Lou. I'm closing early. See you tomorrow."

"Sure. Sure," Lou muttered, shuffling out the door.

Zuke pulled back when Nicole's cries lessened. Cupping the sides of her face, he wiped the tears from her cheeks with his thumbs, studying her for a quiet moment. "Nic. What's going on?"

She retreated, embarrassed for crying on his shoulder. "I'm sorry," she said, glancing down at her hands, avoiding his stare. She was sorry for many things—disappearing for a month and then showing up like a blubbering idiot expecting he would be there for her, making a scene in front of a customer, not telling him about Jesse—for not being a good friend.

He slowly shook his head. "You have nothing to apologize for. I am glad that you feel safe here," he said, reassuring her that she had made the right decision. He pulled a few napkins from the dispenser nearby and handed them to her.

She swiped her runny mascara and tears from below her lashes. "You didn't have to ask your customer to leave."

"Lou? Oh, don't worry about him. He's here every day, hoping to hit the jackpot. He'll be here tomorrow, guaranteed." He sighed. "So, it's been a while since you've been here. I checked in on you with Claire a couple of times. Made sure nothing serious happened."

An inward grin coasted across her face. *I knew it. My security system worked.* "I'm sorry I showed up on your doorstep unannounced, crying and expecting you to drop everything. That's not fair to you. I had a shitty morning and needed a friend. I didn't know where else to go."

"Want to talk about it?"

She perked up a little. "Can I get a coffee first?"

"Is that what this is about?" He raised an eyebrow. "You missed my coffee?"

She cracked a smile. "Kinda." Nicole followed him to the counter and watched him make her a coffee just the way she liked it—her usual. Trying to shake off her morning and distract him from her tear-stained face, Nicole attempted small talk. "I heard on the news the other night that scientists were studying the effects of coffee withdrawal on humans. My question is, who stops drinking coffee?"

"I'm banking on none of my customers," he cracked. She had only been around him for a few minutes and was already feeling better.

"I think a better question for researchers would be, what are the benefits of drinking good coffee? Turns out there's a lot of swill out there."

He shot her a playful look. "Your love runs deep, doesn't it?" he asked, handing her the coffee she had craved for weeks.

"Let's just say, when Juan Valdez is ready to hang up his serape, I'd be willing to take over and spread the good coffee word." They shared a good, drawn-out laugh. His was hearty, hers unrestrained.

She inhaled the dark roast, letting the steam drift through her sinuses. "I'm sorry I didn't tell you about Jesse," she said, clutching the cup like it was the last one on Earth. "It happened soon after our . . . dinner. I didn't know how to tell you. I didn't want it to be awkward between us."

"Nic. I'm a big boy. We can be friends when you have a boyfriend," he said, leaning his hips against the counter behind him. "If I'm being honest, half of me was relieved. You were the first woman I kissed since Gianna's accident. I wasn't sure I was ready." He paused. "But you're on my mind all the time."

She felt her entire body blush at his words. Nicole was committed to Jesse, but if she was honest with herself, part of her wondered what life with Zuke would be like. "You should have heard it from me, not him."

"Did something happen between you two? Is that why you are upset?"

She dug her teeth into her bottom lip. "This morning, I went for a walk in the park across the street from my office and ran into a guy from college. Triggered some bad memories."

"A friend?"

A quiet laugh shivered out of her. "Not quite," Nicole said before taking a sip. She closed her eyes, basking in the warmth and flavor as it coated her throat. Her body visibly relaxed, stripped of any reservations about telling him about her past. "He was the guy that I think raped me in college."

She recounted her last ten months, starting with Wheeler. She even admitted that her daily routine of seeing him was the only thing that got her out of her apartment last summer. "I thought I was good after Model Mugging. And up until this morning, I truly believed I had my life back." She took a long sip. "But then I saw Rob."

A kindhearted look crossed his face.

"I thought if I confronted him, if I knocked him out, showed him that he couldn't hurt me anymore, that I'd feel better and be able to put it all behind me. But I don't feel better. When I accused him, he had this stunned look on his face, like he had no idea what I was talking about. He hoped I got the help I needed and then jogged away. So, now I'm not sure it was him."

Nicole pushed back the tears brimming in her eyes. "There was a sick comfort in thinking it was him. It kept me from thinking that every man that passed me on the street was a possible suspect," she cried. "But if it wasn't him, who did this to me? Who hates me that much?" She turned away. "I'm so tired of crying about this. It's been almost a year. I want to move on already."

She sensed Zuke's eyes but was afraid to meet his expression. She had said a lot. Nicole grabbed a fresh napkin from the dispenser and took a few moments, wiping her nose and regaining her composure. "Was this coffee or truth serum?" she joked, looking at the bottom of her cup.

"You've had a hell of a morning. You should give yourself some grace. It took a lot of courage to share that with me."

She met him in the eye, finding a look that said, 'I'm so sorry this happened to you. You don't deserve any of it.'

"You know you're only the second person I have told out of all my friends and family." There was a lightness in her chest that could only come after revealing the truth.

"Boyfriend?"

Nicole quickly jerked her head. A pang of guilt pulsed inside of her. "No. My sister, Jamie," she said, looking away again. "I can't bring myself to tell him yet. I'm scared it will change the way he thinks of me. Damaged goods?" She blew out a breath. "I'm sorry. I shouldn't be talking to you about that."

"Whether you tell him or not, what happened to you doesn't define you. What defines you is what you have done to overcome it. You should be proud of yourself, Nic. And if he loves you, he'll be on your side. If anything, he should love you more for how strong you are and how you have handled it on your own. Anything less than that, then he doesn't deserve you."

She sniffled. "Thank you."

"You can fight me on it, but the way I see it, you keep living up to that name of yours."

The corners of her mouth ticked up. "Victorious."

| 35 |

Jamie

Faint scents of fresh-cut flowers filled Vows Bridal Salon. Jamie stood before the floor-length gold lacquered mirror and rubbed gloss along her bottom lip with her pinky. She puckered at her reflection. "I can't wait to try on my dress," she said, scrunching her salon-inspired curls. "Just need everyone else to get here so we can get started."

"I'm excited to see you in your dress," Nicole said. "Nervous?"

It was less than two months before Jamie's big day. Despite it being *her* wedding, she was sure Karen specifically picked everything Jamie didn't want—from the white lily centerpieces to the Back Alley Cats jazz band to the buffet-style service. Her gown was the only decision that was hers.

"I want to get through this as unscathed as possible," Jamie said, shaking out her hands. "I barely got any sleep, worrying about what Karen will think of the dress. Or worse, what she'll say. It's the only wedding responsibility she gave me. It has to be perfect." She blew out a long, shaky breath. "If she's not impressed, I'm not sure what I'll do."

Jamie's posture stiffened when Nicole gently grabbed her by the shoulders, her expression dripping with empathy. "Jamie, I love you, so you need to listen to me. You don't have to take her abuse. You have choices. Have you told Randy how much she hurts you?"

"I've tried to talk to him."

"And?"

Jamie shrugged.

"I know this is not what you want to hear right now, but you helped me when I was in crisis, and now I want to try and help you." She let out a breath. "I'm worried that Karen is going to mentally ruin you. I see what a toll this wedding is taking on you, and she is just getting started. I know you love Randy, but Karen and her controlling, manipulative bullshit come with Randy. You have to ask yourself—is this the life you want?"

The question poked at the needling doubt that was building in the back of Jamie's mind. The night before, she had floated the idea of her and Randy running off to Town Hall and scrapping The Sullivan again. But Randy quickly dismissed her—again. "Hon, you're overreacting. I told you already, she loves you. It's just her way of helping. Come on," he said, rubbing her arms, "you're stressing. Everything will be fine," he patronized.

She might have felt better if Randy had listened to why she wanted to elope before turning her down, but he didn't. He was quick to take Karen's side and end their conversation.

Is this the life I want?

A confusing rush of anticipation and dread whirled inside of Jamie. She knew she was not the kind of woman Karen wanted for her precious Randy. Karen wanted him to be with someone like herself—born from money, inherently knowing which side the fork goes on, conservative, socially strategic . . . *boring.*

Jamie was also second-guessing having to give up her life completely. Randy recently sprung on her how he was excited to have kids. A lot of them—and soon. She wanted kids, too, but thought they'd have more time together as a couple first. And surprisingly, she enjoyed going to work every day. She was good at her job. And as cranky as Mr. Riley was, he was real, which she appreciated, unlike the phony, shallow women at the country club who were only concerned with perceptions.

Jamie shoved her doubts away. Other women would kill to have her promised life. She was being dramatic. Besides, she had already made her decision. It was too late. She was at the bridal salon to try on her wedding dress, for Christ's sake.

"I'm overreacting," she said, dismissing her feelings. "I have an idea. Tell me something to distract me."

Nicole gave her a long look. "I'm here for you, Jamie. No matter what happens."

Jamie tilted her head toward the ceiling, trying to keep her tears at bay. "I know," she whispered. "But you're still talking about it. I need a distraction."

"Okay . . . How about, I think tonight's the night," Nicole said.

Jamie's eyes snapped wide. "As in, *the* night?" Nicole nodded, stifling a giggle. Jamie grabbed her wrists. "I'm officially distracted. Tell me more."

"Jesse has a big day planned for us in Lake George this afternoon. He hasn't given me all the details—wants to keep it a secret. All he said was that I should bring a sweater for later. I think he chartered a sunset cruise."

"He's such a romantic—so good for you." Jamie lowered her voice. "Does he know that . . ." Her voice trailed off.

Nicole cut her off. "Absolutely not. I haven't told him anything. I don't want to think about it at all today. I've made a conscious decision to rewrite May eighteenth in my life. Today is about the future—your wedding and Jesse and I moving our relationship forward. I have no interest in going backward."

"Does Jesse know how amazing you are?"

"He's learning." Nicole let out a giddy laugh. "My twelve-year-old self would never believe I'm in love with Jesse Young."

"I'm so proud of you, Nic." Jamie pulled Nicole in for a hug. "You deserve all the love. I've got a good feeling about you two."

Over Nicole's shoulder, Jamie saw her mother and Karen walking in the front door. "It's showtime," Jamie whispered under her breath.

I won't let Karen ruin my day today. I won't let Karen ruin my day today.

Anne threw her arms around Jamie. "Hi, sweetie!" she said, her apple pectin shampoo scent engulfing Jamie's nose.

"Hi, Mom. Thanks for coming."

Anne clasped Jamie's hands into hers. "Are you kidding? I wouldn't miss this for the world." She beamed. "You look beautiful, sweetie."

"Thanks, Mom."

Jamie stepped toward Karen, who clutched her purse like she was worried someone might steal it. "Hi, Karen. Thank you for coming!" Jamie said in a 'please don't hurt me' tone.

Karen met her with a distant embrace. "Hello, dear," she said, barely touching her.

Breathe.

"This place is so beautiful. I love the mood here," Anne said, scanning the salon. "The soft music. The fresh bouquets. The white velvet couches. It's all so serene and chic," she cackled, shimmying her shoulders. "It's perfect for a nervous bride."

"She has nothing to be nervous about. She's marrying my Randy," Karen chimed in.

Jamie swallowed her words. *Randy's not the one I'm worried about, Karen.* "Well, let's move inside. I'll let them know we're all here." Jamie led the three women to the couches.

"How did you find this place, Jamie?" Karen asked, eyeing the racks of wedding gowns covered in clear plastic garment bags lining the walls.

"Word of mouth. They've got a great selection, and the people are wonderful. You'll see."

Karen swung one of the dresses out. She was poker-faced. "When I told my friend Evelyn from the club that you got your dress here, she gasped." Jamie rubbed the back of her neck while Karen flipped through the rack, making disapproving noises.

Anne shot Jamie a concerned look. "I'm excited to see you in your dress, sweetie. It's so exciting!"

"You all can help me pick out my veil, too." Jamie cleared the nerves from her throat. "Let me see if the bridal consultant is available. I'll be right back," she said before escaping to the front of the salon.

At the check-in desk, Jamie found her consultant, Cleo, pouring glasses of champagne. She looked every bit of her name—heavy blue eye makeup, black eyeliner, pin-straight black bob grazing her shoulders with heavy bangs. "Can I take one of those?" Jamie asked, downing one of the glasses without waiting for permission.

"Mother or mother-in-law?" Cleo asked.

"Mother-in-law."

Cleo refilled Jamie's glass. "Ignore her as much as you can. You get to play dress up today. It's going to be fun." But ignoring Karen was getting more challenging by the minute.

"I don't think she knows what fun is. She's treating this wedding like a business conference."

"Well, hopefully, the champagne will loosen her up."

"Cheers to that," Jamie said, downing the second glass in one gulp.

Jamie led Cleo to the couches where the women were sitting. "Everyone, this is Cleo. She's going to help us today."

"Hi! So lovely to meet all of you. Would anyone like a glass of champagne?" she offered.

"Oh, how fun. Yes, please," Anne said, taking a flute from the tray.

Nicole took one, too. "How fancy. Yes, thank you."

Cleo offered the last glass on the tray to Karen. "Champagne?"

"Is it really champagne? Or just a domestic sparkling wine?" Karen asked.

"Um," Cleo said, with furrowed brows, "I don't... I'm sorry. No one has ever asked me that before. They usually just take a glass."

Karen waved her off. "I'll pass, dear. I'll have a bottle of water, please."

Uneasiness swirled in the pit of Jamie's stomach. *Come on, Karen. Stop being so... Karen.*

Cleo smiled politely, but the 'Are you for real, lady' expression on her face said it all. "I'll be right back."

A minute later, Cleo appeared with the water. "Ladies, please make yourself comfortable. I'm stealing the bride now." She turned toward Jamie. "You come with me. It's dress time!"

Jamie gave a small applause. "Yay!" she squealed. Jamie's nerves were bubbling over like the two glasses of champagne she had downed. "Let's go."

In the dressing room, Jamie kept her back to the mirror, letting Cleo tuck, pull, adjust, zip, and button her into her gown. When Cleo was done, she gave Jamie a pair of heels to get the full effect. "You ready?"

Jamie nervously nodded. "I think so."

"All right. Turn around," Cleo said, swiveling Jamie toward the mirror.

Jamie sucked in a breath at her reflection. She had never felt more beautiful in her entire life. "Oh my God," she cried, clapping her palm to her chest. "It's better than I thought. Oh, God, I can't cry. I am going to ruin my makeup." She waved her hands near her face as if the breeze would help dry her tears. "Cleo, is it as amazing as I think it is?"

"Better," she said, peeking over Jamie's shoulder into the mirror. "You can't go wrong with a classic strapless ballgown. All eyes will be on you walking down the aisle, that's for sure. Fits you beautifully."

Eagerness spread through her limbs. She couldn't wait to see everyone's faces when she walked out into the salon. "The moment of truth," Jamie said. There was no way her dress wouldn't win Karen over. "Let's go show them."

The taffeta and crinoline underneath her dress rustled as she promenaded her way back to the women. Her mom and sister were quietly chit-chatting while Karen was disengaged, sitting like she had a ramrod surgically implanted in her back.

"Oh, sweetie," her mom said first, clapping her hands to her mouth.

"Jamie!" Nicole followed.

Cleo held Jamie's hand and guided her onto the carpeted pedestal before the floor-to-ceiling three-way mirror. Jamie gathered a handful of the skirt, giggling, and did a twirl for them. With the chandelier overhead projecting mood lighting in the salon, she was more glamorous than in the dressing room. She felt like a princess.

Anne pulled tissues from her purse and blotted her nose. "I know I was pushing for the mermaid style, but sweetie, this dress is the most beautiful thing I have ever seen. You look stunning." She stood next to Jamie, running her hand along the train. "I love how the beading covers the entire bodice and fades into the skirt."

Nicole added, "Jamie, you are glowing. Randy's jaw will hit the floor when he sees you."

"I know, right?" she said, her voice choked with tears.

Jamie felt the weight of the elephant in the room. She took in her reflection one last time and then did a one-eighty to face Karen. "So . . ."

Karen remained seated, purse welded to her lap, and looked at Jamie sharply. "Did you have a second choice? I'm not sure this is *the one*."

An indescribable sound sprung from the back of Jamie's throat. For a second, she wondered if she had been shot. She opened her mouth to say something and then snapped it closed. She couldn't form any words. Her knees were about to give out. She was unstable on the pedestal. "I want to get down," she said quietly to Cleo, gathering her dress. "Now," she snapped.

Cleo ran over to her side and caught her hand. The room was silent, with all eyes on Karen. "What?" Karen's face crumpled with a scoff. "Would you rather I lied and let her wear that?" she said, motioning to Jamie's dress.

Anne stepped forward. "I would rather you leave."

Jamie was stunned. She had never heard her mother speak like that to anyone.

"Leave?" Karen questioned.

"Yes. Right now," Anne said.

"Why?"

"Because I won't let you ruin today," Anne said. "Don't you see how hard Jamie tries to please you, and you continue to cut her down at every opportunity? Isn't it enough for you that she makes your son incredibly happy, and he adores her?"

Karen scoffed in her condescending way.

Anne repeated herself. "You should leave."

Jamie's eyes grew at the same time the corners of her lips twitched. She had never seen anyone stand up to Karen like that. Certainly not Anne.

Burn!

Jamie avoided eye contact with Nicole, fearing they would crack up in Karen's face.

Karen rose to her feet, clearing her throat along the way. She rolled her shoulders back and looked at Cleo. "May I please use your phone to call my husband to pick me up?"

Jamie and Nicole waited until Cleo escorted Karen out of the room before they said in unison, "Mom!" Jamie's body turned limp with relief.

Anne pushed up the sleeves of her shirt. "Someone needed to say it. I have never met anyone so unlikeable in my entire life. And that says a lot coming from an elementary school teacher who deals with parents every day," she said, pushing her hair out of her eyes. "Today is all about you, sweetie. You are the most beautiful bride I have ever seen. I am not going to let her take that away. Now get back on the pedestal, and let's find you a veil."

An hour later, with her mom's and Nicole's help, Jamie completed her wedding look with a veil, shoes, and jewelry. She only needed a few alterations to her dress, and the salon seamstress assured her it would be done well before her wedding day.

Back in the outfit she wore to the boutique and ready to leave, Jamie thought about Randy. She knew she would have to tell him what happened with his mother before Karen got to him, but she was giving herself a moment to enjoy her morning of playing dress up. It was everything she wanted it to be once Karen left.

Still grinning like a loon, gliding to the front of the salon next to Anne and Nicole, Jamie asked, "Mom, can you give Nicole a ride home? Randy is picking me up in a few minutes to go to . . ." Jamie stopped mid-stride, clutching her chest when her heart slammed into her ribs from the inertia.

Karen sprung from the purple velvet bench by the door and rushed to Jamie's side. "Jamie, dear. I am so glad I caught you before Randy got here. I have good news. Problem solved." She smiled, patting Jamie's hand.

"Good news?"

"While I was waiting, I called Evelyn and got the name of the bridal salon her daughter used in Saratoga—Xaviers. I've already spoken with their manager, Lucy. Lovely woman. Anyway, I explained your situation and time crunch. As luck would have it, they have an opening tomorrow morning at eleven. Something about a cancellation. It would be tight, but if you find a dress you like in their salon, they can alter it in time for your wedding." Karen handed her a piece of paper with a number written on it. "Give them a call to confirm the appointment."

Jamie's mouth opened and closed like a fish out of water. It was a new low for Karen. "Why would you do that? I already have a dress."

At that moment, Randy and his father walked in the door, full of smiles, after their round of golf. "Oh, hey, everyone," Randy said, waving to the group. "Hi, Hon. How'd it go today? Ready for lunch?" he asked, walking toward Jamie to kiss her.

Both women kept their stare on each other, ignoring the men. Karen swiveled her head in disappointment. "After all this time, you still don't see what a big deal this wedding is, do you? Let me make it simple for you. Your dress is cheap. People at the club will talk. When you look back, do you want to see pictures of yourself walking down the aisle in a beautiful designer gown or a bargain-basement Jessica McClintock prom dress?"

"Stop! Please stop, Karen!" Jamie pleaded. She was unraveling like a spool of ribbon. The room was quiet. Even the music from above had stopped. Jamie lowered her voice. "I have kept my mouth shut, pretending to be what you want me to be. I've let you make all the decisions around this wedding. I'm done," she said, grinding her teeth.

"I told you before, you don't have a choice, Jamie. It's my money," Karen said smugly.

Jamie raked her hands through her hair, ruining her perfect curls. "No. Not today, it isn't. I used *my* money. You told me my dress was my responsibility, and I found the perfect dress."

Karen shrugged one shoulder. "I think you can do better."

"I can do better?" Her voice strained.

"Jamie. You're overacting. Please don't make a scene," Karen said. She twisted her pearls around her index finger, closing her eyes as if she couldn't bear to watch.

Jamie was too heated to worry about making a scene. "When you say I can do better, are you still talking about the dress, or are you talking to Randy about me?" she asked, pointing her finger at him. "Since the day you found out I wasn't a country club girl, you have looked down your pointy nose at me. You have never given me a chance. You always assumed Randy could do better. News flash, Karen. He cannot. I am the best thing in Randy's life, and he loves me. Get used to it. I'm not going anywhere."

"Hon," Randy said, reaching for Jamie's hand, "let's get some air. Cool down."

Jamie swatted Randy's hand away. "Get some air? Cool down?" Her chin quaked. "Please don't tell me you're okay with how your mother is talking to me." She glared at him. Her heart stopped for a full second as tears skipped down her cheeks.

Randy turned to his mother, pinching the bridge of his nose. "Mom. You need to back off."

"Randy. Please. She's having a tantrum. Don't encourage her," Karen said flippantly.

"Mom, Jamie is going to be my wife—the mother of my children—your grandchildren. You can't talk to her that way. You shouldn't talk to anyone that way."

Jamie squared her shoulders, giving her restarted heart room in her chest to do a victory lap. There was the man she had always hoped she was marrying. *Yes!*

Karen clutched her pearls. "Randy. I want what's best for you."

"And that's Jamie," he said, slipping his hand into hers. "Today was about her, Mom. Not you. And if it's going to be a problem, then maybe she and I should just go to Town Hall and get married there," he suggested, squeezing Jamie's hand. She squeezed back. *He was listening.*

"Oh please, Randy. You don't mean that. Everything has already been planned. Invitations have been sent. You can't cancel now. Think about your reputation. The firm's reputation. You don't want that kind of publicity," Karen said.

Jamie affectionately looked up at Randy, anticipating another comeback, but caught a slight hesitation at his mother's words instead. It was brief, and maybe no one else noticed, but in that nanosecond that he wavered, Jamie knew that Karen would always have a grip on Randy, no matter how much he loved her.

She glanced at Nicole, who offered a small, empathetic smile before looking away. Was Jamie ready to give up her voice, her independence, for a life where her feelings were an afterthought at best? An impossible sadness weighed on her heart. She knew the answer.

"Randy," Jamie said quietly, squeezing his hand. He turned away from his mother to face her flooding eyes. "Randy, honey. I love you so much." She sniffled. "But I can't do this. Not like this. Not with your mother making all the decisions."

His eyes crinkled into slits. "Jamie. I said we could go to Town Hall."

"I know, Randy." Her face softened. "And I love you for it. But I know deep down you don't want to get married at Town Hall any more than your mother wants us to. She'd make your life a living hell if we went through with it. It'd be easier to do what she wants. She knows that. And I know that because that's how I have lived for the last year. Sitting quietly and suffocating. But I can't do it anymore."

"What are you saying?"

"I can't marry you right now. I'm sorry." Randy's eyes inflated. She hated hurting him. But she hated the pain she was in more. She needed to stop waiting for Randy to stand up for her and start doing it herself. "It's not forever. I just need more time. To see what life is like when I am the one making decisions for myself. You know?"

His face was frozen in disbelief. "No. I don't know." Her stomach knotted with guilt. She never meant to hurt him.

"Oh, this is getting ridiculous, Rand. Take me home," Karen said to her husband, slipping her arm through his and leading him out the door.

Jamie forced herself to breathe, ignoring Karen. "I'm so sorry, Randy. Let's go talk. Alone."

After all her agonizing, it turned out Jamie had the strength to stand up for herself after all.

| 36 |

Nicole

"Well, that was an unexpectedly eventful morning," Nicole said from the passenger seat of her mother's car. "I'm so proud of Jamie for speaking up."

"I didn't think she had it in her. She's too much like me sometimes. But I am so happy she found her voice today before it was too late," Anne said, pulling out of the salon parking lot.

Nicole scrunched her face. "What do you mean, 'Too much like you?'"

Anne came to a complete stop at a red light. "She's been so focused on playing housewife and living this charmed life. I'm worried that if they ultimately get married, she'll dismiss the importance of having her own friends and money and won't see the risk of relinquishing all control over to Randy until it's too late."

"So, hope for the best, but plan for the worst?"

"I sound so jaded when you say it like that. I hope the worst never comes," Anne said.

They turned onto the highway and headed north toward Nicole's exit. The intermittent clusters of pine trees and freshly mowed fields lining the road streaked by the windows in varying shades of green as they gained speed. "No. Of course not. But I agree with what you're saying. I've told her she needs to be more independent," Nicole said.

"Independence is important. Of course, it is. And rewarding. Look what being fiercely independent has done for you—you put yourself through college, you're making a name for yourself at your firm, you've taught yourself how to refurbish a rundown apartment and make it into a home. Not every woman has that kind of drive in them. You should be very proud of yourself. I know I am." Nicole saw the gleam in her mother's profile.

A rush of validation ran through her as Anne's words sank in. "Thanks, Mom. That means a lot coming from you."

"But . . . sometimes too much independence keeps you from asking for help when you need it the most. That's my biggest worry for you. I hope you know you don't need to take on everything alone. There is no shame in asking." *I'm still learning.*

"I've gotten pretty good at figuring things out for myself." Nicole's heart sank. It was meant to be a moment of personal pride, but it came across as an insensitive jab toward her mom.

"After your father died, I know I wasn't there for you girls like I should have been. You were forced to grow up so fast. I'm sorry I wasn't stronger." Her breath hitched. "You deserved a better childhood."

"Mom." Nicole gently squeezed Anne's arm. "That's not what I meant. I'm sorry you took it that way. You had a lot thrown your way all at once, too. I know in my heart that you did the best you could at the time." She squeezed again before putting her hands on her lap and gazing at a break in the tree line. "You know, a friend recently told me I should give myself some grace—not be so hard on myself. It's probably good advice. Maybe we should both think about taking it." They both nodded in quiet agreement.

Exiting off the highway, they drove down the few blocks to Nicole's neighborhood in silence. In a moment of clarity, Nicole recognized that if her mother could have done better, she would have. Of course, she would have. She loved her and Jamie unconditionally. And as Nicole was painfully aware, sometimes, anything more than backward was progress.

Anne waited at a blinking traffic light for an oncoming car to pass. "Honestly, Mom, I think how you handled it made the three of us stronger in the long run."

"Thank you, sweetie. That is certainly a positive spin on it. I hope you're right." Anne pulled her car along the curb in front of Nicole's apartment behind a blue sedan.

"That's Jesse's car. He must be inside already," Nicole commented.

"He has a key?" her mother asked, arching her eyebrow. "You must be getting serious."

Nicole felt her ears getting hot. "Part of me hates to admit it, but I am crazy about him," she said. "It's scary."

"There is nothing like a new love," her mom said, giving her a gentle smile. "Enjoy it."

"We were supposed to go to Lake George today," she said, craning her neck out the window. "Although, it looks like it's going to pour any second. Hopefully, it passes. He had a special day planned for us." Nicole had plans, too.

"Well then, I won't keep you. I love you, sweetie. I'm glad we had a chance to talk," Anne said, giving Nicole a hug and a motherly kiss on the side of her head.

"Me too. Thanks, Mom. I love you."

Nicole climbed out of the car and waited for her mom to pull away before rushing up the stairs to see Jesse. Her emotions, like butterflies, fluttered around her heart, colliding with each other—validation and love from her mom, confidence in herself, and the anticipation of being with Jesse.

***

Nicole pushed the door open to find Jesse sitting on the couch, zoning out to the TV. Noodle jumped to the floor with a *thump* when Jesse stood to greet Nicole. "Hi!" they said in harmony.

"I'm not going to lie, Jesse. I kinda like coming home and seeing you here." Her smile widened with approval when she noticed how hot he looked in his chambray shirt and khaki shorts.

He met her smile. "I kinda like being here when you get home," he said, wrapping his arms around her. Her body naturally molded into his when he pulled her in for a hard kiss, sending a jittery burst of excitement on her tongue like a handful of Pop Rocks.

For a minute, she was distracted enough that she forgot about her morning. But then it slid back into her thoughts, and she pulled away, lightly clapping her hands on his chest. "You are not going to believe what happened." Her voice was energized.

"Tell me," he said, his arms still around her. He dipped his chin and drew his nose down her profile, whispering, "Have I ever told you how much your lavender shampoo drives me crazy?"

"No, wait." She giggled, playfully pushing him away. "We can talk about my shampoo in a minute. You need to hear this."

He backed her to the door and slid one of his hands up the side of her neck, coiling his fingers into her hair. "Um, hmm," he said, pinning his hips against hers, hovering his mouth along her bottom lip. "I'm listening."

"No, seriously, I want to tell you what happened," she said, turning her head.

His shoulders collapsed. He stepped back and sighed. "What?" His voice was riddled with annoyance.

"What?" she asked right back, confused.

Jesse cast his hands out. "I don't know, you tell me."

She snapped him a look. "I was excited to tell you about Jamie and my conversation with my mom on the way home. What's wrong with you?"

"Nothing. I'm fine." He made an about-face and moved into the kitchen.

She threw her hands up, exasperated. "Here we go. Silent Jesse," she said, hurling him a side-eye.

"Give me a break," he said under his breath.

Nicole didn't understand. One minute, they were kissing and loving on each other, and the next, he was pacing in the kitchen, annoyed. *What the hell?* "Did I do something to upset you?"

He cracked his knuckles in a familiar sequence. *Pop. Pop. Pop.* "Not everything is about you, Nic. I just need a minute," he barked. *Pop. Pop.*

Actually, today is about me. About us. "Fine. I need to change. I'll leave you alone," she said, stomping into the bedroom and slamming the door behind her.

She leaned against the wall. *Come on, Jesse. Snap out of it.*

Nicole spent almost twenty minutes deciding on the red floral sundress in the front of the closet that she had already picked out the night before. Ironically, it wasn't so sunny outside. *Or inside.* At least a dozen times, she told herself that whatever was bothering Jesse would blow over. It always did. But the silent treatment was getting old.

Standing in front of the mirror, Nicole smoothed the front of her dress. After her morning, May eighteenth was already memorably rewritten, and she wanted to keep the momentum going with Jesse. But her hopes were beginning to dwindle. He was pacing the apartment, and outside, the heavy rain was pelting against the windows.

Nicole was on her knees digging around the closet floor, searching for her other sandal, when she heard a quiet knock at the door. She stood up, flung her second shoe onto her bed, and opened the door to Jesse, leaning his shoulder against the door jamb. His face was apologetic.

She shot him a withering glance. "Yes?"

His eyes bathed her in approval. "You look beautiful." The corner of his mouth ticked up the way it always did when he flirted with her.

"Sweet talk will get you nowhere," she said, crossing her arms over her chest.

"Then tell me about your morning."

"The moment passed."

He leaned his head against the doorframe, his hands tucked under his arms. "I'm sorry."

She bobbed her shoulders. "What happened?"

He dragged a hand down his face. "My boss called me this morning." He sighed.

"On a Saturday? That can only go one of two ways. What did he say?" She already knew the answer based on his earlier mood and irritated body language.

"He told me he wanted me to hear it from him first."

She raised her eyebrows at him in disbelief. "Did he say why?" Her heart broke for him. She knew how much time and energy he had put into his training and how badly he wanted the job.

"I don't know. Some bullshit about this guy Martin having seniority and that they had to give it to him. I stopped listening after that," he said, glaring down at his boat shoes.

"Jesse . . . I'm so sorry. Did he say when another opportunity might come up?"

"I didn't ask. I was too pissed."

Nicole looped her pinky around his and squeezed it. "I'm sorry, Jess," she said quietly.

He squeezed back. His mouth pressed into a white line, still avoiding her stare.

She searched for something to say to change the mood. "Wanna head up to Lake George? I'll let you beat me at mini golf?" She offered up a grin, poking his side.

"Let me?" The subtle raise of his eyebrows put a giggle in her belly.

"Well, we both know that I hold the Around the U.S. in 18 Holes record, but I can throw a few holes if it would make you feel better."

His mouth cracked into the beginning of a smile. "You have quite a knack for making me feel better."

"It's a gift, really," she said, tipping up one of her shoulders. Jesse's lighter tone told her that he was coming around. She hoped that meant they were getting back on track with their plans when a loud clap of thunder ripped through the apartment. They both flinched. "Whoa, that was close."

"It's raining harder than before," he said, glancing over her shoulder out the bedroom window. "You might get to keep your title for another day."

She laced her fingers into his other hand. "I was looking forward to the special day you had planned."

"It's still early. Maybe the storm will pass, and we can go later."

"What should we do in the meantime?" she asked. Her knees felt hollow at the suggestion of what she was offering.

They had been together for over five months. Wheeler felt like a lifetime ago. There was no question that Jesse made her feel safe and loved. But she had to ask herself one last time if she was ready to take the next step. He was a part of everything good in her world. She had made him wait so long and even practiced with her toy a few times, testing her body's reaction. She just needed to get out of her head, let herself go, and be in the moment with him. *What am I waiting for? It doesn't get more perfect than this.* Her pulse quickened.

He let out a quiet chuckle. "You're the one with the gift to make me feel better, Nic." Jesse dipped his head, sliding his mouth down the curve of her neck. She closed her eyes, tilting her head back as he grazed his teeth along her collarbone. His lips hovered at the front of her throat before landing an inch above the gap between her breasts. "What do you suggest?" The breath of his words tickled her skin, leaving goosebumps in their wake. She felt electric.

Her heart pounded at his nearness. She wanted his hands on her. To touch him. To taste him. "I have some ideas," she said, sliding her hand up his chest. She reached for a handful of his shirt, feeling his warmth through the thin material.

"Take your shoes off," she playfully demanded, leading him to her bed.

He quirked his lips. "Yes, ma'am."

With his docksiders kicked off, she gently pushed him onto the mattress and stood over him, wedged between his legs. He looked up at her and skimmed his hands up and down the back of her thighs, grazing his fingers under the lace hem of her panties, sending a wave of heaviness between her legs. She climbed on his lap, letting her dress flow past her thighs, straddling his, and unbuttoned his shirt. She liked being on top of him. She felt powerful—more in control. Confident.

"You sure?" he asked.

She glanced at him through the fringe of her lashes and nodded.

His warm green eyes anchored on her. "We won't do anything you're not ready for," he said reassuringly, then cast his eyes on her lips.

"Thank you," she uttered quietly, running her fingers along his bare chest like a mallet on a xylophone. "And for the record, if we do this, there is no way I'm letting you win at mini golf later." She exhaled a chuckle.

His hands ran up the curve of her back, pulling her closer. "Deal," he said, panting a laugh that draped around her neck. Want drowned out any fears still left in her mind—*Today is my day. Our day.*

They melted into each other, exploring one another. He drew back, kissing his way to her shoulder, easing off the straps of her dress with his teeth. Her top fell open, exposing her breasts. She gripped the back of his rocklike biceps. Steady, she offered herself to him. "Jesus, Nic, you're so beautiful," he whispered, sweeping a hand along her torso, brushing his nose past her pinched nipple. Her breath hitched when he skated his tongue between her breasts. She wanted more.

Nicole swept her hair to one shoulder and locked her eyes on his. She watched his lips skim across her chest, closing over her nipple. Her thighs tightened in reaction to his wet, circling tongue. "Jesse," she whimpered as he started to suck. She wound her arms around his neck, the heat between her thighs became more insistent.

He kissed his way up her neck until their mouths collided like two railcars being coupled together, seducing her. She sighed into him, spreading her knees wider, bringing herself closer to him as they tasted each other. A cry flowed out of her. She rolled her hips against his shorts, feeling his hardness beneath her. "*Fuck*, Nic," he groaned.

Their foreheads pressed together. She could feel his breath on her lips. "Please tell me you brought protection."

He smiled against her mouth, nodding. She sat taller on her knees, sliding off him. He reached for his wallet in his back pocket, pulled out a condom, and tossed it on the bed.

Slowly, he crawled toward her, gently easing her onto her back. She was trembling with expectancy as she unbuttoned his shorts, sliding her hand inside his boxers and putting her fingers around his shape. His abs clenched at her touch. He sucked in a breath and waited. "You're driving me crazy. You know that?" he huffed out.

The corners of her mouth tugged into a smile. "That's the idea."

He hovered over her for what felt like an eternity before giving into his shaky arms and pressing his bare chest to hers. She felt the full weight of him on top of her. He kissed her eagerly, hiking up the bottom of her dress. "Nic," he murmured into her ear. "I've waited so long to be with you." He spread her legs apart with his.

Nicole's insides went numb, and she froze. "What?" she said quietly.

"I've waited so long to be with you," he said, his eyes closed. He lifted her thigh to his hip, moving against her.

I've waited so long to be with you.

"Wait," she said.

He lifted himself onto his elbows. "What? What's wrong?"

"I'm sorry," she said, trying to sit up. "I need to stop." Panic settled in her chest. Nausea curdled in her stomach. "I need to get up."

Jesse rolled off her, groaning, mumbling something that resembled, "Are you fucking kidding me?" He was irritated. She couldn't blame him.

He pushed himself up, sitting on his heels. In a huff, he buttoned his shorts and shirt while Nicole slid the straps of her dress onto her shoulders.

"I'm sorry," she whispered. She turned away to wipe her eyes, hoping he didn't see her. She was embarrassed enough. Sitting in silence, her hollowed gaze lingered on her white duvet, then sharpened on a small round object near the unopened condom. From a distance, it resembled a nickel. She picked it up and flipped it over in her palm. It was an old button. *Where did this come from?*

She turned to find Jesse's glare. His usually hazel eyes weren't warm and green. They were black as onyx. "I have been so patient with you.

How much longer are you going to make me wait?" he snarled. "It's been a fucking year, Nic. When are you going to move on?"

Her eyebrows pinched together. "What's been a *fucking* year?"

Pulling at the cuffs of his shirt, he gave Nicole a sidelong glance.

"A year? We've only been together five months . . ." She stopped. Her throat was closing, cutting off the air feeding the unplausible tale weaving through the grooves of her brain. *I've waited so long to be with you . . . It's been a year.* "No, no, no, no, no, no," she said in rapid succession, trying to drown out his words ringing in her ears. She jerked herself to her feet.

"Nic," he said, reaching for her hand. "I'm sorry. I was frustrated that you stopped."

"It was you?" she said slowly, swatting his hand away.

"Me, what?" he said, but his voice flattened.

"That night. At Wheeler. When I was raped. *One year ago.* 'I've waited so long to be with you' —that's what he said. The way you pulled my leg against you—" Panic constricted her throat. "It was you, wasn't it?"

He stood. "What are you talking about? You were raped?"

"If you don't know what I am talking about, help me explain this?" She opened her fisted hand to show him the button she found on the bed near his wallet. "I was wearing a tartan plaid skirt that night. When I got back to my dorm, I was missing two buttons, exactly like this one."

He stiffened. There were a million signs—his eyes fell, Adam's apple bobbed, weight shifted, but it was the musky arousal scent permeating from him that awakened a dormant memory from that night so intense that it pushed her against the wall.

"How could you do that to me?"

"Nic, c'mere." He held out his arms. "Let's talk about this."

She slid along the bedroom wall to the doorway, not taking her eyes off him, and escaped to the kitchen. Jesse was right behind her. She began to pace, but horror was unfolding in her mind.

"Talk?" she asked. She stopped and spun around, studying him. She could barely get the words out, raising her voice above a whisper. "What part do you want to talk about, Jesse? How you raped me next to a dumpster? Or how I fear for my life every time I walk out the door? Or the saddest part of all . . . how you duped me into falling in love with you?" She felt faint and feverish. Her hands and feet were cold and clammy.

He inched closer to her. "Nic."

She jerked out of his reach. "Don't come near me," she warned, holding up her hand.

His shoulders slumped with the weight of his hands in his pockets. His expression was suddenly hard, saying, 'Are you serious?'

"I know it was you, but what I can't figure out is why." Her front door was in her peripheral vision. *I've got to get him out of here.*

"I don't know. I had a bad night." He shrugged. "I was walking home and saw you in the driveway."

Nicole's pulse throbbed in her ears, her palms, the soles of her feet. "You had a bad night? Tell me, Jesse, what was so bad about your night that you had to ruin my life?"

"Ruin your life?" He stopped in his tracks. His eyes welled up. "You have always been able to take care of yourself no matter what happened—losing your dad, your absent mother, even how you've dealt with this. You were already the strongest, most positive person I knew. I didn't think you could get any better, but I watched you grow more confident and beautiful this past year. Nic, you're amazing. That's why I love you so much." He inched toward her.

"Love me?" she sneered, backpedaling closer to the door. She was equally tortured and sickened at the thought. "That's not what people who love each other do."

He reached out to touch her and then pulled back with a twisted expression as if she was no longer worthy. "I have loved you since that first summer you and your family moved into our house. No matter what I did, you only saw me like a brother." *Summer siblings.* "By the time we got to Wheeler, I had given up trying, so I avoided you. It was easier that way because just being your friend sucked. And then . . ." He paused. His body straightened.

"And then that night at MacArthur's, you appeared out of nowhere. I was so happy to see you. For a second, I stupidly thought you were happy to see me, too, and maybe that was the night we'd leave together. But no. You were using me to get away from your sleazy ex-boyfriend. You treated me like some loser—a throwaway. I was so hurt . . . and angry." His jaw visibly tightened, popping the muscles along his neck. She watched his hands flex open and close into tight fists.

Her chin quaked, remembering the cold, wet pavement ripping away at her cheek as he violently forced himself in her, tearing away at her insides—the searing pain. She knew what he was capable of. *Please don't hurt me again. Please.*

"I have never once thought you were a loser. I went to you as a friend," she said through a desperate cry.

He shuffled toward her. "I don't want to be your *friend,* Nic."

The truth felt thick and suffocating, hanging in the air like an oppressively hot and humid summer day. She was fighting more waves of nausea.

Nicole took three repelling steps away from Jesse. When she reached the door, she threw it open. "Get out! Get out, now!" The rain raged outside.

"No," he said firmly. He took another step closer. "I'm not leaving until we talk about this. You taught me that, remember? It's better to talk than keep it bottled up." He gave her an unblinking stare.

"I said, get out. Don't you dare come near me!"

He stepped forward again. "Nic. I love you."

"Would you have ever told me it was you?"

"Why would I? You never told me you were raped." His eyes softened. "And for the record, it wasn't rape. It was love."

"This is not love, Jesse. This is you feeling incredibly guilty because you got caught. You're not sorry for what you did." Tears streamed down her face. "Get out of here. I don't want you here."

"Nic." He moved closer, angling his body between her and the door. She was trapped inside. The hair on her arms stood in response to his closeness. Her heart clambered in her throat. She had missed her chance to get to safety. "Please. We love each other. You can't seriously be saying we're done over *this*. It's just a fight." His voice was low and calm.

"This is not just a fight, Jesse." *Don't engage!*

"You're going to throw us away over something that happened a year ago? Something that some would say you brought on yourself."

"I want to leave. Move out of the way. Let me go," she screamed, attempting to force her way past him in the doorway. He was too strong and pushed her an arm's length away.

"You're not going anywhere," he yelled, outstretching his fist toward her just before punching the door. Nicole sucked in a sharp breath. "We're not done here," Jesse said, drilling a dangerously intense gaze into her.

And then, as they replayed that terrible night, Nicole remembered something else. Something better. A choir of thundering voices cheered her on—Jamie, Zuke, Leia, Jose, Kristen, Donna, Amanda, Anne—even Blade. *Center!*

The edges of her mouth pulled into a contrived smile as she opened her stance. Jesse's shoulders relaxed under the touch of her hands. His eyebrows unfurrowed. "That's more like it, babe . . .," he whispered.

Then, using her grip for leverage, she rammed her knee as hard as she could into his groin, one time, then two, then three. "No! No! No!"

Jesse dropped to the living room floor, writhing in pain. She didn't wait to see if he was alive or dead. *Don't engage. Just get to safety.*

She sprinted out of her apartment barefoot and empty-handed into the torrential downpour, leaving Jesse the same way he had left her one year ago—crumpled in a ball.

A groundswell of adrenaline rushed out of her pores like surging flood waters as she ran down the block, listening for the slapping of incensed footsteps chasing after her. *Nothing.* She whiplashed her head over her shoulder to see if her eyes picked up something her ears missed in the thunders of the storm. *No one.*

She slowed to a hurried walk, her chest heaving, her lungs burning. Steps away from safety, she ached to find the edge of the blue mat and hear the celebrated melody of Leia's whistle. But it wasn't an exercise, and there was no whistle, only validation in her winner's spirit that was reaffirming, empowering . . . *victorious.*

EPILOGUE

May 18, 1997 – One Year Later

A gentle spring breeze floated around Nicole as she rounded the corner of the brick building. Her brain was jumpy, bouncing between the night before and her day ahead. "Nic!" an enthusiastic voice called out as she dropped her keys into her sunflower-embroidered mini backpack.

Nicole's face sprouted into a wide grin when she spotted Jamie waiting for her in front of the YMCA.

"Hi!" Nicole said, skipping up the few steps to meet her sister on the stoop.

"Hey, I left you a message on your answering machine last night. I never heard back from you," Jamie said.

Nicole blushed. "Oh, sorry. I didn't get it. I wasn't home last night . . . or this morning," she said, biting back her smile.

Jamie raised an eyebrow. "I've never seen you wear that before," she said, watching Nicole slide a pendant along a gold chain hanging around her neck. "A gift from a special Italian chef, maybe?"

Nicole's heart expanded, remembering what Zuke—*my love*—said when he clasped it around her neck the night before. "The laurel wreath is a symbol of victory, just like you. If you ever doubt your courage or strength, just run your fingers over the leafy crown and remind yourself how hard you have worked to get where you are."

Nicole could feel her eyes smiling. "He wanted me to have something I could wear that was a constant reminder of how far I've come."

"He is *so* sweet," Jamie said, resting her hand over her heart.

"If anyone knows, aside from you and Dr. Goldman, how my last two years have gone, it's him. He understands how important today is for me."

Up to that point, Nicole had kept her circle of confession small. And that may be all it ever ends up being. Therapy helped Nicole understand that whoever, whenever, and how many details she shared was her decision and her decision alone. "There is no one-size-fits-all approach to healing," Dr. Goldman had taught her.

Beyond telling her mom that she and Jesse had broken up, she didn't offer many details other than, "He wasn't the guy I thought he was." After countless therapy sessions, Nicole couldn't find any personal benefits in telling her mom the whole story. She only found ways it would hurt Anne. Not only would it burden her with worry and guilt, but it would put a strain on, if not ruin, her friendship with Jeanie—the very person Anne would need to lean on the most to get through her crisis.

"That's why I love Zuke. He has been in your corner since the day you met him. I'm sorry I ever doubted him," Jamie said, pulling Nicole into her arms. "Well, I don't have a gold necklace budget these days, so you'll have to settle for a hug from me. I love you. I am so proud of you."

"I'll take your priceless hugs anytime. I love you too." Nicole relaxed into her sister's arms, breathing in her warm and familiar jasmine scent. "You said you called me. Everything okay?"

Jamie pulled back. "I wanted you to be the first to hear my exciting news." She paused for emphasis. "I got my certification in the mail yesterday. I'm officially a Title Agent," she cheered.

"Jamie! That's amazing. So that means you'll get the promotion at work, right?"

"It sure does," Jamie confirmed with pride.

"First, your own apartment, and now this. Independence looks good on you." Nicole threw her arms around her again.

Not long after Jamie postponed the wedding, she moved out of her and Randy's shared apartment into a small one-bedroom in Saratoga.

She had confessed to Nicole that she was falling back into her habit of putting Randy's needs first, mostly out of guilt for blindsiding him at the bridal salon. She needed her own space. A month later, Randy and Jamie ended their engagement and went their separate ways. He was too hurt, and for the first time since she was fifteen, Jamie didn't have anyone else to take care of except herself. And she was enjoying the hell out of her newfound freedom.

Nicole checked the time on her watch. "Oh! We're gonna be late," she said, opening the door.

They rushed down the hallway. Nicole chugged the last sip of her favorite coffee and tossed her cup into the nearby garbage before turning toward the basement stairwell. A toddler sporting a hot pink bathing suit ran out of the frosted glass pool exit with her mother in tow, stopping the sisters. The heavy smell of chlorine seeped out the door and engulfed Nicole's sinuses, triggering thoughts of Jesse. Her muscles tensed.

Since that day in her apartment, he had left a total of three messages on her answering machine. The first two were left days following the incident and were mostly filled with Jesse in various stages of denial, begging Nicole to give him another chance. The third message was left a few months later, letting Nicole know he was moving to Boston to work for another engineering firm and promised never to contact her again.

Nicole touched her necklace, releasing her breath, which naturally loosened the tension in her body. With Jesse in another state, chances were less that she would see him again, but if their universes ever did collide, she knew she would survive. She already had. Which was exactly what her day was about—celebrating her survival and paying it forward by empowering other women to stand up for themselves and live their lives without fear. Because if women don't lift each other up, how could they expect men to?

The sisters made their way down the stairs to the bottom floor. "You ready to take your first class?" Nicole asked.

Jamie huffed. "Ready is a strong word. Nervous. Terrified. Anxious. Probably more like it."

"I think once you get started, you'll get a lot of pent-up feelings out on the mat. Just think about Karen." Nicole chuckled. "I already warned Blade that he might want to wear extra padding."

Outside the studio door, Jamie's face lit up at the poster-sized sign that read *Welcome to Model Mugging* in Nicole's slanted handwriting. Wearing a proud, big sister smile, she said, "Well, Miss Certified Instructor, I should ask you . . . are you ready to *teach* your first class?"

Nicole ran her thumb along the jagged edges of her pendant. The path she had set for herself two years ago wasn't supposed to bring her to the basement of the YMCA, but there she was, living outside her comfort zone, challenging herself, thriving—building character every day.

"I am. But I'm not afraid to ask for help if I need it."

No more shame.

RESOURCES

If you are a victim of sexual violence or know someone who could use assistance, please visit **RAINN** (Rape, Abuse & Incest National Network): **https://www.rainn.org** or call the National Sexual Assault 24/7 Hotline: **800.656.HOPE** (4673).

To learn more about **Model Mugging** programs and locations/schedules near you, please visit: **https://modelmugging.org**

ACKNOWLEDGMENTS

This book would never have happened without the support of the following people and two adorable fluffers. I love you all and am humbled by your support and faith in me and this book.

Bry, thank you for your unwavering love and support of all my creative endeavors. I know it isn't always easy on you. And, of course, for sharing your little brother woes, which only added to the authenticity of Jesse's character.

Lukey, thank you for driving home with me that Memorial Day weekend. Our most honest and unexpected conversation 1000% inspired this book.

The Elsas, thank you for enduring my endless ITIK streams of consciousness. Your champion puzzle-solving skills helped me make sense of all my thoughts.

Mom, thank you for insisting that I take Model Mugging 20 years ago—going so far as to pay my tuition! It is the definition of a gift that keeps on giving.

David, thank you for reading my really early rough drafts and still being one of my biggest cheerleaders despite them.

Jeanette, thank you for being my dear friend and confidant since 4/6/99.

Coco, thank you for sharing your love of dark and disturbing stories and breakfast foods.

Jessica, thank you for designing a beautiful cover. You truly captured the essence of ITIK.

ACKNOWLEDGMENTS

Libby, thank you for your handholding, coaching, and unfiltered feedback. I would never have gotten here without you.

Caroline, thank you for skillfully editing ITIK and assuring me (and reassuring me and reassuring me a few more times) that I really am a writer.

Emily, thank you for going above and beyond beta reading ITIK. Your feedback was invaluable.

Secret Book Club (you know who you are), thank you for continuing to open the aperture on my reading choices. I am a better writer for it and a better person with all of you in my life.

Nick & Ed, thank you for your unconditional support and willingness to help me in any way possible. Your kindness continues to blow me away.

Mark, thank you for your time, expertise, and devoted commitment to an ever-growing and desperate unmet need. I wish there were more like you out there.

Theo & Rocco, thank you for getting up early and staying up late with me. You make writing a less lonely endeavor.

ITIK ARC Reader Team, thank you for being so honest and raw and helping me make this book the best it can be. My heart is overflowing with your love and support, and I am forever grateful for our connection.

And finally, to my readers (I have readers—pinch me!) for making my dream a reality. Cheers to this being the first of many books to come.

ABOUT THE AUTHOR

Melissa Trombetta is a wife, mother of two teenagers, and a long-standing member of corporate America. While she is both a mom and an accountant, she strives not to dress like either. Writing in her free time and dancing at country music festivals like her kids aren't standing next to her are her guilty pleasures. Many of the stories in *I Thought I Knew* were ripped from her personal headlines, helping her build resilience and candor, which she hopes to have only added to her character.

Sign up for Melissa's Flawed & Funny newsletter and stay up on all her latest life antics and book news. **Website:** https://flawedandfunny.substack.com.